to Steve
& Maureen

2076
REAGAN'S LAST WORD

Michael Santos

2076
REAGAN'S LAST WORD

A novel by

Michael Santos

Copyright © 2010 by Michael Santos.

Library of Congress Control Number: 2010902945
ISBN: Hardcover   978-1-4500-5671-7
        Softcover   978-1-4500-5670-0
        Ebook   978-1-4500-5672-4

All rights reserved. No part of this book may be reproduced or transmitted in any form or by any means, electronic or mechanical, including photocopying, recording, or by any information storage and retrieval system, without permission in writing from the copyright owner.

This is a work of fiction. Names, characters, places and incidents either are the product of the author's imagination or are used fictitiously, and any resemblance to any actual persons, living or dead, events, or locales is entirely coincidental.

This book was printed in the United States of America.

To order additional copies of this book, contact:
Xlibris Corporation
1-888-795-4274
www.Xlibris.com
Orders@Xlibris.com
74032

Of all tyrannies, a tyranny sincerely exercised for the good of its victims may be the most oppressive.

—C. S. Lewis.

Prologue

Ronald Reagan approached the podium. He was about to address the 1976 Republican National Convention. He lost the nomination for president of the United States to his rival, Gerald Ford. He did not have prepared remarks since he was not supposed to speak. There was no written speech to give, but he did have a message. The same message that first made him go into politics. It was the message that would drive his presidency. His ability to deliver it made him into a transformative leader. It was a message of freedom.

Professor Calvin Marshall enjoyed listening to Reagan's speeches. He had a large collection of them, probably the most comprehensive in America. This was his favorite speech.

He reached for the whiskey on the rocks that he prepared and looked back at the screen.

Ronald Reagan started to deliver his message. The people at the convention came into view, and Professor Marshall could tell that the speech was grabbing their imagination. Reagan was seizing them and making them look into the future. "Someone asked me to write a letter for a time capsule that is going to be opened in Los Angeles a hundred years from now, on our Tricentennial."

He saw this video so many times that he could repeat each word by memory. He had shown it to his students many times, but that was years prior, when it was permitted to show this kind of thing. When he was still allowed to teach American history, as he knew it.

"It sounded like an easy assignment. They suggested I write something about the problems and the issues today. I set out to do so, riding down the coast in an automobile, looking at the blue Pacific out on one side and the Santa Ynez Mountains on the other, and I couldn't help but wonder if it was going to be that beautiful a hundred years from now as it was on that summer day."

He thought about the morning and his drive down along that same coast. His last class of the morning had been on ancient Greece, and after that, he left to go see his doctor. He left the Santa Barbara City College and drove down the coast with the pacific off on one side and the Santa Ynez Mountains on the other. It was a beautiful view. Marshall was going for a routine physical, and he was feeling fantastic.

He focused his attention back on the video, sitting in his home office, finishing a glass of whiskey. The people at the convention looked as if they were hooked to every word. He could relate. Reagan established a connection with them that only he was capable of. It was one of the reasons he was to be called the Great Communicator.

"Then as I tried to write—let your own minds turn to that task. You're going to write for people a hundred years from now who know all about us. We know nothing about them. We don't know what kind of a world they'll be living in."

Reagan was concerned about the world of the future. He was worried about the America that would get to read his letter. Professor Marshall felt sad. He knew Reagan would be disappointed. After all his efforts, his beloved America still finished the way he feared. And in the modern socialist America, there was no room for Reagan's message.

He wondered if the people in the audience realized how prophetic the message was. "The erosion of freedom that has taken place under Democratic rule in this country, the invasion of private rights, the controls and restrictions on the vitality of the great free economy that we enjoy. These are our challenges that we must meet."

He wondered what made him watch the video. It was a sad day. Why make it worse? He received terrible news at his visit with the doctor. Up to that morning, he had been a healthy seventy-one-year-old; then his doctor gave him shocking news. He had a hard time believing it. But he knew right away that it was a death sentence. He left his doctor's office before hearing any of the options he had, for he knew there were no options. Nothing could save him.

"And suddenly it dawned on me, those who would read this letter a hundred years from now will know whether those missiles were fired. They will know whether we met our challenge. Whether they have the freedoms that we have known up until now will depend on what we do here.

"Will they look back with appreciation and say, 'Thank God for those people in 1976 who headed off that loss of freedom, who kept us now a hundred years later free, who kept our world from nuclear destruction?'"

"Thank you, Mr. President," Professor Marshall said. He smiled as he pressed the pause button. Reagan did keep the world safe from the Soviet Union. Safe from nuclear destruction. He had done his part to keep those freedoms alive. Marshall would tell his students it all started with that speech. The Republican Party was transformed that day. That convention of 1976 saw a new beginning. Gerald Ford would continue as the nominee of the party for that year's election. However, the party had a new leader. He stood there in front of them. The speech he delivered was a call to arms, a call to go forth from there with the determination to do the hard work to keep America free. The audience knew they were part of something special. They were foot soldiers of that man and his crusade for freedom. The Reagan Revolution was given birth before their eyes.

A successful revolution that collapsed the Soviet system and increased freedom in America. It was not Reagan's fault that it all disappeared. It happened well after his watch. After he was taken by Alzheimer's.

Professor Marshall felt sad again. He did not know if it was due to the failure of his country to live up to the promise of the speech he was listening to or from the news he received that day. Not only was he given a death sentence by his doctor, but he also saw the awful news as soon as he walked into his home office. He had the web page open in his computer screen to his right. He fought a tear as his gaze moved from the screen playing Reagan's speech to the computer. His good friend, Senator Frank Thomas, was taken to the hospital the day prior. It was reported that he was in critical condition from a stroke and not expected to survive.

Senator Thomas was his same age, seventy-one years old. Marshall knew he was next.

The window with his friend's last e-mail was open. He received it a few days prior. He read it again. "If the Consumption Chip Bill passes, freedom will die and tyranny will rule America."

He had warned his friend a long time ago that it was coming. He looked back at the screen, at the image of Ronald Reagan, which was frozen. He pressed pause again and listened to the conclusion of the speech. The remarks ended with a warning. The always optimistic and cheerful leader had a troubling concern about the future. It sent a chill down Marshall's spine.

"And if we failed, they probably won't get to read the letter at all because it spoke of individual freedom, and they won't be allowed to talk of that or read of it."

Part 1

What kind of a world they'll be living in

Chapter 1

May 25, 2076
Levittown (Long Island), New York

Michael saw his mother at the end of the hallway. She was smiling. It was rare to see Mom smile. He walked up to her with a grin of his own. Her happiness was contagious, and he felt a thrill, an excitement he had not felt in a long time. The same feeling he used to get as a kid at Christmas time, before finding out what Santa brought him. When he was closer to her, he realized why she was in high spirits. She was holding a small baby in her arms.

"Shh . . . Mike. The baby is sleeping." She walked toward the crib and carefully placed the baby down. She was gentle, displaying warmth that conveyed there was nothing to worry about.

"Can I hold him, Mommy?" the small Michael asked.

"No. He is too small. One day when he is bigger." She smiled at Michael, caressing his cheek. "You're going to be a great big brother."

Michael heard a loud noise, turned back, and saw a man coming down the hallway. He did not know who it was, did not recognize him.

Michael turned toward his mother, but she was gone. He became petrified, and knew he could not run and leave his little brother alone. The man pushed him aside; he fell on the floor and started to cry. The screaming by the baby was deafening and made him stand up.

He was no longer in the room, no longer a child. He was looking into the room through a window. The man was holding his baby brother and looking at him.

He spoke to Michael, but at first, he did not understand what was said. Michael usually did not comprehend any of it. This time he heard the last part clearly.

"We have decided this baby costs too much. He is going to consume and waste resources the rest of us need. There can't be economic equality when there are too many people using limited resources." The man smiled at Michael. "Sorry kid, social justice cannot be denied."

The man approached the baby's crib. The baby was quiet, and Michael wondered if he was alive. He hit the window as hard as he could, but it did not matter how hard he tried; he could not break it.

The man took a straw, and he bent over. Michael knew the ending. He had seen it too many times. He shut his eyes, refused to see it again.

Michael Adams woke up soaked from a cold sweat. It took him a moment to realize he was in his apartment in Levittown. It was Memorial Day, a day that brought painful and unpleasant memories for him. It was inaccurate to call it that since that holiday was abolished fourteen years prior, replaced by Community Service Day. Regardless of the name, it was a weary day. Every year his symptoms were the same. He would wake up at night with the same recurrent nightmare. During the day, a terrible headache with nausea did not allow him to concentrate and get anything productive done. The symptoms lasted four to five days around that last Monday of May. A few years back, he considered seeking medical help for it but then decided against it. His symptoms only bothered him for a few days. He felt he could deal with it. The last thing he needed was to have a medical record with a psychiatric history. It could be used against him someday.

The way he dealt with his problem was to stay home and get some sleep, catch up on some reading, and his headache would go away.

On this day, he was unable to do that. Ms. Olga Parker needed to see him in her office. She was the head of the journalism department, and to cancel on her was inconceivable. Even if he felt like crap.

Michael felt better after a shower, reached the bus stop at the New York Institute of Technology in Old Westbury, in good spirits. He walked toward the journalism school.

One thing he liked about his school was the campus. A serene wooded setting gave it a peaceful feeling. It made him feel better. His headache was gone as he walked.

He enjoyed the view from the glass elevator. The school of journalism was placed in what he felt was the best part of the campus, surrounded by trees and a large pond separating it from the Osteopathic Medical School behind it.

He walked out at the third floor, immediately noticed the glass door to the administrative offices with its sign: "Katie Couric School of Journalism." The third floor was the one place on campus he tried to avoid as much as he could.

A strong smell of new paint received him. He liked the color, a light cream, which gave the administrative offices a new look.

He walked straight to Parker's office, knocked, walked in to find her busy, looking at her computer screen.

"Please have a seat." She continued to read her screen without bothering to look at him.

Michael felt nervous. He looked past her at the wall and noticed she had a framed poster of her three golden rules. The "Rules of Excellence in Journalism" as she called them. Next to it, she had a blue and red portrait of former President Barack Obama. He also noticed the portrait of the current President, George Wilson.

"What are you doing on this Community Service Day?"

"I didn't get a good sleep, so I might just go home and take a nap."

"Wanted to talk to you about the next issue." She finally looked at him.

The next issue of the student e-letter was due to come out the following Monday. She had to review and approve it. He was able to post it only after her final blessing. If she had concerns, they were communicated to him via an email or a tweet message. It was unusual to have him come to her office.

"Anything wrong?"

"There is a lot wrong with it." She looked down at her screen. "You wrote this editorial about the upcoming Fourth of July, asking if we still know what it means to be an American."

"It is our nation's Tricentennial. I thought it was an appropriate time to have that discussion."

"Parochial displays of patriotism do nothing but harm. They are empty gestures. That's what they are. Our students understand they are citizens of the world. We don't need a discussion on what it means to be an American." She looked at him.

Michael knew it was not over. There was about to be a long lecture.

"If you want to honor your country, you go out and help your community, as you should be doing today. Instead of staying home, sleeping."

He looked at her golden rules. Number three had been violated—"strive for the common good." He picked a subject for his story that, in her view, did not benefit the general welfare of the public. "I just thought it was a good idea to analyze the importance of our Tricentennial. It only comes once every three hundred years."

"I told you specifically to write an editorial about the upcoming vote on the Consumption Chip Bill being discussed in Congress. There is some uneasiness out there about it. We need to reassure people that it is a good idea. You love to be critical, so I was hoping you would expose, criticize those in Congress who are halting progress by their opposition to the bill."

Michael thought about writing such an article. The problem was that he liked the arguments the opposition of the bill were making. He knew that if he wrote it, she would reject it.

"If you felt you had to do this story, then you have an obligation to focus the story. To tell your readers it is important on a day like that to remember the progress this nation has had in the last three hundred years. That we have gone from a nation fascinated with greed, selfishness, and materialism. To one where our citizens understand they are their brother's keeper."

His gaze went back to her framed rules. He violated the second rule. "Focus your story. How can this story help the common good?"

His interpretation of the rule was that any story needed a good spin, so it would better accomplish progressive objectives.

"Since we already have a holiday to increase awareness of community service, I didn't think it was necessary for me to transform the Fourth of July into another such holiday. I don't understand why I can't analyze the significance of the day."

She stared at him. He knew that when she called a student to her office, it was to say how to do things, not to have a dialogue.

"You want to be a journalist. Your job is not to ask why. The job of a journalist is to report news that helps society achieve a common purpose."

"But why . . ." He did not finish the question. The look she gave him told him it was time to be quiet.

"You take too many liberties. You know why I made you editor of the e-letter?"

He wanted to say he was a great writer and smarter than her other students but bit his lower lip. "I thought I was doing a good job." He said after an awkward pause.

"I made you editor in your junior year because I had a lot of hope for you. Now you are about to start your senior year, and I am having doubts about that decision. On the semester you spent in India, you wrote some excellent articles about life over there. Some of them very critical."

He knew why she enjoyed those articles. Criticism of India fitted her political views well. After the passing of the new Constitution of the People's Republic of Japan, India became the only recognized country in the world with a system of democratic capitalism. He was impressed with how much the standard of living was increasing there. The country was progressing in ways that even its most ardent critics could not deny. However, some of his articles were critical, but he felt he was just being objective. If anything, he was appreciative of the freedom he had there to say anything he wanted to.

"Let's also be realistic. Your father's position was a big influence in my decision. I felt if you were as dedicated as he is that you would make a great journalist one day."

He knew what she meant by dedicated. Dedicated to the party, not the truth.

She turned her attention back to the screen. "This is the worse part of this editorial."

His hope that she was done evaporated.

"You say here, that in our Tricentennial, in Los Angeles, a time capsule is going to be opened that contains a letter written by President Ronald Reagan one hundred years ago. 'How exciting it will be to hear the message from someone who seemed to understand so well what being an American was all about.'"

The specific paragraph was at the end of his piece. The release of a letter written a hundred years back by a historical figure did seem to be a big deal. Why was she objecting to its mention?

"This is rubbish. Don't know where you get this, what kind of right-wing radicals you are hanging around with, feeding you this crap. First, there is no such letter. What made you make it up is beyond me. You can never be a good journalist if you are going to be making up stuff. At least check your sources and make sure they are not making up stuff."

She was accusing him of breaking the number one rule. The one rule that he agreed with. "Always be accurate." Michael felt angry. He touched his hair, a habit he had whenever he was nervous.

"Second, even . . ."

Michael did not let her continue, he stood up—it was his turn to talk. "I did not make anything up. Ronald Reagan wrote a letter in 1976 that is to be opened this year, on our Tricentennial." She tried to say something else, but he ignored her and went on. "I understand you disagreeing with the substance of my editorial or my lack of spin on it, but you can't accuse me of lying. I have three golden rules of my own. Accuracy, accuracy, and accuracy."

"Sit down, Mr. Adams!" She looked as angry as he felt. "I have been very lenient with you. After all, you are here to be educated."

Not from her, he thought.

"Effective immediately you are suspended as editor. I will be getting myself a new editor."

Chapter 2

Michael went straight home. He tried to sleep, but the obnoxious exchange he had with Parker prevented it. Removing him as editor was going to affect his future career goals. His father was not going to be pleased.

After a few hours in front of his computer, he was able to get some sleep, but the next morning, he was like a zombie throughout all of his classes.

At lunch, he sat in the cafeteria, staring at his food when his best friend approached him.

"Hey, buddy."

He was lost in his thoughts but acknowledged his friend as he sat across from Michael. "Hi, Craig." Right away, he was drawn to the T-shirt. "What's that? Don't tell me you have to wear that all the time." He shook his head as he noted the T-shirt. It made it simple to spot a community organizer. They all had to wear their traditional uniform with a blue t-shirt and the NACORN (National Association of Community Organizers for a Responsible Nation) emblem in its upper left side. They were a civilian national security force, their shirt made them visible and a constant presence.

"It's so cool, buddy. You don't know how much respect people show you when you're wearing it."

"I still can't believe you joined them." Michael had tried to convince his friend not to join. He spent over an hour explaining to Craig their mission—how they carried it out. He disagreed with everything they stood for.

Michael explained that in theory they did a good service for the country, involving themselves in all aspects of daily life. They believed everyone to be entitled to good housing, free health care, permanent jobs, and to live in a safe neighborhood. To accomplish their goals, they used tactics that he found reprehensible. It was intimidation.

They made sure people knew where to get the services and products they needed and that working conditions were optimal. More importantly, they made certain that those responsible to produce and provide the needed services were doing so. In addition, that no one was trying to profit from their labor. That was where he felt their tactics bordered bullying, to say the least.

"Hey. You know how many carbon credits I've received just for joining? I'm getting my bike today. It's an old one, but it's so cool. Do you have a bike?"

Michael laughed at the double standard. Everyone received a standard stipend from the government on carbon credits. To try to profit from your labor was a sign of greed and lack of a social consciousness. Community organizers exposed people like that immediately. However, it was cool to earn extra carbon credits by being a community organizer and intimidating those that actually produced something.

"If this is what I have to do to get a bike. I'll walk."

"Funny. You should be careful what you say now. I'm suppose to inform them of anyone who is saying anything fishy about us or the government."

"Oh no. They've brainwashed you already. That was fast." Michael knew his friend was trying to be funny. He took it seriously. Craig's new friends were in the lookout for anyone who did not share their notions of social justice and equality. "Now I'll have to watch what I say in front of you."

"Come on, buddy. Where is your sense of humor? I'm kidding you. I would never get you in trouble. But you do need to be careful of what you say. There are a lot of others around here."

"I know. They're everywhere."

Community organizers were everywhere. There were multitudes of them in all major cities. Their numbers grew over the years as their mission evolved and were entrusted with other functions.

They were involved in organizing people to come out and vote. Educating the public on who was the right candidate to vote for, the candidate who shared their agenda of continued reform for a more just and equal society. They also ensured that people volunteered their time for indispensable community projects.

"I went to my first event last night."

Beat up some poor soul that dared say something critical of the government, Michael thought. For the first time since he met his childhood friend, he bit his tongue and did not say what he was thinking. "What was it?"

"There was some protest going on in front of the house of some congresswoman. She is supporting this Consumption Chip Bill Congress is debating."

"The protesters were against it?"

"Yea. The leader of the protest was some right-wing radical. Some nutcase. Spreading misinformation to the public."

That was the thing Michael hated about NACORN the most. Harassing people that had an honest disagreement with what their representative was doing. What harm was there in allowing the protest to go forward? It was not as if the congresswoman was actually going to listen to the protesters. She knew better. All congresspeople knew better than to oppose the desires of NACORN. At the national level, NACORN made sure that candidates subscribed to their agenda. Those who did would receive the support and votes they needed. No party member with any serious political aspirations could ignore them.

Michael realized it was better to change the subject. He was going to end up angry with his good friend. Besides, there was someone else he found more annoying than any community organizer. "You'll never believe what that Parker bitch did to me."

"What happened?" Craig asked.

"She removed me as editor."

"Shit. You're starting your senior year, how can she do that? Why?"

He tried to eat some of his rice, which was getting cold. "It was an editorial I wrote for next week, about the Fourth of July. I mention in it a letter written by Ronald Reagan, which is to be released in July in LA."

"Who's Ronald Reagan?"

The question surprised him. "Our fortieth President. Don't you know any history?"

"Not if I can help it," Craig said. "And he wrote a letter? To whom?"

"Well, back in 1976, he wrote a letter that was placed in a time capsule to be opened a hundred years later. That's this year. This coming July."

"Oh, that's pretty cool."

"She accused me of making it up! She says there is no such letter. She called me a liar to my face and suspended me as editor. That bitch." Michael realized he was raising his voice. Several people in the cafeteria were looking at him.

"Watch out, buddy, you don't want to get suspended from school. It's your senior year. Don't get so angry."

He knew he sounded angry. It was how he felt. He was fuming. How could he come across any other way? "It is not anger you know. It is righteous indignation."

"You sure this letter exists?"

"I'm sure. Reagan himself said it. I saw a video of some speech he gave in 1976 where he mentioned the letter."

"Then just send her the link of the video so she sees you weren't lying."

"I tried last night. You can't find the video anywhere. Not easy to find much about Ronald Reagan. But that video, I can't find it anywhere or any mention of it or any mention of the letter."

"Where did you see it then?"

"Jackie." Michael displayed a smile as he mentioned her name. "I went with Jackie last year to LA. Her grandfather is a history professor over there."

"You haven't seen her in a while, no?"

He pretended he did not hear the question. "Her grandpa has this collection of Reagan memorabilia. He has a bunch of videos and books on him. That's where I saw the video."

He had been thinking about that trip to Los Angeles. Jackie was the best part of the trip. Thinking about the two weeks he spent with her brought him pleasant memories. Watching the videos and asking Jackie's grandfather questions was another enjoyable aspect of his visit. It was a collection impossible to see anywhere else.

"What is she up to these days?"

He took a bite of his chicken and talked. "I haven't seen her since then."

"She is still upset at you?"

"Probably. I don't know why, we had already gone our separate ways." Several times, he considered calling her and trying to patch things up but never did. He felt she treated him unfairly.

Michael realized he had been given a good excuse to get in touch with her. "I'm going to call her."

"I've heard that before," Craig said.

"I need that video her grandpa has. I will call her and ask her how to get in touch with him."

"And what is she doing Saturday night?"

He smiled at his friend, feeling more relaxed. Jackie made a better topic of conversation than community organizers.

"When I get the video, I will then send it to Parker. At least she won't be able to call me a liar. She won't make me editor again . . . I knew she was looking for an excuse."

"Your dad is not going to like it."

Michael pushed his tray away; his appetite was gone, and he was done with the food. For a moment, he glanced at his friend. "No he won't be too happy." There would be time to worry about that later. His father was the last person he wanted to think of. "What about your dad? He won't like that." He pointed to the symbol in Craig's shirt.

"I know. What has all his criticism ever got him? Nothing but trouble. At least, I'm getting a bike."

"Did your folks move already?"

"Yes. They left for Alaska on Sunday." Michael remembered Craig's dad had spoken for years about moving to Alaska. He called it the last bastion of freedom in America.

"What did they do to your house?"

"It's still there. Still officially ours."

"You are not afraid the government will take it away now that it's empty?"

"Who would want that old, crappy house? I wish someone would just blow it up."

Chapter 3

May 26
East Meadows (Long Island), New York

Jackie Perez hated what was about to happen. She was doing medical rounds with the rest of her team, which consisted of an attending physician, two fourth year medical students, and another intern like her.

"Dr. Perez, why don't you tell us about the patient?" Her attending physician asked. He stood right next to the bedside, smiled, and held the patient's hand.

She saw the sweet smile of the patient. She felt pity for him as she took her tablet PC, with his information in front of her, and started to discuss his medical history. "He is a fifty-five-year-old man with a past medical history of Down's Syndrome. He also has diabetes mellitus, non-insulin requiring, and has developed diabetic nephropathy with a creatinine of 1.8."

"What other complications can we expect?" The attending started to drill the students with questions.

Jackie kept looking at the patient, feeling awkward with the situation.

"Dr. Perez, you want to answer that question?" She realized she was not paying attention to the discussion.

"I asked if Downs's Syndrome hadn't been cured." One of the students said.

"No new babies are born anymore with Downs's Syndrome." The attending answered the question, looking inpatient with her delay. "The prenatal test for Down's is now mandatory, and if positive, then of course the mother goes ahead with an abortion."

Jackie never met a person with Downs's Syndrome previously. Since the day her patient was admitted to the hospital, she became attached to him. She felt he was a sweet fifty-five-year-old little boy.

"The care of a patient like this used to place great financial and emotional strains in the family and society."

"Should we be talking like this in front of him?" She interrupted her attending. He looked at her and continued, "It is also unfair to him, to be condemned to such a difficult life." He looked down toward the patient and smiled. "He is one that fell through the cracks, and the mother was never tested. Now with his new complications and problems, the family realizes how much hardship they are in for, and they have agreed to proceed with the euthanasia."

A nurse came in and gave the patient an intravenous medication. He went to sleep.

"That was sodium thiopental. It is a sedating agent and will induce coma quickly."

He was describing the procedure to the students when the nurse handed another syringe to Jackie.

"That one is pancuronium bromide. It is a muscle relaxant. It will paralyze him, including his diaphragm, and he will stop breathing. It is also given IV and needs to be administered by a doctor." Her only thought was that she was the one who was about to kill him. She looked at the syringe in her hand and at the patient who was peacefully sleeping. She went closer to the bed and looked at her attending. "But why are we judging that his life is no longer worth living? He was happy. What right do we have to take that away from him?"

"He has no quality of life to look forward to," her attending said.

"And what about an alcoholic or drug addict? Do they have a better quality of life than him? Why does his life have less worth?" Jackie saw her attending was getting frustrated.

He moved closer to her. "An alcoholic and a drug addict can get better. They can be treated. He will never get better. Only has medical complications to look forward to."

Jackie had taken an oath to do no harm. The words sounded like complete hypocrisy to her. She looked again at the syringe—at the deadly medication she held in her hand. "We are supposed to do no harm."

"Exactly," her attending said. "If he continues to live, we harm his family and society in general. Every human will expel within his lifetime eight hundred million pounds of carbon dioxide into the atmosphere. It increases global warming, causes harm to all of us. And he wastes precious time and resources that can be used on someone who has some quality of life to look forward to." He extended his hand for her to give him the syringe. "Dr. Perez, let him die. His family agreed. We are following their wishes."

She held on to the syringe. She knew there was nothing she could do. There was no way to talk him out of going forward with it. "His family agreed because we convinced them that this was the only choice they had," she said.

"The board has recommended it. They would never approve any other treatment." He looked annoyed. "Dr. Perez, give me the syringe, and please wait outside."

Jackie stood outside in the hallway, relieved that she was not taking part on what was going on in the room. Her attending did not take long in coming out.

"We will discuss what happened in there later." He reached out for the sanitizer dispenser, which was outside the patient's room. "Did you get to discharge Mr. Smith yesterday? He is still showing up in my rounding list."

Jackie looked down at her tablet PC. She brought up her list of patients. There was no need to look; she knew Mr. Smith was still in the hospital. After a deep breath, she faced her attending. "No, he wasn't feeling well yesterday, so I kept him one more day."

"You know . . ." He stared at her and was visibly angry. "The length of stay for a patient with CHF is two to three days. He has been here now for six days. Go discharge him. Now!"

She did not wish to get into another argument with her attending but knew she was right. Her patient had shortness of breath when she saw him the previous day. That morning, prior to rounds, she examined him and felt he was not ready to go home. His blood pressure was elevated, had significant edema of his legs, and his lungs had rales at the bases—telling her he was still overloaded with fluid. Her attending turned away, but before he was able to get far, she spoke to him. "He is not ready to go home yet. I just made some more med adjustments this morning."

"You did not understand me. I said go discharge him. The last thing I need is a call from upstairs asking me why I am not moving these patients out when we desperately need the beds."

"He will be back tonight if I discharge him still sick like this."

"Fine. If he comes back, he comes back. We have limited resources. We do the best we can to the most people that we can. He is never going to be 100 percent better. Let him go." He did not give her a chance to say anything else. The rest of the team joined him, and he walked away to the next room and the next patient.

Jackie's phone rang, and she moved toward the elevators where she was able to take the call. "This is Jackie . . . What do you mean you can't get me the meds . . . ? I am desperate. You were my last chance . . ." People were coming off the elevator. She lowered her voice and walked toward another hallway, trying to stay away from the nurse's station. Last thing she wanted was for anyone to overhear her conversation. "What am I going to do now? I need those meds . . . He is just going to get worse . . . What do you mean send him to Texas? Do you know how difficult it is for anyone to get into Texas? Might as well send him to Antarctica . . . Okay, thanks. I will see what I can do. Bye." She put away her phone. "I need to find a way to get those meds," she murmured.

Chapter 4

Michael found the coffee shop not far away from his place. It was located across the Nassau County Medical Center in East Meadows. He had called Jackie's mom and pretended to have lost her daughter's number. Her mom told Michael she usually went to the coffee shop in the evening, after finishing her work in the hospital, to do some studying. That is where he found her.

He saw her as he came in, sitting by herself in the far corner, reading an e-book, looking as gorgeous as when he last saw her. Her long black hair and shapely figure were unchanged. She had a short black dress, and his gaze went directly to her crossed legs. Michael wondered whether it was appropriate for her to work in a hospital showing off her legs like that. No complaint from him. Not when he appreciated looking at them. Besides, she was a serious person. Unlikely anyone would dare make any comment directly at her. She would put them in their place right away. That was the Jackie he remembered. Never afraid to speak her mind.

He felt nervous going up to her after a long one year. She did not notice him coming in, so he went over to the counter first. "Could I have a light Mocha?"

"We're out of milk."

"What?" Michael noticed the look of annoyance by the kid taking his order.

"Don't you care about the children? They needed more than you, buddy. I can give you a black coffee."

He hated black coffee, but it did not make sense to come in and not order anything. "Fine, give me a small one."

The kid seemed annoyed again.

"I mean tall . . . A tall black cafe with two sugars."

"I can only give you one sugar."

It was Michael's turn to look annoyed.

"What can I say? It's the end of the month. We're running short in supplies."

Jackie looked up and saw him. She smiled and waved. Any doubts of her being happy to see him or not were gone.

Michael picked up his coffee and pressed his thumb against the digital display. A couple of carbon credits would be automatically removed from his account.

"Hi, Jackie."

"Long time, no see. How are you?" She stood up, kissed him on the cheek, and they hugged.

"What a coincidence to see you here."

"Please sit."

"What are you studying?"

"Just reviewing. It's Harrison's, an internal medicine book." She grabbed her e-book and sat down.

"That's right you are a resident now, right?"

"Yes, finishing my internship. Next month I will start my second year of Internal Medicine."

Her smile made him regret his initial hesitation to contact her. Maybe she forgave him after all. It was not his fault; he reminded himself once again. They had already decided to go their separate ways.

"What about you? You must be finished," she said.

"Not yet, I'm starting my last year of Journalism."

"I thought you would be done by now."

His smile was gone. "I should have finished by now, sure. If I hadn't been forced to volunteer for community service after high school and then spent another semester doing more forced volunteering."

"Well, some of that time wasn't all that badly spent."

Michael smiled. Indeed, some of that time was well-spent. He met someone wonderful. Michael thought about telling her that but then remembered why he was there.

"How's your grandfather?"

Jackie looked surprised. "Why do you ask?"

"Well, I was doing an article about Ronald Reagan and . . . Well, I just wanted to ask him some questions . . ."

He stopped when he noticed Jackie shaking her head.

"What?"

She chuckled.

"Why are you laughing?"

"You are something else. We haven't seen each other in more than a year and you . . ."

"Me what?"

"You know, my mom called me and told me you called. And she told you I was here. Here I think you were coming in because you missed me and you wanted to apologize. It's nothing like that. It's just some homework assignment you have."

"Apologize for what?"

Her smile was gone as she looked straight at him. Michael knew right away the question was a mistake.

"Apologize for what? You have the nerve to ask me that?"

"You are the one that said you wanted us to go our separate ways. You had this hang up of me being younger than you."

Getting into an argument with Jackie was the last thing he wanted, what he was determined to avoid at all costs coming into the coffee shop.

A lady, who was sitting nearby, stared at him and asked him to keep his voice down.

"I said that because you were being immature," continued Jackie. "You insulted my mentor. And then you proved me your immaturity by sticking your tongue down another girl five seconds after we broke up."

So she was still hurt about that, thought Michael.

Jackie stood up. Whatever happiness she had felt when he came in seemed long gone, and she looked ready to leave.

He felt sad; their meeting had started off so well and deteriorated so quickly.

Michael spoke with a softer tone. "It wasn't five seconds. It was a few hours, at least." That was not a good thing to say.

She took her purse and her e-book—"I hope you still have her number"—and walked away.

After a moment, he looked to the lady who was still staring at him. "That didn't work out too well. I guess Saturday night is out of the question."

The lady smiled and agreed with him.

Chapter 5

"Do you know why we've asked you here?"

The man speaking was the communications officer for the New York Institute of Technology. His job was to make sure that information being presented to the students was balanced and diverse. He reported directly to the communications department in Washington DC.

"We are concerned about your recent browsing history." He continued.

"It's not what it looks like," Michael interrupted. "Those naked pictures meant nothing to me."

"Do you think this is funny?" Olga Parker asked.

Michael had been called to the office of the communications officer. It was his second visit to the third floor in just a few days. He was sitting at a conference table, with the communications officer sitting across from him, Olga Parker was to his right, and his history professor sat to his left.

Michael had spent the entire previous day browsing the internet and reading anything he could find about Reagan. He had sent an email to his history professor asking for recommendations on books about Ronald Reagan, and he sent him an extensive list, which Michael downloaded and read, but was not able to find the answers he was looking for.

"All I did was read most of the books you linked me to." Michael pointed to his history professor. "They're all very critical of Ronald Reagan. Not one author seemed to have anything remotely good to say about him. I don't see why that's a crime."

"And who said you've committed any crime?" The communications officer said. "You are here to be educated and get a balanced education. It is hard to argue it is being balanced when you are reading so much about the same topic. If some right-wing radical is brainwashing you, giving you misinformation about Reagan, making you think he was a great president, then that concerns us."

"It is common belief that he was a terrible president. He spent too much money, initiated an era of greed that at the beginning of this century led to a financial collapse." The professor loved to hear his own voice, to give lengthy explanations, even when no one had asked for one.

"Yes, that's what I read. Makes you wonder how he got elected twice," Michael said.

"Popularity has nothing to do with it. He was a charismatic speaker and got away with convincing the American people what he was doing was right. It wasn't until years later that it became obvious what a reckless administration he conducted."

Michael did not want to hear the same anti-Reagan rhetoric that he spent the previous day reading about. All he wanted was to find a reference to the letter that Reagan wrote in 1976. If he knew it was going to lead to getting a lecture from these three clowns, he would not have bothered. Then again, why not? It should not be a crime in America to want to find out information about a former president.

The professor prevented Michael, and the others, from saying anything and continued with his lecture. "In foreign policy, he was even more reckless. He started an arrogant foreign policy that planted the seeds for the hatred toward America that we would be victims of in the early decades of this century."

Michael decided it was better to stay quiet, let the professor go on with his long lecture. It was all part of their game; he knew that all too well. They pretended the purpose of the meeting was just to make sure he was getting a diverse education and not listening to a one sided point of view presented to him by some outside influence. The real reason for the meeting was to teach him a valuable life lesson, never to bother asking why, never seek boldly the truth. If only they knew he had access to a source of information not one of them could dream of. But he did not dare go there. He thought about accessing it the day before, but wisely, he chose not to. Michael would be in real trouble if he had dared.

"You obviously have a well-versed professor here. In the future you might just want to ask him anything you need to know about Reagan." The communications officer finally spoke, ending a ten-minute rant about Reagan.

"Yes, you can ask me anything you might need to know. Turn of the Century American history is my passion."

"I was interested in Reagan's speeches." Michael knew he should not be baiting the professor in going off on another long lecture, but he could not help it. It was time to test if the professor knew as much as he was pretending to. "One speech in particular. The one he gave in 1976 at the Republican National Convention, where he mentions that he wrote a letter for a time capsule, which is supposed to be opened this year. I cannot find that speech. Or any reference to that speech. Or any reference to that letter."

Michael prepared for another anti-Reagan monologue.

"When the Reagan Library closed down twenty years ago, a lot of his letters and speeches were saved away. Most of them are no longer available electronically because . . . again, some of it is for lack of interest, also because the government can only save a limited amount of electronic information—so it has to make some tough choices, and ultimately his speeches are not considered to serve the greater good."

"So the government has shot down anything that contained any of his speeches," Michael said. All eyes in the room zeroed in on him. He made a mental note to learn how to keep his mouth shut.

"Be careful, Mr. Adams. Don't go around saying something like that. Our government does not censor."

Michael wanted to laugh at that statement. Sitting in what he felt was some kind of a censorship board, being sold the lie that censorship did not exist. What was next? Were they going to try to convince him that the government did not torture political prisoners?

"So you don't know anything about that speech he gave in 1976 or if he might have written a letter for a time capsule?" Michael asked.

"A letter for a time capsule? I never heard of that one before," said the professor, looking as if he was pondering the question.

"Even if he wrote such a letter, I don't imagine there would be any enthusiasm to find out what it said. Probably some message to go and make a profit and screw anyone that gets in your way. Why would we want to hear that?" the communications officer said.

"Mr. Adams. I thought I was clear to you the other day when I said there is no Reagan letter. Then you turn around and start making all these inquiries." Parker broke her silence.

"I am a journalism student. You accused me unfairly of getting my facts wrong in a story, and I was doing research to double check and see if I did or did not." Michael knew he did not get his facts wrong and wanted to tell her that, to tell her what a bitch he thought she was. But he did his best to avoid looking angry.

"You are a journalism student, and your job is to report news. News that are important and can help improve society. Your persistence in inquiring about a letter that does not exist from a discredited politician makes you seem to be advocating a political view. That will not be tolerated from one of my journalism students."

She was overreacting; Michael knew that. Making him feel as if asking about the letter was a national crime. Then again, she was a control freak and did not appreciate anyone disagreeing with her.

"If you were not your father's son you would be in deep trouble by now. Stop this, or I will make sure he finds out."

Parker's stare left little doubt in Michael's mind that she meant it. What she did not understand is that he had not gone into journalism to feed the people propaganda in order to make the world a better place. Ever since he was a kid, his dream was to expose a government cover-up such as Woodward with Watergate a hundred years prior. Michael loved mysteries. And if she thought that threatening him with his dad was going to shut him up, she was mistaken. All she achieved was to increase his curiosity and determination. If the standard government line regarding the letter was that it did not exist then it was never going to be released. Not on the Fourth of July, not ever. Michael would never get to hear its message. But why? He wondered. And now, more than ever, he was going to find out. What was it about the letter or about Reagan that was so threatening? If he was just some fool that became president by a combination of good looks and charisma, then why worry about anything he said in a letter. He was going to find a way to contact Professor Marshall and get some answers.

Chapter 6

Michael's original plan was to relax the rest of the evening. Forget Parker, Reagan, history, the letter, everything. He had planned a visit to the gym for some kickboxing to reduce the stress. It was what was needed after a tense day.

Kickboxing was his favorite exercise. He loved hitting the heavy bag at the gym, helping him keep in great shape and also to relax.

A call from Jackie changed his plans. She was sorry about their argument, and they ended up having a pleasant chat. He lied to her, told her he was still at the university, which was walking distance from her house, and she invited him to stop by.

She lived in Old Westbury, Long Island. He rode the same bus he took every morning. From the bus stop, it was a short walk to her house.

Her neighborhood was charming with grand old houses in vast lots and enormous oak trees that made it such a serene place to walk by. It felt as peaceful as his college campus. It was considered an exclusive neighborhood, a residential area for the privileged. Once upon a time, it used to be a place only for rich people. But that was back when there were rich people. Then, it became a place to live for the well-connected.

Jackie's dad, Tony Perez, was an architect. A likeable guy who Michael met a couple of times. Tony gave him a history of the neighborhood when he went to visit once before, when he met Jackie's family for the first time, before going with her to Los Angeles. Tony told him he did some work for some influential people in town. When one of the houses became available, they pulled some strings, and Tony was able to get it. His application pulled ahead of many others.

Unfortunately, for Tony, he did not get to enjoy the house for long. He divorced Jackie's mom shortly after moving in and went to live by himself in Queens. A small apartment that Michael also had a chance to see once.

The house was bigger than they needed. That was one of Jackie's complaints. Having a house with all the luxuries anyone could ask for was a danger, especially with so many empty rooms. One day it could be decided that one of the rooms had to be given to someone that needed the space. Their house, being so close to a university, which was growing larger every year, raised the possibility they would have to take a student into their home. A student who would be in need of space and be a complete stranger to them.

Michael felt tired from the last hill before the house. It was a tougher walk than expected, but he was happy to be there especially as Jackie came to the door to receive him.

"Hi, come in please."

"Nice neighborhood."

"Thanks, want something to drink?"

"Orange juice will be fine."

"Here, don't forget your thumb," she said.

He went over to the security system panel next to the entrance and placed his right thumb on the digital display.

"Adams, Michael." The security system correctly identified him. It asked Jackie if this was an intruder or a welcome guest. She had fifteen seconds to press yes, which she did right away. If she failed, or a stranger pressed the yes, the house would be locked down and the police dispatched. The police appreciated the system, which among other things kept an electronic record of who entered a house. It was a useful tool in criminal investigations.

Michael sat in her living room, relaxing, while she went to get some juice.

"I wanted to apologize for my outburst the other day." Jackie handed him the orange juice.

"No need."

"I meant to call you on Monday. I remembered what day it was . . . You were probably not feeling good."

He took a sip of the juice. It was touching for her to have remembered. "Thanks, that's thoughtful."

"You still have the nightmares?"

"Sometimes."

He noticed Jackie parting her hair from her face. She used her hair loose, requiring her constant attention. Michael loved it like that. Sitting in front of her reminded him of everything he found attractive about her. The beautiful lips, the easy smile, those expressive brown eyes. "I am really glad to see you again," he told her.

She smiled and they continued a pleasant conversation. They talked about her residency, if medicine was everything she expected, if journalism was everything he expected. Inevitably, they started to talk about the time they first met.

"It was so different in India," she said.

They met in India. She was a medical student doing volunteer work as required by her school, delivering care to a small village outside Agra.

He was doing a semester of community service. Traveled to Agra with the Peace Corps to help in the same free clinic where she worked. While there, he kept a travel blog. About once a week, he posted a commentary on life in a small village in India. Some of those posts, the ones critical of the Indian government, were posted in his school's weekly e-letter. One of them was even published in the government-owned New York Times. In the travel section, but still a significant achievement for a young journalist. Only a matter of time before he made the front page.

"How was it different?" he asked.

"I don't know. Over there it was straightforward. People were sick—you gave them a medication or did something to make them better. It's different here. Sometimes you don't feel like you are doing what's best for the patient."

"You sound disappointed."

"I don't know. I think it will get better. Once I finish my training, I'll probably join Doctors without Borders. I'll get to travel and practice medicine. Hopefully even help some sick people."

"Don't tell me you are going to become like that guy . . . What was his name again?" Michael chuckled.

"Don't start with him," Jackie said, trying to suppress a smile of her own. "You know how much trouble you got me into with him?"

"The man couldn't take a joke."

"I still remember the argument he got into when you told him you were a slave." She shook her head in disapproval.

"I was. He told me it was great I was there doing volunteer work. I told him I was not a volunteer. Who were we kidding? It was mandated. I had to go. It was mandatory volunteer work." He remembered back then Jackie had been upset with him for that exchange. Told him he was immature for getting into an unnecessary argument. Especially with an attending physician she needed to impress. Now, they were enjoying the memory of the incident. "I told him when you do work for someone and you are obligated to do it . . . And you are not being compensated . . . That's servitude. I looked him straight in the eyes and told him . . . Yup. I am a slave."

Their conversation went on for an hour. He enjoyed bringing up the funny things that happened in India and reminding her of so many annoying things he saw her attending physician do. The man had an exaggerated view of self-sacrifice.

"You regret your stay there?" Jackie asked.

"I would not say that. I didn't appreciate that I was forced to go. But I learned a lot about me, life, and . . ." He paused and looked at her for a couple of seconds. "I met you. That was the highlight of my stay."

The laughter of the moment was gone. Her expression turned serious.

"Jackie, I've never been able to forget you."

"It would never work out between us. You are younger than me."

"Come on, you talk like you are an old woman. You are a couple of years older than me. That's no big deal." It was a big deal in her mind, and he knew it. Sometimes he felt anything he said or did was proof to her of his immaturity.

"We had a nice time there but . . ."

"You remember that day at the Taj Mahal?"

Michael remembered well the time he invited her to go to the Taj Mahal. It was not far from where they were working.

"Of course, I remember. What a romantic place to go on a first date."

"How many couples can say they had their first kiss at the world famous Taj Mahal." He remembered it as the happiest day of his life. Their first kiss, exchanged in front of the raised marble tank, with the reflection of the Taj Mahal behind them.

"We are not a couple. We had a wonderful time in India. And I had a lot of fun with you when we went to Los Angeles together. But we have very different lives now. It would never work out between us."

Michael could not hide his disappointment. That was not the response he was expecting.

"Don't give me that long face. We can still be friends. That's why I invited you here today. There was no need to get upset at you like that when we are just friends."

Her last statement hurt more than anything else. Since it made it clear why she called. Getting upset at him at the coffee shop showed she still had feelings for him. So she called to make sure he understood there was no romantic interest.

"I had a nice time tonight, but it is getting late. I have class in the morning." He tried, in vain, to pretend it did not bother him to be "just a friend."

Michael came out of the house and was starting his walk toward the bus stop when Jackie's mom pulled over.

"Hi Mike."

"Hi, Ms. Perez."

She came out of her car, looking happy to see him.

"It's Ms. Marshall, and you can just call me Abigail."

He remembered well she preferred Ms. Marshall, but at that moment, he did not care.

"How have you been? It is good to see you," she said.

"I'm pretty good. Came by to chat with Jackie, but I have to get going. Don't want to miss my bus." There was a bus passing by every thirty minutes, and he did not want to get into a long conversation, which would make him miss the next one.

"I won't keep you then. But please don't be a stranger."

Michael only took a few steps down the driveway before she pulled his arm.

"Jackie needs some distraction. All she does is read those medicine books all day, every day. Take her out. She needs to have some fun."

"Well, I don't think she is all that interested."

"Nonsense. She has never liked a guy as much as she liked you. You two were in love—she still is. It's so obvious."

"She didn't seem interested."

Michael wished there was something he could say to break off the exchange. Then it occurred to him, he had not asked Jackie about her grandfather.

"You need to be persistent."

"Ms. Marshall, I would like to get in touch with your father. How can I do that?"

Michael was a surprised at her expression. She looked as if he had just insulted her ancestors.

"Why do you want to know about him? Is that why you came here? To find out where he is?"

"I came here to chat with Jackie."

"Sure, you came here to find out if she knows where my father is."

"What do you mean where he is?"

"Please go. You are not welcome in this house."

Chapter 7

Carbon Credits (CC) became the official monetary system throughout Europe and the United States in 2020. It was more than just a new currency. It was an entire new way of conducting financial transactions. Paper money was gone, replaced by an electronic monetary system.

The advocates of the new system had a simple goal. To reward social and environmental responsibility rather than greed. They wanted a system that would even out the economic playing field for all social classes. They needed a system that would be stable and not subject to previous ups and downs.

All Americans had an account with the government, based on the previous social security system, and were allotted a specific amount of carbon credits. This was not based on the type of job. A doctor could get the same amount of credits as a construction worker.

There were ways to increase the allotted amount. If someone were involved with community activities, that person would get a larger amount. People that lived in more environmentally friendly cities received larger amounts. In 2076, the average American worker received fifty thousand CC.

All necessities were guaranteed. Health care, utilities, a home to live in, were all entitlements provided by the government.

Deductions on consumption were based on the negative impact a product had on the environment. The higher the carbon footprint of a product or service, the higher the deduction would be. Prices were no longer guided by principles of supply and demand.

Saving money was not required. Doing community service was encouraged for anyone who wanted to increase their carbon credits account.

Retirement was no longer a concern for senior citizens since they would continue to receive a yearly amount. Productivity was not rewarded. However, disobedience was punished with heavy deductions. People were expected to work until they were seventy, and an early retirement would lead to a significant reduction in the allotted credits. The accumulation of money was no longer the driving force to work. Rather, it was the responsibility to contribute to society.

Human activities could be better regulated using the carbon credits system. Traveling by air was an activity with a large carbon footprint. Airplanes consumed an unacceptable amount of fossil fuel. There was an electric airplane developed once, fancy, with solar panels in its wings. On its "main voyage" from New York to Los Angeles, it crashed shortly after takeoff. No one wanted to get aboard an electric airplane after that, and the aviation industry continued using fossil fuels. To discourage air travel, the government implemented large carbon credits reductions.

The accepted way to travel was by the high-speed rail system, which connected most cities within the continental United States. The Obama-Rail could reach speeds of two hundred miles per hour, considered the fastest and best way for domestic travel.

The electronic monetary system also made it difficult for illegal transactions, since there would be an electronic footprint to every exchange. Every transfer of credits from one person's account to another had to be justified.

"What do you mean four thousand? I don't have those kinds of credits." Jackie sat in her family room, trying to relax by reading a book, but a phone call interrupted her reading. "I really need those meds." She stood up and dropped her e-book reader. She paced the room, listening to her caller. "How would I even make the transaction? Those meds are illegal . . . Fine, I will see what I can do . . ." She noticed her mother coming into the room. "No, I can't send him off to Texas. I wouldn't even know how to do that . . ." She said hi to her mom. "No, I don't know any one that works in the government. I don't have those kinds of connections . . ." Her mom asked her who she was talking to. Jackie signaled for her to wait. "I'm gonna let you go. I'll get back to you and let you know what I'm going to do. But I need those meds."

"Who was that?"

Her mom sat down, took off her shoes; she looked tired from a long day at work.

"I'll tell you later, Mom. I want to go take a shower and get some sleep."

"I saw Mike was here."

"Yes, he left a few minutes ago." She picked up her e-book and headed for the stairs.

The lights went off, and the whole house became engulfed in darkness. Jackie looked around and saw a red light blinking.

"What happened?" she asked.

Jackie's mom went over to the temperature panel; the blinking red light was coming from there. "You didn't see this? You have the temperature down to seventy-two, how could you? We're going to get a big fine."

She adjusted the temperature up to much more environmentally friendly seventy-eight degrees. However, the damage was done. They exceeded their power usage for the day, and now their power would be off, likely for the rest of the evening. Her mom went back to the sofa.

"Sorry Mom, it felt a little hot. And since we had company over, I lowered it."

"Yes, company, I don't like him."

Jackie was surprised to hear that. Her mom insisted many times she should call Michael. Kept telling her how much she enjoyed meeting him the first time Jackie brought him over.

She stepped down from the stairs to get a better look at her mom. Her eyes were adjusting to the darkness. "Why? What happened?"

"Is Grandpa here?"

"Yes, he's downstairs in his room. Said he was going to sleep early."

"Did Mike see him?"

"No. He's been in his room, why?" She could see her mom looked annoyed.

"He asked me about Dad. I found it very strange. Did he ask you anything?"

"Not today, but he did the other day. Why is that odd? He met Grandpa. They hit it off when we were in Los Angeles. You know how much Grandpa likes to talk. Mike enjoyed very much listening to him." Jackie felt, as usual, her mom was making a mountain out of nothing.

"I think it's odd that he does not call you, and right at this moment, he comes looking for you and asking about Dad."

Jackie tried to interrupt her mom, but it was to no use. Her mom raised her hand—she had more to say, and Jackie had to listen.

"I'm just saying, watch out. He could be fishing for information. We don't need headaches right now. Doesn't his dad work for the government? All these government kids are the same—they'll sell out their parents if they have to."

"Mom, you are . . ." Jackie paused for a second as she realized something. "You're right. His dad is high up in the government." She was all smiles now. "He might be able to help."

"Help?" her mom asked.

"Yes. If you have a government waiver, you can actually get meds from abroad. It's otherwise illegal. But there are waivers available for government officials." She sat at the edge of the sofa close to her mom.

"I just told you not to trust him. Now you're going to go and volunteer information about your grandpa and ask him if he can help?"

"Mom, you don't know Mike. He is a sweet guy. He might be a little immature sometimes, but you can trust him."

"I don't trust him. Please promise me you won't tell him anything. We already had an agent here yesterday. You know how anxious I was after that. If they even suspect your grandpa is here, they'll come back. And they won't ask nicely next time."

Jackie headed again for the stairs. She talked back to her mom as she walked away, "Come on, Mom, don't be paranoid. It's not like Grandpa is some kind of a criminal."

Chapter 8

Michael noticed a blue Obamobile pulling up next to him, as he walked from his place to the bus stop, on his way to school. It was an egg-shaped two-seater. The smallest and most common car in America.

"Need a ride?"

He recognized the friendly face of Jackie. He smiled and went up to the car, pressed his thumb on the fingertip recognition panel for the door to open.

"Hello, my friend, how are you?" she said.

"Surprised to see you." He said with a big smile.

The car had turned off, so she pressed her thumb on a panel next to the wheel for the car to restart. The fingertip recognition system would only allow its main user to start the car. Other drivers could use it as well, if the main user entered their data prior to their use.

"Want a ride to school?"

"Sure, but aren't you headed the opposite direction?" Michael pointed west on Hempstead turnpike toward her hospital, which wasn't far from where he lived.

"I'm early. Your school is by my house, so I can take the same route without problems and just let you get out up front."

She pressed the screen on her navigation system, letting it know she was driving back home. Sometimes Michael felt happy he did not have a car. The idea of having to get permission from a machine to go anywhere was troubling.

The standard navigation system allowed five different addresses to be saved in the system. Every user had the right to enter one non-saved destination per month. If the user tried to go anywhere other than those destinations, the car would not go. It would come to a stop. This was for the good of the owner since it decreased theft and the good of society by decreasing unnecessary congestion on the roads. It promoted saving energy by discouraging needless trips for which mass transportation could be used. The vehicle could only function within a fifty-mile radius of the user's home address. It would shut down if taken beyond that distance.

"New car, right?" he asked.

"Yes. Like it?"

"I don't like that it gets to decide where you can or cannot go. Other than that, I like it. I'm trying to accumulate some credits, see if I can get one."

He was close to the amount he needed. Just recently, he had gone for a test drive. At the test drive, he drove one exactly like hers; the salesman gave him a complete lecture about the car. The Obamobile was the most widely available car in America, the salesman told him. It came in a two-passenger compact and a limited four-door sedan. It was an electrical vehicle with a maximum speed of sixty miles per hour, but the manufacturer did not recommend exceeding forty-five. It required recharging after approximately forty miles.

The name of the car was intended to commemorate the president that nationalized the automobile industry. That opened the doors for small and environmentally friendly vehicles. It came in blue or red.

"You look very nice." His attention turned to Jackie. Happy to see her, even if all she wanted was to be friends. Then again, maybe he did have a chance to earn back her heart, to get her to change her mind about their relationship. She was worth the effort.

"Thanks." She had her eyes on the road but did turn for a second to give him a big smile. "Why were you asking about my grandfather? I'm just curious."

Grandfather? What grandfather? Her smile was the only thing occupying his mind at the moment.

"Will you go out to dinner with me tomorrow night? I know this great Portuguese restaurant."

"I told you yesterday. Let's keep it as friends only."

"Friends can have dinner together." He saw her smile. Her gaze focused on the road ahead. She did not look at him but seemed to be considering it.

"Just dinner. Not a date. Right?"

"Absolutely. Just dinner. I won't even bring you roses."

She chuckled. In one of their first dates, he brought her a dozen red roses. She loved the gesture. Told him "no one buys roses anymore." If he was trying to impress her, she said back then, roses were a step in the right direction.

"Definitely not roses," she said.

Traffic along the Long Island Expressway was moving well that morning. The sea of blue and red Obamobiles was flowing without delays. Not congested, as it was the usual. His exit was coming up, and they would soon reach their destination.

"Where's the famous Long Island traffic when you need it," he murmured.

"Sorry?"

He shook his head and smiled. "Nothing."

She had to stop to recharge the car. After ten minutes, they were back on the road.

"How come you don't have enough carbon credits for a car?" she asked him after he complained of how long it took to recharge it. It was one of the reasons many people found cars impractical, preferred to use mass transportation to go anywhere.

"I've been living irresponsibly, so it is hard to accumulate the credits."

"What about doing some community service?"

He looked at her and gave her a sarcastic smile. "I'll just take the bus until I can get a real job. At least I'll feel like I've earned it."

Michael saw the sign in front of them: "New York Institute of Technology."

"We're here," she said.

He leaned toward Jackie and kissed her cheek. "Thanks, I'll call you later. Tell you where we're going."

"We can just meet there." She smiled. "Since it's not a date. Just text me the name of the place."

She drove away. As he walked to his class, he smiled, thought about their "not a date" date. It was a step in the right direction.

If he was able to romance her once before, he could do it again. He would sweep her off her feet, just as he did before. Then, it occurred to him he was going to need some roses.

Baron West's latest assignment sent him into Long Island. Traveling all over the country was part of the job, so he was used to it. This was a small and unworthy assignment as far as he was concerned. His previous case had been high profile and far more interesting, but it did not turn out well. Not his fault, of course. But it did lead him to this mission. This one he was confident he would be able to wrap up in a couple of days.

The traffic was light on the Long Island Expressway, which was unusual. Tended to be a parking lot on most days. It made it easier to keep track of the car he was following. He was curious to know whom she picked up. Why did she turn around?

It was a hot day, and the air conditioner was broken. That irritated him. In the afternoon, he would have to visit the local field office and request another car.

She stopped in front of a university, and the kid she picked up came out of the car. He would have to review her file again. However, he was convinced that kid was not in her file.

The file described her as a loner, highly dedicated to her career and studies, with few friends. However, this was the second time he saw her with the same kid. The night prior, he had seen him visiting her house.

She drove away. Maybe it would be worth asking the kid some questions. Most college kids were willing to be cooperative and informative.

West drove toward him and stopped his car. He was sweating, and it was noticeable through his shirt. In spite of the heat, he put his suit jacket on so that he would not feel self-conscious about the sweating.

"Good morning."

The kid was tall, probably about six foot two, well built, the type to be engaged in sports. Maybe weight lifting. With black hair and blue eyes, most likely he was popular with the girls. Definitely the type that runs for fun and away from trouble.

"What's your name, kid?" Agent Baron West showed his identification.

Michael looked at it for a couple of seconds. West saw the same wide-eyed look of surprise he elicited so many times before.

"Agent West, FBI. Let me ask you a couple of questions."

"Sure," Michael said.

"What's your name?"

"Michael. Michael Adams."

He did not look nervous to be talking to an agent. No hesitancy in his voice. Unusual for a kid his age.

"What's your relationship with Jackie Perez?"

"Is she in trouble?" Michael asked, looking concerned.

"I'll ask the questions if that's okay with you." West stared into his eyes. He did not detect fear. "Do you know her?"

Michael admitted he did. Told him he used to date her. That they were just friends now.

"She has a grandfather. An old man by the name of Calvin Marshall. Do you know him?" West had no clues as to where the old man was. He disappeared, leaving no trace behind. But, he was close to his granddaughter; it made sense he would try to make contact with her at some point.

"Calvin Marshall?" Michael looked thoughtful. He repeated the name twice. "No. Doesn't sound familiar."

"You dated the girl and she never mentioned her grandfather?"

"If she did, I never paid attention," he said with a big smile. He looked proud of his answer. "She is very cute. I have sometimes a hard time paying attention when she talks."

He was lying. And there was nothing West hated more than a lying punk. He probably thought he had to protect his girlfriend.

The heat continued to bother West. Damn global warming, he thought.

"All right. Try to remember that name. Calvin Marshall. I just need to have a little chat with him. Nothing serious. If you find out anything . . . Here's my card. Give me a call. I'll make it worth your time."

Michael picked up the card and said yes while looking at it. West walked back to his car feeling satisfied. The kid was lying, no doubt about that. But that meant he was moving in the right direction. Not many people dared lie to a federal agent. Too many scary stories going around of what could happen if you were dishonest with the authorities. If he had the nerve to lie, then there was something important to hide. It would be worth to do a little research on who was Michael Adams.

Chapter 9

First, Jackie's mom reacted in a weird way when he asked about her dad. Then, a federal agent came asking if he knew the old man. There was something going on with Professor Marshall. Michael was due for an Ethics in Journalism class but instead went straight to the library and sat in front of a computer.

He needed to do a little research on the professor. Knowing that his browsing history was subject to scrutiny, he considered for a moment logging on using his father's account. Quickly he decided against that. It could get him into serious trouble, especially with his dad. He decided instead to send a text to his friend Craig, asking him to join him in the library.

In the meantime, he logged on just to check the news. The school's web page came on, and he first checked if the change in editor had been updated. It certainly had. Parker did not waste time.

He noticed the main headline in the national news. "Consumption Chip Bill passes House vote." If he had written an article about that instead of the Fourth of July—if he had not mentioned Ronald Reagan, he would still be editor. Playing by the rules was something he needed to learn.

He clicked on the headline; to see how it was being reported, doubting it was being covered objectively.

The article went into detail on what the new law guaranteed. It would make mandatory the use by everyone of a microchip, less than one centimeter in size. This chip could be placed under the skin, and among its principal functions, it would track the amount of calories consumed by the person. It would allow the government to send a warning to anyone who was overconsuming.

Repeated offenders could face big fines. The chip was a great opportunity to decrease everyone's carbon footprint, reduce any excessive use of resources, which lead to economic inequality, and end the health crisis of obesity.

The chip would contain detailed personal information, including the person's own health record. This would make it easier for medical or emergency personnel to have immediate access to important information. It would decrease medical errors since the information would be up to date and always available with the person, no matter where.

Remote access would allow parents to know where their child might be at all times. Also, caregivers could track elderly folks they were caring for—they would be able to know if grandma took her medication. How wonderful, thought Michael. Everyone will be so well taken care of from now on. "Maybe someone will send me a reminder if I forget to eat lunch," Michael murmured.

Michael noticed there was not a single negative comment, nothing about the concerns that some might have. It mentioned that the vote was in favor of the bill's passage by a wide margin; giving the impression that it was not a controversial issue. That everyone agreed the chip was a positive thing. The fact that the government would have easy access to personal information and know where anyone was at all times did not seem to bother a single person.

At the end of the article, it mentioned the bill was now headed for the Senate, where at some point it was felt it would face a tougher time. However, the tragic absence of a Senator Thomas had killed whatever opposition it faced.

"Hey, you're supposed to be in class."

Michael turned around to see his friend Craig walking toward him.

"Come here."

Craig sat in a chair, and Michael asked him to get closer. He did not want to be loud since the library was full of students and in total silence. Everybody sat in front of a computer, busy in whatever they were doing.

"You know, last night I went to Jackie's house."

"You did? How did that go?"

"Well, let me tell you something," Michael whispered. "I ran into Jackie's mom, and when I asked her about her father, Jackie's grandpa, she freaked out."

"Why?"

Michael gestured for Craig to keep his tone down. "I don't know. But there's more." He moved closer so Craig could hear him better. "This morning a federal agent stopped me to ask about Jackie's grandpa."

Craig sat up, moved away from Michael. "Oh no. That's not good. You better stay away from him or from Jackie. They're probably in trouble. You don't want to get mixed up on it."

"Right," Michael said. He turned back toward the computer. "I need you to log me on. I have to find out what's going on."

"Don't get involved on this, buddy. I'm telling you. My dad . . . When he refused to upgrade the house, you know to get the new security system. He made a comment that he had a gun at home. That was the only security he needed. Federal agents came home to ask him questions. You don't want to mess around with them. You don't need that."

Michael did not pay attention to the friendly and unsolicited advice. He insisted his friend help him. Once Craig did log on, Michael started his search.

"Got it."

"What is it?"

"This is the Santa Barbara City College website," he said, picking up Craig's phone and dialing the number. "That's where I remember he works. He is a history professor there." Michael did not want to use his own phone. If they had been checking on his internet activity, it was safe to assume they could monitor his phone calls.

"Why you calling them? You're looking for trouble."

"Hi I need the history department please . . ." He covered the phone with his hand and told Craig not to worry. "Hi, I'm looking for a professor Calvin Marshall. May I speak with him please?" Michael listened; the lady he was talking to told him there was no one there by that name. "Are you sure? I'm pretty sure you have a professor Marshall there . . ." He looked at Craig and covered his phone again. "They put me on hold—yes, hi . . ."

He listened without saying anything. "Well, thank you. I really appreciate it."

"What did they say?"

Michael was looking straight at the computer. He thought for a moment before answering his friend. "He said they don't have a Professor Marshall anymore. He left suddenly. They believe he had some medical issues. They heard he was refusing treatment and then disappeared. He has been taken off the faculty on a medical leave. That's all they know. They haven't heard from him."

"So he is a sick old man refusing treatment. Leave it alone, man." Craig stood up; he was ready to get out of there.

Michael logged off and stood up. "It doesn't make sense. A federal agent would be looking for him because he is refusing treatment." He smiled and grabbed Craig's arm. "You know who will know?"

Craig shook his head. It was obvious he wanted him to drop the whole thing, but it was not Michael's nature to do so. He had to find out. Asking Jackie was out of the question. Last thing he needed was for her to think he was going out with her just to solve the mystery of what happened to her grandfather. Especially if she was trying to protect that mystery.

"Tony. Jackie's dad. He is an architect, but he is actually working—running a construction company. He's a really cool guy. He'll know what's happened and won't tell me to get lost like Jackie's mom did."

Chapter 10

Calvin Marshall felt helpless. He understood he needed to stay home, but he was feeling claustrophobic in that basement. It was the safest place to be. The security system was useless, since it had malfunctioned, and Tony had never managed to get someone to come in and fix it. Faulty sensors could not detect his presence, and he could go and come as pleased. He had a room and a bathroom down there; his granddaughter brought him down anything he needed.

After a few days, it was easy to feel suffocated. All he wanted was to get some fresh air. He went for a walk and found a mall. There was no need to buy anything, but it was a busy place, easy to get lost in a crowd. Walking in the mall, up and down the stairs, would give him the exercise he needed. The past few days had been too stressful for him. His biggest worry had become Jackie. When he came to stay with his daughter and granddaughter, the last thing he wanted was to bother them. Now, Jackie was going through the trouble of finding medications for him. Medications he had no intention of taking, no matter what she said.

His daughter was nervous, concerned there would be a federal agent knocking on their door again. It did not help that she was suffering from generalized anxiety disorder. She was taking anxiety medication ever since her mother died. If her mother were alive, things would be different.

He went into a store to check out some shirts. If only he could buy something, he thought. But, he could not afford to use his carbon credits and be identified in any way by making a purchase. They would find him.

"Excuse me."

He placed the shirt back and turned around. An old lady was coming his way.

"You gotta help me," she said. She looked to be in distress. "They wanna take me away, put me to sleep like some useless dog, please help me." She had tears in her eyes.

"Who wants to take you away?" Marshall asked. Then, he saw two community organizers approach them, a man and a woman.

"No. Go away, please get away from me," the old lady told the woman as she came up to her.

The man looked at Marshall and another lady standing nearby "She got away from the hospital. She is a little confused. We're taking her back," he told them.

"No! Get away from me." The old lady pushed the woman aside.

Marshall went up to the old lady. "Please, let me talk to her. She's frightened."

The man pulled Marshall's arm. "Sir, please don't interfere. She is just a confused lady, needs to be in the hospital, on her medication."

"Let me just talk to her." Marshall tried to get around the community organizer.

The man stood in front of Marshall; he was looking annoyed at this point. "I said, let it go, old man. We need to take her back to the hospital. Now move along."

"She looks so frightened."

The community organizer looked angry. "I don't think you understood me. Stay out of this. Don't you have some shopping to do? Or are you lost too?" The man took out his electronic pad. "Let me see your thumb, let's see who you are."

It was over; Marshall knew it. To be identified meant it would be him on his way to a hospital. Him who would be asking for help. He should have stayed in that basement.

"Help! Help!" The old lady ran away from the woman and was getting the attention of everyone at the mall with her yelling.

The man, seeing that his partner was not able to manage the old lady on her own, went over to help her. As bad as Marshall felt for the predicament the old lady was in, he needed to take advantage of the moment and get away. He turned around and walked away from the scene as fast as he could.

He went inside a store, deciding to spend some time there, until he felt it was safe to walk back home. If the community organizers saw him outside, walking home, they might go up to him again. He had to stay away from them.

The section for men's cloth seemed like the perfect place to blend in. There were some jackets on display, and he tried one of them. As he stepped up to a mirror to check himself out, the image in front of him was one he did not recognize. There was an old man looking back at him from the mirror. How did that happen, he wondered. "When did I get so old?" he murmured.

Marshall noticed a man in a suit looking at him. Did he really look his way? He was not sure; it happened too fast. It was better not to take any chances. He placed the jacket back in its hanger and walked out of the store.

The man with the suit also came out. Was he being followed? Was he being paranoid? He went down the stairs, walked as fast as he could without running. The exit of the mall was toward his left, and he headed that way. He looked back and saw the man coming down as well. If he was after him, he did not seem to be in a hurry. Marshall picked up his pace, convinced he was being followed.

As he came out, he saw the sign of a university next to the mall and walked on that direction. There were lots of students. He walked through the lawn of the school, straight to where they were. An old man walking in a campus full of students in their twenties was not the best place to hide. He kept walking and did not dare look back. If he saw the man again, he would have to start running.

Cutting across a parking lot, he saw a forestlike area with tall trees, seemed like a good place to hide. Once he reached there, he ran and moved diagonal through those woods, ran for half a mile, and decided to stop behind one of the trees. He felt short of breath and dizzy. It took him a while to get the courage to look back. No one was following him. Feeling relieved, he sat down for a moment. A few minutes of rest were needed before he could start walking again.

Suddenly, he realized he had no clue where he was or how to get home from there. Was he really becoming forgetful? Maybe they were right, and he was losing his mind. Lost and without a way to call anyone to come get him was not the way his trip to the mall was supposed to end. Even if he could get a phone, the last thing he wanted was to make a call.

Chapter 11

Saturday May 28
Mineola, New York

Roses turned out to be a great idea. Her smile of approval made it all worth it. Michael sat at the restaurant, admiring her beauty. Proud of his choice, of the restaurant he picked for their first date in more than a year. It was a Portuguese restaurant. The music, the paintings of sea ships from the Age of Discoveries, and the traditional Mediterranean food made him feel as if he was in Europe. They loved the music. There had been a lady singing a fado, a melancholic, passionate, and time-honored song from Portugal. The specialty of the house was seafood, and she was pleased with her meal as was Michael who ordered cod fish. It was rich in calories, made with potatoes and eggs. It was delicious.

"More wine?"

"Sure." Jackie extended her glass. "That was a nice gesture. I can't believe you remembered."

He poured the wine in her glass. A Cabernet Sauvignon that he knew was her favorite.

She was touched he remembered her preference. "With that memory of yours, I shouldn't be surprised you remembered. Still. It was a nice gesture."

They clicked their glasses and exchanged smiles. She looked as he remembered her on their first date. They went to the Taj Mahal for a day of sigh seeing that turned out to be a day of romance. He impressed her by his knowledge of the Taj Mahal. Michael could picture the look in her face when he talked about its history. How it had been built by the Shah Jahan in memory of his dead wife. At that moment, she did not look like the serious medical student who wanted nothing but a career. Rather, she was a sweet girl who believed in romance and everlasting love. He could see that same look again.

Michael could not comprehend why he allowed a year to go by before calling her. He took more wine, gazing directly into her eyes. "I should have called you a long time ago and apologize. I guess it was immaturish of me."

"Immaturish? Is that a word?" She smiled.

"You were right. I went out with that girl right after we broke up just to spite you."

"I know you did. And yes it was immature of you." She picked up her glass and drank some more wine.

Michael was happy to see she was enjoying it.

"But, I shouldn't have broken up with you like that. We just came back from having a great time in Los Angeles. Falling in love in India then coming home and taking off together to Los Angeles. Everything was moving so fast. I was scared. Then starting my residency and I knew how busy I would be. I didn't think I was going to have time for fun or romance."

Michael was pleased, as the night was going better than expected.

The waiter approached them. "Any dessert?"

Jackie took the digital menu and looked at the choices. "I'll have a lemon meringue pie," she said.

Michael knew exactly what he wanted. "I'll have the chocolate mousse."

The waiter looked at his digital pad, "I'm sorry, sir. That's above your ACI."

Michael looked up at the waiter in disbelief. The allotted calorie intake (ACI) was a mandatory restriction, in all restaurants, of the maximum amount of calories a customer could consume during a given meal. He was not a fan of the restriction.

Michael was irritated, and he knew it was evident in his face. He looked at the waiter and continued to point to his choice of dessert in the menu. "I don't care about the ACI. I've had it before, and I've survived."

"I know, sir. They have recently decreased the amount of calories allowed per customer."

The evening had gone perfect; it was better not to make an issue out of this. He did not want to create a scene in front of Jackie. After all, it was not the waiter's fault; he was just following the law.

"It's this obesity epidemic. That's why they have increased the restrictions. To make sure people start consuming fewer calories," Jackie said.

Michael understood it and still did not agree with it being done. "I know. I work out every day. I do kickboxing and burn a lot of calories. I have a very low body fat. I don't think I need to worry about eating a little chocolate once in a while."

"But your eating habits will continue as you get older and less active. That's when people get obese."

"Sir, if I might make a recommendation. We have this delicious sugar-free flan. It's low in calories but still very good." The waiter pointed to the item in the menu.

Michael looked up slowly to the waiter, annoyed at him, whether his fault or not. "I don't like . . ." He paused and stared for a second. "Flan." He took a deep breath and smiled at Jackie. A smile of resignation. "I wanted the chocolate mousse."

"I'm sorry, sir. It's for your own good."

"Just bring me a cup of coffee." He handed back the menu display. "What?"

She was shaking her head and smiling. "Same old Mike." Her phone interrupted them. "Yes . . . This is Jackie . . ."

Her expression turned serious. It was the look she had when talking about her studies and career.

"You have the meds . . . Wonderful . . ."

Michael figured she was talking about a patient.

"Okay. I'm on my way then."

He had the feeling their night was coming to a premature end.

"I'm sorry, but I have to go."

"I didn't know you were on call today," Michael said.

"No. This is not a hospital thing. It's personal."

She did not seem to want to elaborate, and Michael was not going to push it. Their evening was delightful even if it ended hastily. He enjoyed her company and felt she did as well. There were no questions about her grandfather, and that was done on purpose. Not wanting to give the impression their dinner had any other agenda, other than enjoying her company.

"I had a great time tonight, but I do have to go," she said.

"No problem. I'll take care of the bill."

"We should split it. After all, this was not a date."

It felt like a date to him. "If you are in a rush, go. I'll take care of it as friends. You can treat me some other time, and we'll be even." Perfect, he thought. Another date was needed, so she could treat him.

"Thanks. Bye." She leaned forward and gave him a kiss on his cheek and rushed out. "Thanks for the roses," she said as she walked out of the restaurant.

The waiter came back a few minutes later. "Here's the lemon meringue pie."

"She went to the restroom to freshen up a little," Michael said. "She said to tell you she changed her mind. She doesn't want the lemon meringue pie. She wants to try the chocolate mousse. If that's okay with you?"

"No problem, sir. I'll be right back." The waiter picked up the pie.

"Make it to go, please. And bring me the bill." He smiled, satisfied he had won a battle in the struggle for freedom. At least the freedom to eat chocolate mousse.

Chapter 12

It was late, almost midnight, but at least Jackie did not have to get up early the next morning. She was glad about that. Losing sleep was something she did regularly, yet even after one year of internship, it was difficult to get used to.

She was headed home, driving along the Long Island Expressway, after what had been an interesting evening for her. A nice and enjoyable dinner with a great friend had been the highlight. She looked down at the passenger seat and smiled, seeing the dozen red roses Michael gave her. She wanted to ask him why the questions about her grandfather. But it all became irrelevant as the evening went on, as she enjoyed his company so much.

Her mom was overreacting anyways. Jackie knew Michael well enough to know he was no government informant.

She came off the highway, stopped at a red light, and looked down at the package next to the flowers. It had been the source of her headaches for the past few days, and now it was finally taken care of. At least temporarily. Her pharmacist friend called and told her he had the medications. He gave her a three-month supply but warned her he would not be able to keep doing this on a regular basis. Jackie still needed to come up with a long-term plan.

She wanted to ask Michael about his father, to see if he could pull in some favors. Making a request like that was not easy. Especially with a friend she had not seen in a year.

Her life had become so complicated since her grandfather showed up at their door, telling them about his illness. At least now, she could get him started on a treatment. In the package, there was aricept, which her grandfather would have to take every night, and also namenda, which he would need to take twice a day. These were medications she was not used to prescribing. She never had to. They were expensive medications and no longer used in the United States, made illegal years prior. They were not considered the standard of care for the treatment of Alzheimer's dementia, since they were not a cure. All they would do would be to slow down her grandfather's symptoms. That was fine with her. She wanted to enjoy his company for a few more years.

His symptoms were getting worse. He gave her a scare the day prior when he went to the mall for a walk and got lost. Did not find his way back home until late at night. Did not even remember their phone number to call, to ask someone to go pick him up. He said he did not want to use a phone. Jackie knew he was compensating. Patients started to do that as their memory failed them. They would rationalize their memory loss and make excuses, convince themselves there was no problem. It was going to be a struggle to get him to take the pills.

He had left Los Angeles refusing to get treatment. However, that she could understand. She did not agree with the standard way of treating Alzheimer's. Taking the meds would be different, not a cure, but they would help with few risks of side effects. She would convince him to take them. If all else failed, guilt was a powerful tool. After all the trouble she went through, how could he not take them? She smiled knowing she was the only one that could convince her grandpa to do something he did not want to do.

She wondered if she could convince him to go to Texas. Her pharmacist friend reminded her the best research program for the treatment of Alzheimer's was located in Houston. She didn't know how to get that accomplished, even if Grandpa agreed. Getting to Texas was impossible. Not even Michael's dad would be able to help with that, no matter how well connected.

When she turned the corner into Northern Boulevard, five minutes from her house, she noticed a car following her. The white sedan had been behind her since she came off the highway. She accelerated and the white sedan matched her speed. She was getting nervous. Why would anyone be following her? Could anyone know she was transporting illegal medications?

"Come down, Jackie, don't be paranoid." But the white car was getting closer, tailgating her. She pressed the accelerator and as she reached a speed of sixty miles per hour, her rearview mirror revealed the red and blue lights. It was a police car.

"Oh no." Jackie's car slowed down as the police officer, through remote access, took charge of her vehicle.

The car was pulled over to the side of the road. She took the package and hid it under the seat. If the cop found contraband like that, she would be in trouble. At least a fine. Even a suspension of her medical license. It would get her pharmacist friend into a mess. If they asked who the medications were for, her grandfather would be in trouble too. She lowered the window as the officer approached her car.

"License, please."

She placed her thumb on his digital pad, and he was able to pull up her driver's license. The system would do a background check. First, to make sure she was the registered owner of that vehicle. Then, any felonies, misdemeanors, or traffic violations, he would know about in a few seconds.

Her record was clean. Not a single infraction.

"You know why I pulled you over, Miss?"

"Was I going too fast?" If so, it was not her fault. He was the one who scared her by tailgating and made her accelerate. Then again, he would know if she had been speeding before that. Even before pulling her over he must have accessed her trip itinerary and would have known exactly where she had gone and how fast.

"No. Do you know how many miles you've driven today?"

Jackie looked at the dashboard. "I didn't get a warning." The navigation system was supposed to warn her if she exceeded her daily allowed mileage.

The cop flashed his light at the dashboard. "The new restrictions have probably not been downloaded yet. I'm sure you are aware of the power shortages."

"Yes, sir."

"It's because of people trying to squeeze every last mile, waiting right until they get a warning, that we now have this tougher restrictions."

"I was having dinner with a friend and then I received this call, I kind of had to go meet someone right away."

"And there was something wrong with the bus? The train?"

He started pressing his pad, and she knew she was not getting away from a fine. After getting the meds, she was running low on credits. A fine would take her over her limit. Next month she would have to pay a fine just for going over her limit.

"You are not far from home," he said when he was done, "so please go straight there."

"Okay, officer."

"Good night."

The police car sped away, ahead of her. She noticed her hands were shaking. It was not just about the fine. Her grandfather, getting illegal medications for him, having a federal agent coming to their house asking questions about him—it was all adding up. Even Michael was asking questions about him.

But she knew there was no reason to be freaking out like this. Her mother was transferring her anxieties to her daughter. With her grandfather refusal of medical treatment and subsequent disappearance, it was normal for the authorities to be concerned of his whereabouts, to be in the lookout for him. It was probably just a health department official, and her mother was behaving as if he was some federal agent looking for a wanted criminal. After that day, and after her mom's overreaction, she had been feeling as if someone was watching her. That was why she freaked out when she saw someone following her.

She felt calmer and resumed her drive home. No one was following her. It occurred to her it was not a bad idea to try and get Grandpa to Texas. He would get the treatment he needed, and her mother's anxiety would improve.

Jackie's dad was an architect who traveled all over the country to approve and supervise different projects. If anyone could give her a brilliant idea on how to get Grandpa to Texas, it would be him.

Chapter 13

June 1, 2076
Old Westbury, New York

Baron West found his way back to the campus of the New York Institute of Technology. He made an appointment to speak with Olga Parker, director of the journalism program, and the person to talk to about Michael Adams.

"What kind of student is he?" West was looking at the e-reader she provided him, where she had pulled Michael's school chart.

"He is smart. Does very well with minimal studying."

"Does he have a problem with authority?" West asked.

She thought about the question, sat back on her chair; crossing her legs.

West noticed she was wearing a short dress. Leaning back like that, it was obvious she wanted him to check out her legs. And she was just his type, a smart lady in great physical shape. She had short and bright blonde hair with deep blue eyes. To top it all, beautiful, full lips. Everything he needed for a pleasant stay in Long Island.

"You can say he does. I had a recent incident with him," she said.

"He is the type."

She didn't volunteer more, just looked at him, waiting for him to ask further questions.

"You've noticed his radical appearance?"

She looked surprised and leaned forward on her chair. "How so?"

"He is in his twenties. Does not have a single visible tattoo or piercing." He spent only a few minutes with Michael, but it was enough to take notice of every detail. "Don't you find that odd?"

"Never noticed."

"Can you name me any other kid his age that does not have a tattoo or a piercing?"

She looked thoughtful. "Not off the top of my head." She paused for a moment, hesitated then went ahead, "maybe he has them, and you didn't notice."

He looked up to her. "It's my business to notice. I wouldn't have missed it." He placed the electronic chart on her desk. "No. Let me tell you why. He does not like to conform. He does not like to do what others are doing. He wants to rebel but doesn't know how to. So he does small personal expressions like that. He is the most dangerous type. An individual who likes to go against his peers, do his own thing. One day he will go rogue and do something unexpected and dangerous, I assure you." The kid needed to be put in his place, for his own good. To learn to conform to the will of others. To abandon his hate for society. "I bet you he has intense workouts, so he can take his hate out on something physical."

West was impressing her; he was sure of it. He could see it in her face. "I am a psychiatrist, you know?"

"Oh really?" Her expression of amusement became more apparent.

He noticed no wedding ring in her left hand. Definitely his type of lady. "Yes. I was in the last class to graduate from NYU. Before the evacuation." It felt good to be talking about his favorite topic: himself. "Then I did my residency in psychiatry upstate. After that, never went into practice. Was recruited to join the FBI and have been with them ever since."

She looked impressed. Getting her to go out with him would be a piece of cake. If he decided he wanted to.

"Is there anything else you can tell me about him?"

She shook her head. "No."

"You mentioned you had an incident with him? What happened?"

"He wrote this editorial. He was my editor for the school's weekly letter."

West saw he had been editor until recently. Either fired or quit, it was another sign of insubordination, just as he figured. "Why no longer your editor?"

"That was the result of the incident." She leaned back on her seat. "I reviewed the editorial he wrote, as I always do. He usually does a decent job, finds interesting stories to comment about, gets the other students in the team to write thoughtful pieces. But sometimes he goes off in the wrong direction." She reached out for the chart he was holding. "Let me show you that editorial he wrote. I attached it to his file." A couple of clicks and she handed him back the e-reader.

West read it. And it was indeed, a most interesting editorial.

"He discusses the upcoming Fourth of July," she said. "I felt the article was too patriotic, in a weird way. It felt like, what a great country we were in the past, and that we have lost something. Rather than what a great country we are now, in spite of how lousy we used to be. It is not the kind of article I want my students to write."

"Does our generation still know what it means to be an American?" West stopped reading for a moment and looked at her.

"See? That's what I meant. It was too right-wing for my taste," she said.

He went back to reading it.

"And there's that mention at the end of the article of some letter Ronald Reagan wrote a hundred years ago," she continued. "I thought bringing up Reagan on the Fourth of July was inappropriate. It taints the holiday."

West read the editorial with increased interest. "Did you ask him how he knows of this letter?"

"No. Never even heard of such letter. Thought he made it up. My attitude was, even if it exists, who cares? Who wants to hear anything Reagan had to say?"

Agent West placed the chart back on her desk. He had not seen it in its entirety, and there was more he could ask. But he had seen enough. The kid knew more than he had let on, just as he suspected. He stood up, ready to leave, "I think I need to chat with Mr. Adams."

Chapter 14

June 1
Long Island City (Queens), New York

Going up to the one hundredth floor of a building under construction was a frightening idea. Especially in a shaky service elevator. But Michael came to see Tony Perez, to find out if he knew how to get in touch with Marshall, and Tony was a busy man, with no time to spare. He told Michael to come along if he wanted to ask some questions.

"We were hoping to have finished it last year. It has been under construction for more than ten years," Tony complained.

It was hard for Michael to pay attention when he was so busy looking down at the nearby buildings, which were becoming distant and smaller. An uneasy feeling was growing stronger with each floor. Finding out about Mr. Marshall could not be this important.

"How high are we?" Michael asked.

Tony looked amused. "We're here. One hundredth floor. Please don't tell me you're going to throw up."

It felt better to be off the elevator. The one hundredth floor was half finished. The roof was done. A far wall was completed. Divisions were being made for future offices. Tony walked over to a table in the middle, where a fat guy was standing. That guy was not keeping up with his allotted calorie intake, Michael thought.

Tony went up to a computer, completely ignoring the fat guy, and seemed to be checking out something important. Michael noticed frustration on Tony's face.

"Anything wrong?" Tony asked the fat guy.

"Everything is wrong. Pedro told me he came by asking you for a job, and you turned him down, again. We wanna know why."

"You mean besides he is just so damn slow, incompetent, and doesn't give a crap about anything?" Tony was shaking his head.

"He needs a job. He's got a family, you know? You think he likes going downtown every month, having to explain why he don't have a job? One of these days he's gonna get fined for not working. Is that what you want?"

"If you don't mind getting the fuck out of my face, I have a building to complete. It won't be built with my feelings about Pedro and his family. Actual work will need to be done." Tony returned his attention to the computer screen.

The fat man grabbed Tony's arm, "Don't think we're not keeping score, brother."

Michael moved toward Tony, but he raised his free hand, signaling for Michael to stay back.

"You think you're a big shit. Big time architect," the fat man continued. "But you got no wings. It's a long way down with no wings." The fat man stared into Tony's eyes and then walked away.

Michael thought about suggesting he take the stairs for some needed exercise, but he kept quiet, since he also had no wings and no desire to take a shortcut to the first floor.

Michael did not know what to say after witnessing a threat like that. He stayed quiet while Tony finished what he was doing.

"That's why nothing gets done," Tony was addressing Michael after a few minutes had gone by. "Why it's taken so long to complete this. You're forced to hire incompetent people." He was shaking his head, not looking pleased at all. "Sometimes I feel they don't want me to finish building it. This is just some kind of a jobs program for them."

Michael felt he came at a bad time, but he needed to know, and Tony could help.

"That's why nothing gets done," Tony repeated himself. "Ever wonder why there are so many homeless people, even though the government guarantees housing to everyone?"

"There's no one to build houses or repair old ones."

"Exactly. When you hire based on the need of the worker, and not based on how competent the person is to do the job, that's what happens. Everything gets delayed, nothing gets done right."

Michael looked at Manhattan in the distance. There was no way it was like that back when all those skyscrapers were built. Back then, it seemed America could build and do such amazing things.

"This is the world we live in, Mike. I'm sure Howard Roark would not approve. If he was forced to live in this world, he probably would jump out this hundredth floor voluntarily."

"Who is Howard Roark?" Michael asked and made a mental note to look up that name.

"I'm sure you didn't come all the way here to hear about my construction problems. What's in your mind?"

"I know you're busy, but I wanted to find out about Jackie's grandpa. I want to get in touch with him but haven't had much success. Jackie's mom freaked out when I asked her about him." Noise from the elevator interrupted them. Michael saw that it was coming up. Hopefully it was not the fat guy, coming back after getting a doughnut, for his promised flying lesson.

"Abigail freaks out about everything. It's her nature," Tony said, looking back at his computer.

Michael was in front of him, not able to see what Tony was doing. It involved a lot of clicking.

"Why do you need to talk to him?"

"He has this collection of Reagan, and I'm writing this article and needed to get some information from him. I don't seem to be able to get it anywhere else."

"Yes, he loves that collection. He's been able to get a lot of stuff over the years. He used to have a connection, some senator. He was able to get a lot of stuff through him."

Michael could tell Tony was dealing with important work, and he felt, once again, that he was in the way. Tony was reading and typing, and whatever it was, it was making him angry.

Once the typing stopped, Michael proceeded, "I called his university, but they told me he disappeared. That he was in some medical leave. You know anything at all?"

Tony moved away from his computer and walked toward Michael. "He was diagnosed with Alzheimer's. All I know is that they wanted to admit him to the hospital for some treatment, and he disappeared."

"Alzheimer's?" Michael paused for a moment, trying to remember where he had read something about that disease. "I read somewhere that they had a cure. Why would he refuse treatment to cure him?"

"The treatment is not meant to cure him."

Michael heard the familiar voice. It did not sound like the fat man. He turned around and saw Jackie coming off the elevator.

"Daddy!" She walked past Michael and embraced her dad.

Tony seemed to forget all of his frustrations in one instant. He hugged his daughter, lifting her a few inches off the ground. "Good to see you," he told her.

Jackie looked at Michael; if she was happy to see him, he could not tell. Her expression was all too serious. "Why are you asking about Grandpa?"

"I was telling him that he was diagnosed with Alzheimer's," Tony interrupted. "I think Mike went to ask your mother about him, and she freaked out as usual."

Jackie looked at her dad as if to tell him not to go there.

"Why did he refuse treatment that could help him?" Michael asked.

"Because he doesn't want to die yet . . . It's a long story really," Jackie said, pondering what to say next. She seemed to be hesitating, as if she did not want to go into any details.

Michael, for his part, was itching to hear more. At the same time, he wanted to avoid pushing her too far with questions and getting into an argument with her.

After a brief pause, she continued. "Have you heard of the Alzheimer's project?"

"I read about it. A government program to develop a cure for Alzheimer's." He remembered reading a short summary. It was not a detailed article and left Michael with more questions than answers.

"That's right. I did not know much about it. They don't really teach some of this history in medical school. It was after Grandpa was diagnosed that I looked into it. Actually, he knew more about it than me."

"Too bad he is losing it. The man is a walking encyclopedia," Tony said.

"Dad, don't talk like that." She moved away from him and closer to Michael. "The Alzheimer's project was a program put into action in the twenties, back when they discovered the exact genetic code that makes you predisposed to develop Alzheimer's in your old age." She stood by the center table and leaned on it. "They tried to develop some medications that could target those genes. Unfortunately, only the government was doing any significant research."

"All of the drug companies went out of business," Tony interrupted. "Like in everything else, they removed the incentive to do very hard and important work."

"It is expensive research for a very difficult disease," Jackie explained in detail how a patient with Alzheimer's loses all cognitive functions. The deterioration is slow, day by day becoming dependent on others to do the most basic of activities.

"As you can imagine," she continued, "it is a disease that consumes a lot of resources. These patients used to go to nursing homes, where they would need care almost around the clock. They would get a lot of complications. Fall, break a hip, get infections, you name it. With the population getting older, it became a very expensive condition to take care of."

"What about the cure?"

Michael noticed the sun going down in the distance. It would be dark soon. He still had to take the bus, and it was not the safest part of town.

Jackie, for some reason, did not seem to want to elaborate further. "Well . . ." After a moment, she went on. "They approved a test mandatory for any expectant mother. It is one of the mandatory tests you must take to be able to get a license to have a baby. If it comes positive then you know your baby will be predisposed to Alzheimer's at an old age."

"And be a burden to society," Michael said.

"Yes. So if it comes positive, the fee for the license is outrageous, and . . ."

"Encourages the mom to have an abortion," Michael completed Jackie's sentence. He understood and appreciated why Jackie had hesitated to go into this topic. She knew how Michael felt about abortion.

"That's not it," she continued. "The test is now also mandatory for any adult after the age of sixty-five. If positive . . . They are sent to receive end of life counseling. The poor prognosis and burden placed on the family and society is explained. Euthanasia is offered. They are not given any other choice. That's why medications to slow down the progress of Alzheimer's are illegal. They don't want the patient to feel like there is an alternative to euthanasia."

Michael was disgusted. "That's the treatment they wanted to give your grandpa? Euthanasia?"

"Yes," Jackie said.

"What kind of a cure is that?"

"The cure is not for him. It is a cure for society. We're getting rid of Alzheimer's, not from individual patients, but from society in general."

"I hope you're not defending that," Michael said; still feeling disgusted.

"Of course not, I hate euthanasia. To end a human life like this, it's the most malicious thing I have ever seen."

"No wonder he doesn't want to be treated." It seemed sick to even call it a treatment—no matter what spin it was given, to make it sound like a great benefit to society.

It was getting dark; Michael knew he had to go. Maybe Jackie could give him a ride home. But first, Marshall. He knew why he was hiding but not where. "Where is he? I still would like to talk to him."

Jackie's face became stern. "Why?"

"It's a long story."

"When someone like Grandpa refuses treatment and disappears, they place an alert. Anyone with information to contact the authorities."

"You don't think that's what I'm after. Find out where your grandpa is so I can call the police or something and tell them."

"It is a little suspicious that as this alert went out for information on him, that's when you show up asking questions about him."

Getting a ride home from her was now out of the question. Walking all the way home would be a better alternative. "You know, Jackie, I do like you. But unfortunately, you seem to be willing to think the worse of me."

Michael did not wait for an apology. "You don't need to tell me where he is. It's dark, getting late, and I have to go." He waved at Tony. "It was good seeing you again." He walked away.

Chapter 15

The mirror was lying. He could not believe how old he looked. Calvin Marshall was seventy-one years old, but standing in front of the mirror, unshaven and with lack of sleep, he could pass for someone in his eighties.

As he shaved, his gaze moved to a picture of his granddaughter on the counter. It was a picture he took of her the day she graduated from medical school. He was so proud of her.

He thought of the danger he had brought her. It was a mistake coming to New York, no doubt about it. But where else could he have gone?

The events of the last few days confirmed how much his family was in jeopardy. An agent had come asking about him. He had to be suspicious he was there. How much time before he came back and searched the house?

Venturing outside the house was the worst mistake. He needed exercise and ended up getting lost. His daughter's anxiety had reached a tipping point with the incident. What if she had called the police? They would find him. And what would happen to his family?

He splashed water on his shaven face. "Yes, that's what I'll have to do," he told the mirror. The best course of action would be to disappear. Jackie and Abigail would be spared any further danger. Besides, how long could he continue to hide in a basement?

"Grandpa?" Jackie's voice startled him.

"One moment."

He finished getting dressed and came out of the bathroom. Maybe he was not looking any younger, but he felt better especially after making his decision.

"Good morning, sweetie." He kissed her forehead.

"Did you take your pills?"

"No, I don't want them. I don't need them."

"Grandpa. I went through so much trouble to get you those pills. They won't cure you, but they will help. They will slow down your memory loss."

The pill bottle was sealed on his bedside table. He wished she had not gone through any trouble. It was not necessary and further proof that he had become a burden in her life.

"You shouldn't have bothered. I am creating you nothing but trouble."

"But I care. I want you to be with us. To share your wisdom with us for many more years."

"That's probably not realistic."

"Come on, don't talk like that."

She sat next to him, placed her arm around his shoulder. She meant well; he knew that, just trying to give him encouragement, but he did not share her optimism.

"You know, I went to talk to Dad last night."

The tone she was taking was the same she had when, as a little girl, she would try to convince him to let her get away with doing something she wanted to do and was not suppose to.

"Texas has one of the best research centers for Alzheimer's. It's in Houston. It's supposed to be the best one in the world."

"I'm not going anywhere near Texas." Not even Jackie could get him to do that.

"Listen to me. They might be able to help you."

He stood up. "Even if you are right . . ." He could not believe she was even suggesting it. "How would you get me there? It's impossible."

"That's why I went to talk to dad. His work takes him all over the country. I thought he could help."

"There is nothing Tony can do. The only people that go to Texas for medical care are relatives of politicians. Party members. The well-connected."

She looked determined to convince him as she stood in front of him. "That's what Dad said. He actually suggested I talk to Mike. Remember my ex-boyfriend?"

"Sure, I remember him. He was in my house in LA. A curious and bright young man."

"His father is a high ranking official in the government."

"And you think he can help me? I hope you haven't asked him. This is not something you ask someone unless you are 100 percent sure they will help. Or at least keep it to themselves that you ever asked."

"I haven't asked him. I actually insulted him yesterday, didn't mean to, but I'm going to call him and see what he thinks."

The idea of asking help from the son of a government official was not appealing. His own plan was best; it was better to just get away. "Please, don't ask him anything. Let me at least think about it. Give me a little time." Time to disappear.

"Of course."

"What is it?" He could see she had something else in mind.

"Dad suggested for you to stay with him for a little while. At least until we can see if we can get you to Texas or not. You will have a lot of privacy. His apartment has no security system, and no one will know you're there. Dad is rarely home. Just goes there to sleep. Sometimes not even every night because he goes out of town so much."

Finally, an idea he could love. Staying at Tony's apartment would take him away from his daughter and granddaughter, keeping them safe, and next time Tony went out of town, it would be the perfect time to disappear.

"That's a great idea. When do we go?"

"Today," she said.

Chapter 16

Agent West was irritated after spending his entire morning looking for Michael. One of the kid's classmates informed him he was probably at the gym and that was where he found him, in a backroom punching a heavy bag. There were two other kids there engaged in some kickboxing. Michael had boxing gloves on and was hitting the heavy bag with everything he had. He was throwing strong uppercuts and hooks and making the bag shake with every punch.

"Impressive, you can throw a strong punch." West then looked at the other two and showed him his ID. "Get out," he told them.

Michael looked surprised to see him. "May I help you?"

West walked toward the bag and stood in front of him. "You did not tell me the truth the other day. You lied, and that can get you into a lot of trouble. Lying to a federal agent is a very serious offense."

Michael did not seem scared. Not a problem, West knew how to make him afraid.

"What did I lie to you about?" Michael proceeded to hit the bag, continuing his workout as before.

West grabbed his right arm just as he was about to land an uppercut on the bag. "I need you to pay attention to me." He looked him straight in the eyes. If this kid thought this was some kind of a joke, he was going to find out how wrong he was. "I am looking for Professor Marshall. You know who he is, and you lied to me. How dare you lie to your government?"

"I don't . . ."

"Spare me! You know who he is." He stared for a few more seconds before proceeding. "You recently wrote an article about a letter that Ronald Reagan wrote. That nonsense could only come from Professor Marshall." He let go of his arm, expecting to now get full cooperation. "So where is he?"

"Why are you looking for him?"

Why? Who did this kid think he was? Who dared ask a federal agent the why of anything? He obviously was not aware of who he was dealing with. West sent a right-handed punch straight to Michael's abdomen.

The punch took him by surprise. He lost all his air and took a couple of steps back. West felt satisfied, seeing the previous smile replaced by a frown.

"See? That's how you throw an effective uppercut to the body. It's not about power. It's all in the hip."

West approached Michael who looked as if he would be throwing a few punches of his own if he was not dealing with a federal agent. He took Michael's face with one of his hands, squeezing as hard as he could. "Listen to me very carefully now. I am with the division on antisocial behavior of the FBI. I am called in to deal with some of the worst outcasts of our society. I don't get impressed with juvenile punks like you."

Michael did not utter a word. It seemed like it was starting to get into his head the gravity of his situation.

"Your friend, Professor Marshall, has an illness. It has made him paranoid, delusional, distrustful of everyone around him, including his government. He is a danger to himself and society." After he allowed that to sink into Michael's head for a few seconds, he continued, "Do you admit that you know who he is?"

"I probably met him once when I was dating his granddaughter. I have no clue where he is. I'm not dating her anymore."

"You've seen her recently. Did she mention him at all?"

Other people were coming into the kickboxing room. West ordered them to get out. Whether they were attracted by the scene developing there or by exercise did not matter; they could not stay.

"You're wasting your time. I've told you in perfect English, I do not know where Mr. Marshall is."

"When did he tell you about the letter?"

"What letter?"

"Don't play dumb with me kid." He pressed his finger against Michael's chest. "I do not play games. We can finish this conversation somewhere less pleasant if you want to play games."

Someone walked in again. "Mike, are you okay?"

"He's fine." He stared at the other stupid-looking kid. "This is federal business. Move along." His attention returned to Michael. "When did he tell you about that letter?"

"I don't remember. I don't remember who told me about that. I read so many things. Besides, my journalism professor told me the letter does not exist, and I listen to her. She is a wise woman," Michael said with a smile.

West's anger was bursting, and he could not contain the impulse to slap Michael's face. The smile was out of the kid's face, once again. "You are one stupid kid. You probably think you can get away with lying to a federal agent. Nothing is going to happen to you. You're so wrong." He considered slapping Michael one more time; instead, he just pointed his index finger directly at his face. "Don't think we're not keeping score, kid. You cannot even begin to imagine what kind of trouble I can get you into just for pissing me off." West brought the finger to his mouth, signaling Michael to stay quiet. "You had your chance to talk. You lost it." It was his turn to smile. "I'm going to pay a visit to that girlfriend of yours. I am sure she will be more cooperative than you."

There was finally a look of concern in Michael's face. He knew it was just a matter of time before it turned into full fear.

"You will be seeing me again, Mr. Adams. I do not tolerate liars. You should know better than to try to cover up for a right-wing radical like Professor Marshall. Right-wingers like him . . . and you. Tend to die lonely deaths in a hospital bed, with no one giving a crap about your selfish life."

West could finally detect some fear. "You spend your whole lives standing in the way of societal progress, for your own selfish purposes, but one day you get run over, and you realize, social justice cannot be denied."

Chapter 17

Michael rushed into the locker room and attempted to call Jackie but there was no response. He took his gym bag, changed into jeans and a T-shirt, with no time to take a shower before leaving.

"Who was that?" His friend Craig came in.

He was finishing packing his sweaty clothes in the gym bag. "That was that agent I told you about. Came in here asking me about Mr. Marshall again."

"You see? I told you not to get involved. This guy is going to get you into trouble."

"I'm already involved Craig—can I borrow your bike?"

"You are kidding, right? My brand new bike?" He chuckled. "Where are you going?"

Michael stood in front of his friend, wishing he would just give him the key card and not ask questions. Questions that would take too much precious time to explain. He had to rush if he was to beat West. "I have to warn Jackie. The agent went over to her house to question her. I have to go and warn her."

"Buddy, don't get involved. I'm telling you. You can get into a lot of trouble."

"Are you going to report me?" The moment he said it, he realized his mistake. It was evident he hurt Craig's feelings. "Sorry, shouldn't have said that. But I told you I'm already involved. Please, let me just borrow your bike." Taking the bus was not an option; he would never make it on time. Even by car, he could not make it. Using the bike was the only way.

"Just call her. You're getting too worked up about this whole thing."

"I tried calling her. She's not picking up. I have to get there before he gets there. This guy is trouble. He is with this antisocial division of the feds. I've read about these guys. They're political assassins."

"You're exaggerating." In spite of his skepticism, it looked like Craig was going to give in. He went toward his locker to open it. "And you are going through this trouble after she insulted you. How do you know this professor didn't commit some real crime?"

The thought did cross his mind but disappeared after his conversation with West. "Jackie gave me the impression they were looking for him because of his Alzheimer's. Because he is supposed to be hospitalized for treatment." A treatment to eliminate the professor. Hard to grasp that was accepted as the standard of care.

"What's Alzheimer's?" Craig asked.

"It's a disease in which you start losing your memories, your mind."

"Oh, the old man is losing his mind. That's good reason for the antisocial whatever to be looking for him. He probably is a threat to society."

"I don't think that's it though. An FBI agent looking for a sick old man? Even if he is displaying antisocial behavior, it just seems too much to send an agent. And he warned me to stay away from this right-wing radical. Gave me a lecture about the dangers of being a right-winger. Why did he say that? I think he is looking for him because of his political views."

"That's more reason to stay away from this. You don't want to be branded a political radical or be helping one out. Your career will be over."

Michael looked at the time; the minutes were ticking away. The thought came to him that soon West would be interrogating Jackie, maybe even taking her away somewhere, for some unpleasant questioning. Michael knew what they were capable of. She would be branded a political radical for her audacity of defying her government, daring to help her grandfather at his time of need. And what could Marshall have done that was so dangerous? With his death imminent, had he become outspoken about his political views? If so, that should not be a crime in America.

"If that article I wrote had been for a real news publication, I probably would have had an agent knocking on my door. That's just not right." His thoughts returned to the time. He had to end the conversation if he was to have any hope of making it on time. "It would be me being called a right-wing radical." He reached out with his hand to Craig. "Please. If you are my friend, let me borrow the bike."

"I am your friend. I'm just concerned you're getting yourself into trouble. My dad has gotten himself into this kind of trouble before, and it's not pleasant."

"I have to help. Mr. Marshall is probably innocent. My instinct tells me he's done nothing wrong. He is just a voice of dissent, an innocent victim of an ill-conceived notion of societal justice. I have to try to help."

Craig handed him the card key.

Michael smiled with gratitude toward his friend. "Thanks, buddy."

He was getting out the door of the locker room when he heard Craig talk.

"I want to see that bike again. Without a scratch."

Michael stopped and looked back at his friend. "You will. I will see you later." As soon as he said the words, he had the sudden feeling that he would not see his friend again for a long time.

Chapter 18

Michael took longer convincing Craig than he liked. He was thankful to be able to use the bike, but could he make it to Jackie's house before Agent West? If the agent was trapped in traffic, he still had a chance.

The bike was right outside the gym. He got on, and without further waste of time, he sped away.

He made it to the expressway in less than five minutes. The traffic was bumper to bumper, as hoped. He tried to beat the traffic by driving between lanes. Changing from lane to lane was not the safest way to go, but it was fast.

It was fun driving the bike without any of the fancy electronics of a car. It was old, with no GPS, no fingerprint security system; he could drive it anywhere. And it went so much faster than any car.

Getting his own bike had to go up on his list of priorities. It felt so good to be riding one. He would want an old one, which would not be easy; they were becoming harder to get. The newer models, especially with all those gadgets, were a big disappointment.

The exit to Jackie's house was coming up, and as he moved into the right lane, a car suddenly changed into the same lane in front of him. He almost hit the car. He slowed down and missed it by a hair. After a deep breath, and a quick glance on both directions, he raced toward the exit, full speed ahead.

Off the highway, he tried not to go as fast since he knew there was a risk of being pulled over for speeding. He hoped he had done good enough time on the expressway to get there before West.

At Jackie's house, he noticed her car was not there. Unless, she had it inside the garage. At least West was not there either, which was a relief.

Michael rang the bell twice before the door opened. Ms Marshall stood at the door and stared at him. She was trying to hurt him with some sort of vision power, he thought. He swallowed and tried to be cordial, "Hi, is Jackie home?"

"I thought I told you not to come back here."

"I understand why you were suspicious of me the other day. You are worried about your dad and about the government finding him. Trust me—I'm not a government informant."

She appeared skeptical.

"I had an agent come in and ask me questions about Mr. Marshall. This was just a little while ago. I told him nothing, but he said he was on his way here to question Jackie. I tried to call her, to warn her, but she is not picking up her phone."

"He's coming here?" The anger in her face was gone, replaced by panic.

"Yes, he'll be here any minute. I need to talk to her."

"She's not here." She was softening up. "And she forgot her phone."

"Where is she?"

She looked lost in her thoughts. Maybe she was considering whether to trust him or not.

"Ms Marshall, trust me. Where is she?"

"She went to her dad's place."

"Tony? I know where that is. Don't tell the agent anything. Just tell him you think she's still working. If she calls you, have her call me, and tell her I'll meet her at her dad's place."

Michael, within seconds, was back on the bike and speeding away. A car that was approaching the house almost hit him as he came off the driveway. He was too distracted to notice who was driving it.

Baron West reached Jackie's neighborhood after a painful drive through traffic. This was his second visit, and it better be his last. Someone was going to tell him where the old man was. The stage of playing games was over. If he had to tear the house apart until he found clues of where the professor was hiding, he would do it.

He was approaching the house, but before he could pull into the driveway, a motorcycle came out at full speed. He hit the brakes and barely missed hitting it. "God damn it!" He had just exchanged the old car with a defective air conditioner for a brand new one. Last thing he needed was some idiotic kid messing it up.

At first, he did not notice but then he realized it. The motorcycle pulled away so fast that he hardly had a good look. However, he was sure it was he, the stupid kid. "Mr. Adams. What were you doing here?"

West smiled. From the start, he knew what kind of rebellious punk Michael Adams was. "Let's see where you're going."

Chapter 19

"Why are you doing this?" Michael asked out loud as he drove into the Northern State Parkway, on his way to Tony's apartment. A day prior, Jackie insulted him; a day later, he was speeding through the highway trying to warn her. To inform her that a federal agent was looking for her and her grandpa. In a way it was kind of fun to oppose the government, but could he get away with it? Most people were too afraid to even try. How much trouble would he get into? No matter what, he would never ask his dad to bail him out, no way, never. Well, maybe, if it was absolutely necessary.

He was protecting a source of a story he was working on. That was a good reason to do what he was doing. His dad used to be a journalist, he would understand. Maybe.

He smiled and wondered if this was how it felt like to be a real reporter, not like the ones he was learning from but the ones from a different time, from back when there were real reporters. Before the government started controlling all information.

Michael came off the highway and stopped at a red light. He needed to recharge the bike. It was running low, but the line at the charge station was too long. There were a few larger cars, which could sometimes take up to ten minutes to charge. It had created a long line. It was unavoidable; he would have to risk it and try to make it with the power he had.

A beep in his earpiece signaled an incoming call. He answered and heard Jackie's voice. "Mike."

"Hey, I've been trying to get in touch with you."

"Mom called. She told me you were there. That some agent came asking you about Grandpa."

At sixty miles per hour, it was hard to pay attention to her and the road. "Yes, came and asked me if I knew him and where he could be. I told him I didn't know, so he said he was going to go find you and question you."

"Well, no one has been there so far."

That was strange. West should have already reached her house, even with bad traffic.

"Why is a federal agent looking for Grandpa?" Jackie asked.

"I don't think he is after him because of his disease."

"What do you mean?"

Before he was able to answer her, a truck cut him off. It went right in front and forced him to switch to his right lane to avoid a collision. The horn of a blue sedan warned him there was a car coming fast on that same lane. Michael had to maneuver back toward the truck and drove in between both the truck and the blue car.

"Mike, you still there?" Jackie asked after a few seconds.

"I'm here."

"Listen, drive safely. Are you on your way here? To Dad's place?"

"Yes."

"We'll talk when you get here."

"I'll be there in five minutes."

"Michael . . ." Her voice was soft and pleasant.

Another car came in front of him. It was distracting to talk to her; he was going to crash soon if he did not end the conversation. His heart was pounding fast, a result of his near-accident. "Yes." He felt short of breath as he spoke. "I think is better we talk when I get there."

"I didn't have a chance yesterday to tell you I had a really great time Saturday night."

He smiled. "Me too." A few more minutes would not hurt.

"I shouldn't have said what I said." She sounded apologetic. "You are a great friend. I just have been so worried about Grandpa."

Want to have dinner tonight? Michael thought, but it was probably not the best time to ask.

"Anyways, we'll talk when you get here. See you soon." She ended the call.

Michael was distracted, thinking about Jackie, and did not hear the ring tone of another incoming call. Once he snapped out of it, he answered right away. "Jackie?" He wondered why she was calling back.

"Not Jackie, Mr. Adams."

Michael recognized the voice. The annoying voice of Agent West. He remained quiet, not sure what to say.

"I am right behind you, pull over. You and I need to chat before you get to see your girlfriend."

He looked at his rearview mirror and saw him. West was in a two-door Obamobile. He was in a different car the first time they met; Michael was sure of it. How long had he been following? Did he follow all the way from the gym? Did he listen in on his conversation with Jackie? Regardless, he now was leading him straight to Jackie and her grandfather. How could he be so stupid? Jackie was not going to be happy about this. And he was upset at himself for being so careless.

Michael did not slow down or acknowledge West. He did not know what to do, felt trapped, and knew he had to think of something fast.

"I won't ask again. Stop the bike."

"Hello? Hello? Please speak up! I can't hear you! Is that you, Jackie? I told you, stop calling me! I am not interested in you anymore. It's over!" Michael cut off the call before West could say anything. He saw him through the rearview mirror. He was accelerating. Michael increased his speed. "Shit. I won't be able to get away."

Michael heard the sound of a train. Up ahead, a block away, cars were coming to a stop for the Obama-Rail. The fast-speed rail was supposed to decrease its speed to about fifty miles per hour within residential areas. It seemed as if it was coming a lot faster than that. With the cars slowing down ahead of him, there was no way to avoid West. He was trapped.

"Let's see how fast you can really go." Michael accelerated, passing the recommended maximum speed, driving between several cars. As the intersection approached, he felt he made a bad decision. The train was coming too fast. He was not going to be able to pass on time. "Can't go back now!" He kept the accelerator pressed at its maximum, asking the bike to give him every ounce of power it had left. As he came closer to the speeding train, he could hear West's words. "One day you'll get run over." There was no going back. At that last moment, all he could think of was Jackie. Would he ever get to see her again?

Part 2

They probably won't get to read the letter at all

Chapter 20

Jackie enjoyed hearing Michael's voice. She had been unfair to him, and in spite of that, he was trying to help. Her father had been right. He told her she had been harsh with Michael and then suggested she call him, not only to apologize, but to see if he could help her get Grandpa to Texas. She knew his dad was influential and as the good friend he was, who cared about her, he would be willing to at least try and see what his dad could do.

"What time will Tony be here? There's nothing to eat." Marshall spoke from the kitchen.

Her grandfather was already making himself at home; that was an encouraging sign. Harmony would soon return to her life. If her grandpa got along well with Tony, they could take their time deciding where to go next. The only downside was she doubted if Grandpa was going to take his pills. If she was not there to remind him every day, he would not take them. She was sure of that.

"That was Mike," Jackie said as Marshall came back from the kitchen.

"What did he say?"

"He's on his way. We didn't talk much. He was driving." She was standing by a large window, overlooking the street below. There was yet no sign of Michael. "He said a federal agent came asking him questions about you. And that the agent now went off to look for us."

"You sure we'll be safe here? What if the agent comes here?"

"He said he doesn't think the agent is after you because of the Alzheimer's." Jackie paused for a moment, pondering a question, she looked at her grandfather. "Why else would he be looking for you?"

She could see he was becoming nervous.

"I should disappear. I shouldn't have shown up at your mother's house. It was a mistake. I'm jeopardizing all of you."

She felt he was about to break into tears. She walked over to him and put her arm over his shoulder. "Is there something else going on you haven't told me? Is there any other reason why they would be looking for you?"

"I should disappear. I've endangered you. That's the last thing I wanted to do."

"Did you get into some kind of trouble back in LA?"

"This government . . . You have no idea what they are capable of doing to shut anyone down. Any voice that has anything to say contrary to their propaganda is shut down immediately and absolutely."

For Jackie, the picture was becoming clearer. Her grandfather had strong political views. He had always been a reserved person and kept his views mostly to himself. Now with the Alzheimer's, he was probably becoming more outspoken. He must have said something controversial, and it got him into some trouble.

She remembered, when she was a little girl, he had provoked some controversy back then. She did not remember all the details but knew that it had kept him from being allowed to teach his favorite subject—American history.

"Is that what's going on? You've said something you shouldn't have?"

He shook his head, turned toward Jackie. "It's not my voice they want to silence. I'm nobody. Just a crazy old man now. Who would listen to me?"

"Don't talk like that. I still listen to you." She gave him a hug. "Whatever you said that's gotten you into trouble, they do have to consider you have Alzheimer's. You're not a threat to anyone. You need to take care of your health. I'm sure if they knew you have Alzheimer's, they would leave you alone."

Marshall looked his granddaughter in the eyes and took a deep breath. "Jackie," he paused for a moment, "I don't have Alzheimer's."

Chapter 21

Michael closed his eyes as he was about to pass the railroad crossing. One second after going through, the Obama-Rail made its way past him, almost getting him to lose control of the bike, but he was able to keep it straight. He stopped and looked back. Hard to believe the stunt he had just pulled. West was not going to be a happy assassin. He was definitely in deep trouble now. There was no time to stand still and think; he had to rush to Tony's apartment.

He reached the building, parked the bike in front, ran up the stairs to the fourth floor, and rang the bell. Jackie opened the door. "Hi, welcome." She looked serious.

"Hi." As he came into the living room, there he was—standing in front of him, the man he had been looking for the last one week, the man nobody seemed to know, or wanted to tell him where he was. "Mr. Marshall. I've been asking about you."

"And why is that?"

"Grandpa, why did you say that?"

Michael had the sense he had interrupted an important conversation. Marshall did not answer Jackie; he seemed to be more concerned with Michael's presence.

"Why have you been looking for me? Are you helping the government find me? If not, then why come looking for me?"

"I came to warn you guys. A federal agent came asking me about you. It was the second time. And I don't think it has anything to do with your Alzheimer's."

Jackie's attention now turned to Michael as well. With a puzzled look, she asked him, "Why did he think you would know anything about my grandfather?"

"I think because of my article." Michael could tell this was going to turn into a long story. But there was no choice; Professor Marshall did not trust him, that much was evident. And who could blame him? In his shoes, with a government assassin after him, he would be the same way. It was hard to know who to trust.

"What article?" Jackie asked.

"I wrote this article about the upcoming Fourth of July, our nation's Tricentennial." Michael went over to one of the sofas and sat down. The ride from Long Island was stressful, and he felt exhausted. "I still have those books you gave me," he told Marshall. "About our Founding Fathers. And I've been thinking a lot about the way America used to be."

"Want some water?" Jackie asked.

She could read him well; he definitely felt thirsty.

"Sure," Michael continued, "anyways, to make a long story short, I wrote an article about the Fourth of July and what it still means to be an American, and I end up mentioning a letter that Ronald Reagan wrote in 1976."

Jackie handed him the water and sat down in front of him.

He took a sip, thanked her, noticed how beautiful she looked in her short blue dress, and returned to his explanation. He reminded Marshall that he learned about the letter in his house, in Los Angeles. It was there he saw the video of the 1976 convention where Ronald Reagan talks about the letter. "I have since found out that Reagan is a taboo topic," Michael said. He explained to them the trouble his editorial caused him and how in school, they wanted to know who did he learn the nonsense about the letter from. "I tried to look for that video or any other mention of the letter."

"That's a waste of time," Marshall interrupted. "The government has gone through great lengths to make sure they eliminate any material that could be considered . . . controversial. Anything to do with Ronald Reagan is considered divisive and unacceptable. Most of his speeches have disappeared, removed from the internet, from libraries, only critical material has survived, or private collections like mine."

"That's why I wanted to find you. I figure if anyone would know about the letter, it would be you. I understand their bias against Reagan, but I did not appreciate being called a liar."

"I don't get it." Jackie jumped into the conversation. "Why you writing about Reagan would lead to a federal agent coming to ask you about Grandpa?"

"I think they were looking for him, and when I wrote the article, and don't ask me how this agent found out about it because that I do not know, but when he saw it, he realized I knew your grandpa. How else would I know of the Reagan letter?"

Michael looked at his watch. He was getting nervous, wondering if West knew where he was headed. "You know, he was following me."

"Who was following you? The agent?" She looked surprised.

Marshall seemed to be in shock. Maybe he should have mentioned it when he first arrived. If he was trying to earn the professor's trust, he was not making the right moves.

"He followed you here? We have to get out of here. Now!" Marshall headed for the door.

Jackie stood up and held his arm. "Wait, Grandpa, we have to wait for Dad."

"Relax, Mr. Marshall, I'm pretty sure I lost him." Of course, it was a matter of time before West figured out he was on his way to Tony's apartment.

"If he is coming this way, I don't feel comfortable being here. I'm putting you all at risk. I need to leave," Marshall said.

Michael stood up and walked toward Marshall. "Why is he looking for you? Is it really just because you have Alzheimer's?"

"I don't have Alzheimer's."

Michael, hoping to get some answers, was instead getting more confused. He looked at Jackie who seemed to be bewildered.

"How can you say you don't have it after you told me you did? After you told me they wanted to put you through euthanasia. Please tell me you didn't lie about that."

There was sadness in his face. It looked as if he was trying to fight back tears. "I never lied. I never said I had Alzheimer's."

Jackie tried to interrupt, but he asked her to let him continue. "What I said was true. They wanted to put me through euthanasia. I went for a routine physical with my doctor, and I was shocked when he looked in my chart and saw a consult from a doctor I have never seen in my life. This doctor diagnosed me with a rapidly progressing form of Alzheimer's. That's when my doctor told me he had no choice but to refer me to the palliative care team, to discuss options with me and my family . . . Specifically euthanasia."

Michael saw Jackie's look of disbelief. He could relate. He felt it too. "You mean they made it up?" he asked.

"I have never complained about my memory, no one has ever complained about my memory, my doctor has never referred me for any memory testing."

"That's impossible, Grandpa. No one can alter a medical record just like that. There are many safeguards in the system that don't allow for tampering."

Mr. Marshall laughed as if he was being told the funniest joke of the year. "The government controls the medical records. It is all centralized. They can tamper any record if they choose. If they want to eliminate you. It's the easiest way to eliminate a political dissident."

She shook her head. Michael could tell she was not convinced. To him the story did not seem all that far-fetched; he was never surprised with how far the government could go.

"Why would they want to go through this much trouble to silence you?" she asked. "What could you possibly have said that was so bad to make them go through that kind of trouble?"

"I told you. It's not my voice they're trying to silence."

Michael was over by the window, looking down, making sure the bike was where he left it. He would not forgive himself if anything happened to it. Craig would never forgive him either.

"Whose voice then? Are you trying to cover for someone?" Jackie asked.

She looked tense. All the days she had spent being worried about her grandfather's health then finding out his health is fine; the government just wants to eliminate him.

"You know," Michael interrupted, "being my dad's son, I can tell you, the government will, sometimes, do outrageous things to silence a voice that says something damaging to their agenda."

"Especially his voice. The voice of such a great communicator."

"Who are you talking about?" Jackie asked.

Michael understood right away who he was talking about.

"Ronald Reagan. It's his voice that they're trying to silence," Marshall said.

"Ronald Reagan? He's dead," Jackie said.

But a dead guy could still have something left to say, Michael thought, one last word for the country he so much loved. He walked back toward Marshall. "The video about the letter, it was real, right? Ronald Reagan did write a letter to be released this year."

Marshall smiled. "Yes he did. He wrote a beautiful letter that speaks of individual freedom. A beautiful message of freedom meant for all of us to hear. A message this government is determined to suppress. Not to allow it to be heard."

Jackie was about to say something, but Michael interrupted. "How do you know that it's a beautiful letter? You speak as if you've read it. The letter is in some time capsule in LA, to be opened in July."

"You're right. I have already read it."

"How did you get to read it?" Michael asked.

Marshall reached into his right pocket. He took out an envelope. Michael had not seen one in a long time. With society going completely paperless, there was no use for envelopes.

"I have the letter with me. I have the Reagan letter." He held the envelope in his hand.

Michael was shocked. "How did you get it? Isn't it supposed to be in Los Angeles? In a time capsule? How did you end up with it?"

"Grandpa, you didn't steal this, did you? Is that why they're looking for you like this? You have stolen some government document?" Jackie looked shocked.

"I did not steal it," he said.

"How did you get it?" Michael asked.

"It's a long story."

"You have to give it back." Jackie tried to reach for it, but Marshall placed it back in the safety of his pocket. "If you just give it back, I'm sure they will stop bothering you. It does not belong to you anyways. It's from a former president. It belongs to the government."

"No, it certainly does not." Marshall walked away from her, took a few steps, and turned to face his granddaughter. "Ronald Reagan wrote this letter for us. For us, the people of this generation, to read it, and for him to be able to share his ideas about freedom with us. He did not write it for the government. If anything, he was worried this exact thing would happen. That a government that no longer believes in freedom would not allow us to read it."

"Please, I know you're passionate about this. But if they want the letter back this badly, what can we do? You're not going to be hiding forever, or get yourself killed, just for some letter."

Marshall shook his head. It obviously was not just some letter to him. "It is a historic letter. Written by one of our most important leaders. About the most important subject that has defined for centuries what this country is supposed to be all about. Freedom. I don't know if anyone will ever get to read it as he intended it, but the least I can do is make sure it does not fall in the wrong hands. In the hands of the government." Tears came down his cheeks. "I have nothing left. The things that I used to own, my collection, it's probably all gone now. I don't even own my own medical record. It all belongs to the government. I feel, sometimes, I am their property too."

Jackie tried to hold her grandfather's hand, but he took a step back.

"Not this. Not this letter. This does not belong to them. It's mine. I won't give it away. They will have to take it from my cold, dead hand. Ronald Reagan would have wanted me to have it. He did not trust the government back then. Imagine how much he would distrust this oppressive one we have."

"That's fine. No one will make you give it away," Michael said. "Now we have to think that agent is very serious about finding you and likely to find us here. It might be a good idea to go somewhere else."

"Not before Dad gets here."

"Let's go find a place to eat," said Mr. Marshall. "There's no food here anyways. We can call Tony from there."

"We should go then," Michael said.

Jackie did not move. She seemed lost in her thoughts. It was a lot of information to absorb. "I still find it hard to believe they could alter your medical record like that." She looked at her grandfather who was moving to the door, eager to leave. "If there was a consult there by another physician then you must have seen that doctor. Maybe you just didn't know he was evaluating you for memory problems."

Marshall shook his head. He did not seem to have any doubt. "No. I've been very healthy. I have not gone to see anyone, other than my primary care doc. I would have recognized the name. Never heard the name before. Never talked to him in my life."

"Professor?" Michael asked. "Do you, by any chance, remember the name of the doctor that they say diagnosed you with Alzheimer's?" He was not sure why he was asking; it was a hunch.

Marshall thought about it for a few seconds. "Yes. I remember. I'm good with names. It was Doctor Baron West."

His answer sent a chill down Michael's spine. He turned pale and reached for the door. "We better go."

Chapter 22

The name gave him an immediate sense of doom. Baron West was the doctor that altered Professor Marshall's medical record—making up a diagnosis of Alzheimer's dementia. A diagnosis that required him to undergo euthanasia. His worst fear about West was well-founded. If he tried to eliminate the professor back in Los Angeles, he was not coming to have a friendly chat; he was coming to finish the job.

"What's wrong? You've turned so pale. Have you heard that name before?" Jackie asked.

"Baron West is the name of the federal agent that came asking me about your grandpa."

It was her turn to lose all color from her face.

"Are you sure?" Marshall asked.

"I remember the name. He told me he works for the division on antisocial behavior in the FBI." If Marshall's facial expression was any indication, he knew what Michael was talking about. If so, he knew he was a dead man walking. "If he had access to alter a medical record like that, you can bet he has orders from high up." He did not want to worry Jackie, at least not more than she already was, but he didn't want to minimize the situation. "If his goal was to eliminate your grandpa . . . We're all in deep trouble."

Michael could feel his abdomen sore from the punch he received at the gym. West would not hesitate, he would kill them, Michael thought. They were wasting valuable time. They were in danger and in need to get out of there. The feeling of imminent trouble was growing stronger each passing minute.

"I am risking everyone's life. I can't ask you guys to do this for me. I will surrender to him. I don't want any of you to get hurt. Or let me go, and I'll try to disappear."

"Come on, Grandpa. Don't say that. We are in this together. We are not going to let you go through this alone."

Michael agreed with her. They had to help him. Marshall was not going to die just because the government wanted to censor a political letter. It seemed so unfair, so un-American. "We'll find someplace to hide," he said. Some place to hide from the bastard and then figure out what to do next. He felt determined, with that sense of doom gone. There had to be a way to avoid such great injustice. "Let's go then. We've wasted enough time."

Michael stepped outside Tony's apartment with Marshall and Jackie right behind him. He went to the elevator and pressed the down button several times—trying to make it come faster, without success.

"The elevator is not working," Jackie said with a smile.

"The stairs it is."

"Nothing works anymore," Marshall complained as they walked toward the stairs. "People don't want to get things fixed. If they do, there's no one who knows how to fix them. If you find someone who knows, they take their sweet time fixing it."

Michael went ahead, and as he was about to take the first step down he sees West coming up. He took a step back with Jackie banging into him.

"Mr. Adams. I hope I did not keep you waiting too long."

West had both hands behind his back. His stare made Michael nervous. Made him take two more steps back. West kept smiling at him, ignoring the others.

"That stunt you pulled back there with the train . . ." West shook his head. "The train came to complete stop because of it and held up traffic. Everyone was cursing you. That was very dangerous behavior you displayed. Definitely a menace to society."

Michael tried to figure out what he could do. West was blocking their only way out of the building. His only hope was to waste time and see if someone came by then, maybe create a distraction and try to get away. "I really had to go to the bathroom. You know, when you have to go you have to go."

West did not seem to find him funny. He looked past him to Jackie and then Marshall. "Professor, it is so good to see you again."

"I have never seen you in my life."

"You forgot. You came to see me, sent by your primary care doctor because you were having some problems with your memory. You probably forgot. That's part of your diagnosis. It is expected to have lapses of memory like this." He paused and looked at Jackie. "You should know that, Dr. Perez."

"There is nothing wrong with my memory, and you know it," Marshall said. He moved a few steps closer to West, standing next to Jackie and Michael, anger clear in his voice and face.

"I didn't come here to have a medical discussion. Mr. Marshall, you're sick and in need of medical attention. I'm here for your own good. To make sure you get the help you need. I'm going to have to insist that you come with me."

"I'm not going anywhere with you."

"All we want is to take him for a second opinion. He is not a threat to anyone," Jackie said.

"I can easily arrange for a second opinion once he is safe in a hospital."

"He doesn't—" Michael tried to interrupt.

"Shh, kid." West placed his index finger in front of his mouth. "Adults are talking now." His gaze returned to Jackie. "You seem to be the only reasonable one in this group. You know this is routine. He needs to be hospitalized, and he can be evaluated there. We'll give him the help he needs."

"What kind of help? Euthanasia?" she asked.

"Whatever help he might need. He is a threat to society right now. You say he is not a threat to anyone? Look at the kind of problems he is getting the two of you in. This stupid kid just disobeyed an order to pull over. I should have him arrested right now." He pressed his finger on Michael's shoulder.

Michael thought about telling him where to stick the finger. Jackie would not approve. It would earn him back the label of immature, so he kept his mouth tightly shut.

"This kid even ran in front of a train. He could have been killed. And for what? Because you grandfather, in his demented state, has been brainwashing him, transforming him into a hatemonger, filling him with lies about who Ronald Reagan really was."

Jackie expressed her concern about the way it was being handled. How unfair it was to her grandfather. However, West was not persuaded.

"Unfair would be for you to lose your license," West said. "You don't think I know you've been trying to buy illegal meds for him? Another example of the bad influence he is having."

Michael listened while West repeated his story. How Marshall was a threat to society, how it was better for all to have him committed to a hospital. Jackie was playing his game, trying to win the argument.

Michael was getting tired of the exchange. "Enough!" he screamed, hoping the neighbors heard him. "Let's cut this bullshit." Michael took a step toward West. His eyebrows came together with his anger becoming evident. If West wanted a hatemonger, Michael was willing to give him one. "You are not looking for Professor Marshall because he is demented and needs medical attention. That's bullshit. You know why you are looking for him. We know why. And you know that we know. So don't play this game with us."

Agent Baron West did not say anything for a few seconds. He looked at the others who were quiet, looking nervous. He reached inside his suit and took out a gun. "Very well. No more games then." He smiled and pointed the gun to Marshall. "Professor. I'm afraid I'm going to insist you come with me. It would be such a headache if you resist arrest, and I have to shoot you." He shook his head and rolled up his eyes. "The reports I would have to file would be terrible. Such a waste of my time."

Everyone froze. Michael stared at the gun; he wanted to say something, but the gun encouraged him to remain silent.

"See, Mr. Adams, this letter Mr. Marshall has shown you, or his ideas about freedom, it's all nonsense. A joke. True power comes largely from the barrel of a gun."

Michael wished there was something he could do to wipe the smirk from West's face.

"Soon I will destroy the letter, and you too will get the joke."

He felt it was unacceptable to allow Marshall to go anywhere with West. Michael knew he would never see him again. The letter would be lost forever. He probably would never get to read the letter at all. And the America Marshall first exposed Michael to, that America would slip away.

"I'm coming with you. I don't want you to hurt anyone, but to get the letter, you'll have to kill me."

"As you wish," said West.

Marshall walked toward West. As he took that first step, Michael lifted his right knee up into his chest and sent his heel to West. The kick hit him in the middle of the chest. The impact made him step backwards, slipping and falling down the stairs.

Michael grabbed Jackie's arm. "Let's go," They ran down the stairs.

West sat and tried to get back up. Michael jumped the last few steps and landed in front of him. Jackie and her grandfather ran past them and continued down the stairs. West was able to get up fast but received a right uppercut from Michael. It hit him in the abdomen and took all his air away. Michael followed it with a left hook to the face. That punch should have knocked out West, thought Michael; it was delivered with such strength. It did not happen. West was still standing.

Michael threw another right uppercut to the abdomen. This time it was expected, and West caught it. He tried another left hook, and his arm was caught by West's right hand. They stared into each other's eyes. Michael tried to get his arms loose; West held them as hard as he could.

West pushed Michael and threw a punch. Michael felt as if the right side of his face exploded. It made him lose his balance, and he fell toward his left side. He fell down the stairs, his face making hard contact with every other step until the bottom of the staircase.

Michael got up, ignoring his pain. West was coming down the stairs. He did not seem to have his gun with him. It looked like a good time to make a run for it. He went down the stairs two to three steps at a time. When he came around the last set of stairs, he jumped to the bottom. He lost his balance and fell at the bottom but was able to get up and rush out of the building.

Michael came out and at first did not see them. He looked right again and saw them running toward 71st Avenue. He ran after them with West coming fast behind him. Michael looked back once, and it seemed as if West was limping.

Michael caught up with them. "Come on, this way." He pointed to an entrance to the subway and they ran in that direction. They crossed in the middle of the street, with cars coming in both directions, but they managed to make it to the other side safely.

Jackie and Marshall caught up with Michael who was running ahead of them. He let them go into the subway ahead of him while he looked back. He looked to the other side and saw West standing there, not crossing the street yet.

There was a train coming, Michael could hear it. He rushed down the stairs. Marshall almost slipped down, but Michael reached him at the right moment, holding him by an arm, letting him regain his footing. They made it on time to the subway car by a few seconds, just as the doors closed.

Michael took a deep breath. They were safe. But for how long? Attacking a federal officer, even if he was a bastard, was going to make it hard to hide anywhere.

Chapter 23

Humiliation, what a horrible feeling. West felt humiliated. He saw them go into the subway entrance on 71st Avenue. It was going to be a short ride for them. He would get them, he was certain of that. Nonetheless, to be beaten down like that was embarrassing. That punk was going to regret it for the rest of his short life.

It was all because of the stairs. If he kept his balance on those stairs, they would all be in handcuffs, and he would have been spared this disgrace.

West felt an intense pain in his right ankle. There was no choice; he needed some assistance. He saw a Community Organizer standing a few feet from him and went up to him.

He disliked approaching them. At least, if he could help it. They were used as a civilian security force, but nonetheless, they were amateurs, too much for his taste. They carried out their duties with a lack of professionalism. However, they had strength in numbers. That was what made them a force hard to ignore. Sometimes it was necessary to use them. This case was perfect for them, since they could be found everywhere especially in major cities. They were the eyes and ears of the government, on the lookout for right-wing activities, making sure neighborhoods were safe, that people were doing their social duty. It was time they beware of Michael Adams and Professor Marshall.

The one West approached could have been spotted anywhere, even without the uniform; he had the NACORN symbol tattooed on his right cheek. There was no doubt he was proud of his chosen profession. He had a multitude of other tattoos, with only his eyes and hair spared.

"I need your help." Baron West took out his identification and showed it to him. He explained the situation.

"The old man is very sick and in need of medical attention . . . And this young man and his girlfriend have kidnapped him. The young man too has psychiatric issues and needs to be approached with caution."

He gave him a detailed description of Michael, Jackie, and Marshall. "I last saw them going into the 71st Avenue entrance." He pointed across the street.

The community organizer was typing a text message. All other community organizers in the area would receive it. They would all be on the lookout for the escapees. West was satisfied. They would not be able to go anywhere without being spotted. If they thought they could get away from him, they were dead wrong.

He walked back. First, he needed to retrieve his gun. Then, his ankle was in need of attention. He took out his phone and made a call.

"Hi, Baron West. Remember me?" The pain in that ankle was excruciating. It was bothering him more all the time. That punk had to pay for this. If the ankle was broken, he was going to have to come up with a special way of killing Michael. "I need to see that file on Michael Adams . . . Yes. Can you see me at my hotel?" His hotel was the place to be. Rest the ankle, get some ice and a painkiller, and that should take care of it; the police could hold on to his fugitives until he felt better. He would take care of them later. Besides, he could continue to monitor their progress from his car and then the hotel. He had tapped into Michael's phone, therefore, wherever the kid went to, he would know it.

"I'll see you later then." The phone went back to his pocket. He was satisfied he was going to see Olga Parker. His first encounter with her had been short but enjoyable. Or, to be precise, she had been enjoyable to look at. It was good he had an excuse to see her one more time. Maybe, he could turn it into a social occasion. Why not? A day that had been frustrating deserved to give way to a satisfying evening.

Chapter 24

The day started like any other. Jackie woke up early and rushed to make it on time for rounds at the hospital. It was not a busy day, and she made it home early. She took her grandfather to her dad's place. She was waiting for her dad to get home, considering where to go for dinner, when all hell broke loose.

A call by her mom telling her Michael had been home. A federal agent was on his way to ask questions. Michael came over, sounded and looked so concerned. Her grandfather provided some shocking news for the evening—he did not have Alzheimer's. It was all part of a government plot to destroy him because of a letter he had in his possession. A letter that exposed her grandpa as a political radical, an enemy of the State. How did he even get that letter? He had kept that to himself. An agent provided the fireworks by showing up. She was trying to reason with him when Michael decided to attack him. In a flash, she found herself in the subway, on the run like a fugitive.

The doors closed in front of her. For the moment, they were safe, out of harm's way until the next station. She looked around her; there were so many people. Nobody looked at them. Everyone seemed to be in their own world, thinking about their own problems.

Her gaze met Michael's. "Nice going," she told him. Michael seemed surprised, not understanding what she meant.

"You attacked a federal agent . . ." She looked around; no one seemed to have heard her. She lowered her voice and got closer to him. They were both holding on to the same pole. "You attacked a federal agent, how do you expect us to hide anywhere now?"

Her grandfather sat for a moment trying to catch up his breath. He stood up next to Jackie. "There is no where we can go now. They will find us," he said.

The subway stopped. The main lights went off. It startled her for a moment. This was natural, since it was rush hour, and there were likely other trains ahead. There could also be malfunctions. A common occurrence. The subway system was falling apart due to lack of maintenance.

"What do you think I should have done? He was going to take your grandfather away. We would never see him again."

"You don't know that. I still don't buy this whole conspiracy by the government over some stupid letter." She felt claustrophobic with the train standing still as it was. She wished it would move, but there was nothing she could do, just wait.

"It's not a stupid letter," Marshall said. "But you're right, you should have just let him take me away. I've brought you so much trouble already."

"Don't say that. I am glad he did not take you away." She should have chosen her words better. The letter meant a lot to him, not a stupid letter to him; that was obvious. And Michael was probably right. That agent would have taken him away, and she would never see him again. There was also no guarantee the two of them would have been left off the hook. At least, she and Michael would have been taken in for some questioning.

The train was not moving, and she tried to fight the feeling of discomfort. How much longer before it started to advance? Did West have it stop because of them? Was the police on its way to get them off and arrested? Her anxiety was increasing. It was better to keep talking, to stay distracted. "Why this interest in that letter? Why was he so willing to kill you just like that? How did you get the letter anyways?"

Her grandfather looked around; he was about to say something then shook his head. "This is not the place to talk. It's too crowded."

She nodded. They had already said too much. Who knew who was listening? "Where do we go from here? If this thing ever starts moving again," she said.

Michael did not answer, looked the other way. She did not realize what he was looking at. After a few seconds, she realized he was not looking at anything in particular, just ignoring her. He was most definitely immature. Kind of cute but immature.

"Mike, I'm sorry. I didn't mean to insinuate this is your fault. He was the one with a gun, not you."

Her apology was sincere. To blame each other was not going to get them anywhere. They had to keep in mind who the bad guy was. Who it was that was trying to kill her grandfather. She also should not forget Michael was mixed up on this because of her, because she introduced him to her grandpa, because he cared about her, and was trying to help her. She held his hand and smiled at him. "There was no reason to blame you. You're my good friend."

Michael returned the smile. "Well, you're right too. If I hadn't come looking for you guys. He wouldn't have followed me there."

The lights came back on. They went off again. Her hope that the train would move lasted only a few seconds. Her attention returned to the conversation. "Sooner or later he would have found us. We were not going to hide there forever."

"Where can we realistically go? They must be out there looking for us. Any ideas?" Michael asked.

She tried to think of a safe place to go. She felt clueless. There had to be a place they could sit for a few minutes. "Next station is Queens Boulevard, right?"

"Yes," he said.

"Let's just find some place there to sit and talk. Maybe eat something. A quiet place."

"Is there such a place in Queens?" Marshall asked.

"And after that?" Michael asked.

"I don't know. I still think it might be a good idea to call that West guy and negotiate something. If the letter means so much to him, we can surrender it in exchange for him leaving us alone."

Even before she finished her sentence, she knew her grandfather disagreed. He was as stubborn as ever. It was going to be difficult to convince him to give up the letter. If he were determined to keep it safe, it would be impossible to convince him. She had to make him understand, if it was the only way out of the mess they were in, it was what they had to do.

Chapter 25

The train was moving. Michael observed everyone remained expressionless, the same they were when it stopped and while it was standing still.

"There is nowhere we can hide," Marshall said.

Michael considered what Jackie said. She was right about turning the letter in. Contacting West was a different thing though; death itself could not be worse than talking to him. Lucifer at least would have some interesting old stories to share. He needed a better idea. "We'll find a good place to hide and then we'll contact my dad," he said. "If we're going to make a deal with the letter . . ." He stopped when he realized Marshall was shaking his head. The idea did not seem to be going well with him. Michael could understand how he felt, he too did not like the idea of allowing the letter to be destroyed, but was it worth it their lives? It was the wrong place to argue the point. "Let's just contact my dad. He will be the best person to give us some ideas. He has influence. He can help."

Marshall leaned forward and whispered, "And in the meantime, where do you think we'll be able to hide?"

For a whisper, Michael felt anyone interested could have easily heard them.

"There are cameras everywhere," Marshall continued, "in this train, in all the stations, out in the streets. You can't make a phone call without the government knowing you're calling and who you're calling. They control all forms of communication. You can't send a text or an email without alerting them it's you. You can't even get food anywhere, without the government knowing it's you."

Michael knew he was right. He looked up front and saw a camera pointed in their direction. He touched his phone and remembered West's unsolicited call earlier. If they tried to buy anything, they would need to use fingertip identification. The second they did that, they would give away their location.

"We can't take interstate trains. How would we get a ticket? They will know that we have and where we're going. We can't drive. All this modern cars can only be programmed to go so far. And they would know it's you driving it," Marshall said.

They reached the Queens Boulevard station. Michael moved toward the door and gestured for the professor to follow. They had to go and take their chances.

Marshall stood in front of him. "Then you have those community organizers. They're everywhere. If they have been alerted to our presence and to look out for us, then we cannot stay in any public place."

The look of concern he was displaying was contagious. Michael himself started to feel the same way.

The doors opened, and he stepped out. "You're really painting a grim picture." He told Marshall as they both walked into the platform.

The professor stopped, looked at him, and waited for the other passengers to walk past them. "It's not a grim picture, it is reality. This government believes itself to be God. And tries to behave like it. There is nowhere we can hide from it."

Michael saw Jackie ahead of them, waiting, looking inpatient. "How did you make it all the way from LA to New York without being found?"

Michael looked around. There were cameras overlooking them, one in each side, covering both directions. If someone was motivated to look for them, it was easy to find them. The head bunt Michael gave West was, more than likely, strong motivation to use all possible tools in his search.

"When I decided to escape, I went home and took the letter. It's a long story, but I knew the letter was the main reason they were coming after me. I changed into some old clothes and took some food with me. I first went to a friend's house. He lives by the beach. No security system in his little place. I stayed there for a week. One night, I took the Obama-Rail. The nonstop from

Los Angeles to New York. My beard had grown long. I had not showered, and my clothes were dirty." Marshall was smiling, seemed to be amused at his adventure. "In the train, I sat next to a homeless guy. I stayed with him all the way to New York. People thought I was just another homeless guy. I got off in the station at Westbury and walked to my daughter."

The professor did have some ingenuity, thought Michael. It was time to keep moving. They needed to go and find a safe place. They joined Jackie and walked toward the exit.

"I was lucky I was able to stay under the radar like that," Marshall kept talking. "Now they'll be looking for the three of us. We won't be able to pull that off."

Michael looked up to the end of the stairs, and he saw them. Two community organizers were standing there, checking out everyone that came off the subway. They looked down and saw Michael. For a moment, he thought they might not be looking for them. They saw Jackie coming right behind and then noticed Marshall who was next to Michael.

"That must be them," one of the guys said.

"Shit." Michael turned around rushed back to where they came from.

Marshall did the same thing, returned to the platform they had just left, except there was no subway there anymore. Michael ran ahead of them. Jackie and her grandfather picked up their pace and without much delay, caught up with him. It was a waste of time. They were running to a dead end.

Michael reached the end wall and looked back. Jackie was just a step behind him. In the distance, he saw the community organizers walking toward them. They kept a slow pace, not rushing at all. They seemed to know there was nowhere to run. One of the guys, who had to be more than six feet and some two hundred and fifty pounds of muscle, was talking on his phone. Probably alerting others that they found them. The second guy had a stunner gun in his hand, standard use by all community organizers. It was a defensive weapon, of course, incapable of causing any real harm. Just enough to immobilize someone that needed to be dealt with. They were necessary defensive weapons since, being so involved with the community, sometimes it was required to maintain the peace.

They were close, and Michael knew he could not take them both. It was questionable whether he would even be able to take the big guy if he was the only one coming. He would not be able to run past them either. Well, maybe he could have, but the professor or Jackie, or both, would not be able to.

Michael felt trapped once again. It was becoming the norm of the day. The previous times he had figured out a way to escape, and he had to this time as well. He looked down to the track, in both directions, saw there was no train coming one way or the other. "I must have freedom." He jumped.

"Mike!" Jackie screamed.

"Come on, jump, quickly," he said.

Marshall sat at the edge of the platform and jumped. He fell on the tracks. Michael helped him up, and Jackie jumped just as the big guy was about to grab her. She fell and let out a scream that sent panic into all those who were there. The reason for her scream was right in front of her. Michael saw it as well. A large rat was staring at her.

"Come on." Michael helped her get up, which she did fast.

"Run, let's move."

They ran. Michael was sure he had never ran this fast. The disgusting rats, the community organizers, and a possible train, were all giving him the energy and motivation he needed. If subway running ever became an Olympic sport, he would win gold. Michael slowed down a bit as he looked back. He saw the big guy who was arguing with his friend. They were not going to follow; that was for sure. The rats were too much for their sensibilities.

"I don't think this was such a good idea." He heard Jackie say.

It was not just the one rat, the one that made Jackie scream. There were rats on both sides of the tracks.

"The next station is just half a block away. We can make it." Michael could see the next station coming up. There was no train coming in either direction.

Michael heard a noise behind him and turned. Marshall had fallen. He was on the floor, struggling to get up.

Michael rushed back to help him. "You keep going," he told Jackie. It looked like Marshall hurt his knee. He could see some blood. "Can you stand up?"

"Yes." He seemed to be in pain as he tried to stand on that left leg. He could not do it. He then tried to lift himself up with his right leg. "Just give me a hand." The discomfort was obvious.

Michael heard the noise of an incoming train. It was stopping in the previous station, but in a few seconds, it would be coming their way.

"Let's go!" Michael moved forward with the professor limping next to him. It was not going to be easy to make it to the platform. They were so close, and yet it felt like it was a world away.

Jackie made it to the platform. She screamed at them to hurry.

Michael tripped and fell. He realized he had stepped on a rat. "Disgusting," he said and saw the rat moving next to his foot. He jumped. It was the highest jump in his life. That too had to be an Olympic record. "Come on, we can make it." He grabbed the professor and walked with him as fast as he could.

The unmistakable sound of the train departing the previous station sent them into a panic. It was coming their way. "We have to run."

Marshall ran for his life; the terror seemed to numb all of his knee pain.

They reached the platform. Michael saw the train getting closer. Death was literally around the corner. He bent down and wrapped his arms around Mr. Marshall's thighs. With his right shoulder supporting the professor's legs, he lifted him up in the air. It was enough of a lift that Marshall was able to step into the platform with Jackie's help. Michael placed both of his hands on the floor of the platform to push himself up. He made the mistake of looking one more time to his right side. The train was a few feet away from him. With all of his strength, he pulled himself up and pulled his legs out of the way, half a second before the train had a chance to crush them.

He was lying down on the floor; staring at the ceiling. His heart was pounding. It felt like it was going at two hundred beats per minute. To his surprise, his mind drifted not to the train that almost ended his life. Instead, he was thinking about the disgusting rat he stepped on that made him trip and fall.

"Let's not do that again," Jackie said. She was squatting next to him, displaying a smile. "I'd rather be captured."

"They have rats in jail too," he said.

"Euthanasia is not looking all that bad," Marshall said.

The subway doors opened and a multitude of passengers came out. No one bothered to look down at Michael, who was lying down on the floor. Just another homeless guy taking a power nap.

Michael was reflecting on something as he remained on the floor. He stood up with a new sense of urgency. "Let's try to get out with the crowd."

It was a large mass of people, as expected during rush hour, and they were in the middle of it. They reached the stairs, and Michael turned to Marshall. "Let's keep a little distance. Walk on the other side as we go up the stairs." Michael reached for Jackie and wrapped his arm around her waist, bringing her next to him.

"What are you doing?"

"Just play along, honey."

At the top of the stairs, there were two community organizers, just like in the previous station. Going back to the rats was not an option. He had no choice but to go forward and pray for the best. If they could make it past those two, they might have a chance to call his dad for advice and help.

Chapter 26

The community organizers were checking everyone as they came out. Michael had his arm around Jackie's waist, and Marshall walked on the other side with a crowd of people between them.

Michael brought Jackie's face up to him and gave her a kiss on the lips. They walked past them, still kissing. Just a happy couple, in love, walking by.

A few feet away, they broke off their kiss.

Jackie looked at him with a smile. "You do have some imaginative ways of getting out of trouble."

He returned the smile, but before he was able to say anything, he noticed Marshall catching up to them. "How's the knee?"

"It's sore as hell, but I'll live. I would like to clean it a little."

The professor's pants were ripped at the level of his left knee. It looked bloody and dirty.

"Let me take a look," Jackie said.

"Not here."

Two other community organizers were at the end of the street, standing at the corner.

"These guys are everywhere," Michael said. It was daylight, but it would soon get dark. They had to find a place to hide and quickly. They needed to stay out of sight, at least until the night. He thought at night they might have a better chance to get around.

"Why are they always in pairs?" Jackie asked.

"They don't know what it's like to be alone," Marshall said. "To be an individual. Their entire existence consists of being part of a collective, a group. They wouldn't know what to do on their own. How to function."

They were coming not because they had seen them. It seemed they were just walking in their direction.

Michael bumped into a guy who was trying to show him some digital display.

"Come on, man. Want to see some nude girls?" The obnoxious man said with Jackie standing right next to Michael.

He looked down and saw the picture of a topless woman. "What?" It was not a surprising occurrence in Queens Boulevard.

"Couples are welcome," the man said.

Michael looked over the man's shoulder and saw the entrance to the strip club. The windows were all blacked out.

"No, thank you." Jackie pushed the man back so she could continue to walk.

Michael saw the community organizers walking toward them. They were busy talking to each other and had not seen them yet. But they soon would. "Actually, I think it's a great idea. I've always wanted to check out a place like this." Once again, he grabbed her arm and pulled her to follow him.

"What are you doing?" she asked in disbelief. "I'm not going in there."

"No time to argue, just follow me."

Marshall had a confused look but followed them in without protesting.

The place was dark with dim lights with a strong smell of alcohol. There was a tall brunette dancing up on the stage. Her top was coming off. Michael scanned the whole place and saw it was half-empty. Or half full, depending on how he looked at it. He saw a booth, all the way in the back, next to the backdoor exit. "Perfect. Let's go sit there."

Michael and Jackie sat down next to each other. He felt awkward to be there with her and her grandfather but desperate times did call for desperate measures.

Marshall stood in front of them. "You don't think it looks a little odd for me to be here with both of you?"

Michael laughed. He took a deep breath, feeling as if his heart was coming down to a normal rate. "Come on, Mr. Marshall. This is New York. Trust me, they probably have seen weirder things here than the three of us."

Marshall saw a restroom, excused himself to go freshen up, and clean his wound.

As soon as he left, a blonde waitress came up to them. Michael noticed right away her beautiful body. She was wearing only a red see-through dress that left little to the imagination.

"Hi guys. You guys want something to drink?"

"I'll have a Diet Coke," Michael said.

"Me too."

"If you guys want a lap dance, the dancers will be coming around."

"Can't wait. Thank you," Jackie said with a sarcastic smile. When the waitress was gone, she turned to Michael, her smile all gone. "Of all the places to hide you had to think of this one?"

"It's perfect. There are no cameras. All the windows to the outside are black so no one can look inside and see us." He smiled. She had to agree it was a good place to hide. "And who is going to have the idea of looking for us here? An old man, his granddaughter, her boyfriend, this is the last place anyone would look."

"As I said before. You have some imaginative ways of getting yourself out of trouble."

The waitress came back with their drinks. Michael smiled and thanked her. Jackie pressed her thumb on a digital display she provided. The drinks were triple what they would cost in most places.

As soon as the blonde left, Michael reached for his phone, searched in both of his pants' pockets but found nothing. "I think I dropped my phone. Probably in the subway when I fell." The image of the repulsive rat chewing his phone came into his mind. It was going to take a while to forget that horrible rat. He couldn't decide who he disliked the most, the rat or West.

"You want to call your dad?"

"Yes. But now I can't do it."

"I don't have my phone either. I left it home. Maybe someone can let you borrow one."

He reflected on that for a few seconds. "No I can't," he said.

"Hi guys. What a lovely couple. You guys want a lap dance?" A topless and busty redhead stood in front of Michael. With her long fingernails, she started to caress his face. She did this while looking at Jackie. "Now sweetie, why don't you get your boyfriend a lap dance?"

"He's not my boyfriend. And he's gay."

Michael's eyes almost popped out as he stared at Jackie. She made him completely forget the gorgeous redhead standing in front of him. Then, he decided to play along. "We're actually here for her. It's her birthday and she loves redheads."

Jackie looked as if she could slap Michael in the face.

As the dancer moved toward Jackie, Michael stopped her. "She is a little shy. Let her finish her drink, and she'll loosen up a little bit."

"I'll be back in a few minutes then." She winked at Jackie and walked away.

Jackie stared at him for a few seconds.

"You started it." He broke the silence.

"Weren't you going to go and make a phone call?"

"I can't."

"What do you mean you can't? I'm sure if you go up to the front they'll let you borrow a phone."

"I don't know my dad's number."

Jackie finished her drink and placed it on the table in front of them. "What do you mean you don't know his number?"

"Well, he has a new number. It's saved in my phone. I have never actually dialed the number myself, so I don't know it."

"You mean you forgot his number."

Another lady was approaching them. It was the brunette that a minute prior was dancing up on stage. Michael signaled no, and she kept walking to another booth.

"I did not forget anything."

"What happened to Mr. 'I'm incapable of forgetting.'?" She tried to mock his voice.

"I am incapable of forgetting as I've told you before."

"Several times," she interrupted.

"But, you have to read something at least once to be able to remember it. I had his new number beamed into my phone last time I saw him. I've never actually had to dial it, so I don't know it."

"Excuses, excuses. Maybe it's not Grandpa's memory we should be worried about."

"My memory is fine. And don't make fun of it. You're the only one I've ever told I have a photographic memory."

Marshall came out of the restroom and stood there, looking at the stage where the redhead dancer was now performing.

"You really think your dad will be able to help us?"

"If he can't, we're doomed."

"What does he do anyways? You told me he works for the government, I don't remember if you told me what he does."

"And you talk about my memory." He stared at his empty cup, feeling thirsty, but thinking it was not prudent to be ordering anything more. He continued talking with Jackie. "My dad was just promoted. He is the new communications czar. It is one of the most important positions in the country."

"That's nice."

"He has meetings with President Wilson all the time."

Marshall returned to their booth and sat next to Michael.

"How's the knee?"

"It's good. I cleaned it. I made a kind of bandage with some tissue paper. It feels good for now."

"We were talking about how we were going to call my dad. I lost my phone, and I don't know his number."

"We can't use a phone," Marshall said. "They'll be monitoring any calls you make to your relatives or friends. And if you had your phone and used it, they would know your location right away. We have to stay away from using any electronics."

"Then we can't get in touch with him. We can't just stay here forever." He saw the redhead coming back their way. "Even if it's tempting."

After a moment of reflection, whether he was thinking about the redhead or his dad was hard to tell, he turned to the professor. "We'll just have to risk it and try to make it down there?"

"To your dad's place?" Marshall asked.

"Yes."

"And exactly where is your dad's place? Please tell me is like ten minutes from here."

"No. Not at all. We're going to Obama City."

Chapter 27

"Obama City?" Marshall's voice was loud; with the music and the cheering going on, no one noticed. "Are you crazy?" He tried to lower his voice. "We're trying to get away from the government and you want to take us into the lion's den—are you serious?" He was interrupted by a dancer who came and stood next to Jackie.

"What about it, sweetie. You ready for that dance?"

Jackie looked away from her grandfather and blushed. "That's okay. Not right now. Give me just a few more minutes."

The redhead walked away looking disappointed.

Marshall could not believe what trouble he had created for his granddaughter. A smart, brilliant and young physician was sitting in a strip club, hiding from the government, and it was his fault. If he had disappeared, she would have been spared the whole ordeal. "This is all my fault. I should not have gotten you guys into this trouble. Now I'm going to get you guys killed, trying to get to Obama City."

"Come on. Don't talk like that," Jackie said.

"You guys ready for another drink?" A petite waitress interrupted them.

"I just want some water," Marshall told her. When she walked away, he turned back to Michael and Jackie. "As soon as she brings it, let's get out of here." He did not feel comfortable being there, no matter what a great place to hide it was. To be there with his granddaughter and Michael troubled him.

"How did you come to have the letter? Why are they so concerned that you have it?"

"Jackie . . . This government just does not tolerate any voices of dissent. Period." The blonde brought him water with a smile.

"Is that all for now?"

"For now, yes. Thank you," Marshall said. He took a sip of the water and continued to talk. "I'll give you the short version. A few years ago, a time capsule was opened in LA, when they were rebuilding after what they called a manmade disaster or as I would call it a terrorist attack. It contained the Reagan letter and was handed to the communications department. The communications czar, a Miss . . ." He tried to remember her name but it was not coming to him.

"Faulkner," Michael said.

"Yes, you are right. Ms. Faulkner. A devil of a woman. She hates anything to do with Ronald Reagan. She believes anything he said to be dangerous for our way of life. So she ordered the letter be destroyed. Any mention of it, any speech that Reagan gave about the letter, had already been eliminated." He took a gulp of the rest of his water.

"Please go on. We need to go," Michael said once Marshall finished the water.

"A friend of mine, Senator Frank Thomas. He was one of the few good ones left. He still went along with the administration on most issues but still overall, a more reasonable fellow. He had been a professor of history with me at Santa Barbara before getting into politics; that's where we became great friends. Our wives died around the same time; they used to be good friends too. He shared my passion for history and collecting historical documents. He was especially fond of documents the government decided to destroy."

"So he got a hold of the letter," Michael said.

"Yes, he did. He was the chair of the communications committee in the Senate and he received a tip from a department official. He was worried Faulkner would find out—she does not like her orders disobeyed, so he asked me to keep it with my collection."

Another dancer, a tall brunette, was coming their way. Marshall wished he was there alone. It had been a long time since he had seen such a beautiful woman.

"Are you guys going to order any lap dances or just sit back here?" She looked annoyed.

"We were waiting for that gorgeous redhead to come back." Michael pointed to the stage where she was performing to the delight of the crowd. "Please continue," he said as the brunette walked away.

"That was a few years back. I kept the letter in my collection, hidden. Never showed it to anyone." His gaze kept shifting toward the redhead on stage. It was a distracting place to talk. "A few weeks ago I sent an email to Frank, following up in a conversation we had, reminding him that it was 2076, that we should make the letter public, as Ronald Reagan would have liked. I sent the email from a group account in the history department. There was no way to know it was me. Except the senator. He would know it was me. He would understand what letter I was talking about."

"What was his reaction?" Michael asked.

"He was outraged by this Consumption Chip Bill before Congress, that it marked the very end of our liberty. He felt it was the right time to remind Americans the kind of Nation we used to be and what we have become. His intention was to read the letter in a speech on the floor of the Senate. A speech in opposition of the consumption chip and about the erosion of freedom in America." Marshall felt a sense of sadness coming over him as he thought about the fate of his friend. "One morning, I heard in the news that he was taken to the hospital, and he was diagnosed with a stroke. They said he was alive but delirious and not expected to survive. The next day is when I went for my physical and my doctor told me of that consult I never had with Dr. West, saying I had Alzheimer's." The redhead was done on stage and was walking toward them. "Sitting at my doctor's office, I had this feeling that it was all a set up by the government. Somehow, they knew his plans, about the letter, about me having it. There was no other reason to come after me. I've lead a quiet life especially after my wife died. So I knew they were coming after me because of the letter."

"That redhead is gonna come here next. We really should leave," Jackie said.

"Hard to believe they were bold enough to go after a sitting senator." Michael did his best to ignore the redhead who was now finishing a lap dance two tables away from them.

"The administration was upset about his growing loud opposition of the Consumption Chip Bill. When they found out about the letter or so-called stolen letter, as they would say, they probably realized they had a legitimate reason to go after him."

The redhead reached their booth. Before she was able to say anything, a heavyset man came behind her.

"Is there a Michael Adams here?" he asked them, holding a phone in his hand.

"That's me," Michael said.

Marshall was the first to notice. He looked toward the front of the establishment and saw, standing at the counter, a police officer, and right away, he knew they were trapped.

Chapter 28

Michael took the phone. "Yes . . ." He recognized the voice.

"Mr. Adams, I am watching the video of you at the subway. Too bad you missed the train or rather, the train missed you. It would have saved me the trouble. I hope you and Dr. Perez are enjoying your Diet Coke . . ."

Michael dropped the phone and grabbing Jackie's arm, he headed for the backdoor.

He came out into a back alley. It was deserted and full of garbage all over the place. He went toward his right with Marshall following behind.

As they approached the street, he saw a patrol car coming their way. He turned around right away, did not see if the officers were looking in his direction. "Wrong way. We go that way."

"Do you have any brilliant ideas of where we can hide next? I know. Maybe next we can hang out with some drug dealers," Jackie said.

Michael ignored her sarcasm. Besides, that was not a bad idea. They would be safe if they were with some drug dealers. It was not as if the police were searching for real criminals.

He came out into the street, looked around, and did not see any police cars or community organizers coming their way. It was ten minutes to sundown.

"Let's just hang out somewhere until sundown." He walked back to Queens Boulevard. It was a busy place, day or night. They had to try to get lost in the crowds.

In Queens Boulevard, Michael saw police cars driving about. He also noticed another couple of community organizers walking nearby.

"We need to get out of here, Mike. Every corner of Queens Boulevard is under surveillance."

Marshall was right—there were cameras everywhere. Up, above them he saw one pointed in their direction. "Let's keep moving." Michael crossed the street and saw an American Electric Mega store around the next corner. "Let's go in there."

He was walking too fast and had to stop to wait for them. "Let's go into there. It's very crowded. We can try to get lost with the crowd inside, at least until night."

"What difference does it make? This place has so many lights. There is no difference between night and day," Marshall said.

"The back streets are less lighted. We can go look for some place to hide. Maybe a church or something like that?"

"A church? God help you finding one of those around here."

Michael wished the professor could be more optimistic. The odds were against them, but it was counterproductive to be looking at things in such a negative way. Nevertheless, it was hard to blame him. Even if they found a place to hide, it was hard to take a cab or the train, hard to imagine how they would ever manage to make it to Obama City.

"Let's separate," Michael said as they entered the store. "So we don't look so suspicious."

Jackie headed for the upper floor; Marshall went toward the home entertainment section in the back of the store.

Michael saw a community organizer close to where the professor was. He was checking out the TVs, not looking at anyone in particular.

Michael went to Marshall and made conversation, pretending he was interested in the gadgets. "You think there have been many advances in the past few years?" he asked.

"The only advances are in centralizing information in the hands of the government." Marshall walked toward the TV sets. The volume was loud and no one could hear them talking. Michael was close enough that he could. Marshall pretended to be checking out one of the TVs and pointed to the AE logo. "American Electric used to be a private company. The government took it over in the second decade of the century, when everything was being nationalized. It became the official supplier of any electronics to the public. Iphones, security systems, home appliances, TVs—everything is supplied by AE. Even the electronics in your car or the fingertip recognition technology you find in guns and other things. AE provides it all; the government controls them and through them maintains surveillance over your life."

The community organizer was moving in their direction. Michael took Marshall's hand and walked to the other side of the store. The store was crowded, and it was hard to move with so many people. There were several surveillance cameras in the store. He felt exposed even though it was hard to distinguish them in such a large crowd.

"Look." Marshall pointed to a security system pad. The display read: "The home of the future."

Michael remembered seeing the same exact display when he was kid. Back then, he was excited about getting a fancy system like that.

"Look at this. This type of security system is now standard in all modern homes. No new home is allowed to be build without it." He opened the pad. "Anyone that comes into the house will either open the door through the fingertip recognition pad at the door, or if more than one person is coming in or a guest that's coming in, they would have to place their thumb here to be recognized by the system. If this is not done, the system will recognize through sensors throughout the house that there is an intruder in the house. This is, of course, done for the security of the family. But, the system is under surveillance by security personnel who works for the government. Through this, the government knows exactly who is in your house at all times."

Michael turned pale; the community organizer was coming their way. He pushed Marshall inside the "house of the future" display, toward the kitchen area. "Look at this fridge."

"It also opens through fingertip recognition," said Marshall. "It can order your supplies via the internet. The downside is they can know how much food you are taking, what you're consuming. They can create a profile about you and your family. How many calories you consume, how likely you are to become obese, how much negative contribution you are making to the environment. The more you eat, the more carbon dioxide you produce and the more you will pollute the environment."

Michael glanced back. No one seemed to have followed them.

"They can restrict what you can order. They are obsessed with this obesity epidemic and what to do with diabetes. There have been no new treatments developed in this backward health care system of ours, so they want to control what people eat and how much you eat," Marshall said.

Michael thought about the chocolate mousse. With a fridge like that, he would not be able to have it, even in his own place.

He saw Jackie coming down the stairs and noticed two community organizers behind her. They were busy talking and laughing at each other. It was dark outside, a good time to leave. He walked toward the center of the store.

"Look." Marshall stopped him. "They want now to push a new law to make this mandatory." The professor was pointing to a small chip in the "phone and communications" section. "The chip will have all of your phone information, so you can always have access. It's always with you, so you will never be without a phone anywhere. It will contain your personal health records for easy access and for your convenience. It will decrease medical errors, since it will be the same record no matter where you go. It will have your financial records, so you can make your transactions easily. And its main purpose is to help you keep track of how many calories you consume, what your carbon footprint is. So you can make changes, live a healthier life."

"Sounds like you could get a job here," Michael joked. He was keeping an eye on Jackie who had moved away from where they were standing. The two community organizers were another story. They were coming their way. He lowered his head and prayed they would not notice him. Good thing the professor was sounding like a salesman.

"If this becomes law and everyone is required to carry one of these chips, then the government will know where you are at all times. What you're doing."

So much for sounding like a salesman, thought Michael. "Keep it down," he said, hoping the antigovernment talk would not give them away.

"They will know what you're buying, where you're going. They'll know everything about you. Your conversations, who do you talk to, what you talk about, what you look at in the internet. Everything. They will keep profiles of you and your preferences, so they can study you and decide if you are in some way a threat to society. If you need to be referred to the antisocial division. Or if you are being a productive citizen, doing your part for a better community."

Michael was about to tell him that the law making the chip mandatory had passed the House a few days back. That absence of his friend, Senator Thomas, seemed to assure it would have a smooth sailing in the Senate. It was obvious that the professor had not seen recent news. He decided to keep him in the dark. It was the wrong place to see him fuming at the government.

"And Michael, when someone is not doing whatever it is the government wants you to be doing, they are considered a threat to society. They don't hesitate to eliminate you then. They believe there's overpopulation anyways. There are too many people, and it's a threat to the environment. So it's better to eliminate people that are a burden to society. And that's not just the chronically ill but people whose political views makes them a threat to a progressive society."

Population control was a topic Michael wished to avoid. He turned to see if he could find Jackie. He saw her standing by the home entertainment center. The two community organizers were now by the entrance, talking to a cop. "I see Jackie. Let's go get her."

"I'm sorry. When I start talking about this, I just don't seem to be able to stop," Marshall said.

"That's okay. It was informative. Wish we had more time." He walked slowly, not wanting to rush and catch the cop's attention. "Mr. Marshall . . ." He paused and looked back toward the entrance. They were moving about the store, definitely looking for someone. He felt some relief when he saw them headed for the stairs. "Why do they want this control over our lives?"

The cop was going up the stairs with one of the community organizers. The other one had split and was headed in their direction.

"They want power over our lives." Marshall continued to talk as Michael pulled him, walking fast toward Jackie. "They want social and economic equality. We are all equal, but we should also be all free. If people are free, then you can't have equal outcomes. People make different choices. Some people will make bad choices. Some people will have bad outcomes when they make bad choices. That's the price you pay for a free society."

Michael reached Jackie. "Want to get it?" He was standing behind her as she looked at a flat screen TV. "We need to go," he told her.

The news was on. Michael was turning away and heading for the exit when he saw his face on TV. The news commentator stated he was a wanted fugitive that attacked a federal officer in Queens. He felt light-headed.

Jackie grabbed him and pulled him away. "We need to go."

"Hey. That's him!" A teenager who was standing close by screamed. Almost everyone in the store turned their heads, looking in Michael's direction.

"Shit," Michael said.

"Someone grab him!" The kid screamed.

They stepped outside into a pouring rain. Some people were coming out of the store behind them, including a community organizer. Michael saw two police officers coming from his right side. He started to run to his left and turned the corner. They stayed in the store longer than they should have. He shook his head, feeling angry with himself. He was going to have to look for a place to hide, in the rain, with cops after him. Not to mention, his picture all over the local news.

Chapter 29

The rain came down hard, made his visibility limited. Michael could not see any place where they could go in and hide. They were running down a street with apartment buildings on both sides. He looked back over his shoulder. Marshall was falling behind, and in the distance, two police officers were running their way. A police car, with its lights on, was coming from the other direction. "They're gonna get us."

"There's nowhere to go," Jackie said.

Michael saw someone coming out of one of the buildings. He rushed and grabbed the door before it locked. "Thanks. With this rain, no time to get the key."

The lady who was coming out did not even bother to look at him. She did not even say hi. Typical New York snobbishness, thought Michael. He went in and held the door open for Jackie and Marshall.

He ran for the elevator. Its doors were closing, but before they did, he stopped them with his hand. The elevator opened and they all got in. Michael pressed for the top floor, the eleventh, and as the doors closed, he saw two police officers at the entrance of the building.

"What's your idea now? They'll call backup and have us trapped in this building," Jackie said.

"I know." He was clueless on what to do once they made it all the way up. Maybe go back down and hope the cops had gone up. No, that was a bad idea. There were more cops on the way.

The elevator opened, and he came out, saw that the other elevator was on its way up, already by the fifth floor. "That's probably them." A staircase to the roof was ahead; he decided it was the only way to go. "Let's go up."

The rain was still as heavy as before. Michael went to the front of the building and looked down. Three patrol cars, with their police lights on, were down there.

He looked at Jackie, hoping she had any ideas.

"We can't get out that way. That's for sure," she said.

He ran to the back of the building and immediately noticed how close the next building was. He jumped without hesitation. "Come on, Jackie."

She held her grandfather's hand, and they both jumped. They ran toward the back of that building. The next one over was also close but a floor shorter. It would be a tough jump especially for Marshall.

"We have to do this."

"Grandpa won't be able to do it."

Before she was able to say anything else, her grandfather ran and jumped. He fell hard on the floor of that next roof. They did the same and managed to have a safe landing. Michael helped Marshall up to his feet, and they went toward the staircase.

"Let's take the elevator down," Michael said.

The elevator stopped in the first floor. There, Michael went toward the stairs. "Let me just see if there's someone by the front door." When he saw that it was clear, he signaled for them to come down.

They rushed out the door and came out into the pouring rain. Michael looked around, searching for any more police. A taxi was coming down the street. He stepped in front of it, signaling for the cab to stop, and they got in.

"Make a U-turn, and step on it," Michael said.

The driver followed the instructions and drove away fast. As they passed the first intersection, Michael saw a couple of patrol cars going on the opposite direction. He felt better, but the question of where to go next remained. Wherever it was, they would have to leave the taxi without paying. Otherwise, they would give away their location. Their driver was going to be pissed off at them. He could join the club. It felt like no matter what he tried to do, it was impossible to make a real escape. They were going from one dead end to another.

"Mike, where are we going? He's asking you," Jackie said.

Michael had not noticed the driver was talking to him. "I'm thinking. I don't know yet."

"You don't know where you want to go, man?" the driver said with his Jamaican accent.

He was driving fast, in the rain, making Jackie uncomfortable with the speed. With the kind of day they were having, an accident was probably in the cards, thought Michael.

"I'm gonna keep driving around 'til you make up your mind," the driver said.

"Drive to Long Island City, please." Michael had just had an idea. If they could get there alive, without dying of a car accident, it was the perfect place to hide, at least for the night.

The driver made a sudden right turn, almost losing control of the car. It did not seem to bother him at all. He pressed the accelerator even harder, running through a red light as if there was no tomorrow. If he kept it up, with all likelihood, they would not see a tomorrow.

"Could you slow down a little? You're going to get us killed," Jackie said.

"Lady, he said step on it. I'm stepping."

A couple of other fast turns, with the same high speed, and it seemed the he was determined to get them to their destination in record time. Maybe he just needed to use the restroom, wondered Michael.

"We're going to get pulled over for speeding," Marshall said. "And with the entire NYPD now looking for us, that's probably not a great idea."

The driver hit the brakes, and Michael hit his face in the back of the front seat. He could hear the tires screeching and felt as if the car was going to start spinning.

The taxi driver turned toward them. "Man, you're hiding from the police?" He did not wait for an answer. "Get out, man. Get off. I don't want no pay. Don't need proof I had fugitives. Out!"

They came out of the taxi as fast as they had gone in. All of them thankful they had made it alive. Michael was the last one to come out. As he did, he noticed Jackie was standing still, staring at something. He turned to see what she was looking at. He saw it. The taxi dropped them off in front of a police station.

Chapter 30

Her lips tasted as good as they looked. Her body felt even better than it looked especially with his arms wrapped around her. She was in her late thirties or early forties but she had a terrific figure. With short blonde hair and deep blue eyes, Olga Parker was his type of woman.

"Excuse me . . ." He broke off their embrace to answer his phone. "This is West . . ."

He listened to the excuses while he continued to admire her naked body. She had come to his hotel room wearing a tight and short blue dress. She gave some excuse about dinner plans for being dressed up. He felt she dressed like that for him. If her intention was to get his attention, she succeeded. The high heels, especially, were a nice addition. It made her toned legs look longer and better.

"They can't just disappear like that . . ." He walked away from the bed. "They have to be somewhere, keep looking . . ." His excitement was gone. The mood of a few seconds ago disappeared as his mind was back on the job, wondering where Calvin Marshall and his young friend could be.

Olga Parker walked toward him, "Where were we?" she asked.

"Give me a moment." He went back to the bed, where he had his palm PC, and opened the file on Michael Adams. "Is there something more you can tell me about Mr. Adams?"

"He hasn't been found yet?"

"No. I thought I had him trapped at some strip club, but he escaped. Then, he was spotted at the AE store in Queens Boulevard, but somehow he managed to disappear."

West was clicking, bringing something up on the screen. "This kid is starting to annoy me." He felt the pulsating pain in his left ankle. Michael was going to pay for this insult.

"This is interesting." He shook his head. How could he have missed it? He had taken the assignment too lightly. That's why he was making these sloppy mistakes.

"What is it?" She sat on the bed next to him.

"His father is George Adams."

"Yes, the new communications czar. That's really the only reason I made him editor. Well, back then he was not the czar yet, but he was one of the people believed to be next in line."

"And with Faulkner pushing past her eighties, you figured he would soon take her place."

"I was right, wasn't I?"

"It is very interesting. This is going to be an embarrassment for his old man. The president is not going to be happy his new communications czar has a fugitive son accused of antisocial behavior and right-wing radicalism."

"Yes, it doesn't look good."

He smiled and looked up to Parker. "He probably thinks Daddy is going to get him out of trouble. And I agree that it could get a little tricky with the daddy involved."

"You think he'll try to cover for his son?"

"I don't know. He is hard to predict. He is no Faulkner, that's for sure."

Parker was breathing on his neck, looking over his shoulder, and he was enjoying it. Taking pleasure on the smell of her feminine fragrance. Whatever perfume she was using, was tuning him on.

"You guys have a file on him?" she asked.

"We have a file on everybody."

"You want a drink?"

She walked over to the mini bar, stopped at the bathroom first to take a bathrobe then picked up a bottle of whiskey and prepared two glasses with ice and water.

"Thanks." He took a sip of his whiskey. "Does Michael Adams have a medical history that you know of?"

"Not that I know of. I reviewed his health history last year before I made him editor, and he had no history. That I can remember."

He brought up a screen with Michael's health record. His administrative password gave him full access. He clicked on the section of the past medical history, talked to her as he typed. "It says here he has a history of bipolar disorder . . ." He typed some more.

"Really? I didn't know."

"That explains some of his behavior. When you have bipolar disorder, you can go through a manic phase, become hyper, lose control over your actions. You can do things on impulse such as attacking a federal officer. You can also have a phase of hypomania, when you look sad, with a depressed mood." He looked up to her. "Do you remember him exhibiting any of these symptoms?"

She thought about the question for a few seconds. "Now that I think of it. The last time he was in my office he did look a little down, sad if you will."

"Yes, he was probably in his depressed phase then." He clicked into another section in the chart. It was for the current medications. "He's probably not taking his medications. That's what it is. According to his record, he's supposed to be on Lithium, six hundred milligrams, BID." He looked back at her. "BID means twice a day." He returned to the previous section, the Past Medical History. "Oh, I missed that. Not good."

"What?" She asked.

"He has a history of suicidal and homicidal ideation." He closed the electronic chart, satisfied he had checked out everything he needed to. "Definitely in need of some inpatient psychiatric care."

"Even his daddy will have to agree with that." She had a full smile in display.

He took another sip of his whiskey while looking at her. When he was done, he opened her bathrobe. "So, where were we?"

Chapter 31

The rain stopped, but their problems did not. They stood in front of a police station. Michael could hardly believe the bad luck. It had been that kind of day.

"Mike, standing in front of a police station when the police are looking for you, is not a great idea."

Michael took her hand and pulled her away to the other side of the street. Thankfully, no cops were outside and no one had seen them. At least, as far as he could tell. They walked about a block before Michael recognized their surroundings.

"We're in Long Island City already, aren't we?"

"Yes," she said.

"I think your dad's building is this way. Let's try to make it there."

"That's a good idea."

"What's a good idea?" Marshall asked.

"Dad is working on this skyscraper being built not far from here. It's maybe 70 percent finished. It's empty. We can stay there the night."

Michael noticed how tired Marshall looked. They would not be able to go much further with him. All the running and jumping was too much for his age. Tony's building would be a welcome break, with plenty of finished floors where they could hide, without worrying about construction workers, at least for tonight. If they could meet with Tony in the morning, he could get them some supplies—even help them get away.

"Maybe we can run into your dad in the morning."

"He comes in very early. We should be able to see him."

"Hey, where you guys going?"

Michael heard it, but at first, he did not see who said it. He then saw on his left side a tall man with a blonde beard. He looked dirty with torn clothes, walking toward them.

"You guys should not be walking at night like this. Without some . . . protection."

The man was staring at Jackie. Michael estimated he was about an inch taller than him and the same weight.

"Oh my, what have we here? A babe. You're so fine. Isn't she fine?"

Michael saw another man coming from behind the first one. The man with the dirty beard, answered him, "Oh yea. She look good." He touched Jackie's right breast, which sent her left hand toward his face for a slap. It did not meet its destination. The man had good reflexes and held her wrist with his hand.

Michael leaped forward and tackled him to the ground.

He stood up just in time to be punched on the face by the second man. A second punch was coming his way; able to dodge it, he threw a hard right uppercut straight to the man's jaw. That man fell to the floor, but the guy with the beard was standing in front of Michael with a knife out.

The second man stood up and was coming toward Michael, cursing him. Jackie threw a kick right into his groin area. His gaze was focused on Michael; he never saw the kick coming. The look on his face was priceless. He fell on his knees, looking at Jackie. The man with the beard took his eyes off Michael to look at his kicked friend. By the time he looked back at Michael, a right hook landed hard on his left cheek.

With both men hitting the floor, Michael and Jackie left the scene. They were on the run again, with Marshall trying to keep up with them, with limited success.

The two bandits were after them, and the blond guy was gaining. Michael then saw the building they were looking for. It was a block away; they could make it. He was worried about the professor who was falling behind.

"Come on!" Michael was waving for him to run faster.

They made it to the building, found a gate with a lock and chain keeping anyone from coming in. The homeless guys were still after them. At least, they stopped running; they were not in the best shape.

Michael pushed the gate open as much as he could. The chain made it difficult but he created enough of an opening for Marshall and Jackie to get in. It was not enough for Michael. He saw the two men running again, getting closer. "Go Jackie. Get the elevator."

The two men were just across the street. Michael jumped up, climbed the fence with the same urgency that had been the norm the rest of that crazy day. The top part of the fence had barbwire. He reached as high up as he could without touching the barbwire, then jumped to the other side. He fell, unable to keep his balance, scratching his face. The pain on the left side of his face was intense. No time to think about it. He rushed back up and ran toward the elevator.

The two men were trying to get in through the gate. One of them managed to get in and came running toward them. The service elevator, which went up alongside the building, moved slowly. The homeless guy could go get a cup a coffee, come back, and still catch the elevator before it even reached the first floor. That's how slow Michael felt it was moving. He could catch them, there was no doubt, and he still had a knife.

Chapter 32

The man with the dirty beard was running toward them. Michael could see the knife in his left hand. He pressed the up button desperately, as if that would make it go faster.

It was pointless; they would not even be past the first floor before he reached them. Michael jumped down from the elevator.

"Come back here!"

Jackie's scream was of no use; he was running toward the side of the building. His assailant was going after him rather than the elevator.

Michael found a large hammer against one of the walls. He tried to pick it up, but it was bigger and heavier than it looked. He managed to lift it to his waist, and when the man was close to him, he swung it, hitting him right on the stomach. The man dropped the knife, fell to the floor. Michael lifted the hammer over his head. He could kill him with one blow. No. No way. That was not his way.

He lowered the hammer down; in the distance, he saw the other man coming. He went into the building through one of the unfinished windows, found a staircase and ran up the stairs, keeping the hammer with him. It was his insurance policy if they tried to come after him. Hopefully, with that strong blow to the stomach, he would lose interest.

When he reached the tenth floor, he felt exhausted. He considered himself to be in great shape, but going up those flights with a heavy hammer was too much. Especially after the kind of day he had.

Twelve floors were the most he could do. He went toward the front of the building where the service elevator ran. He missed it.

It had just passed his floor. He went to another staircase behind him and rushed up two more floors. Fourteen was his lucky number. He reached the service elevator and was able to join Jackie and Marshall.

"You okay?" Jackie asked him.

"Yes. I'm fine. This thing weights a ton." Placing the hammer down, he sat on the floor. "What happened to those guys?" He asked while looking down to the ground below. If they were around, he did not see them.

"After you hit him with the hammer, his friend talked to him. They seemed to lose interest and went away."

"Or they went to get their friends," Michael said.

"What should we do now?" Jackie asked. "With the police looking for us, this is probably the safest place to spend the night. But not with those crazies after us."

The height was making him nervous. Too high for his comfort. "If we go all the way up, we should be fine. I think this is the only elevator that goes all the way up there."

"They could take the stairs," she said.

"One hundred floors? I don't think so." Michael was exhausted after ten; he could not imagine those two attempting to go all the way. "We should be fine."

Past the fortieth floor, he started to feel the strength of the wind, with the elevator swinging from side to side. He tried not to look too nervous.

"You look nervous," Jackie said.

His eyes were closed as he prayed. Jackie and her grandfather also sat on the floor, jerking the elevator as they did.

"I hope this thing is made to hold the weight of all three of us," Michael said.

The elevator finally made it to the one hundredth floor. Everyone stepped out right away. Michael picked up his hammer and hit the motor, which was next to the elevator. One of the cables came loose as he hit it a second time. The entire elevator fell down one hundred floors.

"Why did you do that?" Jackie looked surprised by his action.

"No one will be able to come up now."

"And we won't be able to go down either," Marshall said.

"It's easier for us to go down the stairs than for anyone to come up."

Marshall felt as if he received a beating. Every muscle of his body hurt him as he went down the stairs. Every step he took, he did so with great difficulty. It was nighttime, they had been in the building under construction for over one hour. No one had come looking for them so far.

Michael had gone down to check out the other floors, see what he could find, came back and told him he found a kitchen that was being used about ten floors down. It seemed some of the construction workers were using it as a break room during the day.

In the kitchen, he found Michael and Jackie sitting at a table. Thankfully, the kitchen had working light. He ate some apples and bread; less than a gourmet dinner, but he was starving. They chatted for a while; the mood much more relaxed.

"There are some carpeted offices in this floor. I saw some chairs in a conference room. It will be a good place to sleep," Michael said.

They finished eating. Not a single apple was left. They left some bread for the morning, to have with their coffee, and headed for one of the offices.

Michael found an office that was spacious, with a bathroom inside, and a window, so they could wake up with the daylight. In addition, he found a laptop that was still logged on.

"We should send a message to your dad."

"That's a good idea, I can send it to his phone, have him meet us here."

"Don't do that. They will be monitoring his communications," Marshall warned.

"You're right," Michael said. "Let's send something only he could understand." Michael reflected on that for a minute. "I got it." He looked at Jackie who was ready to type the message. "Okay, here it goes. Who is Howard Roark? I too have no wings to fly from one hundred." Jackie was looking at him with a confused look. "Trust me, he'll understand. He'll know it's me." He then continued dictating the message. "Bad memory and fair lady still with me. Tonight I sleep. In AM I must fly again."

"Want to send one to your dad?" Jackie asked.

"No. That would be too suspicious. Two emails going from here, one to your dad, one to mine. And why would anyone email my dad from here?"

They then settled down in one of the offices, trying to make the best possible sleeping arrangements they could.

"It's perfect. The carpet is soft. I'll wake up with a terrible backache, but I'll survive," Marshall said.

He could not help but to think about the trouble he had brought for Michael and Jackie. However, he knew that giving away the letter was not a solution. It would just reward coercion; it was in fact accepting that America was now a land of tyranny. He was not ready to accept that.

"I don't think it's a good idea at all to try to bargain with the feds. This letter is too much of a threat to their existence. From their perspective, it must be destroyed and we with it." Marshall wanted to sleep, but it was important to convince them of how important the letter was.

Michael sat up, the moonlight reflected on him as he sat against the wall. "I still don't get why this letter means so much to them? Reagan is dead. Even if people really like the letter, so what, it's not like he's going to follow it up with any actions."

"Let's try and get some sleep, please. I'm so tired," Jackie said, lying down on the opposite side of the room.

Marshall sat on one of the chairs in the conference room and rolled it to where Michael was sitting. "Words matter. They don't have that utopia they had hoped for. It can't happen because you can't control the individual. This chip they want to force on us is an attempt at that goal."

Marshall stopped. For a moment, he thought he heard a noise outside. "Did you hear something?"

"No," said Michael.

The professor continued, "It's an attempt at controlling the individual. They have total control of everything else. But, when you have this much control, you want even more because you still don't have that utopia, because people just continue to be individuals and want to do their own thing. At that point, when you control everything else, you realize that people themselves need to be controlled. The individual is that last variable, that last problem that needs to be dealt with. Opposition that is getting in the way of progress needs to be removed. People who are not or cannot take care of themselves, or are born with too many inadequacies, need to be eliminated. That is the only way they can have that ultimate utopia. Then, they can have that equality and social justice they dream of."

Marshall realized he had caught Jackie's attention. She was sitting up, looking at him.

"It's just not possible to sleep when people are talking." She did not look upset. "Go ahead, Grandpa. Don't worry about me, I'm listening too."

He turned his chair in Jackie's direction. She would find interesting what he was about to say. "This chip, it is the first version, once it passes and gets implemented, upgrades will come. One of the things being talked about is to be able to dispense medications through it. You will go to your doctor and let's say you have blood pressure, they will be able to give you medication that will be timed release. At the right time, the chip will do its thing, and the medication will be released into your bloodstream. You will never have to worry about forgetting to take your medication. You'll never will. And since you have the chip, you can't hide the fact that you have blood pressure or diabetes problems. All that information will be in the chip, and they will know it." He had their full attention; sleep was now the last thing in their mind. "This has many implications. When I went to my doctor and was diagnosed with Alzheimer's, and they referred me to the palliative care team, they could have given a medication that later that night, or in a few days or weeks, would be released, and I would die in my sleep. Expectant mothers could have medication added that, if they are expecting an imperfect baby, will induce a spontaneous abortion."

"I didn't know any of that. Where did you learn all of this?" Jackie asked.

"This is what Frank knew. He was outraged about this. That's why he was so opposed to it and why they went after him. The Reagan letter is a distraction they can't afford at such a critical time. This chip will be a dream come true for progressives. And will transform us from one of the most benevolent nations in history to . . ." He shook his head, could not bring himself to say it, to believe it. However, it was hard to deny, the evidence was all around them. "These progressives have been, for the last seventy years, fundamentally transforming the United States from being the last best hope on earth, to becoming an evil empire."

The room remained silent for a while. Marshall had spent so many years watching out what he was saying that it was a strange feeling speaking so openly. When teaching, he had to be careful about accusing the government of intolerance. Such talk was not tolerated; it could get him into trouble.

"Reagan was worried we were headed for an oppressive society." He broke the silence after a few minutes.

"When did it become this vicious? Physically silencing your opposition like this," Michael said.

Marshall thought about that for a moment. "In the early part of the century, there were a lot of voices of dissent, radio programs, some TV commentators, they were critical of the government's policies, and the gradual decay of our freedoms. At first, they tried to marginalize them, said they were not real news organizations, or that the commentators were radicals, hoping America would fail. People that were protesting the government were made to look like dangerous extremists who were inciting violence." He paused for a moment, trying to remember details he had not discussed with anyone in a long time. "There was a famous case with this radio personality. He was very popular back then . . ." He paused again, trying to recollect the name. "Glen Berk, I think it was. After some group was discovered to be plotting to bomb some government facilities, it was found out that they listened to his show regularly. The media, on behalf of the government, made a big deal about it. He was taken off the air and eventually ended up going to jail for inciting rebellion. I believe he died in jail just a few years after his incarceration." Marshall took a deep breath. He was tired and his back was bothering him.

"This is not surprising," he continued. "True progressives, those who are truly committed to their cause, understand that individual freedom is a clear and present danger to their way of thinking."

Marshall looked at them; they both seemed exhausted. He wished he could tell them so much more, but sleep was important too.

"Grandpa." Jackie approached her grandfather. "I appreciate how passionate you are about all of this. I confess I never knew things were this bad." She had an arm around his shoulder. "We cannot afford to be heroes right now. We are hiding here, running for our lives. Freedom is good, and all that, but what good is it if you're dead? I don't want you to end up like that Glen Berk guy. We have to try to stay alive. If Michael's dad can help us out and we have to surrender the letter . . ." Jackie faced him and looked him in the eyes. "If that's what we need to do to stay alive, then it is what we have to do. I don't think we have a choice right now."

Marshall remained silent. He did not see eye to eye with Jackie on this one. Life was important, of course, but not at the expense of freedom. That was no life at all. That was existence under someone else's terms. However, he felt guilty about getting her involved. If he could spare her from any more trouble, he would.

Maybe, what his granddaughter needed was to have that hope that all could be resolved by surrendering the letter. Hope that would help her keep going, stay alive. "Let's get some sleep, and we'll see what Michael's dad can do for us," he said.

Chapter 33

June 3
Long Island City, New York

A restless sleep due to a nightmare and snoring from her grandfather made her wake up early, feeling tired. Jackie was unsure how much she managed to sleep, but as she stood up and looked outside, she saw it was still dark. She searched for her watch; it was 4:30 in the morning. Too early to get up but futile to try to get any more sleep.

She left the room and went up the stairs to get some fresh air. The place was empty and quiet. The feeling that someone could come at anytime and arrest her was persistent. The last twenty-four hours had been so stressful. Hard to believe she was a fugitive from the law. The other residents at the hospital, and her attending, would soon begin to wonder where she was. Her patients would have to be cared by doctors not familiar with them. She felt terrible to be abandoning them.

She reached the top floor. The breeze felt good. There was only one wall finished, with the rest of them still being built. She could see Manhattan over to her left side.

A tear came down her cheek. The thought that her life was never going to be the same kept recurring. Her career in medicine, all the effort, all the sacrifices she had made over the years, was all for nothing. All being destroyed for some political letter she could not care less about.

She was angry—not at her grandfather that's for sure—but at angry at someone, and she was not sure who. What her grandpa did, taking the letter with him, trying to protect it, she could understand. He was trying to do what he felt was the right thing. Trying to prevent an injustice. His motives were noble. She had learned that from him, to always try and do what she felt to be right, no matter what the consequences. To do what she believed was true, no matter what pressures she felt from others.

Her anger was not toward Michael either. He ended up involved in this because of her. He tried to protect them from the agent because of his concern for her. If not for him, her grandfather would be gone, and she would never see him again.

Agent West did make her angry. After all, it was his appearance that turned her life upside down. It was his attitude, his unwillingness to listen to reason, the obstinate determination to take her grandpa away that sent them on the run.

She couldn't pinpoint the anger she felt on him alone. There was something more. Maybe it was all that talk her grandfather did the night before, all the implications of that consumption chip.

She thought about her attending, who, just last week, wanted her to end the life of another human being. Yes, she was angry at him. In a way, she felt that he, more than anyone else, ruined her medical career. West ruined her ability to practice medicine by making her a fugitive; her attending had already destroyed her desire to practice it. Her naive notion that medicine was a noble profession had been shattered that day.

Do no harm. An oath she took once. One she took seriously. Now, she realized she would not be able to keep it. Sooner or later, she would have to violate it and do harm to one of her patients for the good of society. She would never be able to do it. Her career was over even before becoming a fugitive.

She cleared away the tears. She had to be strong and keep her mind clear. The most important thing was to try to stay alive. Her grandfather and Michael were all that matter for the moment. Helping them was her only concern. As soon as they woke up, they would have to figure out a way to get down to Obama City. That was the only thing that mattered—to make it to Mike's house alive.

She was startled by a noise. Someone was coming up the stairs. She went to hide behind a table at the center of the open floor. Coming up alone was not a good idea. If it turned out to be those same bandits from before, what could she do all alone?

How could she defend herself? She saw a large wood stick in the floor close to the staircase. She went to get it and stood right behind the stairs, holding it over her head. Whoever was coming up was alone; she heard only one set of steps. She had to be fast. Jackie lowered the stick with all of her strength as someone stuck his head through.

Chapter 34

Michael did not see her anywhere. He woke up and did not see Jackie in the room. Checked the bathroom, the kitchen, and found no trace of her. He became concerned, wondering where she might have gone. They had agreed to stay together in case someone came looking for them. He decided to go up, see if she had ventured there.

He went all the way to that top floor under construction, still feeling uncomfortable about being at such altitude. Up that high gave him the sensation he was going to fall. And it was a long way down.

As he reached the top floor, he noticed in the corner of his eye, Jackie and a stick.

"Hey!" He caught it with his hand, just before it hit his head. "Ouch!" The impact did hurt his hand.

"Mike!" Jackie looked frightened. "I'm sorry, I got scared when I heard someone coming up. Didn't know it was you."

"What were you doing up here?"

"I was enjoying the view." She walked to the edge, looking off toward Manhattan, signaled for him to go join her.

Michael felt tense seeing her so close to the edge. "Aren't you getting a little too close there?"

"It's a beautiful view. Come join me." Her smile of encouragement was almost impossible to resist.

"I can see fine from here. Yes, wow! What a great view."

"Come on, don't be afraid. I won't let you fall, promise."

He remained without moving. Of all the women in America, he had to fall for one who loved heights.

"Look I'll take a step back," she said.

One small step but a giant leap to make him somewhat comfortable. He stood next to her and wrapped his arm around her waist. "It is a great view."

"Yes," she said, leaning her head on his shoulder.

"Did you ever go there when you were a kid?" He pointed to Manhattan.

"I was seven years old when it happened. My dad was working in Manhattan at the time. We were so scared. We didn't hear from him until night. I don't remember ever being that scared. The thought that he had been killed too . . ."

"Was he anywhere near the bombings?"

"No. There were, I think, six dirty bombs that exploded throughout the city. He wasn't close to any of them. The problem was the panic afterwards. When people found out that they were dirty bombs, and the fear of radiation, everyone wanted to leave the city."

"From what I read, more people died trying to get out than because of the bombs."

"I don't know if that's true. My dad told me a lot of people died with those bombs. He says some of the buildings completely collapsed with thousands of people in them. The worse man-made disaster in American history."

Michael looked into the distance. He could see areas where there used to stand some of the tallest buildings in the world. There was just rubble in their place. Rubble that was there since the city was completely evacuated, following the disaster, with no major cleanup effort ever undertaken.

"Did your dad think back then that one day the city would be rebuilt? Or did he imagine that it would still be in the dark like this? So many years later."

"I think everyone was worried about the levels of radiation back then, so I think he knew it would be many years before anyone attempted to do anything in there."

Michael's gaze switched from the city to Jackie. She had just woken up, had no makeup, and her hair was a complete mess. Nonetheless, she had the same lovely face. She was a natural beauty.

"Did you ever go?" Jackie asked.

"Once, when I was maybe three. I don't remember anything."

"They used to call it the city that never sleeps."

"I read that somewhere."

"Now it's the city that sleeps permanently. Wonder if it will ever wake up?" She said.

Michael remembered something. "I read an article once that said the levels of radiation in Manhattan are minimal, even at the sites where the bombs went off. That people could live there without problems."

"Really? I thought it would take decades for the levels to go down."

"According to what this guy said, no. The article was very detailed, mentioned that the type of bombs that went off did not actually carry the level of radiation enough to justify any kind of evacuation anywhere in Manhattan."

"Where do you read this stuff? Everything I read is the opposite. Peer-reviewed articles in medical journals, which talk about the health dangers with the level of radiation still present. I was actually a little worried with my dad working this close to Manhattan."

"Well, I have my sources. The information I read is reliable."

She looked at him with a smile. "Talking like a real journalist."

"After the bombs, people evacuated out of panic mostly, and he says there was no reason for the government to have sealed all entry points into the city. And to keep it sealed for the last twenty years."

Jackie took a slight step forward, which made him conscious of the height; he did not move or look down.

"So the government is lying about this too?" She asked. "But why?"

"This guy said . . ." Michael was distracted, looking down, and it took him a few seconds to remember the article. "He said that back then, the government was opposed to building new nuclear power plants. The environmental lobby was against it and wanted to kill any such efforts. When this disaster happened, they used it as the perfect excuse to educate people about the dangers of nuclear power, nuclear waste, radiation, all of that."

"So they helped feed the panic."

Michael nodded. Jackie took another step forward, her arms crossed in front of her. Maybe she was enjoying the great view and the cold breeze. He was not.

"Please step back a little." He took her by an arm and pulled her back.

"You are probably one of those guys that can't even get in rollercoaster." She smiled and sat down on the floor.

He followed her down, "I don't even like to fly. Heights are not my thing." There was one other thing he disliked as much as heights. "Heights and rats. That's two things I can live without."

She leaned on him and lowered her head on his right shoulder.

"So, anyways . . ." Michael continued to recollect the article he read. "He argues that environmental groups manipulate the data to produce reports that exaggerate the level of radiation and the potential harm to humans. Supposedly, they did it also decades ago, to scare people about global warming."

"That's a shame. It would be so great to see it come back to life. The Big Apple, as it used to be called."

"As long as they keep Manhattan like this, as an example of the dangers of nuclear radiation. They know no nuclear plant will ever be built in this country."

"In the meantime, we have all these electrical shortages and restrictions on how much electricity we can consume."

They sat quietly for a few minutes, looking at the city, enjoying the view, as the sun was announcing its arrival.

Then, Michael had a thought. "What if we go hide there, in Manhattan? For a few days until they stop looking for us. Maybe we can even call my dad from there."

For a moment, Jackie stared at him. Staring as if he was some crazy guy she did not know.

"Are you crazy? Just because of some article you read, we're going to risk our health down there, be exposed to all that radiation. I still want to have children one day, you know. And did you forget we need to eat, like three meals a day. Where would you get food?"

"Maybe that was a bad idea."

"How do you know this guy who wrote the article knew what he was talking about?"

That was a good question—one he considered before. "The article was censored, never released. That to me was a red flag, that it was accurate."

"Did the government go after him too?"

"He was very critical of the response to the attacks and the political games played with Manhattan in its aftermath. I don't know if the government went after him, but I never read another article from him again."

They sat there, without talking, for a few minutes. In spite of the height, he was finally enjoying the view and her presence. He knew they were in a lot of trouble. At the same time, he felt that as long as she was with him, everything would make sense. It would all work out, one way or the other.

"Do you believe in God?" he asked her.

"Of course."

"I think he has a plan for all of us. That's why I don't think his plan is for us to get captured and die. If we keep focused and have faith, I think we will be all right. We'll find a way to get out of this mess."

She attentively looked at him, her head resting on his shoulder. When he was around her, he ended up telling her personal things that usually he preferred not to share with anyone.

"I hope you're right," she said.

Their eyes locked for a few seconds. Michael felt as if he was drowning in those gorgeous eyes. "You have the most beautiful eyes."

He lowered his head toward her and brought his lips right in front of hers. Her soft, sweet lips touched his when someone startled them.

"What are you doing here?"

Chapter 35

"Daddy!" Jackie ran and wrapped her arms around her father's neck. "So good to see you."

"You scared us, didn't know it was you." Michael approached Tony and shook his hand.

"I didn't get your message until this morning, rushed over as soon as I could." He smiled. "Mr. I-too-have-no-wings. Very clever."

Jackie hugged her father one more time. After the events of the previous day, she was comforted to have him there. "You'll never believe the kind of day we had yesterday." She spent the next few minutes giving her father a detailed account of everything that happened. Tony shook his head in disbelief.

"And who destroyed my elevator?" he asked.

"That would be me. I'm sorry."

"Why?"

"There were people following us last night. We did it so they wouldn't come after us. It's too many floors to come up." It occurred to Michael, Tony had come up the stairs. "Did you come up one hundred floors?"

"No," said Tony, "there's another elevator in the back. It goes up to the eightieth floor."

"I didn't know," Michael said. Good thing those guys last night did not know either, he thought.

"You guys are lucky no one found you up here." Tony explained it was common for homeless people to break in and sleep inside, in spite of security guards watching the building. "Didn't you see any guards last night?"

"No," Michael said.

They went down, back to the break room, to have some coffee. Tony brought them up to speed on the news bulletins, on the reports that Michael had psychiatric problems and considered suicidal and homicidal.

Great, wait until dad finds out, thought Michael. The new communications czar having a mentally ill son was going to be an embarrassment in front of the president. "At least your grandpa will have a roommate at the psych ward," he told Jackie.

"Is it true? Are you supposed to be on psych meds?" Tony asked.

"No, I'm perfectly fine. I've never had any psychiatric problems."

Marshall joined them after a few minutes, and Tony was not pleased to see him.

"A fine mess you have gotten my daughter into."

Marshall expressed his deep regret for having exposed his granddaughter to all of this. Had he known it was going to turn out so badly, he never would have come to New York. He said it a couple of times, but Tony remained upset.

"Why don't you just return them the letter, so they'll stop harassing us? Who made you keeper and protector of this letter anyways?" His voice was becoming louder, and Jackie asked her dad to come down a little.

Michael felt uncomfortable to be in the middle of a family feud, but what could he do, he was there. Best thing was for him to stay quiet. It was understandable for Tony to be displeased like that; he had good reason to be concerned about the safety of his daughter.

"I didn't ask to protect this letter, but now that I have it, I will. This letter is that last link we have to a proud past. A past in which we were a nation that did more for the advancement of human freedom than any other nation in the history of the world."

"We're no longer that nation, and you know it." More than upset, Tony was looking annoyed. "And you think a letter is going to change any of that? It's not. All you've done is made you, and now your granddaughter, a target."

Marshall, once again, expressed his deep regret for having exposed his granddaughter to this persecution. He would go back and erase it if he could. Michael felt sympathy for him. He was the victim in all of this, and Tony treated him as if he provoked it.

"If you do care about her," Tony said, "then just give them the dam letter."

"No. They will take the letter from my corpse." Before Tony could interrupt him again, he continued, "I don't buy your premise that surrendering the letter will now buy our safety. The decision that our life is worthless has already been made."

"You know," Michael jumped into the discussion. "I agree with Mr. Marshall. If this Agent West just wanted the letter, he would not have altered the medical record, basically setting things up to easily eliminate him."

Marshall nodded in agreement. "People like that West place no value in human life. The minute you do not conform to his goals, it is not above his pay grade to decide you are worthless and should be eliminated."

"Dad," Jackie now intervened, getting in front of her dad, drawing his attention away from Marshall. "That's why we need to go see Michael's dad. He works in the government, he will be more reasonable and will give us some idea of what to do next."

"I don't want you to go. Let them go, let them risk their lives if they want," he told Jackie.

"I'm not going to let Mike take this responsibility alone, of trying to help my grandfather."

"I'm going with you then." He wanted to drive them himself to Obama City, to Michael's place.

"But it will look suspicious if West comes to ask you about us. If you're off from work, he'll suspect you're out with us," Michael said.

"We won't be able to use your truck. They'll be looking for it," Marshall said, insisting Tony stay behind. He wished for no one else to get into trouble because of him.

If Tony came along, it would make for some tense driving, with the two of them arguing all the way, thought Michael.

Jackie was of the same opinion. She preferred her dad stay behind. "Besides, I had this nightmare last night," Jackie told her dad. "I dreamt you were at Mike's place with us, and you were shot. I couldn't go back to sleep after that. I rather you stay. It's just a few hours drive."

Yes, a few hours drive, thought Michael, what could possibly go wrong?

Tony, with great reluctance, ended up agreeing to stay. Their ride down in the elevator was tense and not because of the height. He agreed to let them borrow his truck. An old Ford pickup, the type no longer made or sold in the United States.

"It has a diesel engine. No electronics. Very basic but runs great." Tony was showing it to them.

"How do you get away with having a dinosaur like this?" Michael asked.

"I have a permit because of work. I do a lot of interstate travel, and those little electric cars are not reliable to be out on the highway for so many miles."

Tony showed Michael a box he kept in the truck with tools that could be useful for the road. He also had a medical first aid kit, some duct tape, and the most interesting item of all, a stun gun. Michael picked that up right away and placed it in his pocket.

The parking lot was completely empty, none of the workers had yet arrived, but Michael knew they soon would. "We should get going."

"There is a diesel gas station in South Jersey, probably two hours, depending on traffic. It's five miles from the turnpike. Jackie knows the place. There is a diner next to it. The lady is a friend of mine. I'll let her know you're coming. She will feed you guys and charge it to my account." Tony shook Michael's hand, who was sitting on the driver's seat. "You're in charge. Anything happens to my daughter, I'm finding you responsible."

With that, they were on their way. "Obama City, here we go," Michael said. He tried to sound relaxed, but he was feeling nervous. Not just at what might happen on their way there. He was tense at the prospect of having to face the wrath of George Adams.

Chapter 36

"Are we there yet?" Jackie asked, her eyes closed, shifting her body as best she could, trying to get some rest while Michael was driving.

Michael did not answer her, keeping his eyes fixed on the road, constantly checking the rearview mirror, concerned that at anytime, the police would pull him over and get them all arrested.

"We're lucky the trip has gone so smooth so far," Marshall said.

Michael's heart skipped a beat as he looked into the rearview mirror. "There's a police car behind us," he said. It all seemed pointless. Obama City might as well be all the way in the West Coast. They were never going to make it with police all over the place, looking for them.

"Relax. If they were looking for us, they would have pulled us over already," Jackie said, as she opened her eyes and looked back.

Michael thought whether they could pass for construction workers. Marshall was unshaven, his clothes completely dirty, but looked too old for anyone to buy he did construction work. Michael had a white shirt with all shades of brown; he definitely could pass the part. Jackie—they would never buy it; her dress was not even dirty, not to mention a little too short. She looked as if she had just put it on that morning. It was an inappropriate dress to wear in a hospital, as far as he was concerned, much less to wear for construction work. Her fingernails well manicured, not the hands of a lady working on construction. If the police pulled them over, there was not even a need to lie; they would never buy it.

He kept at the speed limit, and prayed no one was looking for the Ford pickup. It felt strange to be driving down the New Jersey Turnpike and not just because of the police tailing him. Interstate travel by car was a rarity. When Michael was a kid, he wanted to go on a road trip across the country, driving from state to state. His hope was that one day he would see all fifty-seven states. Well, fifty-six if you didn't count Texas. The trip had never taken place. Few people, if any, ever took a trip like that across America, unless it was by train. Why did it have to be so difficult to travel anywhere? "Mr. Marshall, when did it happen? The books you gave me, they seem to be from a very different America. When did it become this oppressive?"

The professor took a deep breath. "That's a good question. I have wondered about it many times. At which point did we stop being the land of the free?"

Michael looked back at him, through the rearview mirror, trying to get his mind off the police car still following them. He wished they would pull him over if that was their intention, the tension of having to drive with them behind was worse.

"Our country was unique among all nations. The history of the world is marked by violence. The norm has always been oppressive governments. That's what the Founding Fathers of our country understood. That the history of the world was marked by this continuous and ugly desire of men to control other men. They set out to form a country unlike any other in the history of the world. A country where people would be able to be free to govern themselves. To control their own lives, their own destinies."

Hearing about the Founding Fathers was a unique experience. So little was learned in school about who they were and what they believed in. The motives and ideas behind the American Revolution were not taught to him in school. All Michael knew about them was what he read in books Marshall gave him a year prior. The irony of hearing about the Founding Fathers at a moment, when he was being persecuted just for carrying a letter with a message of freedom, did not escape him.

"At the beginning of the last century, a progressive movement started to change America. They started playing on people's fears that they would not be able to get ahead in our capitalist society, that they would just be tools of the rich. They started to convince the American people that the government needed to be more involved. Slowly, year by year, the government became more and more involved in each aspect of our lives."

Michael was getting nervous with the police car behind. He saw an exit and took it, but the police car stayed right behind him.

"Where are we going?" Jackie asked.

"I'm going to take another route, through some local roads. See if that cop keeps following."

Michael felt tense, tried to pay attention to Marshall, to get his mind off the police. "Please, continue. I'm enjoying the history lesson."

"The government became bigger and involved in all aspects of our society. By the end of the twentieth century, we were at the edge of socialism. Society had become too complex to be left to the individual. Experts running the government were needed to plan our lives. That's when he came around."

"Ronald Reagan you mean?" Michael asked.

"Yes. He turned it around. He stopped our move toward socialism, and reversed it. He communicated like no one else the evils of centralized governments."

Michael looked back and saw the police car. It was too close for comfort. Stay calm Mike, he told himself, don't speed.

"The worse at that time was the Soviet Union," Marshall continued. "A communist government that controlled every aspect of its people's lives. He exposed it as an evil empire. He understood how incompetent people become in a system like that. Like we have become now. He exposed it and put pressure on them that they were not able to keep up with. They tried to compete with us. No one could compete with Reagan's America. It was a land of freedom and opportunity. And so, they collapsed. He did that. He made it happen. Ended the communism of the Soviet Union and reversed socialism here at home."

The police car finally passed them as Michael made a right turn. He took a deep breath and felt such relief. Now, he could turn his full attention to Marshall. "Then what happened? Why do we find ourselves living like this? Under socialism."

"After Reagan left office, his party slowly started drifting back to the status quo of letting the government grow. The other party at first looked like they had been influenced by Reagan's ideas and had moved a little away from socialism but quickly returned to it. The two parties became undistinguishable. One loved big government; the other one hated it—unless they were running it. There was no real distinction between the tow. That's how we ended up with the one-party system we now have."

Michael wished he could get to the diner faster. It had been two hours since they left Queens; he needed to stretch his legs a little and get some food. He took out the stun gun from one of his pockets and gave it to Jackie; it was bothering him as he drove. "Please, put it in the glove compartment."

"With each party giving the people socialism or socialism at a bargain price," Marshall continued, "it was just a matter of time before a hard-core believer in Marxist ideas came along and fundamentally changed the United States."

"Like President Wilson?" Jackie asked.

"It started way before him, but yes, Wilson is as much a hard-core believer as anyone we've ever had." Marshall looked reflective for a moment. "They've tried to change America into their socialist utopia. And here we are. A land where the ideas of Ronald Reagan . . . the ideas of our Founding Fathers are no longer welcome."

Michael's thoughts were going back and forth between the history lesson and food. The police car threw them off course at the worst time. He needed some food in his stomach. Maybe even a piece of chocolate mousse . . . "You know I ended up having that chocolate mousse?" He turned to Jackie.

Jackie looked as if she did not know what he was talking about; then, she remembered it, and smiled. "How did you manage that?"

"I tricked the waiter." He addressed the professor, looking back at him through the rearview mirror. "When did we get to this point that we can't even eat what we want to eat?"

"Slowly, over years. 'The natural course of things is for government to grow and freedom to yield,' Thomas Jefferson said."

Another police car passed them. Marshall stopped talking as he watched it, as it drove away ahead of them. The tension in the car went up one more notch.

After a few seconds, Marshall continued, "I think the point of no return was when the government took over the health care system. That was one of the worse things that ever happened to our country."

"The worse thing?" Michael asked.

He looked over at Jackie who seemed to have heard this before. She leaned back on her seat and closed her eyes. Too bad he had to keep his eyes on the road, the view on the passenger seat was so much better.

"Once the government controls the health care system, they acquire complete control over our lives because everything we do influences our health." Marshall paused. He seemed to be reflecting, trying to find the right words. "You see, when you say that free health care is a right, you've made a very dangerous statement. If you have a natural right to health care, then the government has an obligation to run and maintain a health care system, to protect that right. That means the government needs to make sure there are enough resources to run that system. So if for example, you are eating too much and making yourself obese, exposing yourself potentially to diabetes or heart disease, you can't say it's your life and you can destroy it like that if you choose to. If I have a right to free health care, then I can say that your eating habits affect me too. Because, if you do get obese and get sick, you are going to waste limited medical resources that could be going to me. Once you start thinking in that direction, society has the right to tell you what to eat."

Michael could see the gas station and the diner coming up. Marshall's lecture was informative but not a substitute for a good breakfast.

"Euthanasia came to be for the same reason," Marshall continued. "A patient with Alzheimer's, for example, becomes too expensive. Developing treatments, drugs to cure the disease, is just too expensive. Keeping those patients alive places a burden on society. So the government feels it has the right to push euthanasia on those people. They don't want to waste good resources into a hopeless situation since it threatens the rights of others to have free health care. The same thing with abortion."

Abortion was the last thing Michael wanted to talk about, especially before breakfast. He thought about changing the topic, but it was too late. Marshall was in full lecture mode.

"Population control is popular among the intellectual bureaucrats. Those that are genetically predisposed to have chronic diseases are their favorite target. That's why they are pushing for couples to go for in vitro fertilization so that parents can have genetically engineered babies. Babies that will be born with no predisposition to most chronic illnesses."

Michael noticed a police car at the diner. As badly as he wanted to stop, he kept driving. He would drive a couple of miles more then return, and he hoped there would be no police then.

"What happened?" Jackie asked.

"There was a cop in there. We can't go in right now. We'll go back after a few minutes."

"I'm starving."

"Me too."

"The health care in the hands of the government ended up having repercussions into everything, even over other issues that at first seemed unrelated."

Marshall did not seem to be concerned about food. Easy to see why he went into teaching; he enjoyed talking and trying to make his point.

"Like what?" Michael asked.

"We used to have a constitutional right to bear arms. It was one of those things that made this country unique. We, the people, used to be in charge. If you are in charge, no one has the right to take away guns that you use to defend yourself and your family. The right to defend yourself is the most basic of all rights. Once you lose that, you can't keep anyone from taking all others away."

"It's illegal to own a gun now," Michael said.

"Yes. It happened back in the twenties. The city of Miami had the highest incidence of gun death and injuries. The governor of South Florida at that time wanted to pass legislation banning all kinds of guns from the State. Back then, that was unconstitutional. The case went to the Supreme Court where the State of South

Florida argued that the expense of gun injuries and death was such that it was jeopardizing the delivery of health care to the rest of their growing population. I don't remember the details of the case, but I know the Supreme Court agreed with them. The right to free health care, being a collective right we all have, was supreme over the right of an individual to have guns. That was the end of our rights. Once government stops fearing the people, they can do to us whatever they want."

"By taking over health care, they completely took over our lives," Michael said, as if wanting to reaffirm Marshall's teaching point. He decided it was a good time to turn around and head for the diner. The pickup was also running low in gas.

After a few more minutes, they reached the gas station. Michael looked around and did not see any signs of police.

"You asked me when it became this bad." Marshall seemed to have remained in his teaching mode, even as he had sat quietly for the last few minutes. He was still thinking of his previous lecture and wanted to finish his explanation before going inside. "When we invited the government to get involved in our most confidential and intimate decisions. When we lost faith that we could take care of ourselves. When we lost the sense that it was our responsibility to take care of our families' health. That we could do it better than any bureaucrat could. When the fear of getting sick and not being able to afford care blinded us to the reality that it would still be us paying for the care, but now with bureaucrats in the middle, guiding and controlling the system. When we surrendered that freedom over our own lives. That's the point where they started treating us as just a part of a system. Our lives became just a budget item. That was the point when we lost our sense of individuality. When we lost the concept of individual freedom. It was at that point that America, the land of the free, ended. That was the point where liberty died and tyranny began."

Chapter 37

"Delicious." Michael enjoyed his egg sandwich and coffee. As hungry as he was, it tasted like the best meal he had in a long time.

"Just tell Tony I say hi," The old lady said with a kind smile. She ran the diner together with her husband who was sitting behind the register up front. It seemed that together with a cook they had in the kitchen, they could run the combined diner/convenient store without much more help.

Michael and Jackie were sitting at the counter, finishing their meals while Marshall was getting some supplies for the road.

"I'll add all of those to Tony's bill. I've already added the gas." The man at register told Marshall.

"And you'll add all of these as well," A man built like a bulldog said as a skinny guy walked right next to him and placed several items on top of the counter, next to the register.

The two men seemed to have taken at least a quarter of everything within the convenient store. Everything they needed to feed a large family. Except, they did not look like family people.

"Who are they?" Michael asked the old lady.

Before she was able to say anything, Michael saw the bigger man had a gun tucked inside his pants. He could see it sticking out his waist. Michael regretted leaving the stun gun in the pickup. Even though, what could it do against a real gun?

"They come here all the time" the old lady whispered. "They take whatever they want without letting us charge them for it."

"And you guys don't do anything about it?" Michael asked.

"And what can we do?" She looked frustrated. "He is going to make us close down. At the end of the month, the government deduces all of our losses from our budget. We end up with so little for ourselves. We'd be better off if we were unemployed and just went through the hassle of filling an unemployment report at the end of the month."

"Do you have my jewelry?" the big guy asked.

His friend was already taking the supplies out to the car.

"Jewelry? You are a jewelry store too?" Michael asked.

"He wants us to take a portion of our profit," she said the word profit with a tone of sarcasm while rolling her eyes, "and buy some jewelry for him that he can then sell."

"How come he has a gun?" Michael asked.

"Why don't you guys do something? Call the police," Jackie said.

The big guy was getting loud. He was obviously not happy with the amount he was receiving. His gun was out, and he was waving it around, calling the old man a cheater. Marshall had taken a few steps away, trying to get away from that spectacle. He was moving slowly, trying not to draw attention.

"The police? He is the sheriff's son," the lady said.

Michael and Jackie looked at her surprised.

"He does the same to all the local businesses, calls himself a community leader. His father became sheriff through political connections. The son shakes down local business. Says he takes from the rich to give to the poor."

"And he openly comes and robs you guys like this?" Jackie asked.

"He doesn't call it robbing. He says he offers us protection in exchange for a service fee."

"Protection from whom?" Michael asked.

"I don't know. He's never said."

Michael chuckled. It was funny to call that elderly couple, running such a humble place, the rich just because they worked hard, and maybe, if left alone, would be able to have a little extra, a little more than what the government thought they deserved.

"What are you looking at, old man?" The big guy was pointing the gun at Marshall.

Michael turned to Jackie. "Go get your grandpa. Tell him you want to show him something and get out through other door. And wait for me in the truck."

"What are you going to do?"

"I need a beer."

She looked at him with mixture of disbelief and amusement.

"What? I'm a little thirsty."

"With breakfast?"

"It's an eye-opener." He turned to the old lady. "A beer please, to go." Jackie was still sitting there, just watching him. "Go," he told her.

Jackie managed to get her grandfather, and they walked out. The big guy was still cursing at the old man and waving his gun at him. It was obvious he wanted to make an impression, hoping it would increase his share the following month. The old lady brought Michael the beer. It was a Heineken.

"I prefer domestic. Let me have a Budweiser. Make it Bud light. I don't want to waste extra calories."

The lady brought the beer and told him she would charge it to Tony's account. Michael thanked her and walked away from the counter, which was to one side of the register, so the big guy had not seen him.

The bulldog look-alike was still harassing the old man. "Just remember what could happen if you piss me off one of these days, and I stop coming around, protecting you. You've seen the news lately? There are right-wing nutcases all over the place."

Michael raised the bottle of Bud light and slammed it on his head, sending him unconscious to the floor. He took the jewelry and tossed it to the old lady. "I hope that covers the meal. When he wakes up, just tell him I stole it. And that I'll come around every month to collect more." Michael took the gun and placed it next to the register. "Keep it for protection," he told the old man.

Michael ran out just as the skinny guy was coming in. He pushed him and threw him on the hood of their car.

Michael looked and saw the Ford truck at the gas station. Jackie and Marshall already sitting inside. He ran and got into the driver's seat.

"Michael. Oscar. Adams. What have you done?" Jackie demanded.

Oh no, thought Michael. Not Mike, not even Michael, but the full thing, even the middle name. A middle name, courtesy of his maternal grandfather who he never met and which he never used. He knew he was in trouble.

"No time to explain, we have to go!"

Michael saw a couple of community organizers stepping out of their car at the charging station next to the diner. They were looking in Michael's direction. Great, now they would be alerted of his presence there.

The community organizers were back into their car. It seemed they had intention to go after him. Not good. Not good at all.

The skinny guy was back on his red Obamobile, backing away. Michael slammed the accelerator, going full force against the little car. The Obamobile was hit from the back and cracked in half. The skinny guy ended up engulfed in a protective foam bubble. The Ford backed out, screeching its tires, and then it was full speed ahead. The community organizers were right behind.

"You figured our day was going well, decided to add some excitement? And did it occur to you, you might have actually hurt that guy?" Jackie sounded annoyed.

"That guy was bully. I hate bullies. It sounded like it was due time someone stood up to him."

"Great, you can tell that to the police when they add assault to your growing list of charges."

"Not now, Jackie. Not now." Michael could see the car, the same blue Obamobile tailgating him.

"We're being followed," Marshall said.

"It's those community organizers," Michael said.

Michael was impressed; they were actually gaining on him. He pressed the accelerator harder, but they were still gaining.

"Tony is going to have to get his truck checked, there's got to be something wrong with it."

Those Obamobiles were not supposed to be able to go faster than sixty miles per hour; they had to be doing more than ninety. More than likely, they added something extra to it.

"Step on it, they're catching up." Marshall was looking at them from the back seat.

"Nice, not only are we going to get arrested but we're being outrun by, as my dad calls them, a toy car."

Michael hit the brakes and came to a full stop. They also stopped, right behind him, almost crashing into him.

"Why did you stop?" Jackie asked.

"You're right. I've had it. I'm surrendering. Besides, I refuse to spend the rest of my life running away from community organizers."

The doors of the blue car came open and its two occupants came out and walked over to the pickup. They were one guy and a lady. She looked tough and mean; he looked like a wimp. Both of them looked like college students, probably being forced to volunteer with their local NACORN chapter. They were nonetheless dangerous; as long as they were in their tail, they were like a government tag—making it impossible to hide or get away anywhere.

The fellow who looked like a wimp stood right next to Michael's door and tapped on the window. Michael lowered it. "Hey, you need a ride?"

"Very funny. Come out of the car." He pointed his stun gun.

"I don't think so. Good luck walking home." Michael said as he stepped on the accelerator and sent the Ford in reverse. He hit the blue Obamobile, sending it all the way against a tree. Through the rearview mirror he saw what little was left of the car scattered all over the place. The only recognizable parts of the car were the two side doors, which were down on the floor.

Michael moved forward, waved at the community organizers as he passed them by. "See you guys."

"They're right about something," Jackie said.

"Right about what?" Michael asked.

"You are crazy."

He smiled, kept on driving, nervous, constantly looking at the rearview mirror to see if anyone was following.

Michael was driving through a residential area when he heard a noise coming from the passenger side. Something felt different from that side of the car. Jackie and Marshall lowered their windows and looked back.

"We have a flat tire," Jackie said.

They were somewhere in New Jersey, not far from the Pennsylvania border. It might as well be Alaska. It just seemed impossible to get down to Obama City. Michael was going to have to change a tire, fast, with the constant worry that police officers were out looking for them. It was the worst possible time to change a tire. What else could go wrong? Michael wondered.

"I just remembered we have no spare tire," Jackie said. "My dad ordered one, but he was complaining just the other day that it had not come in yet."

"Great," Michael said. "No way can we make it to my dad today. Let's find a place to hide the car and somewhere where we can stay for the day and spend the night." He needed a break from the action of the day anyway. Tomorrow, with a fresh mind, he had to figure out another way of reaching Obama City.

"Mike, look . . ." Jackie was pointing at something, but he was not sure what.

Then he saw it. It was a lake with some kind of a forest behind it, with plenty of bushes and trees.

"We can probably hide the car there," she said. "I saw a motel half a mile back. We can go and get a room there."

Chapter 38

The room was not much, but it would have to do. Marshall was happy to be able to sleep, at least for one night, on a real bed. His back would not have been able to take one more night on the floor. There were two full-sized beds in the room. It was the best Jackie could do. She went to get the room, had to give away everything she had in the truck, all the tools, even a bracelet she had. The only thing they had left was the stun gun and the duct tape. With all of that, the motel manager agreed to give her the room with no official charge and no questions asked. For him, it was a common occurrence.

Jackie sat at the edge of the bed; she looked tired of watching TV all afternoon, but what else was there to do? With people out there looking for them.

At least, for the night, she would have the bed all to herself while Michael and Marshall would share the other one.

Michael came out of the bathroom, and Marshall sat up on the bed to talk to him.

"Listen, when we meet your dad, don't tell him I have the letter. Let's wait and see what he says, what he suggests. I know he is your dad, but I don't want to be forced to surrender the letter."

Jackie muted the TV. "We can't put the safety of the letter ahead of our safety. That's all I ask you, Grandpa. We can't keep running like this."

"You can trust my dad. He works for the government, but he's a good guy. At the end, he does the right thing," Michael tried to reassure him.

Marshall could tell Michael was being sincere. Unfortunately, that did not make his dad trustworthy.

"The government wants the letter destroyed. Once your dad gets involved with it, he'll be in trouble too. Just like us."

Michael smiled. "They won't go after my dad. No way. They wouldn't dare."

"What does your dad do?" Marshall realized he had not bothered to ask that question. Not that it matter, he thought.

"My dad is George Adams, the new Communications Czar."

Marshall felt as if he was about to faint. He felt a pressure in the middle of his chest, and his legs felt wiggly. If he were standing, he would have fallen. He tried to stand up, but he did not find the strength. "You are taking us to the house of the Communications Czar?" The chest pressure increased. "Are you crazy? Why don't we just stand by the highway and let a truck hit us and just get it over with?"

"Now, come on, it's not like that."

"It was your father's predecessor, the previous Communications Czar that ordered the destruction of the letter. She decided to erase anything to do with Reagan and his ideas. She forced the closing of the Reagan Library. She has censored any and all voices of dissent and gives orders to silence them permanently. And you're taking me to one of her puppets?"

Michael was unable to say something in defense of his dad. Marshall felt betrayed, as if they were taking him to the slaughterhouse, and everyone knew it except him.

"People who say or write things she does not approve are censored or disappear." Marshall paced the room back and forth and sat on the bed again. Jackie's bed this time. The pressure he felt was uncomfortable.

"That's Faulkner. She's retired. My dad is in charge now, and he's not like her." Michael sounded as if he was trying to convince himself.

"Everyone knows she's still giving the orders. There is no way your dad can distance himself from her wishes." Marshall was upset. He could not help himself. It was rare for him to lose his temper, but he felt he had a good reason.

"Grandpa, don't be unfair to Mike. He's trying to help. It's not as if we have many options. The fact that it is his son that is being treated as a fugitive . . . He will want to help. He's not going to sit around and let his son be taken away."

"I can't blame you for being skeptical. I know every horror story about Faulkner. Some, even most of the public probably don't know. But, you can trust my dad. He hates that woman too. I'm not going to tell you that he would agree with any of your views. He's as far to the left on his politics as anyone, but he has no sympathy for her methods. He knows what a control freak that woman is. If anything, this might give him a chance to show things will be different under him."

The pressure in his chest was getting better. He did not want to say anything else; it was pointless. They were young and did not understand the way things worked in modern-day America.

"He will never let his son be captured," Michael said. As if repeating it would make it a reality. "And I won't let you guys be captured either." As if he had a way to back that up.

Marshall sat there for a few minutes, motionless, mute. "I won't allow the letter to fall in his hands. He will have to remove it from my cold, dead body." His chest pain was gone. Somehow, he did not feel any better.

Jackie sat next to him. "I know how important it is to you. These people want to kill you for this letter. I want you, Mike, me, alive more than anything else. That should be our goal, to stay alive. If we have to sacrifice the letter, then try to understand."

"I understand. But . . . sacrificing the letter is a price too high to pay even to stay alive. I'm not sure I'll be able to pay it."

"You'd rather sacrifice your life?"

He did not answer. "I'm not sure you would understand me even if I explain it." He said after a long pause.

The feelings of guilt were returning. It was more than about getting his granddaughter into trouble. It went beyond showing up at her house. He felt guilty about the kind of country he was leaving her. How to explain to her that the price of freedom had been bought with the lives of so many brave patriots throughout the years. That they had given freedom and that letter its value. Nothing he did could add to it even if he gave his own life. That ultimately, was the heart of the problem. For Marshall, the loss of the letter represented the loss of something large and important, something worth giving one's life. But, for Michael and Jackie, for their generation, what were they losing with the destruction of that letter that had not already been given away? Given away throughout the years by politicians in order to get votes and power. They had diminished its value to the point that a young person like her did not believe it was worth such sacrifices.

"The most important thing for me is to see you out of this, safe and without more problems," Marshall said after a few minutes. He could never forgive himself if anything bad happened to her. Already enough damage had been done to her life and career.

Marshall remained quiet the rest of the night, trying as best he could to get some sleep. As he laid there, in the dark, trying to fall asleep, he could not believe he was on his way to the house of the Communications Czar. To hand the letter to the very people who wanted to destroy it. Something so simple was asked of him—to keep the letter safe. To help preserve a small and simple message of freedom in a country founded in that idea. It seemed like a simple task, yet somehow, it became impossible. Because in the America of his grandchildren, an America that had been fundamentally changed, freedom was no longer part of its foundation.

The last thought in his mind was that no matter what, he would not let the letter fall into their hands. Could never accept it. He had to find a way to protect it. He just had to.

Chapter 39

"No!" Michael woke up from a nightmare. For a moment, he did not remember where he was. He looked around and remembered they were at a motel, somewhere in New Jersey.

He looked to the other bed and saw Jackie sleeping peacefully. She looked so pretty. Nothing at all like a fugitive. He wished he could have slept in her bed. The thought brought him a smile.

She was probably more comfortable sleeping by herself. She had a whole bed.

Michael could not complain, since he too had a bed all to himself. He sat up on the bed and looked to his side. He was not supposed to be sleeping alone. "Where's Mr. Marshall?"

The lights in the bathroom were off, but he went to check anyway. There was no one there. He looked down on the floor; his shoes were gone.

Michael put on his own shoes, looked at the clock, saw it was 5:00 AM. He stepped out into a dark morning.

Standing outside the motel, he looked in all directions but could not see the professor anywhere. If he left after they all fell asleep, there was no way he would be able to find him.

He walked toward the back, looked to both sides again. In the distance, toward his left side, he saw something. Michael ran in that direction.

About a quarter of a mile, he realized it was someone walking away. He picked up his speed, crossed a street without looking, and the honk of a car startled him. He looked to his left side and saw a car that almost hit him. The car, trying to avoid Michael, ended up hitting a stop sign. A young man at the wheel lowered his window, started to curse at Michael. He continued to run.

Michael, by now sure it was Marshall, picked up his speed and was able to grab the professor's shoulder, making him stop. "Mr. Marshall."

"Let me go! Let me go!"

"Come on, don't do this, we're in this together."

"I shouldn't have gone to my daughter's house. I put my granddaughter in great trouble. I put all of you in great danger. If I disappear, they'll come after me. They might leave you guys alone."

"How do you think Jackie would feel? She's doing this, I'm here, because we care. We don't want you to be captured. We don't want them to kill you. That's why we didn't let the agent take you away in Queens."

Marshall shook his head, seemed determined to pursue his current course of action.

"If you get captured now, this is all meaningless. Everything we have been through becomes pointless. Don't do this to us. Trust me, we'll be okay."

"I can't let your father destroy the letter. I can't. It's not right. If the letter is destroyed then it's over. It will be acknowledging what we already know but try not to admit. That the founding ideas of this country . . . that . . . the freedom to say what we want to say, the freedom to disagree, that's something we can no longer talk about or read about." Marshall was crying, kneeling on the floor, in front of Michael. "I hand this letter over to your dad and I will be turning off that last light, that last bulb, in that shinning city upon a hill that we're supposed to be. I feel as if I am handing to your generation a land where liberty is dead. If I give it to him, I am surrendering to your slave masters. How can I look at you and Jackie in the eyes knowing I was born free, and I'm giving you away to slavery."

Marshall was covering his face with his hands, crying.

Michael removed his hands and looked him in the eyes. "I give you my word—and I do believe your word should mean something. I will not let the letter fall on anyone's hands. I will protect it. Whatever we end up agreeing with my dad, the letter will not be part of it. I won't use it to buy protection from the very people who are threatening us."

Marshall did not look reassured. In spite of Michael's most sincere effort.

"I think my dad can help us. I hope my dad can help us. But whatever happens there today, the letter will stay with you. I give you my word."

"Hey, moron!"

Michael looked and saw the car that almost ran him over. The guy driving it looked angry. He was opening the door and seemed determined to get into a physical confrontation. Jackie would never approve of another fight.

"You don't look where you walk! You fucking moron!"

"He's having chest pain. Help me get him to a hospital." Michael pointed to Marshall.

The man went back into his car and drove away.

Michael turned back to the professor. "So much for a Good Samaritan."

"I am calling an ambulance!" The man screamed as he drove away.

"Oh no, we better go before the ambulance gets here." He helped Marshall get up, and they walked back to the hotel. It seemed as if another exciting day was about to begin.

Chapter 40

"There will be an ambulance here soon. We can't afford to be here if they come to the motel and start asking questions." Michael was back in the motel room, updating Jackie who was already awake.

"Where were you guys? I was worried," she said.

"We had to go get some fresh air," Michael said. "But we need to get going. I don't feel safe here anymore."

Packing was not necessary since Michael did not have much with him. He grabbed the stun gun, which was all he needed.

"I need a few minutes," Jackie said as she disappeared into the bathroom.

"You can take a shower when we get to my house. Hurry up—we need to go."

Michael looked outside, the darkness had faded, and sunlight was everywhere. It was time to go.

"Why is there an ambulance coming here?" Jackie could be heard asking from the bathroom.

"Long story."

"Did you smash somebody else over the head?" she asked.

"Not yet," he said. "Day is just beginning," he murmured.

"How are we going to go? Did you forget we have no transportation?" Marshall reminded him. He seemed to have regained his composure.

Michael remembered they left the Ford behind some bushes. No time to go get it, and where would he get a spare tire; he needed another way to get down there.

"Thank God I'm not having a heart attack. I would have died waiting for the ambulance."

"They might not know we are here in the motel. But when they can't find us out there, they might come in asking questions here." Michael was reflective for a moment and then something occurred to him. "I have an idea," he said.

Michael called the man in the motel's office and told him Marshall was having chest pain.

"I don't get it. Now you want them to find us?" Marshall asked.

A few minutes later, an ambulance pulled up in front of the motel. There were two paramedics, one a petite redhead, the other a tall muscular guy. They went into the front office.

"Jackie!" Why was she taking so long, he wondered. Michael turned around and was startled by Jackie standing right behind him.

"I'm ready," she said with a smile.

He looked outside again and saw the two paramedics still in the office. "We're leaving in a minute."

"How?" She asked.

"Oh, I found transportation."

The two paramedics came out of the office and went straight to their room. The ambulance was in the same place they left it, with its engine running.

Perfect, he thought. "Quickly, get in bed," he told Marshall.

"What? Why?" Marshall looked surprised. Did not seem to understand what Michael was trying to do.

"Just do it. Pretend you're having chest pain." He looked at Jackie. "You keep your mouth shut. Unless you have a better idea."

Marshall complied, lied down on the bed with his hands on his chest.

Michael was about to open the door but turned to Jackie first. "Hold his hand, look concerned. He's having a heart attack, you know."

"I'm a doctor, not an actress," she said. Then, she did as told and took her grandfather's hand. "It's going to be okay. It's probably just heartburn."

Michael opened the door and stepped outside. "You guys are finally here."

The two paramedics came inside the room. One was carrying what looked like a cardiac monitor.

"Are you okay? Are you having chest pain?" the lady asked Marshall. He nodded yes. "You have any history of cardiac problems? Taking any medications?" She took a small pill bottle from a box she carried.

The guy was attaching the leads of his cardiac monitor to Marshall's chest. He turned on the monitor. "This is not working again." The male paramedic looked embarrassed. He turned the monitor off and back on a couple of times, perhaps hoping for a different result, but without luck.

"This is a sublingual nitroglycerin. It's going to relieve your pain." The lady turned the bottle upside down but nothing came out. "We're out of nitro. I thought the new supplies came in."

The two of them were looking more miserable than Marshall, who seemed happy he wouldn't have to refuse their medication.

"He's allergic to nitroglycerin," Jackie said, saving the lady paramedic the embarrassment of not being able to give nitroglycerin to a cardiac patient.

"Do you have any other allergies?" she asked.

While the two paramedics were busy doing their work, or being unable to do their work, Michael reached into his pocket. The paramedics had their back to him. He took out the stun gun and made sure that it was at the highest setting. Even at that setting, it would not cause any permanent harm, just leave them motionless for a few minutes. Enough time to get away.

He went first for the muscular guy who was, in a futile attempt, working the monitor, trying to get it to work. Michael pressed the stun gun against his left side, making him scream in pain as he fell on top of Marshall.

The lady paramedic looked down to her partner. She did not have time to understand what happened to him. Just as she turned to Michael, he pressed the stun gun to her abdomen. She screamed in pain and fell, first on the edge of the bed, then to the floor.

Jackie went to her to check if she was fine.

"They will be out for a couple of minutes. We have to go, now!" Michael said.

He helped Marshall get the big guy off him. They laid him down next to the bed.

"Help me take out his shirt."

Michael put it on; it was a little too long but not too bad. Jackie did the same with the lady. They used the duct tape to tie their wrists and ankles, with one final piece going over their mouths, so they couldn't scream for help.

Michael and Jackie went to the ambulance, which was still running. Michael backed it up to the front of the room, so that Marshall could climb in the back, and once he did, Michael drove away.

"Don't you feel terrible leaving those guys like that? Was that even necessary?" Jackie asked.

"They'll be fine. The effect of the stun gun is temporary. It's painful but no lasting effect. Besides, maybe now they'll get a new ambulance with full-working supplies."

He drove to the New Jersey Turnpike, feeling good about the light traffic. On I-95, Jackie managed to sleep for a couple of hours. Michael, too, was feeling sleepy, but he did not dare stop to get coffee; the prospect of getting into further trouble was enough discouragement.

When she woke up, she saw how sleepy he looked and talked to him the rest of the way, making casual conversation just to keep him awake.

They finally saw it. A sign that read: "Obama City forty miles." It was a relief. Their long trip was finally ending.

A couple of miles later, the ambulance shut down.

"No. I knew it was too good to last."

"It's shutting down?"

"Yes."

"It's out of power." Jackie pointed to the energy gauge.

"Impossible." Michael looked at the energy gauge. It was not anywhere near the empty mark. However, he realized it was at the same mark that when he started the trip. It had not moved. It was not working.

Michael had taken this trip so many times, but this one was the longest ever. It was a bad nightmare. One that was never going to end.

"We can't just stay here by the side of the road. What do we do?" Jackie looked as concerned as he was.

"I don't know, but let's get out. If we stay here the police are going to stop and see if we need help."

"Into a highway with fast moving vehicles? I don't think so. And where to?"

"I don't know, we'll walk along the side, but we need to go, quickly. We'll find another way to get home. Let's just go."

Chapter 41

A Good Samaritan stopped by and offered them a ride. It was a challenge getting inside the two-passenger Obamobile, but somehow they managed. Marshall was able to squeeze in between the two seats; Michael sat in the passenger seat with Jackie on his lap. Michael felt that if they were pulled over, that at least the police would have to give them some credit for carpooling.

"This is as far as I can go," The pleasant and talkative Good Samaritan said. He needed to recharge, and his car would not take him even a mile further.

The charge station he dropped them off at was just outside Obama City, probably half an hour from the downtown but just a five-minute walk from Michael's house.

He was nervous to be walking out in the open like that, but it was a short distance, and with luck, they could make it.

"You know? I am having chest pain now." Marshall was rubbing his chest. "Was it necessary to drop a two hundred pound guy on my chest?"

"It seemed like a good idea at the time," Michael answered.

"I'm so tired. Can't wait to get to your house and take a nice hot shower," Jackie said.

Everything was as he remembered it. He could see the financial district in the distance. After the evacuation of Manhattan, most financial institutions had relocated to North Virginia, just a few miles away from Washington DC. It was a practical move, since the government owned them all. It was easier for the treasury czar to regulate their affairs. The move had sparked a great amount of growth and ended up giving birth to what would come to be called Obama City.

Michael's house was in one of the residential areas, where many other bureaucrats lived. Nearly everyone in Obama City worked for the government.

The houses looked new, all with white roofs, solar panels on one side of the roof, and a small windmill on their backyard. This made them more energy efficient.

The sunlight was bothering Michael's eyes. The roads in Obama City were all paved white. The purpose was to decrease global warming, since white roads did not absorb as much heat as the old asphalt roads found everywhere else. One bad thing was that in a sunny day, sunglasses were an absolute necessity. Unfortunately, Michael did not have any with him.

"Do all the houses here look the same?" Jackie asked.

"First time in Obama City?" Michael asked.

"Yes."

"All the houses are identical, inside and out. There is no jealousy here that your neighbor has a better house than you do. Everyone has the same house except for some old houses here and there."

"Must be tough if you get drunk and end up at your neighbor's house." Marshall looked amused.

Michael reached his house and went up to the front door. He could feel his heart racing. There was no reason to be so nervous. His mom, he hoped, would be the most likely to come and open the door. He was about to open it by placing his thumb on the digital display when he remembered he should not let the security system identify him. He rang the bell.

His father opened the door. "Mike!" His father said with excitement. "I'm so happy you're okay." He hugged him. "Please come in."

"These are some friends of mine. This is Jackie."

"Your ex-girlfriend, right?"

"Yes, Dad."

He shook Jackie's hand and smiled at her. "So nice to finally meet you."

"Nice to meet you, Mr. Adams. Mike talks a lot about you."

Michael looked at her, wondering when he had talked a lot about his dad. He then introduced Marshall.

"The alarm system, can you override it?"

"Don't worry about it. It's taken care of," Michael's dad said. "You guys must be so tired. Why don't you freshen up upstairs? Michael will show you where everything is. Once you are all rested, we'll have a nice dinner together."

Michael took his guests upstairs, showed them the guest room and the bathroom. He found some of his mom's old jeans and T-shirt for Jackie to change into. They all took showers and a nap.

Michael felt good to be lying down on his own bed, pleased and safe for the first time in the last three days. It all seemed as if it had been a nightmare. Now, he was back at home, and everything was going to be fine.

After two hours, he woke up feeling rested. He would have slept more except he was starving. He went to his parent's room to wake up Jackie. He found her awake, sitting up, watching TV.

"Did you get any sleep?"

"Yes, woke up twenty minutes ago. I'm starving. Can we get some food?"

"Sure."

"Your dad is so nice."

"He's not usually this nice."

"He probably has been so worried about you."

Worried enough that he did not ask anything. And where was Mom? Better not to worry Jackie with that. "Let's go eat," he said.

His dad came into the room. "Great, you're awake. Get Mr. Marshall and meet me downstairs to eat."

Marshall joined them and they went down. Michael's dad was waiting by the living room. Michael could see that his dad was looking concerned.

"Where's Mom?" Michael asked as he came off the stairs.

"She is at your uncle's. She'll join us later. But first thing is first."

Michael's dad went to the formal dining room. The sliding door to the dining room was closed. It was rare for the dining room to be used, unless it was a formal get-together or a dinner party for political people his dad was trying to impress. Otherwise, all meals were consumed in the kitchen.

"There are some good friends that I want you to meet," his dad said.

He opened the sliding doors, and Michael felt as if the house was collapsing around him. The floor was opening to swallow him—the walls, the roof, the furniture, it was all coming at him. He felt light-headed. He could not believe his eyes. Agent Baron West was sitting at the end of the dining table, smiling and looking straight at him. There was an old woman sitting to the right who he did not recognize.

"Mr. Adams, what took you so long? You should have just taken the train. It's so much faster."

Chapter 42

The cigar filled the room with smoke. He was enjoying it. It had been such a long time since he had been allowed to take pleasure in a good cigar. He held it in his hand and smiled. A good cigar, even one as fine as the one he was enjoying, could not make up for what happened to him. At least he was safe, but his friend had him worried. With the passing of his wife and his son, he did not have any family left. His other so-called friends were all politicians and well-connected government officials, attracted to him for his power, and he knew it.

He took another puff of his cigar. As he exhaled, he looked at Ronald Reagan's picture. It was strange to see one displayed openly like that. He wondered if his hosts would let him take it. The door opened, and two men walked in. He took another puff.

"Enjoying the cigar?" one of the men asked.

"Absolutely," he said.

"We found your friend," the other man said.

It was the best news his hosts had shared with him since his arrival. "Where?"

"He's in Obama City."

"What? What's he doing there?"

"We don't know. Either he has been captured or he's cooperating with them. We have an agent looking into it."

"Cooperate? Calvin? Never."

"You never know. They can be very persuasive."

"I want him out and quickly. They're going to kill him there. Tell your agent to get him out."

One of the two men came around and stood in front of him. He was received by smoke blown directly into his face.

"Are you serious? I'm not going to risk my covert agents just to get a friend of yours out."

"He has my letter."

"I don't care."

"I want that letter. It's important."

"I don't care if he's carrying the original Declaration of Independence. I'm not risking my agents for that."

The tragedy, he thought, was that this obnoxious man was taking away the gratification he was getting from the cigar. He stood up and walked to Reagan's picture. "I need that letter. I want that letter. I won't do anything without that letter. My best friend is in Obama City protecting it for me, risking his life. I want him out." He stared at his obnoxious host. "That's nonnegotiable."

"I don't know if I can do it, even if agree to it."

"We have to assume, if we know he's there, they know too." The other man jumped into the conversation.

"If they know then your friend is dead. It would be impossible to get him out."

Deep down, he knew they were right. He looked at Reagan's picture, wondered how he would feel if he saw his country in the state that it was. A country where carrying a message of freedom was considered radical and criminal. He would be sad but not surprised. He had warned many times that if government continued to grow, to get more involved in people's lives, freedom would be a casualty.

"I won't let my friend be another casualty. I don't care how impossible it is. Find a way, or you can kiss my black ass good-bye." The stare he gave conveyed finality to their argument. "Don't think I'm afraid to go back. I probably should. Let them kill me. The American people are in denial. Maybe if I die, it will wake them up. At least the Senate might wake up. Realize if they can kill me, they can kill any of them."

Silence prevailed in the room for a while. He could see in their faces they did not understand. For them, saving the letter seemed pointless, unnecessary. To them, the letter was not a big deal. Yet, that was exactly what made it such a big deal. America had lost its freedom, even though most Americans recognized freedom as a big deal because it had been stripped from them one small piece at a time.

It was not a big deal to ban smoking, especially when it could save so many lives from cancer. It was not a big deal to tell someone what to eat, especially if it would prevent diabetes or heart disease. It wasn't a big deal to shut down voices of opposition, if it would allow progress to go smoother. It was not a big deal to tell people what to drive, how much energy to consume, how to use natural resources, after all, the well-being of the entire planet was at stake.

It was not a big deal to ban the reading of a letter, especially when it spoke of some selfish notion of freedom.

None of it was a big deal; yet, it all was a big deal. They just didn't understand. The letter was important, and his friend did not deserve to die for daring to read it.

"How do I justify it? Risking my agents to save this professor." The obnoxious man disrupted the silence.

"He could testify too; especially if he's being persecuted," the other man added.

At least he seemed to be more reasonable, the senator thought. Too bad he was the junior of the two, and his senior gave him a stare meant to put him back in his place.

His cigar was coming to an end. His doctor would never forgive him if she found out he was smoking. She probably would get him into trouble. Good thing she was never going to find out. He took one last puff. "I don't care how you justify it. Tell your superiors he's my friend."

"Shit, that's never gonna fly. God, I have lots of friends."

"I don't." The senator blew some more smoke. If he never had another chance to enjoy a cigar, he just wanted to remember how good that one had been.

The obnoxious agent, seeing that he was not getting anywhere with the senator, left the room.

"Senator Thomas," the other agent called out as he was about to leave. "I have an idea. We'll get your friend out."

Chapter 43

June 4
Obama City, North Virginia

Michael stood at the door of the dining room, unable to move. Marshall said something behind him, but he did not register what it was. He was looking straight at Baron West, wishing it were a nightmare. Maybe, he was still up in his room, sleeping.

"Come in, this will be a friendly dinner. We all just need to discuss what has happened. I must insist that you all come in," Michael's dad said.

Jackie was the first one to go in. She did not look at Michael as she walked in.

Marshall was next. He stood next to Michael, looking furious. "How could you? You gave me your word. All along you were bringing us into the clutches of these vultures."

"Don't talk to my son like that." The friendly face that George Adams had exhibited earlier was gone. "Michael, take a seat. Everything will be fine now." His father went in and sat to the left of the agent, across from the old lady. "I don't know if you know her, but this is Ms. Faulkner. It is a great honor that she will be joining us this evening. She has taken time off her busy retirement schedule to grace us with her presence."

Michael looked at Faulkner. She did not look like the witch he had imagined. Then he saw the professor; the look on his face was hard to take. What might he be thinking, sitting at the same dinner table as that woman? Next to her. The woman he blamed for so much of the censorship that had taken place over the years. He remained at the entrance of the dining room, without moving.

"Mike, don't make me ask you again. Come in, join us."

A waiter came in, poured wine for everyone. Michael had lost his appetite. He walked slowly and sat at the end of the table, all the way across West, who was still staring at him. Michael looked at his dad, the shock and sadness replaced by anger.

"Don't look so upset. Our guests are going to think you don't want to have dinner with them." George Adams exchanged a smile with Faulkner.

The new Communications Czar kissing the butt of his predecessor, thought Michael. "I don't want to have dinner with her. I don't want to eat with any of you." His tone was angry; he never spoke like that to his father.

"Watch yourself, young man."

"How could you? How could you betray your own son to these vultures?"

"Michael!"

He was angry and not afraid to show it. "How could you!" He screamed and hit his fist hard on the table.

The waiter who was about to place a plate in front of him took a step back. Michael and his father stared at each other. The waiter then proceeded to place a plate for him, but he took it and threw it to a side. "I'm not hungry. Maybe it's the knife in my back. Made me lose my appetite."

"Mr. Adams, I think we got off on the wrong foot back in Queens," West spoke.

Michael found his voice annoying and nauseating. He spoke so slowly that Michael felt like slapping him on the face, demanding he speak like a normal person.

"I came off too aggressive, and that was my mistake. I should have been more straightforward with you than I was. You are obviously a smart kid and a son of someone of great importance." He nodded to Michael's dad.

These people are so full of each other, thought Michael.

"Mr. Marshall here stole something, a letter. It does not belong to him."

"It belongs to the government, and we want it back," Faulkner completed his sentence. She, too, was getting annoyed at how slow West was speaking.

"So you can destroy it," Michael said.

"That's none of your business. Is my department now supposed to check with you on what is appropriate or not to release to the public?" His father was getting angry. "We will review the letter. If it's appropriate for public release, we will. If not, we won't. And it will be saved as a historic document to be studied by historians who can better place its message into context."

"Reagan's words might sound very nice, but his actions were a different thing. You are too young to understand that," Faulkner said.

The waiter, who wanted to take her dinner order, interrupted Faulkner. She ordered some wine and so did Michael's dad who then asked him to leave them alone for a few minutes.

"I don't think anyone is ready to order dinner yet." He looked back at his son. "Michael, this man has stolen an important document, and you have been helping him. He wants that letter for propaganda, to instigate the people against the government." He took a deep breath and continued, "Now I have talked to Agent West here, and he is going to drop all charges. All he wants is the letter and my assurance that all of this will remain between us."

"It was all just a misunderstanding," West said. "If you just tell us what you have done with the letter, we can all just have a pleasant dinner," West said, looking at Marshall who sat in silence.

West then turned to Jackie. "Ms. Perez . . ."

"Dr. Perez," she corrected him.

"Fine, if you want me to use obsolete titles."

"I worked very hard to earn that title and even harder to deserve it," she said.

"Dear Dr. Perez, you were right to want a second opinion for your grandfather. I will personally make sure that the best neurologist in town sees him. If there is anything wrong with his memory, we will discuss his options."

"There are treatments available to us, you know, government officials, not available to the general public," Michael's dad said.

"There is nothing wrong with my memory. I would appreciate if we dropped the pretense that there is."

Michael felt another burst of anger. He took a deep breath, deciding there was no point in losing his cool. To keep his mind clear was imperative. A promise was made that morning to Marshall, and no way was he going to let the letter fall in anyone's hands. He needed to find out how far his father was willing to go to get the letter. "Dad, why did you betray me? Isn't family more important to you than impressing your former boss?"

His father did not like being questioned like that. "You're embarrassing me in front of these people."

"Not the first time you're embarrassed by one of your sons. Maybe you should get rid of me too."

His father turned red and stood up. "How dare you?"

"I thought you only had one son," Faulkner said.

"You're wrong, he has none," Michael said.

"This concept of family, it's so old-fashioned," West said. "There are no more families. We encourage couples to have children through in vitro fertilization. In vitro children can be obtained by single mothers, single fathers, women couples, men couples. Who needs a mother and a father? It's better to let the upbringing of children to the experts, the State."

"I have always taught you that your first loyalty is to your country. It's only through the government that we can achieve the greater good. Alone, we're nothing. Together, we're so much more than we can ever hope to be individually." His tone had come down. He seemed focused on trying to convince his son to see things his way.

Michael was not buying any of it. "Spare me, Dad. There is no good, great or small, being achieved here today."

"When one individual is being disruptive, we can't allow it," George Adams said. "Otherwise, we have to allow it for all. Soon everyone wants to move in their own direction, and society cannot make any progress. We have made so much progress over the last seventy years. And you want to disrupt all of that for what? To impress your girlfriend here?" He shook his head. "I expected more from you. You have disappointed me."

Chapter 44

Marshall sat quietly, not wanting to speak. The last statement from Michael's father had to be challenged. "Individualism made this country the greatest nation in the history of humanity. We achieved more success, more progress in our first two hundred years than had been achieved in the world in the previous five thousand. Now you are going to claim that collectivism is better. That collectivism can achieve better results. What evidence do you have?" Marshall looked at Michael's dad and West, ignoring Faulkner to his side.

"That's the right-wing propaganda you're helping this man release out into the public," West said.

"Which part of what I said do you disagree with?"

"You right-wingers are all the same. Always trying to twist things. You talk about this country being founded on freedom, but you forget to mention slavery. Or, how the rich, the haves, used to enslave the have-nots. It is we, the progressives, who have repeatedly improved this country. We took down big business, the rich, those who oppressed the have-nots." West became animated with the conversation, finally showing some emotion.

Marshall thought about staying quiet. What was the point of arguing with idiots? Nevertheless, he felt he had to answer what West was saying. "You took down people all right. It wasn't just the rich. You took down the whole nation. You turned classes of people against each other. You forgot to tell the average Joe that while you were promising to tear down the guy in front of him, who had a little more, there was someone behind with less, waiting to tear him down as well."

"You . . ." West tried to interrupt.

"You point out our mistakes as some kind of indictment on freedom. Yes, in a free society people make mistakes. People are free to make mistakes," Marshall continued. "Freedom does not eliminate the existence of bad people. They are there regardless. And freedom does not transform someone bad into someone good. Freedom allows good people to live to their fullest potential. It gives us the power to overcome the bad. It is the greatest contribution of our country to civilization, the concept and the power of freedom."

"Freedom, freedom, freedom. You right-wingers just don't know any other word." West took a long sip of his wine. "A society as complex as ours needs guidance. It needs a government willing to tackle the complex problems that affects us all. The poor need shelter, the hungry need to be fed, the elderly need to be provided, children need to be cared for. The planet needs to be saved from humanity. These are all things that individuals are powerless to overcome. Together we can. Yes, we can!" He looked at Faulkner, a pupil showing his teacher he read his homework. "Yes, we can end poverty. Yes, we can end hunger. Yes, we can provide for our children and elders. Yes, we can save the planet. Only a radical would deny the advances we've made in the last seventy years solving these complex problems." He softly tapped his glass of wine against Faulkner's.

She smiled and finished her wine. Marshall could see the pride in her face. Not pride of West's words but pride of the cause she had spent her entire life fighting. The fight she joined as a young community organizer, determined to follow Saul Alinsky's methods and teachings. He was not surprised to see her there; this was her final victory. A few years back, on the one hundredth anniversary of the publication of *Rules for Radicals* written by Alinsky, she ordered the destruction of the Reagan letter. The symbolism of her action was powerful. Alinsky and his radicals won; they had transformed America. Reagan's America was forever gone.

Marshall could not just sit there and let them celebrate the advances that their radicalism had brought. "What advances?" He knew he could only bring more trouble by talking, but he had to. "People are poorer than ever. We're all poor now. We are all hungry—you restrict what we can eat. And care for children and the elderly? You want to kill children even before they are born and get rid of the elderly when they become a nuisance." He knew he was not going to convince anyone at that table, but it was his last chance to confront a progressive, and he was determined to make his point. "America used to be a country of such wealth; we could not only feed and provide jobs for our people, but we were actually helping feed the poor around the world. That kind of wealth and greatness was not created with your collectivist ideas. It was created because this country unleashed the power of the individual like no other nation before. We became a great country not because we were a "yes, we can" nation, the motto of all you Alinsky radicals. We were founded as a "yes, I can" nation. Yes, I can work to provide me with what I need. Yes, I can feed myself and my family. Yes, I can provide for my children and my parents. Yes, I can give a helping hand to my neighbor when he needs me and not because the government forces me to be compassionate."

"Well said." Michael clapped, expressing his approval.

"Enough! I will not sit here and listen to this anymore," Faulkner said. She stood up and asked the waiter who had come back in to go back to the kitchen until he was called. "This kind of talk is treason. You are in open defiance to your government. Maybe you think you're old, and it doesn't matter what happens to you. Very well. Your granddaughter is here, and you have brought enough trouble to her. She is just starting her medical career. Is she to throw it all away so you can continue your right-wing propaganda? So you can turn this Reagan letter into some kind of symbol of a better time? Mr. Marshall, you know no one is getting out until we get the letter. At the same time, we have no desire to escalate this to the point that it becomes a scandal. And an embarrassment here for George. Where is the letter? No charges have been filed against your granddaughter. She was just trying to help her sick-old grandfather. No harm intended. Give us the letter and she can walk away, go back to her normal life."

Marshall looked at Jackie; her involvement in such a mess was a tragedy. Were they serious about letting her return to her normal life if he surrendered the letter? Probably not. However, they would hurt her or even kill her in front of him, just to make their point. It was part of Alinsky's rules. It did not matter who they destroyed as long as their objectives were achieved.

Marshall knew there was nothing he could do. Not without risking Jackie. He took the letter out of his pocket and handed it to Faulkner.

Chapter 45

Michael looked at the letter. Faulkner was holding what she wanted badly enough to target Marshall for death. To target all of them. Marshall gave it to her because she made him an offer she knew he could never refuse—the safety of his granddaughter. Using his compassion and love for Jackie against him. She now had her reward, her prize.

"Wise choice, freedom man," West mocked his voice.

Her smile of triumph was in full display. She looked so very proud of herself as she walked toward the door. Michael stood up and took the letter from her hand. The pride was gone; indignation had taken over. He actually swallowed hard with the stare she gave him.

His dad stood up. "What are you doing? Give that letter back," he told his son.

Michael placed the letter in his pocket. His jeans had large pockets on the sides. "No. I won't give you the letter." He sat down, turned to his dad. "I'm hungry now. Let's eat."

Faulkner continued to stare at him. If she could shoot him, she probably would, thought Michael. She would not do it, not in his dad's house. She had to save the Communications Czar, and the administration, a scandal.

"It's all right, Mike. There's nothing else we can do. They have all the cards. Just give them the letter," Marshall said, a tear coming down his cheek.

Faulkner stood right in front of Michael, turned his chair around. Michael was surprised; she was stronger than she looked.

"Do you really think I'm going to allow you to keep that letter? You think we're afraid of you? You certainly know I can take that letter from you anytime I want to."

"Oh I know that. You can take it from me. You have the guns. Use them."

"Mike . . ." Jackie reached out for his hand, but he removed it and pointed a finger at Faulkner.

"Any looter could come in here and steal from me. If he comes armed, what can I do but comply? I am not going to play your game and pretend you're doing something civil here." Michael stood and stared back at her. "You want the letter? Take it by force like the thief you are."

"Michael!" his father said. "That's enough, young man! I don't know what has happened to you."

His father was embarrassed about his behavior—it was obvious. Michael was beyond the point of caring about that. Then, his attention went away from his dad to West. He was showing his true self. West took out a gun and pointed it at Michael.

"I knew this was a waste of time," said West. "You have an old man who doesn't care if he dies, who dreams of a better time. And you combine him with a young punk, who thinks there is something wrong with the world around him. It's a recipe for trouble."

"Put that gun away. It's not necessary."

"This is not in your jurisdiction, Mr. Adams. Your son is dangerous, a right-wing loner, who is now displaying antisocial behavior. I must take him in."

"I don't know why my son is behaving like this."

"It's all in the upbringing," West said. "You let them grow up thinking they can have ideas of their own. That their dreams are more important than their social obligations. You do that, and this is the result. A kid like this. That is why I say upbringing of children has to be left to the experts. Parents just don't understand what's best for their child. They can't be objective."

"I am not going to get into a discussion on parenting skills with you. Put the gun away. Now!" George Adams looked at him with an intense seriousness—he was in charge, the one with power, and West should have no doubt about that.

There was complete silence for a few seconds.

Michael's dad finally broke the silence. "Please, everybody, step out into the living room. I need a few minutes alone with my son."

Michael heard a shot and closed his eyes, praying, expecting soon to be dead. Pain did not come. He had not been shot. Jackie's scream made him open his eyes, and he saw the face of pain and shock of his father and the blood. "Dad!" Michael looked at West, smoke still coming out from the gun. The agent shot his father! "Dad!" His father fell down on the table and then to the floor, breaking a couple of plates in the process.

Michael was not able to go to him. West's gun was pointing straight at him. Besides, he had proven, beyond a reasonable doubt, he was willing to use it.

Chapter 46

He was tired of the whole thing. A stupid kid showing such arrogance, defying the government, maybe thinking bullets would bounce off him. The father, not showing the discipline and leadership expected at such a critical time.

"You bastard!" Michael screamed at him.

"I told your father this was going to happen. I ran your profile through our behavioral simulation software, and there was an 80 percent chance you would go rogue and do something unexpected to protect this stupid letter." West pointed his gun back at Michael. "As you have seen, I'm not afraid to use it. Don't make me use it again."

George Adams was dead with a gunshot to the head. Jackie and her grandfather seemed to understand the message, Michael continued to look defiant; it was of concern to West. Faulkner was standing next to Michael without saying a word, her expression of neither approval nor disapproval.

"How could you just shoot him like that? He was one of yours," Marshall said.

"I actually ran his profile too. There was a 55 percent chance he would help his son," West said.

"Unacceptable," said Faulkner. "I turned my own son in when he was no older than you just because I found in his room a copy of *Atlas Shrugged* by Ayn Rand."

"Let my granddaughter go. You said no charges would be filed against her. She is not a threat to you," Marshall said.

West smiled; finally, someone understood the gravity of the situation. He had considered letting her go. "I would, Mr. Marshall. Any job I have ever been involved in, I have never left a body count greater than two. It becomes very complicated after that. People start asking questions."

"Let her go. I'll give you the letter," Michael said. He took a step closer to Faulkner.

"Stay where you are, Mr. Adams. You'll give me the letter. Don't worry." His gaze turned to Jackie. "Unfortunately, Dr. Perez here is not going anywhere. I ran her profile too. I was surprised. She scored almost as high as you Mr. Adams. I just cannot trust her."

"Did you run the letter through your stupid simulation too?" Marshall asked.

West shook his head. "Don't mock our software. Its reliability is without question. And yes, we got some very inconsistent but interesting answers. Depending on the amount of publicity, a significant amount of people would get an emotional reaction to the letter, get nostalgic about all that crap you seem to love to talk about."

"The decision to destroy the letter was not a reckless one as you think," Faulkner said.

"The point is you have no right to destroy it," Marshall said.

West walked toward him. "Rights? There are no rights. I told you before. Power comes from the barrel of a gun."

Faulkner went around the table to look at the corpse of George Adams. West noticed a look of approval from her. Not that he had any doubt.

"This is your fault," West pointed the gun at Marshall. "Coercion, fear, intimidation are all undesirable. Unfortunately, you forced our hand. We have to start getting ugly."

She turned her attention to Michael. "Your father was one of those happy-face progressives."

"He was never willing to use fear or intimidation," West added. He knew how opposed Faulkner had been at his selection to take her place.

Faulkner walked back to Michael; the air was tense. West could tell she was enjoying the fear felt in the room. "When a society has been able to control the means of production and provide for all the services," she continued, "you realize there's still no social justice. You realize you need to control one last variable to be able to achieve it."

"That last variable is the individual," West said.

"Your father didn't understand that," she said.

"People must lose the sense that they are individuals. Only then can they bring their will to be consistent with the will of society, with what is good for the group." Faulkner was addressing Michael as if she was trying to recruit a new pupil.

West walked toward Michael, walking by Marshall. He felt in control of the room. Everyone was within his sight, and they all looked terrified. He wanted the moment to go a little longer. It was the most fun he had in a few days. "Individualism," continued West, "is like a cancer to society. A cancer that just can't be marginalized or kept under control. Cancer has to be eliminated."

"Mao, who is my favorite philosopher, the one I turn to the most," said Faulkner, "believed in absolute obedience to the organization, the group."

"The letter is not what is dangerous. What is dangerous is for you to think you have a choice in whether you get to read it or not," West said.

"That the government tells you it is not acceptable should be sufficient for you. But you ask why. You think that you're free and have a right to ask why. And if you read about freedom in that letter—after we said you couldn't—it reinforces your belief that you're free." Faulkner took a step closer to Michael. "You wanted to be a journalist, but obviously you didn't learn that your job is not to ask why. Why can't I read this letter? No, the job of a good journalist is to report what is in the best interest of all the people. And when you have a progressive government like ours, looking out for the people, it is your job to try to make sure we succeed."

"Reporting propaganda," Marshall said.

West tried to study Michael's expression, see if he finally understood his situation. If he understood, his belief that he was an individual, free to make his own decisions, had now made him one of those cancers of society.

Michael stood in silence, expressionless. It was hard to tell what he was thinking. He would make an excellent poker player, thought West. Hard to read him.

"Your father should have understood that killing you, while tragic and sad, will ultimately save lives, save headaches for others.

If you're allowed to continue letting others know, whether by your words or deeds, that they're free individuals, at some point, we have to intervene to suppress the actions of a large amount of people." Faulkner sounded apologetic.

"Better to kill cancer early before it spreads," West said.

"The cancer analogy is getting a little annoying," Michael said.

West was not amused at the continuous defiance by Michael. He aimed the gun at Michael. "I rather you give me the letter voluntarily so that there is no victory for you. If you die in defiance then there is still a small victory. Nonetheless, I can take the letter from your pulseless body, if you prefer."

Michael remained without expression.

"Trust me. There is no hope, nowhere for you to go." He looked at the others in the room, trying to read their expressions. Would he be forced to kill them all? That could get messy. But, was it sinking into their heads that they were in a hopeless situation? "All I did in Queens was alert community organizers and the media about you. I knew this was the most likely place for you to go, so there was no need to send federal agents after you. If I were to, there would be no place in this country you can hide from me." He raised his gun, still pointing it at Michael. "Give me the letter."

"Very well," Michael said, and reached into his side pocket.

Chapter 47

West had set up the perfect trap. Michael could imagine the news coverage: a right-wing extremist went on a rampage during a family dinner, killing his father, girlfriend, and her grandfather. People would buy it because of the perpetuated impression pushed by the government that right-wingers liked to cling to their guns until one day, their suppressed anger made them snap. West had already documented Michael was not stable, with psychiatric problems, including homicidal ideation. The best he could look forward to was life in a maximum-security facility for the criminally insane. Not good.

What could he do? His judge and jury stood there, gun in hand, having sentenced him for his terrible crime of helping the professor. Of helping preserve a message of freedom. Even if he could escape that room, he was in Obama City, which together with Washington DC, was the most secure city in America. Civilian national security forces were present in significant numbers everywhere. It could be locked down, with no one coming or leaving, within five minutes. Michael could probably make it to the rail station in less than five minutes, be onboard the express to Washington in no time. He knew he could not do that with Jackie and Marshall with him, and he was not about to leave them behind.

Jackie and her grandfather looked frightened. Marshall was probably not surprised at any of this. He tried to warn him, but Michael would not listen. It was a mistake. The worse and maybe last mistake Michael ever made.

"Give me the letter," West said.

"Very well." Michael reached into his pocket. While his mind kept telling him it was a hopeless situation, his instinct, something from deep within his soul, told him not to surrender, not like this, not for this reason. Not without a fight, he thought. He would not surrender the letter, his life, and the lives of his friends. Not without a fight.

Faulkner was standing close to him. He took a step to his left so that she was standing between him and West. He took out the stun gun and pressed it against her abdomen. She screamed and was about to fall down, but he held her up and threw her toward West who was already coming his way.

West tried to hold her but then, when he saw Michael coming, he let her drop to the floor. He raised his gun, but Marshall hit his right hand with a plate, and he lost his handle on the gun. He looked at Marshall, and before he was able to say or do anything, Michael tackled him by the waist and pushed him to the wall.

Michael threw his right fist at him. West saw it coming and ducked, making him hit the wall instead. The pain made Michael take a step back and gave West his turn to attack him, hitting him with a right uppercut to the abdomen. It was even stronger than the one he had given him in the gym and made Michael fall to the floor, on his knees, with all the air knocked out of him.

There was no chance for a follow up; a chair knocked him back against the wall. Jackie had thrown it at him, in what now had become a full team effort. It gave Michael a chance to get back on his feet. He was about to beat up on West when he felt a hand grab his ankle, forcing him to fall. Turning around, he saw Faulkner crawling through the floor like the snake she was, trying to grab him again. She reached out for his ankle but was unable to make any further moves as Marshall had picked up the stun gun and shock her one more time.

Michael stood back up; West had just slapped Jackie across the face and now had his back to him. He happily landed a punch, an uppercut, on the right kidney area. That one had to hurt, thought Michael. West turned around; his expression of pain was priceless. The agony was not over; Michael landed a jab and a cross, a right and left combination, straight on his face, making him lose his balance. West fell on the floor, but immediately, putting his pain aside, reached out to Michael and pulled his leg, making him lose his balance. Michael fell down, landing on his lower back. It sent severe pain down both his legs.

West had no time to rejoice. He received a kick to his abdomen from Jackie while still on the floor, but the kick did not faze him at all since something had caught his attention, and he started crawling fast toward it. Michael saw it—tried to get back on his feet to go for it. The object that both were going for was West's gun. Michael did not get to the gun on time. Neither did West.

Marshall was able to beat them to it and stood in front of West, pointing the gun at him. "I guess we have a change in plans here."

West stood in front of him. "Aren't you forgetting something, old man?" the defiant West said.

"What?"

"My gun has fingerprint recognition."

Marshall pressed the trigger but nothing happened. West reached out for the gun and took it from him.

Michael did not lose a second, he swirled around 360 degrees, throwing a kick to West's abdomen that sent him back against the wall. West managed to get a shot out, but it misfired. Michael wished his kickboxing instructor had seen that kick, he would have been proud, maybe given him the black belt he had missed on his last attempt. He was not off the hook, West still had the gun, and he aimed it at Michael. However, he had followed the kick by leaping forward, and he then sent a second kick right into West's jaw.

West hit the wall with his head but managed to hold onto his gun, and Michael reached for that right arm and pressed it against the wall while he threw a punch into West's abdomen. He delivered it with all the power he had left, and West dropped his gun and brought both his arms down.

"You were right. It was all in the hip," Michael said, following it up with a punch into West's face. With his defenses lowered, it was a direct hit, which tore some skin from West's right cheek, and it was followed by knockout punch. The uppercut with his right arm hit West directly on the jaw. His head jerked backwards fast, and West fell down. Out for the count. Blood was coming out of West's mouth and nose. Michael hoped he had broken his nose. And jaw. If anyone deserved it, it was West, he thought.

Marshall came and pressed the stun gun against West. "He won't be going anywhere for a while."

Michael went over to check his dad's body. No pulse. He was dead, not that he had any doubt.

"We need to leave, or we'll all be dead soon." He heard the professor say.

Michael knew he was right. There would be a chance for mourning some other time. West would not be out for long; they had to go, but his legs just did not have the strength to get up and leave. He kept looking at his dad, feeling an intense sadness that his last moment in life had been spent arguing with his son for political reasons. He had a tear coming down his cheek when he felt someone grab him.

"I'm sorry, but we have to go." Jackie pulled him up and off they went.

Chapter 48

"Let's go through the backdoor." Michael entered the kitchen. There was no one there. The waiter and cook disappeared, probably when they heard the shots. Michael did not need behavioral software to tell him the waiter and cook would never say a word to anyone on what they saw and heard there. At least, not as it actually happened. They would say whatever they were told to say and whatever would keep them out of trouble.

"Where do we go?" Marshall asked.

They came out to the backyard. It was becoming a cloudy day, and the intense sun was gone. It could rain at any moment.

"Let's go this way." Michael ran to the front of his house, made a right turn, and ran ahead of them without wasting a second. Jackie was trying hard to keep up, but she was holding her grandfather's hand, making sure he kept up with them.

Michael ran one block, crossed the street, and went to the front door of a house similar to his own. It was his uncle's house. Nobody opened the door. He rang the bell and knocked on the door hard with force and purpose. The neighbors could probably hear it. Finally, his aunt opened the door, not looking surprised to see him.

"Come in."

Michael paused, waited for Marshall and Jackie to catch up, and he went in after them.

"I'm in trouble—you know where Mom is?" Michael was short of breath. He did not know if he could trust his aunt, but he had few choices.

"Mike."

He turned around and saw his mother.

She hugged him and held him in her arms for a few seconds. "What's going on?" She looked concerned. "Why are they after you? I wish you had called me. I would have warned you they were expecting you here with your dad." She hugged him again. "I begged your dad not to help them until he heard directly from you. I begged him, but he did not listen, sent me here to your aunts so I would not interfere."

Michael was not sure how to give her the bad news. "There's an agent trying to kills us. Mr. Marshall here was his original target, but he now wants to kill all of us."

"Your dad can help. Whatever else he might be, he would never let them harm you."

Michael took a deep breath; there was no good way to say it or a way to lessen the blow. Better she heard it from him rather than the distorted government version. "Mom, he killed Dad."

She turned as pale as the rooftops of Obama City. For a moment, he thought she was going to faint.

"Can't be," she said.

His aunt also had a look of horror, speechless, hearing her older brother was dead.

"These people are serious. They killed Dad, and they intend to kill us." A loud noise interrupted him. A red light was blinking somewhere. He looked at the main door and saw it came from the security system panel.

His aunt went up to the panel and pressed some code. It was not working; the alarm kept making its unbearable sound.

"I don't know why it's going off. I'm overriding it, it's not working," she said.

"An intruder has been detected. Please remain calm. The authorities have been notified, and they will be here soon," said a voice from the panel.

Michael ran up to the door—locked. He looked around the house, with all likelihood, every possible way out was locked. "The system has locked every door, every window." He went to his mom. "I have to go, they'll be here soon. I love you, Mom. Don't believe any of the lies they end up telling you about me."

She hugged him. "I love you, Mike. There's nothing they can say that will change that."

"Don't defend me. Tell them, you are embarrassed about me, ashamed of what I've become."

"Never. I'll never say that."

"Mom, I want you to stay alive. They'll try to hurt you for me. You need to stay alive for me. That's the best help you can give me." He hugged his mom and was about to go when she stopped him.

She went for her purse on top of the dining room table, reached out for a napkin, took her lipstick, and wrote a name and number on the napkin. "This is your uncle in Texas. Your father hated him, and I know you've heard nothing but bad things about him, but he is a good man. He is the only one you can trust. Get in touch with him as soon as you can. Your only hope is to escape to Texas, just as he did. Against your dad's wishes I already contacted him and told him what you were going through."

Marshall grabbed Michael. "They'll be here anytime."

"Thanks, Mom." Michael gave her one last kiss on her cheek. He ran to the kitchen, grabbed one of the chairs, and threw it against the glass door as hard as he could. The glass was shattered. "Let's go," he said. He stepped into the backyard and wondered where to go. West was going to use every tool available to find them. He was in a city full of government bureaucrats, no one sympathetic to his predicament, no one he could trust. There was no realistic way to get out of the city with police and federal agents all over. The murder of a prominent government official would bring a lockdown by the police. They would inspect every car, every train, and every truck leaving the city. All of the modern houses had security systems that allowed the government to know who was inside the house. There was nowhere to go, no place to run.

Chapter 49

Michael stood on his aunt's backyard. For a moment he felt hopeless, unable to think of a place to hide. He thought about taking his aunt's car but realized it would identify him as the driver; the government could shut down the car and trap him inside. Wherever he went to, it had to be walking distance. Where? Even if someone were willing to let them inside their house, the security system would make it impossible to do so. Then, it dawned on him—there was one place he could go. A perfect place to hide, if he could get there.

"This way." He ran the length of the backyard, and when he reached the end, jumped the fence. Jackie was behind him. It was not a tall fence at all, and she had no problem jumping it. Marshall needed help but was able to do it.

"Where are we going?" Jackie asked.

"Just follow me."

They ran another backyard and jumped another fence. As they cleared that second fence, Michael heard a helicopter coming in their direction. He saw the next house over had multiple trees and bushes and went that way. They all had to jump one more fence, moving fast toward the tallest tree.

Michael heard the helicopter flying over them. He figured the trees obstructed their view. After it flew by, he went back the same way, ran toward the next house over. There were no fences separating the next three houses. In the last house, there were a couple of kids playing in the backyard. An old lady, their grandma or nanny, was there with them. Michael changed direction and had to jump another fence. That one proved too much for Marshall, who fell to the ground, landing on his right hip, screaming with pain.

"Are you okay?" Jackie helped him get up.

"I think so."

Michael came back to help. "I hope you didn't break anything." It was not a good time to have to deal with a broken hip.

"I don't think so, let's keep moving."

"We are almost there." Michael went through some bushes, came to the end; there was another fence to jump. It was too much to ask the professor to do it one more time; he was already limping as it was.

A patio table with some chairs was nearby. Michael grabbed one of the chairs and placed it next to the fence. Marshall was able to get over the fence, and Michael was on the other side waiting to help him down, without falling to the floor this time.

"It's the next house over. This way." He ran to the back of the house behind them. He could hear a helicopter approaching.

The last fence had a couple of broken boards, which created enough of an opening for them to get through without problems. Michael looked up and saw the helicopter taking a turn, going on the opposite direction.

They reached a house, which did not look like any of the other ones in Obama City. It was old—the oldest one in the neighborhood. He knew it well, having been to it so many times as a child. A house that dated back to the time before the creation of Obama City. It belonged to a different era. It belonged to his best friend, Craig. An old house, in Craig's family for decades, falling apart, without a security system. Michael knew it was in violation of an ordinance from Obama City, that all houses were required to have a modern security system. Craig's dad, at last, got sick and tired of all the ordinances, all the restrictions, and moved his family as far away as he could. He moved them to Alaska, left the house abandoned.

Michael took a staircase to get down to the basement door. He came back up the stairs. "It's locked."

"Is someone home?" Jackie asked.

"No, they're in Alaska."

Michael went on top of a garbage can, climbed through the wall, trying to reach the balcony that overlooked the backyard. He reached it and pulled himself up. In the balcony, he found the door locked as well. He climbed to the roof of the balcony.

Standing on the roof, he jumped, trying to hold on to the edges of a window. It was a window to a room in the attic. He felt he could get through; he had done it before as a teenager with his friend Craig, trying to sneak in and out of the house. The window opened with ease. He had a hard time getting his hips through but pulled himself in. He went through and fell on the floor, his jeans torn, but otherwise, he was fine.

Without further wastage of time, he went down to the basement, opened the door for Jackie and her grandfather to come in.

"Who lives in this house?" Jackie asked him as she entered.

"A friend of mine, Craig. It's a very old house, falling apart, no security system. His parents just left it a few weeks ago. They didn't bother filling the necessary forms to surrender it to the government. I think they told the neighbors they were going on vacation."

There was a small window, which was at the level of the ground outside, but it did provide the basement with some light so that they weren't in complete darkness. Michael did not want to turn on any lights. He did not want to risk alerting anyone of their presence there. "It's a good place to hide for now," he said.

"For now. And then what? We can't hide here forever. Where do we go from here without being seen?"

"I don't know, Jackie. I have no idea."

Chapter 50

Michael saw his mom at the end of the hallway. She was smiling. It was rare to see Mom smile. He walked up to her with a grin on his face. Her happiness was contagious. He felt a thrill, an excitement he had not felt in a long time. It was the same feeling he used to get as a kid at Christmas time before finding out what Santa brought him. When he was closer to her, he realized why she was in high spirits. She was holding a small baby in her arms.

"Shh . . . Mike. The baby is sleeping." She walked toward the crib and carefully placed the baby down. She was gentle, displaying warmth that conveyed there was nothing to worry about.

"Can I hold him, Mommy?" the small Michael asked.

"No. He is too small. One day, when he's bigger." She smiled at Michael, caressing his cheek. "You are going to be a great big brother."

Michael heard a loud noise. He turned back and saw a man coming down the hallway. He had never recognized him before, but today he looked familiar. How could it be? It couldn't be him. Not here. It was Agent Baron West, coming down the hallway.

Michael turned toward his mother, but she was gone. He became petrified and knew he could not run and leave his little brother alone. West pushed him aside, and he fell on the floor. He started crying. He looked up to see West taking a gun and shooting his brother several times. He stood up but found himself no longer in the room. Michael was looking into the room through a window.

West looked at him and spoke, "This baby costs too much. He is going to consume and waste resources the rest of us need.

There can't be economic equality when there are too many people using limited resources." West smiled. "I told you kid, social justice cannot be denied."

Michael hit the window as hard as he could. It did not matter how hard he tried; he could not break it. West took a straw, bent down, and started sucking the baby's brains.

"No! No!" Michael woke up soaked from a cold sweat, his heart pounding harder, faster than ever before.

"Are you okay? You look like you've seen a ghost," Marshall said.

"Was it the same nightmare?" Jackie asked him.

He realized he was in his friend's house, hiding from federal agents. They were sleeping down in the basement with all the lights off, to at least be together if someone broke into the house.

He took a deep breath, his heart slowing down a bit. He noticed Jackie on the sofa next to him. "Did you sleep?" Last thing he remembered was she was crying late into the night before he finally fell asleep.

"A little," she said. "Until you woke me up. Here, take this." She handed him a glass of water.

"Thanks."

"So was it the same nightmare?" she asked again.

"It was the same nightmare, but now, West was part of it. It had always been some strange face that killed my brother, now it was his face."

"Someone killed your brother?" Marshall asked.

"He doesn't like talking about it," Jackie said, pouring him some more water.

"That's okay." Michael looked at the professor, took a sip of his water, and continued, "I never really had a brother. I was going to have one. My mom told me when I was eight years old that I was going to be a big brother." He smiled. "I still remember how I felt that day. It was like Christmas day, when you wake up and find out Santa brought you your favorite present. None of my friends had brothers. They were all from single-child homes. I felt so special."

Jackie placed a hand over his shoulder. He appreciated her sincere concern for him.

"After she told me that, I remember she started having daily arguments with my dad. I didn't understand why they couldn't be both as happy as I was." He realized Marshall was the second person in the world he was sharing the story with. Most of the time he avoided it, trying to keep the memories and feelings suppressed. "My dad told my mom he would not go and get a license, that it would bring him embarrassment at work. He had been involved in a campaign to convince people to have just one child for population control, to protect the planet, the environment. It was the socially responsible thing to do."

"I still remember when they increased the fee to get a license for a second child. To punish parents if they decided to have more than one. It became more expensive than having an abortion."

"Yes, I know. A second child would have set back his lifestyle," Michael said. He took another sip of his water. "My mom went anyways to try and get a license to have the baby. She was denied and ended up having an abortion." He had a tear coming down his left cheek. "I lost my little brother. A healthy little baby, according to my mom. But he was not wanted in this world we live in. He was bad for the environment." He remained silent for a few seconds. "I still remember the day my mom told me," Michael continued, "Memorial Day. The last Memorial Day ever before it became Community Service day."

"That must have been traumatic for an eighth-year-old," Marshall said.

"I couldn't sleep for days. I was so angry with my mom. I wanted to know more about abortion, but I couldn't find much on the internet." He asked Jackie for some more water; he took the last of it in one gulp. He continued his trip down memory lane, "I found out my dad's account number, and I was able to figure out his password. I gained access to the Communications Department server and was able to find out information that was not available anywhere."

"You could have gotten into serious trouble for that," Marshall said.

"Yes, I did it always in the middle of the night when my dad was sleeping. If anyone was monitoring, they would think it was my dad browsing the internet."

"Want more water?" Jackie asked.

"I've had enough, thanks. Anyways, I looked up abortion. I read about every technique used. I read thesis papers and reports from intellectuals in our government about licenses to have children, population control, the effects of humans on global warming, all that crap. I remember I threw up when I first read it. But I cleaned up and continued reading. It made me sick for weeks."

Jackie handed him a tissue to wipe his tears.

"I'm not crying," he said, taking the tissue from her. "I just have a little moisture around my eyes."

"It must be the humidity down here," she said, suppressing a smile.

Michael felt better sharing the story. "You know, I was very angry back then. Originally, at my mom, but after reading all of that, I realized it was not her fault. She did what she could to save her baby. It was my dad and the government that forced her to have an abortion. I was very angry with my dad for a long time. I became angry at this government and how they control our lives, make decisions about our lives they have no business making." Michael had never before admitted hatred toward the government, not to Jackie, nor even to himself. "When they have no regard for an innocent, helpless life, how can I even think that they will give a crap about mine?"

"Well, remember that the government is not America. There is a difference. Our country has been a force for good through most of its history. Unfortunately, we are off course right now," Marshall said.

"I know. After I met you . . ." He now looked straight at Marshall. "I read those books you gave me about our Founding Fathers. I read Common Sense, American Crisis . . . I read about Washington and Thomas Jefferson. It opened my eyes to an America that used to be so different. That's why I wrote that article, why I asked if my generation knows what this nation is supposed to be all about." Michael reached out for the Reagan letter, which was opened, on a table next to him. "I was hoping with the Tricentennial and the reading of the Reagan letter, that people would talk about it . . . about whether freedom still has any meaning today."

"You read it?" Marshall asked, pointing at Reagan's letter.

"Yes, last night. I couldn't sleep right away. I read it twice."

"Can I see it?" Jackie took it from him.

"He would be disappointed at the amount of control government has gained over our lives. He would be deeply disappointed," Marshall said.

"He seemed to understand well what the founding ideas of this country were all about. That's why I hoped people would get to hear his words," Michael said. He felt better after pouring his emotions out with Jackie and Marshall. It was five in the morning—no point in trying to get back to sleep.

"Aren't some people just not able to make good decisions, and the government has to exert some amount of control, to be able to help them out," Jackie said.

"It is a self-fulfilling prophecy. The government tells you, you can't solve your problem, so they intervene, take charge, and by doing so, take away your initiative and your ability to solve the problem. Once the government is involved, they suppress the ingenuity of the individual and leave nothing but mediocrity in its place."

Jackie handed the Reagan letter back to Michael. He placed it back on its envelope.

Marshall looked at Jackie; he seemed to want to make another point. "This philosophy of progressives, liberals, socialists, whatever they want to call themselves. It is a flawed philosophy, which unfortunately has now penetrated the consciousness of our people. They claim that they want equality for everyone. But, if we are all equal, why would some of us need help to achieve the same as others? Indeed, they do not believe in equality. They believe some people are better and smarter than others. Bureaucrats and politicians have the obligation to tell others how to live their lives."

Marshall was animated, made Michael wondered if this was how he lectured his students. Then again, if he ever gave a lecture like this, he would have gone to jail a long time ago. That was why he was so animated. How many times did he have a chance to speak his mind to young people?

"All men are created equal. That was not a statement of opinion by Thomas Jefferson but a conclusion reached by a mind of reason and logic. It was a statement of fact. It does not mean we will all have the same outcomes. It does not mean it will be fair for everyone. Life hardly ever is. It just means that we all have the same right to succeed or fail to the best of our abilities."

"No one can govern your life better than you can do it yourself," Michael said.

"It was Thomas Jefferson that said, and Ronald Reagan repeated it, 'if we cannot trust people to govern themselves, how can we trust them to govern others?' Wise words, which we have forgotten," Marshall said.

Jackie went upstairs to make coffee.

Michael held the letter in his hand. "He would not approve of the way things are now," he said.

"No, he would be very disappointed."

"This is not what people wanted. I am sure they might have wanted some help in dealing with their problems, but they did not want this kind of total control."

"It happened slowly."

"This government tells us what to drink, what to eat, what to say, how to say it, where to go, how to get there, how many children to have, when and how to die. Enough! Our government has grown way beyond the consent of the governed." Michael looked down at the letter. "Our freedom is in life support, if not dead already. I don't know what I can do, but I have to do something." He looked at Marshall. "I'm going to make sure that this letter, this message, gets out. It will not die with us."

Chapter 51

She looked out the window, wondered when they would be able to step outside. The trip to Obama City had been a total failure. They were trapped, without hope of escape; everything had gone so bad. She had been the type of person who felt in control of her life, determined through school and through her residency to have a career. She never allowed any distractions to get in the way of her professional goals. Even when love knocked on her door, she chose not to go with her heart but to look at her life objectively and make the best decision for her future. The decision might have been a mistake, but it was her decision. Now she felt helpless, with the future out of her control.

"You feel better?" she asked Michael as he came down the stairs from taking a shower.

"Yes, nothing like a hot shower. Are you hungry?" he asked her.

"Yes, I'm starving. I made us a sandwich with the little leftovers I could find."

They sat in the kitchen, enjoying the little food they had, grateful in a way for still being alive.

When Michael was done with his sandwich, he seemed to have something in mind he wanted to share with her.

"What is it?" she asked.

"I want to try and get the letter published," he said.

"Is the day going a little too quietly for your taste?"

He smiled at her. "No, that's not it. I don't think it can get worse than it already is. We're trapped. We can't possibly stay here indefinitely. We're already out of food."

"And you're going to exchange the letter for food?"

"No. Stop being funny. Your grandpa is right, if the letter does not get released, if we allow them to just destroy it, then they win."

Her feeling of hopelessness returned and did not allow her to consider any positive ramifications of releasing the letter. How could they think about releasing it when they did not even know how they were going to stay alive? How they were going to get something as basic as food? "I just think right now we need to stay alive. Your mom was right; we need to try to get to Texas. Once we're there we can see what to do with the letter."

"I think if I release the letter, it might make it easier to escape. They are desperate to kill us, to suppress the letter. If I release it and bring some attention to us, to this struggle to save the letter, then killing us would be too obvious and could make things worse for them. It might give us a little breathing room."

"How are you going to release it?"

"I might be able to log in to one of my old accounts from college, from the e-letter. I created some fake accounts. They might still be valid, and I could email the letter to a long list of contacts I have, maybe post it in some websites. It would come down but not before some people read it and email it to their contacts. It might spread enough that a lot of people will end up reading it."

Jackie was not convinced. She felt the odds were against them; it seemed a futile attempt. "I don't know. It sounds too risky. They'll find us if you try." At that moment, she heard a loud knock on the door.

"Is someone there? This is the police, open up!"

"Shit." Jackie saw a face at the kitchen window, looking in the opposite direction to where they were, toward the living room.

She dropped to the floor, as did Michael, out of sight from the window. There was a second round of knocks, even louder.

"Let's go to the basement," Michael said.

Jackie crawled toward the basement door, in the back of the kitchen. She looked back to see Michael picking up the napkins and bread crumbs they had left behind. He then followed her, crawled toward the basement door.

They ran down the stairs; both almost fell down, and Jackie went to wake up her grandpa who was taking a nap on one of the sofas.

Jackie startled Marshall. "What's going on?" he asked.

There were steps upstairs. There was someone inside the house. This was it, thought Jackie, the end of their road.

"This way," Michael said.

Jackie followed him; she felt it was futile to try to hide. They would be found, no matter what, even if Michael found some hole to crawl under, they would soon be dead or captured. She had to stay rational, avoid panic, which would not help accomplish anything.

Michael went to a room in the back of the basement. At some point, it had been a home theater. Years ago, with the whole place falling apart, Craig's dad started using it for storage. It was still full of junk, which they had accumulated through the years and not worth the effort of taking it to Alaska.

Jackie went after Michael. She climbed on top of two boxes and helped her grandfather up with her. Michael squeezed behind some boxes that were standing against the wall in the far end of the room. Jackie did the same and saw a small hallway with a door at a side. Michael opened it without difficulty and stepped in. The room was dark, even worse once the door closed.

"There probably are rats in here," Jackie said.

"It's probably better that we can't see," Michael said.

"What is this room?" Marshall asked.

"They had a home theater down here, and this was the projection room. Now it's just for storage. If you don't know it's here, it is hard to see it because of where the door is. You can't see the small hallway that comes here unless you are standing right in front of it," he whispered.

"It will be hard with all those boxes," Jackie said.

"Unless they are certain there's someone in the house," Michael said.

She could not see anything in such darkness, but she could hear someone coming down the stairs. The voices felt to be all too close. She could feel her own heart racing. She was petrified with fear.

She heard a voice of someone inside the home-theater room. "Is anybody here?"

"This is all storage." She heard a second voice say. "Anybody could hide here."

Then she heard multiple shots. She reached out to Michael and squeezed his hand. She heard more shots, closed her eyes, expecting at any time that the shots would be coming her way.

"There's no one here. It's just junk," the second voice said.

She could hear a distinct third voice. "The rest of the house is empty. There's no sign of a break-in."

"Let's go, guys."

Jackie felt relief, but thought, how would they know if all three were gone? Could one have stayed behind, waiting for them to get out? She did not feel safe, did not want to let go of Michael's hand.

Nobody dared to move. They all stood there for hours, in the dark, wondering what to do next. She thought of her conversation with Michael and his idea of publishing the letter. After this experience, she could not go through much more. They had to find a way to escape, go to Texas. Michael had to agree; it was the only way.

Chapter 52

West had a great view of Obama City from his office in the twentieth floor; it was impressive. He loved seeing those houses with their white roofs and solar panels, their windmills—present in almost every one. A sight of progress. In the distance, he could see the statue of Barack Obama, his left hand up, as if pointing to the future, to a better America. To a world as it should be, not as it was.

Beyond, he could see the financial district. Not what it once was. That was because of people there who wished to work for their own personal gain, rather than the common good.

The rest of the city understood their roles so well. He wished the rest of the country could be more like it. His latest assignment had taken him away, to Los Angeles first and then Long Island. They were nothing compared to Obama City.

Thus far, he had nothing to show for his trips and his troubles. It started like a straightforward assignment. He was to fly to Los Angeles and talk with Senator Frank Thomas about a letter from Ronald Reagan—a letter he was not supposed to have and which threw into question his loyalty to the State. He preferred talking with the senator at his Los Angeles home rather than in Washington DC, with many curious ears all around. Faulkner, who in retirement still had influence throughout all of government, called his department to give him the tip and asked he investigate. If Thomas had the letter, he had to answer some questions. The letter would also serve as proof of right-wing radicalism, from a senator who was becoming a headache for the administration, with his constant and vocal opposition to the Consumption Chip Bill. Just the fact that he was under investigation by the antisocial division for stealing a government document would help to hurt his reputation.

She wanted him to keep it all low key, but developments made things more and more complicated. The initial refusal of Thomas to cooperate, which forced West to get ugly. He took him to a hospital for some questioning. The senator did not cooperate, but he still found out that a Professor Marshall actually had the letter in his possession. He was able, right away, to access the professor's medical record and gave him a terminal diagnosis of Alzheimer's dementia and recommendation for a palliative care consult, to discuss euthanasia. He figured he had the professor trapped with that. Instead, he disappeared. He should have first run the professor's profile through the behavioral software; he would have known how dangerous he was. He would not repeat a mistake like that.

Then, the senator, too, managed to disappear just when they had announced he was critically ill, not expected to survive. He had no clue as to the whereabouts of Thomas, suspected some outside interference. On the other hand, with the professor, he was confident he had nowhere else to go but Long Island, to his family. There, Marshall received unexpected help, the son of the new Communications Czar. A man Faulkner did not want to see take over her job. To make matters worse, his son turned out to be resourceful, escaping capture in spite of his best efforts.

West was lost in his thoughts, did not hear a knock on the door until it became more persistent and louder. "Come in," he said.

Faulkner walked in. "Working on a Saturday morning?"

"I work every day until my assignment is complete."

"No word on the professor or the kid?"

"No."

"They couldn't have just disappeared like that. We have community organizers looking for them, the police, federal agents. How could they have gone away like that?"

He could sense the displeasure in her tone. She was the person in government—more than anyone else—he wanted to impress the most. This was a simple assignment, which he wanted to complete to her satisfaction. She had the right to be annoyed. He felt the same way.

"I don't think they disappeared. They have to be hiding out there," he said.

"Where? You've already gone to every house, no?"

"Yes, I am as surprised as anyone that we have not been able to find them."

"Does he have any more family there that could be offering him refuge?"

"He has his mother and an aunt and uncle. They don't know anything. We have the mom under custody, asking her questions. She is clueless of where he went. We searched his uncle's house from top to bottom, and there was nothing."

"The satellite images? The surveillance cameras?"

"Nothing. There was one picture of them jumping a fence in a house nearby. I had people search all those homes around there. They did not find anything."

"That's impossible. They have to be somewhere."

"The security systems in all those houses have not revealed anything since the kid left his aunt's house. They must be in some place with no security system, but we looked everywhere. The public places all have surveillance cameras and people on the ground. They could not go unnoticed."

"And they haven't gone anywhere to buy food, get any supplies?"

"No. With all due respect"—he turned to look straight at her—"this is not the first time I've searched for a missing dissident. I know all the methods of finding them. I have not missed anything."

"I don't doubt your ability. It was the reason I requested you take this assignment. But you are being outsmarted by a twenty-four-year-old punk."

She knew how to push people's buttons, insult them where it hurt the most. "The kid found some hole somewhere to crawl into. He is clever, I give him that," West said, walking back to the window, looking into the distance, wandering where Michael Adams could be. "Sooner or later, he has to stick his head out. I have eyes everywhere. He will not escape me. I assure you."

"Very well. Try to wrap this up quickly. We are getting some heat."

He walked to his desk, sat down, tried to read Faulkner. She was not there just to discuss his lack of progress; there was something else. "What kind of heat?"

"The Texans are making a lot of noise about George's death. He was viewed as a moderate voice. He wasn't jamming their signals or promoting anti-Texas propaganda as they call it."

He could tell she was delighted that George Adams was out of the way. The only thing he had done during this assignment, to her satisfaction, had been his death. It had removed a headache. However, he knew it did not make up for his other failures.

"I wished Thomas had not slipped through your fingers." She did not hide her displeasure.

"He had unexpected help. He's beyond my reach now."

"We can't afford to send anyone after him right now. It could draw too much attention. The Texans are already using him, accusing us of persecuting him for political reasons." For the first time, she looked like the old lady she was. She looked fatigued, exhausted of all the political battles she was constantly fighting. "Don't worry, his time will come," she said.

She went over and sat on a chair in front of him, leaned forward, placed her elbows on his desk, spoke softly, as if concerned someone could hear them. "The Texans are going to the UN. We believe Frank is going to testify. He seems to have proof of things I have done to censor and silence dissent. I think he is determined to embarrass us, and they are hoping the scandal will help them. That it will lead to final recognition of their independence."

"They've tried that before."

"Frank is well-liked at the UN. There might be sympathetic ears this time. The president is worried about upsetting his friends at the UN."

West understood. He also saw the danger if the whole thing blew up. If the administration was embarrassed, Faulkner would take the heat, but she would place all the blame on him. After all, she was officially retired, therefore, not able to give any orders. "I understand," he said. "Would you like me to hold back until things cool down a little?"

She looked as if she was ready to slap him. "Absolutely not. What I want is for you to finish this. The president is very upset that letter is still out there."

Her concern made sense now. She was not one to be intimidated by anything the Texans tried to do. The president was a different thing. He was the one putting pressure on her. "I'm doing the best I can," he tried to reassure her.

"Get it! No matter what it takes. And no witnesses," she said. "Don't give those Texans more potential pawns." She stood up. Her point had been made, and she was ready to leave. "The president is putting pressure on the Senate to end debate and pass his Consumption Chip Bill. His hope is he can sign it on the Fourth of July at the Tricentennial ceremony."

"I would love to be there. It will be a historic occasion," he said.

"He will be showing a message President Obama taped sixty-five years ago to be shown on our Tricentennial."

"I didn't know that. Have you seen this message?"

"Yes. It is a beautiful message. He speaks of social justice and equality. Just as we are on the brink of achieving it." The weariness had left her face. Talking about Obama had reenergized her.

"I can understand then the frustration the president must feel," West said.

She nodded. "The last thing he needs is a message from Reagan out there, spoiling such a glorious occasion."

Chapter 53

They spent most of the day in the projection room. They were afraid to come out and find a police officer waiting for them. Around nighttime, Michael decided to venture out, slowly making his way out of the home-theater room. He searched the basement first, went through the rest of the house, came back to give them the good news that there was no one in the house. Upstairs, he placed a chair against the open kitchen door to keep it closed.

It was a tense night for all of them. Every small noise startled Michael, woke him up from a light sleep. He went upstairs three times during the night to check if there was someone.

The next evening, Michael and Jackie were sitting in the basement; Marshall risked it and went to take a nap on a real bed upstairs. They were eating some canned food they found; Michael was trying his best to make Jackie laugh.

"I have another one. A man goes to apply for a new car. He's finally accumulated the necessary carbon credits to get his brand new Obamobile. All the paper work seems to be in order so the clerk tells him 'Come back in six months to pick it up.' The man looks at his calendar, says, 'Will that be morning or afternoon?' The clerk is surprised at the question. 'What does it matter, it's six months away.' The man says, 'Well, I'm getting my roof fixed in the afternoon.'"

She cracked a smile. Her smile had become such a rarity, he was happy he was able to elicit one. She hardly talked after the police left the house. It was obvious the tension was getting to her; it was getting to all of them.

"Thanks for trying to cheer me up especially when you have more reason to be feeling down than me," Jackie said.

"We have to try to stay positive, keep our minds clear and focused."

"I feel bad we got you involved in all of this."

"Don't. Your grandpa didn't ask to get that Reagan letter but he, did. I wrote about it and here I am. Eventually something like this was going to happen to me. Sooner or later, I was going to write something that was going to make me an enemy of the State."

She smiled, moved closer to him, and caressed his cheek. "You've been a great friend."

He had been feeling guilty for bringing them to Obama City, in spite of Marshall's warnings. To hear those words from Jackie meant a lot to him. The tenderness with which she said it made it even more special.

"You might not believe me when I tell you"—he took her hand in his—"you are the best thing that has ever happened to me."

She leaned closer to him, and they were about to kiss. She placed her hand in front of his mouth. "My grandpa could come down anytime."

They were alone in the basement, the lights off, just a candle keeping the place from complete darkness.

"Do you really think we'll make it out of here?" she asked him.

He brought her hand up to his lips and kissed it. "I promise you, one of these days you and I will be in the Taj Mahal together."

She smiled at him. He hoped the memories of that date were as precious to her as they were to him.

"That's a date then," she said.

He moved aside hair that was in front of her left eye. "I can't wait." He looked at her for a brief moment without saying a word. "You have the most beautiful eyes." Even with the dim light, he was able to appreciate her expressive, gorgeous eyes.

Jackie did not say a word or moved. Michael leaned forward and softly kissed her lips. The kiss was brief. Noise from a helicopter interrupted it. It was flying above the house and brought concern back to Michael's face. The idea of making it to the Taj Mahal, or anywhere else, shattered by the reality that there were people looking for them.

Chapter 54

"How do I look?"

"Weird," Jackie said.

Michael stepped into the bathroom to look in the mirror. The dim candlelight barely allowed him to see anything. He looked different, wearing a tight old black shirt from his friend Craig, black jeans, a clip-on earring from Craig's mom, and old eyeglasses from Craig's dad. It was hard to see with the glasses, everything was blurry. He also had a baseball cap and had not shaven since their ordeal began. His own mom would not recognize him.

"I definitely look different," he said, returning from the bathroom.

"What's with your forehead?" Jackie asked.

He removed his baseball cap to reveal what he had done. "I placed some tape on my forehead, to stretch the skin. There are surveillance cameras everywhere. They use digital picture matching. It matches the image they get from you with their picture on file. By stretching my forehead like this, it can cause a mismatch when they try to match my image with whatever picture they have on file."

"Clever," Marshall said.

"I don't like this at all. This is an unnecessary risk. Just a couple of hours ago, we heard that helicopter."

"I have to do this. It's important. Then if we succeed, we'll try to get out of here tonight or tomorrow night. We can't stay here much longer, or we'll have to start eating the rats."

"Disgusting," Jackie said. "What are you going to do once you're out there?"

"I'm going to go to the library—it's not too far from here. I am going to try to log on to one of my old accounts. Once I do that, I will scan the letter and email it to my contacts. I will also post it, ask people to copy it, and email it to their friends."

"The government will remove it right away, track every email you sent it to, and they will delete it." Marshall sounded skeptical.

"That's why it has to be done today. Saturday night and Sunday, the Communications Department has a minimal crew. It could take hours before they realize what's happened. Enough for it to spread."

"Can you make a paper copy while you are at the library?" Marshall asked.

"Paper?" One of the tapes from his forehead came off.

"Back when paper existed, a letter like this could be copied. You could make a few hundred copies and just give it away."

As Marshall talked, Michael went to the bathroom to retape his forehead.

"We are a paperless society now," the professor continued. "Everything is electronic, easier for the government to monitor and control."

He came out of the bathroom and was about to go out when Jackie stood in front of him.

"Don't go. It's too dangerous. Once we get to Texas, you can do this," she said.

"I have to. If something bad happens, at least this will be done. You love what you do and so do I. I will never have a chance to be a real journalist. This is my chance. I will post a quick message letting people know what has been done to us over this letter."

"A journalist uncovering the truth—now that will be an amazing thing." Marshall chuckled as he talked. "All they do these days is deliver propaganda for the government."

Michael wished he could remove the anguish from her face. She looked as if she was saying goodbye to him for the last time. As if she did not expect him to ever come back. "This is my chance to expose a big story." He hoped she could see it from his point of view. "A letter from a former president that's being suppressed by the government. It's a huge story. If I do this, I can be satisfied that at least for one brief moment, I was true to my profession."

Jackie hugged him and gave him a kiss on the lips. "Please be careful out there, and if anything does not look right, come back."

Michael came out of the basement, went up the stairs carefully, did not see anything suspicious, and ran to a large tree in the middle of the backyard. He did not see anyone. He went to the back, jumped the fence, and walked to the sidewalk. He looked to his left then right—no one around. He started his walk to the library.

Michael walked a couple of blocks and saw a community organizer standing at a corner, talking on the phone. He decided to walk right in front of him. The community organizer did not seem to recognize him. He felt good; his disguise was effective.

He made a left turn and walked five more blocks. He saw the library on the opposite side, crossed the street, walked in with his head bowed.

The Edward Kennedy Memorial Library was a large building with multiple conference rooms in the upstairs section. The first floor had numerous computer terminals. In the center, there were sofas with an e-reader available to each side.

Michael looked for an available computer, which was not a problem with such few users at that time. He saw, on his right, a section of classic books—old-fashioned paper books. At the end of that section, there was a statute of the man to whom the library was dedicated—Senator Edward Kennedy.

The web page of the library came on, and a window popped up for him to input his account number and password. He typed the account number he planned to use but without success. Rejected. He tried another account, and it was rejected as well. Two others rejected too. Michael realized all of his accounts were deleted. He was not going to accomplish what he wanted. For a moment, he wondered what else could be done.

A man came from behind. "May I help you, sir?" the man said. "Are you having trouble logging in?"

Michael felt his heart skip a beat. He looked back and saw it was one of the librarians. "It's no trouble at all. I forgot my password, but that's fine, I decided to read a book better."

"That's why we need Congress to give us that chip. No one will ever need a password again. We'll be able to access the internet at will, with no security risks," the librarian said as he walked away.

Michael went to the classics, grabbed the first book he found, sat on a sofa, and tried to read. It was blurry with the glasses, so he took them off. He pretended he was reading it, thinking what he could try next. The book caught his attention. It was fiction, a mystery. A story about a rich man, a powerful politician, who was driving one night, drunk, with a mistress at his side. He was involved in an accident but escaped unharmed, without a scratch while the woman was found dead. Michael put it down. It did not appeal to him. He was not in the mood for mysteries. He had problems of his own he needed to solve. Maybe he should have developed a plan B before coming out. It was best to go back to the house; it was not going to work out.

Then, Michael realized something. "My dad's account." How stupid could he be, he wondered. It was unlikely they would have inactivated it already. Inactivating the account of the Communications Czar would require the highest level of clearance. West could not do it. Faulkner could but unlikely she would want her fingerprints on anything to do with his dad. Once he accessed the Communications Department, he would have access to every email in the nation, he could post the letter in multiple sites at once. Only someone at a higher level could take it off. It was a brilliant idea.

The only problem was the librarian. Michael knew his dad's account number, but the password was a different thing. His dad had to change passwords every six months, and Michael had not attempted to access his dad's account in more than a year. However, his dad was predictable in the way he created new passwords, so Michael was confident he could figure it out but not with the librarian looking over his shoulder.

Just as he was thinking on what to do about the librarian, a blond man sat across from him. Michael pretended once again to be reading his mystery. He looked up after a few seconds, and the man was looking directly at him. He was an overweight middle-aged man. Michael turned a page, pretended he was reading. "I knew it, the fat man did it," he said. Then, he looked up again. The man was staring at him. He placed down his novel and walked away. Without looking back, he went directly to the main entrance, hoping the blond man was not following him.

Chapter 55

Her lips were delicious, exactly what he needed to unwind on a Saturday night. She had perfectly shaped breasts. He was kissing her left breast when his phone interrupted him.

"Yes . . . You found him . . . Where . . . ? Fantastic. Just hold him, and I will be right there. And I want him alive, is that understood . . . ?"

He jumped out of bed. His lover looked so tempting, inciting him to stay a few more minutes, finish what he was doing. As good as Olga Parker looked completely naked on his bed, he had a job to do. He had to admit—she looked even better, more attractive, than when he first met her in Long Island.

"Do you have to go now?" she asked.

"Yes, they found your student, Michael Adams."

She sat up; there was a definite thrill in her face. She looked as excited about the news as he was.

He had expressed to her his frustration about Michael getting away. The main purpose of his earlier phone call to her had been to whine about his failure. She had already told him everything she knew and had nothing more to contribute.

During their conversation, she asked if he had any plans for the night. When he said no, she said she could take the express and meet him for dinner. He agreed with her. Nothing better than a night of passionate sex with Olga to forget his frustrations.

"Where is he?"

"He was seen at some library, not far from where he lives. Probably trying to get some help. Stupid kid, he actually thought we were not going to inactivate his accounts."

"Do you have to go get him now? Can't they just hold him until you get there?" She stretched on the bed, her arms up, making her breasts look so much more desirable.

"I can't risk it. He's already evaded me a couple of times. I can't risk letting him get away one more time. I need to get there and make sure he's captured, make sure we find his friends and the stupid letter. It's time to close this case. It has taken longer than I ever expected."

Chapter 56

Michael came down the steps of the library, looked over his left shoulder. The blonde stranger was coming behind him. He increased his pace, and over to his other side, he saw a black car slowly driving in his direction. It was following him; there was no further doubt, they found him. He had been identified.

Michael went to cross the street; a bus was coming his way. When it passed him, he jumped into its back. He passed the blond man as well as the black car.

He jumped out of the bus and decided to go back inside the library. Better to stay in a public place, he thought. Hopefully they would want to avoid shooting him out in the open like that. He ran the steps of the library and before walking in, took a peak back; the blond man was nowhere to be seen.

Once inside the library, he picked up the book he was reading before. He returned to the classics, stood by one of the bookshelves and pretended to read, standing in such a way that he could see the entrance to the library. Nobody had come in after him. Not yet.

His thoughts drifted to Jackie. Did they identify him once he reached the library or when he came out of the house? If it was coming out of the house, Jackie and Marshall were in danger. Maybe already captured. He wished he could call them. At this point, he would use any phone; revealing his location was no longer a concern.

Someone came into the library. A man with a dark suit followed by two community organizers. They had stun guns out. Michael wished he had his with him, but it needed to be recharged, and he had no way to do it at Craig's house.

One of the community organizers spotted him. Michael moved to the back, trying to walk slowly to avoid too much attention. With two community organizers coming after him with stun guns in their hands, going unnoticed was not an easy task. One of them went to the back, following right behind Michael. The other one went to the front with the agent. They were trying to surround him.

Michael reached the end. Nowhere else to go. They were getting closer. He stood behind the Edward Kennedy statute, trying to figure out the best way to escape. The community organizer coming from behind was morbidly obese; he should be able to outrun him, but the man occupied so much space and had a stun gun. It would be impossible to go around him without getting shocked. The other one was coming with an agent; they both looked in shape. He would not be able to get past them.

The statute did not look too big or heavy. Michael threw his fiction book at the obese guy; it hit him on the forehead. He then pushed the statute forward, making it fall on top of the other community organizers. It also caught the agent's leg under it. He ran to the other end of the library.

"Hey! What is this?" The librarian grabbed Michael's arm.

The out-of-shape community organizer recovered from the book attack and was coming his way. Michael saw an exit sign just in front of him. He tried to move, but the librarian was holding his arm with significant strength.

"You're dreaming if you think you're going somewhere," the librarian said.

"And the dream shall never die," Michael said and slapped him with the back of his free hand. The librarian loosened his grip on Michael, and he ran for the exit.

When he opened the emergency door, a loud alarm went off throughout the library. There was a brick wall in the back. Michael ran to it and jumped, grabbing the top of the wall, pulling himself up and over to the other side. There was no way the fat guy was climbing that wall; he would have to go around.

Michael ran to his left side, undecided where to go. Going back to the house was out of the question. It was too risky. The last thing he wanted to do was to lead them back to the professor, jeopardize Jackie's safety. If he were captured, he would be captured alone. Nevertheless, it was not going to happen. He would not allow himself to be arrested.

A car was coming at him, full speed. It looked like the same black car as before. Michael made the next left turn and ran down that street, determined to get away, one way or the other.

Chapter 57

Marshall looked out the window, slightly pulling the curtain to a side. There was a car parked across the street. It had been there for the last five minutes. There was someone inside the car; whoever he was, he had not come out.

He heard Jackie behind him and whispered for her to come over. "They found us."

She peaked outside to see the car in question.

"We need to go—we can't stay here any longer," Marshall said.

"What about Mike?"

"They probably have him by now. Either they saw him coming out or they found him on his way here. But if they found us, we have to assume they found him too." He looked at Jackie. He could understand how bad she felt; so much had been lost already. The thought of losing Michael was probably too painful for her to bear. "I shouldn't have agreed with him," he said. "Going to that library was a bad idea. They're everywhere. No way was he ever going to go there and come back without them knowing it."

"How can we just leave? What if he comes back? Let's just go back down and hide in the projection room."

"They know we're here. They'll tear this house apart until they find us."

"Where would we go? If he got captured with a disguise by himself, what are you and I going to do that he didn't?"

He knew she was right. His instinct was to go and try to get lost again, but there was no place to go, nowhere to hide. If those were federal agents, they were doomed. Their only hope was to hide, as Jackie suggested, and hope it would work out again. "Okay, let's get downstairs. I guess that is the only hope we have until we can think of something else."

He peaked out one last time. The man in the car had opened his door. He was talking on the phone, looking straight at the house. No further doubt in his mind, that man was there for them. Likely waiting for backup.

He was about to walk away from the window when a pizza delivery car parked outside, right in front. A lady came out of the car, waved hi to the agent across the street. The agent looked surprised. The lady took a large pizza box from the passenger seat of her Obamobile. Must be taking it to the house across, thought Marshall. He was wrong; she turned and walked his way. Why did they send a pizza lady? If she was a federal agent, why was she bothering, pretending to be a delivery person? Why, when they were being so obvious?

Marshall turned to Jackie. "There's a pizza lady coming this way."

"What?" Jackie went to the window and saw her. "Let's go. Let's get downstairs and hide. This doesn't feel good."

Marshall stepped away from the window. He was intrigued about the pizza lady; whoever she was, the best thing was to hide.

He heard a loud knock on the door just as he was about to go down to the basement. He paused for a moment, thought he heard her say something. The pizza lady had said something, but he was too far to hear it. He walked back to the door.

"Grandpa," Jackie whispered loudly enough that he was able to hear her.

Another knock on the door. "Mr. Marshall, we know you're there, open the door," the pizza lady said.

Marshall was barely able to hear her for she was keeping her voice down. If she knew he was there, then why the pretense? Why didn't those agents knock down the door and arrest them?

"Mr. Marshall"—she was whispering—"I'm here to help."

He looked back at Jackie; she seemed surprised as well. He did not know what to make of it. Who could be there to help them? Did Michael send a message asking for help? That was unlikely. Even if he did, it would have taken longer for someone to get there. Could she still be a federal agent? Why offer help?

Marshall did not know what to think but knew his options were limited. They were trapped. The man across the street was definitely a federal agent—there to arrest them, he was certain of that. They were doomed, whoever the pizza lady was. Might as well take a risk, he decided.

"No," Jackie said as he unlocked the front door.

"I'm here to help," the pizza lady said once again.

Marshall opened the door, and she came in.

Chapter 58

A black car was coming at him. They found him, in spite of all the precautions he took, all he did, his disguise, his attempt to go unnoticed—all in vain. He should have known better. Jackie warned him, but he had to be a hero. Now there was no choice—he had to run for his life.

A park across the street looked like a good place to hide. He ran in front of the car that was following him, and it barely missed him. Its driver did not attempt to slow down. Neither did Michael.

Michael ran across the park. In the middle of the day, it was crowded, full of people, he could have disappeared with ease. Since he had chosen the night for his heroics, that was not possible. It was too risky to stay in the park; it would be simple to surround him. It was better to run.

There were a few people in there. Some looked at him as he passed by them; most did not seem to care. He reached the other side and turned right. At that instant, he saw a police car; it flashed a light at him. Michael turned around and ran the other way.

He crossed the street, the police car was getting close—they would catch up with him any second if he didn't do something. He climbed a wood fence and fell on the floor of a backyard with a concrete floor. It was a painful fall. He did not have a chance to think about his pain. Or where to go next. Immediately, he heard a dog barking. A Doberman was coming for him and did not look happy. He rushed to the other side of the yard, jumped toward the fence just as the dog jumped at him. The dog managed to bite his jeans at one of his ankles, and they ripped as Michael pulled his leg over to the other side of the fence.

There was no time to waste. He had to keep moving, so he stood up and ran to the front of the house.

Back on the street, he heard someone shout: "Freeze!" It was a policeman. Michael ran away from him, thinking for a moment he was going to be shot from behind. Only a miracle could keep him alive, he thought.

His prayer seemed answered when he saw a church across the street. Michael changed direction and headed for it. He made a car come to a sudden stop when he crossed the street. He jumped over the hood of another car, slid through it, and ran without stopping.

He went up the steps of the church, looked back briefly, saw the cop still running after him. He would not be able to stay in the church for any amount of time. The back door had to be his immediate destination.

Michael closed the door of the church behind him. As he saw the inside of the church, he froze in disbelief. Where the cross of Jesus should be, and probably had been at some point, there was instead the logo of NACORN. It was not a church but a community outreach center with about two dozen community organizers.

"I pledge allegiance to our leader . . ." The community organizers were all saying in a chorus. They were all standing up when Michael first came in. When they heard the door close, they turned around and saw him.

He stood there, frozen, not knowing what to do, hoping they would not recognize him.

"Isn't that the guy we're looking for?" one of them said.

"Yes!" a couple of others shouted.

They all went after Michael, who went out as fast as he had come in. Stepping out of the church, he noticed right away the cop coming up the steps, with his gun out. Michael jumped on the handrail and then jumped down onto the street. The cop took aim at him but stopped when the community organizers came out running in front of him, trying to catch up with Michael.

He ran for a block then he saw two police cars stopping ahead of him; the cops came out with guns in hand. He couldn't run forward or go back with a bunch of community organizers behind him. He crossed the street, almost got hit by a bus, which missed him by an inch. A car did knock him, threw him into the ground, and he hit his head. He stood up right away, looked around, and saw a movie theater just in front of him. The community organizers and cops were closing in. There was not much of a choice; it would be a night at the movies.

Michael ran past the ticket agent. The multiplex had twenty theaters, with one playing *Obama: The Movie.* He went into that one before any of his persecutors, which now included the ticket agent, could see him. His eyes took a second to adjust to the darkness. The place was packed with people just as he hoped. An open seat next to the far wall, close to the emergency exit, looked like the perfect place to settle before anyone else walked in. The seat was in one of the front rows, and he had to lean back on his chair in order to see the movie.

The actor playing Barack Obama looked so much like the pictures and videos Michael had seen.

"We are the ones we've been waiting for . . ." the actor playing Obama said. "We are the change that we seek. We are the hope of those boys who have little . . . who've been told that they cannot have what they dream . . . that they cannot be what they imagine."

Michael scrolled down as much as he could, pretending to be watching the movie with interest, hoping he would not be seen.

"We are the hope of the father who goes to work before dawn and lies awake with doubts that tell him he cannot give his children the same opportunities that someone gave him."

Michael heard those words and thought how he did not have the same opportunities as previous generations of Americans. No hope of having a standard of living better, or even equal, to that of his parents, of pursuing his American dream. He would never have an opportunity to do for a living what he wanted to do—never allowed to report the truth of the world around him. The freedom previous generations enjoyed and took for granted. It was shattered for him. He would never be able to say he was born in the land of the free and mean it.

"We are the hope of the woman who hears that her city will not be rebuilt, that she cannot reclaim the life that was swept away in a terrible storm."

Michael chuckled. He thought of Manhattan—twenty years and still abandoned. A city that became a political game. He thought of all the abandoned construction, no one competent or willing to get work done, because the government and its vast bureaucracy took away all incentive.

"We are the hope of the future . . ."

A future without freedom—ruled by bureaucrats. A future with young people rewarded for being enforcers of the government rather than rewarded for their hard work and initiative. Where construction was not about building something of quality but a way to reward political friends with a job they were never qualified to do. Where an old couple worked hard to sustain someone who wished not to work at all. A future where it was an audacity to hope.

"The answer to the cynics who tell us our house must stand divided . . . that we cannot come together . . ."

"Coming together by not allowing disagreements," murmured Michael.

"That we cannot remake this world as it should be."

Michael noticed the people sitting around him were watching with such admiration. They had good reason to be inspired, he thought. They lived in the world President Obama created for them. Almost everyone in that theater was a bureaucrat or related to one. Life was great for them. What about the rest of America? The rest of the country had to live under the endless rules created by them. "His dream world is my nightmare," Michael said, looking back at the screen.

"Shut up," some lady sitting behind him said. She obviously heard him.

Michael looked back to see if one of those community organizers had come into the theater. He saw two enter. He stared back at the screen. Hopefully, they would start listening to Obama and forget everything else.

His hope was in vain. They stood at the end of the front row, pointed a flash light at him. "You can't get away," one of them said loud enough that everyone in the theater looked.

Michael stood up, went to the exit door, saw the fire alarm lever. He looked back; the community organizers were coming after him.

"Yes, we can!" the actor playing Obama said.

"Yes, I can!" Michael pulled the lever of the fire alarm.

The alarm went off; everyone headed for the exit. The community organizers tried to get past people, but there were too many standing in their way. Michael came out with the crowd, looked to both sides to see where he could go next.

"You are that guy they're looking for," said a blonde lady next to him.

Most of the crowd stared at him as they came out of the theater. A tall guy reached for his arm and grabbed it. Michael looked over the guy's shoulder and saw more community organizers and police coming.

"No time to chat," he said, tried to go, but the guy held his arm, not loosening the grip. He pushed him, and the guy fell.

Michael was back on the run, on the streets of Obama City, with no idea where to go next.

Chapter 59

Community organizers, police, even Saturday night moviegoers—everyone in Obama City seemed to want a piece of him. He knew the city well enough to know there were not many places left to hide. However, Michael felt he had no choice but to run. As long as he had any strength left in his legs, he had to keep running.

As Michael was about to cross another street, a police car pulled in front of him. He jumped over the hood, and continued to run. A cop shouted for him to stop, or he was going to shoot. He heard a shot—distant—but did not dare look back or stop. He continued to run. Another shot—this time it sounded a lot closer. Michael went on the middle of the street. A one-way street with multiple Obamobiles coming straight at him. He figured the cops would not shoot him there for fear of hurting or killing someone else. The cars swirled past him as they avoided hitting him. One of them came to a sudden stop and was hit by others behind it. Michael did not look; he just kept running.

The statute of Obama was up ahead, about five blocks away. There was a train station there behind it. The express to Washington DC had to be his next destination. It gave him some hope. But Michael had nothing left. His legs felt as if they were going to give in on him. There was no way he could run another five blocks. Soon, he would be captured, under West's custody. And the letter? Destroyed—never to be read by anyone else. Lost to history. Lost to tyranny. "No," Michael said and increased his pace.

Four blocks to go, and the pain in his legs was becoming intense. The words of Thomas Paine came to mind. 'These are the times that try men's souls.' He increased his speed even more. "Don't be a summer soldier," he told himself. People like Thomas Paine and other Founding Fathers had gone through so much, been winter soldiers through the most difficult of times, made so many sacrifices for the sake of America's freedom. They would not be happy with what was happening. Members of the government they created, running after him, to destroy Reagan's letter, to destroy a letter just because it spoke of individual freedom. They would want him to ignore the pain in his legs, the utter exhaustion, and to keep on running. And so he ignored it, ignored the pounding in his chest, and he increased his speed even more.

Only three more blocks left. A cop tried to tackle Michael, but he was one second too slow—instead fell on the ground. The scene was repeated by two other cops—all with the same success.

Just another two blocks, but the beating in his chest was becoming unbearable. Another police car stopped in front of him. He went around it—kept running. He was moving as fast as he had ever moved. Where he had found the sudden new burst of energy he did not know. All he knew was that he was not going to stop; no matter what. Run, Mike, run, he told himself.

One more block. Run, Mike, run. A helicopter was above him, focusing a bright, intense light on him. It did not matter; Obama's statue was a few feet away. He was getting away. He was going to make it.

When he reached his destination, he made a right turn behind the statute. He looked over his shoulder, saw cops running after him, already close enough to shoot. He was not looking ahead when he ran into someone. The collision felt more as if he hit a brick wall. He was knocked hard, and he fell to the ground one more time, hitting his head. The impact almost made him lose consciousness, but he did not. Michael closed his eyes for a second then opened them, looked up, and saw whom he collided with.

"You didn't really think you were going to get away, did you?" It was his nemesis, Agent Baron West, standing, his hands at his hips, with a grin in his face.

Michael tried to push himself up on his elbows, tried to get up. Then, he dropped to the ground completely as machine guns, rifles and handguns were all pointed right at his face. He was surrounded by a multitude of federal agents. It was over, and he knew it. It was the end.

Chapter 60

A couple of agents lifted Michael from the ground, threw him against a car, searched for a weapon. West handcuffed him and threw him on the backseat of the car. At least he still had the Reagan letter, he thought. A small consolation, considering there was no hope of going anywhere with it.

An agent came and sat next to Michael with a gun pointed directly at him.

"Are you comfortable back there, Mr. Adams?" West said as he sat on the driver's seat.

Michael did not answer even though no one had told him yet that he had the right to remain silent. Maybe they did not bother with such things anymore. "Aren't you going to read me my rights?" he finally asked.

"Who said we're arresting you? You're a sick young man. Suicidal and homicidal. We are taking you to a psychiatric facility, where we'll be able to provide you with appropriate treatment."

"Of course," Michael said. "You wouldn't go after me for my political views. That's beneath your values. Better, invent some mental illness I need to be cured of. Hypocrite."

That earned him a slap from the other agent. "Watch it," he said.

"See? You're paranoid and delusional. Typical symptoms of your disease." West looked at the rearview image displayed in the digital monitor in the dashboard. There were many people behind them, making it hard for West to back up the car. "Don't worry," West continued, "you'll be under the care of one of the best medical authorities in the treatment of paranoid ailments such as yours."

"Oh really? Who's that?" Michael asked.

"Me, of course." West looked back at Michael with a broad smile.

The other agent chuckled with the comment. "He'll have you seeing everything clear in no time," he added.

"So you're still pretending to be a psychiatrist," Michael said.

"I am a psychiatrist," West said. "As I told you, I work with the antisocial division of the FBI. We constantly monitor dangerous individuals such as you, who can become at any time, a threat to society."

Michael tried to remain quiet; there was nothing to be gained by further conversation with West.

"The threats vary a wide range. From a loner who is clinging to his gun and religion at home, and could at any time snap, kill his whole family. To a dangerous right-wing activist, who can misinform the people of the good the government does for them, give them fishy information, and lead them the wrong direction." West was finally able to get out and drive away.

There was significant traffic caused by the police presence, and the accidents Michael caused along the way.

"As you can imagine, we do deal with some very dangerous individuals. That's why we must be armed and ready for any eventuality," West said.

Michael wished West would just drive and keep quiet. "If you're going to be talking garbage all the way, can we just skip to the part where you shoot me?"

The other agent punched him in the face. "We have a funny guy with us," he said.

West slightly turned back, displayed a smile, continued his monologue. He was not willing to grant Michael the gift of a little silence. "When we receive tips about people like Senator Thomas or your friend Mr. Marshall, who might be engaging in dangerous behavior, we run their profiles through our behavior software and then decide how much of a threat they might be and how best to deal with them."

Michael looked out the window; they were moving fast now. In the distance, he saw the Edward Kennedy library. He felt so stupid for having gone there. What was he trying to accomplish?

Did he really think he was not going to be caught? Jackie tried to warn him, but he wouldn't listen.

Jackie was probably getting worried he hadn't returned. What would be her reaction when she realized he was not coming back? He felt an intense sadness. The realization that he was never going to see Jackie again hit him hard. Tears started to accumulate around his eyes. He closed them, trying to hold back those tears, hoping they would not come out. There was no way he would give West the pleasure of breaking down emotionally in front of him.

"Every threat is dealt with differently." The annoying West seemed determined to talk nonstop until they reached their destination. "Some people might just need some therapy. Others, like you, need stronger action. You're too dangerous to be left alone."

The other agent punched Michael in the face one more time. "He don't look all that dangerous now. Why don't you show us some kickboxing moves? Let's see you get off those handcuffs."

Michael had blood coming out of his nose. He looked at the agent. "I thought our government never tortures prisoners."

He punched him again. Michael saw the blood dripping from his nose to his shirt and jeans. The taste of blood in his mouth made him nauseous. His entire face hurt as hell.

Nothing that was happening was a surprise to him. They would not torture prisoners in order to defend America's freedom. But to defend their left-wing agenda? That was an entirely different thing. He was familiar with their methods, far more than they could imagine. Once he learned how to break into the website at the Communications Department, accessed their databases using his father's account, he made it a habit to check it regularly. It became his main source of information. He would read reports and learn things that most people, even members of Congress, would never find out because the Communications Department censored it. That's how he learned about many bad things the antisocial division had done. Political assassinations, torture, imprisonment of political dissidents—their objective was to suppress right-wing political views at any cost. "Hypocrites," Michael repeated, expecting another punch, but thankfully, it never came.

"It could have been so different. You have natural leadership qualities." It almost sounded as if West was expressing admiration. "But instead of using them for the good of the people, to inspire them to work together to achieve social justice and equality, you squandered it, for your own self interest. You waste your talents protecting this stupid letter about freedom. You know what Reagan's real message with that letter is . . . You're on your own. That's what freedom really means." West was shaking his head, looking disappointed.

Michael had a sense of fear and doom, which was becoming overwhelming. He kept thinking what might happen to him once they reached the psychiatric hospital. The drugs they would pump on him to make him lose all sense of reality, make him say things he did not want to say. If they had not found Jackie, they would make him confess where she was. He was scared for what was about to happen to him and what might happen to her and her grandfather. He could only hope, somehow, they would be able to get away.

"I give you credit. You are resourceful. That was a clever place to hide. An old house like that. And I don't know how you were able to hide from my agents when they went inside."

His fear became stronger. He knew his friends were doomed. They were about to be, or already were, captured. He was in a situation with no possible escape. It was all over for him and for them.

Don't think like that, he told himself. He was alive and in use of his faculties. As long as that was the case, there was hope. He tried to clear his head and remove all feelings of anger, sadness, or fear. There had to be a way to escape, even if it meant being shot. Once he was inside a hospital, with drugs making it impossible to distinguish reality from fantasy, it would be too late. He had to make a move before getting inside the hospital. Michael looked at the agent sitting next to him, the gun still pointed at him. Any thought of taking the gun, in an escape attempt, evaporated when he noticed it had electronic fingertip recognition. It would not work for Michael, or anyone, other than the agent. His handcuffs also had an electronic locking mechanism, making it impossible for anyone but the agent who put them on to open them.

When they reached the hospital and tried to move him, he had to take a chance. Make a run for it as soon as the door opened. He probably would be killed, but there was always a chance that he could get away. He had to take it. At least, he would not die a miserable death inside a hospital, collaborating with West.

He remembered an old saying he read once. It was once the motto of a state, part of a different America, symbolic of an exceptional era. The saying was: 'Live free or die.' That was his exact feeling.

He closed his eyes and prayed. He prayed and begged God, not so much for a miracle, but that if an opportunity came, he would be ready and would know what to do.

Chapter 61

Jackie froze as her grandfather opened the door. She wanted to scream for him not to do it; instead, she froze. A pizza lady entered the house as soon as the door opened.

She closed the door behind her. "I'm here to help. Get your belongings and we need to go."

Jackie was confused and scared. "Who are you?"

"I don't have time to answer questions right now. There are federal agents out there, and they're here for you."

A voice from outside interrupted them. "We have the house surrounded. Come out with your hands up in the air."

The pizza lady went to the window and looked out. "Is there a back door?"

"In the basement," Marshall said.

"Let's go." The pizza lady placed the box down on a coffee table, opened it.

Jackie was shocked at what was inside. It looked like a bomb. Her confusion and fear increased, and she knew it would be a night she would never forget.

The lady set the timer for five minutes and stood up. "I have a van parked in the back, waiting for us. I will explain on the way." She headed for the basement.

Jackie was not moving. She could not move. Everything was happening too fast, and she did not understand any of it. What was happening? What was to be of Michael?

"You're going to get killed if you don't come with me," the pizza lady said.

Jackie went with her, and they ran down the stairs. There were no belongings to get. There was nothing left but a desire to stay alive, to get to see Michael again. The lady was the first one to come out of the basement.

A uniformed federal agent stood on the backyard, just a few feet away from the steps to the basement. A shot later, he was down, bleeding, and the pizza lady running up the stairs. She did not hesitate and shot another one who fell just a few feet away from them. Whoever this lady was, she was used to shooting and killing people.

The pizza lady looked back at Jackie. "Run!" She took aim at someone behind her and shot again.

The noise from the gun came right next to Jackie's left ear. It probably blew an eardrum, she thought. The lady ran to the fence and told them to climb it. Jackie was getting tired of climbing fences but did it without protesting. She was worried her grandfather would have a hard time; however, he came right after her, aided by the pizza assassin.

A van with its side door opened was waiting for them. Several more shots were exchanged. Jackie heard people shouting behind them, but she did not dare look back. She ran, holding her grandfather's hand, and jumped inside the van. The pizza lady continued to shoot, even as she approached the van. Whether she killed anyone else, Jackie was unable to see. The lady came inside the van, and it sped away. She closed the door. The young man who was driving accelerated to what had to be more than a hundred.

Jackie felt they were going to crash any moment. The van was old and did not inspire much confidence. It was probably from the beginning of the century, she thought. What possessed these people to attempt a rescue in such an old vehicle was beyond her.

There were police lights right behind them. Jackie looked out and saw several police cars following close behind. "Some kind of rescue this is," she said.

The pizza lady just smiled.

"Do you really think we're going to get away in such an old van?" Jackie asked.

The lady did not answer.

They were going to be captured; Jackie had no doubt. Now, they would also be facing charges of shooting, maybe even killing federal agents. And the bomb the pizza lady left behind? Whoever died from that bomb would be added to their charges and to Jackie's conscience. Even if the rescue was successful, could she ever forgive herself for the lives that were lost? Those agents were just doing their job, and now they were shot, maybe dead. All because of them, because they refused to surrender. Suddenly, Jackie heard an explosion in the distance, and everything went dark.

Chapter 62

West stopped at a red light. Michael could see the church a block away. He should have known what kind of place it was—headquarters for the community organizers of the area. A place for them to worship their true god, the State, the government. A helicopter, flying over, was illuminating it, making it look almost holy.

The traffic light turned green, and off they went to Michael's final destination. A sinner being transported to his purgatory, to pay penance for his sins. To be tormented for daring to carry a message of blasphemy.

A blast, loud, came from his right, brought him back to reality. He turned but could not see where it came from. Everything had gone dark, and West was not able to control the car. They crashed against a tree, and he fell forward, hitting his bloody face in the back of West's seat. As they crashed, a branch from the tree fell, broke the windshield, and hit West on the forehead just as the airbag deployed. He cursed and seemed to be in pain.

The other agent had an expression of panic. Everything was dark; it was hard to see, at first, what was causing that look. Then, Michael saw it. The helicopter, which a second ago was flying above them, was crashing against the church. The explosion shattered the windows in the car, sending Michael on top of the agent's lap. The agent pushed him away.

One of the flying pieces of glass cut Michael's left arm. He felt the pain and brought his arm forward. His handcuffs were loose.

It took him a moment to realize every light was off. The car stopped working and so did the helicopter. His handcuffs, which had an electronic mechanism, were also damaged somehow.

"What the fuck happened?" The agent with the gun asked.

Michael looked at the gun. If the fingertip recognition was not working, it was useless. Everything electronic seemed to have malfunctioned. He tested his theory— pushed the door slightly with his leg, confirmed what he suspected—the door was unlocked. The door locks were electronic as well. It was true. He didn't know how, but there was no time to think. It was an opportunity, and he was ready.

"I don't know—the power's off. This thing just died on me," West said.

The agent with the gun opened his mouth to say something. Before anything came out of his mouth, Michael's fist went at it, breaking a couple of front teeth.

"Thanks for the chat, gotta run," Michael said while he reached for the door and stepped out of the car.

The agent with the gun, clueless as to what was going on, picked up the gun and tried to use it. Useless—his gun was dead.

West tried to open his door, but it was distorted from the crash, and he had to force it open. By the time he came out, Michael was on the run.

Most people were running toward the church, to check for survivors; he was running away from there. No one looked at him; they had bigger problems.

Police cars all seemed to be dead with their lights not flashing. The cops were running to the scene of the crash. One policeman, who Michael ran right in front of, was busy with his phone. He was shaking it, puzzled as to why the phone was not responding. He did not notice him.

At the next intersection, a Cherokee SUV pulled right in front of him, opened its passenger door. "If you want to see the morning, get in!" the driver of the Cherokee said.

Michael could not see the driver. He did not know what to do. However, he knew he had nothing left in his legs. How far could he go on foot?

Michael accepted the offer and got in the car. The driver made a U-turn and sped away. All the traffic lights were dead, all cars had come to a complete stop; the Cherokee was the only one moving. Everyone looked at them as they drove by, obviously wondering why their car was working while all others were not.

"What's going on? Why are all the lights off?" The darkness made it difficult at first to realize who the driver was. Once he did, he was shocked and did not know what to feel. The man driving was the blond guy who had been staring at him in the library. Had he been rescued or recaptured?

"The lights are off," said the blond man. "Anything that uses electricity is not working right now within about a ten-mile radius."

"Why? What happened?"

"There was an explosion. It was a small explosive, did not do much damage, but generated an EMP."

"A What?"

"An EMP . . . electromagnetic pulse. It burns anything that uses electronic circuits. It destroys the microcircuits, making them useless. So everything that uses electronics, which is pretty much everything, becomes useless under that ten-mile radius."

"When will the power come back?"

"The power is not gone. The gadgets that use the power are useless. They won't be coming back. The cars, the phones—everything that's electronic will have to be repaired. It's all useless now. All these houses, all the electronics they have—it's going to be a tough few days for everyone around here." He smiled, seemed satisfied on what had been accomplished.

"Why is this car working?"

"It's old, from the turn of the century. Its few electronics have been removed. It's a combustion engine, doesn't even have a working radio. It has nothing electronic that the EMP could have affected."

Michael tried to absorb what was going on. He tasted the blood on his lips. He was glad his situation had improved. Nonetheless, he needed to understand it, to get some kind of an explanation. "Why? Why did you do it?"

"It was the only way to get you out. There's too much security in Obama City, almost impossible to overcome it. Electronics is their most powerful tool but also their Achilles' tendon."

"And who are you?"

"The name is Rick Brown." He shook Michael's hand. "I'm an intelligence officer with the Republic of Texas."

"Texas?" Michael did not trust Texans. Not an abnormal feeling to have for a person his age. The natural result of what he learned in school. He was taught terrible things about Texans. As he grew up and learned even worse things about his own government, he still had uneasy feelings about them.

"Yes, Texas," Brown repeated.

Great, thought Michael, feeling as if he had not been rescued, just captured by another faction. A pawn in a conflict between two nations.

The rest of the drive went under almost complete silence. "You don't trust me, do you?" Brown asked after a few minutes, reading Michael's expression perfectly.

"I don't trust anyone these days."

Brown smiled and looked at Michael. "I can just drop you off at the next police station. Actually, come to think of it, I think there's a reward for information on your whereabouts."

Michael got the point; there was little choice but to go ahead with whatever Brown wanted to do. He closed his eyes, tried to get some rest. He thought about Jackie, her face, their earlier kiss. Before he dozed off into sleep, his last thought was a desire to see and kiss her again.

Chapter 63

West stared at the burning church; his anger could match the intensity of the fire. He shook his head in disbelief; the stupid kid had slipped out of his hands one more time.

His phone was of no use—dead like everything else around him. The car, the helicopter, the streetlights, they all stopped working. The only light was coming from the fire.

"Nothing is working," the other agent said.

The idiot had allowed Michael to get away. West had to hold back, to keep himself from slapping him. "You're fucking brilliant," he said. "Why is nothing working?" He did not expect an answer. He already knew what was going on but did not understand why.

"I have no idea. Even if the power is gone in this block, why would it affect the cars?" The other agent said, looking clueless.

"That explosion we heard was likely a bomb with an EMP. It destroyed every electronic microcircuit around here."

"A what?"

"An electromagnetic pulse."

"Isn't that from a nuclear explosion?"

"We've been trying to develop a small bomb, with minimal nuclear power, that's still capable to generate a powerful and limited pulse. Enough to destroy electronics around a certain radius."

West felt blood on his forehead; it hurt. The sight of blood on his fingers brought back the anger and frustration. He looked at the other agent, puzzled, "What I don't understand is why and who."

"Right-wing terrorists?"

"Of course, but why and who?"

"We can't let that stupid kid get away. We need to send someone after him," the other agent said. He, too, had blood on his face, around the lips. At least one tooth seemed to be missing.

"How do you intend to do that Einstein? Without a working phone or without a car," West said.

"How long does the power stay out with this electromagnetic pulse?"

West ignored him; the ignorance was starting to annoy him. If this was the kind of agents being produced, they were in trouble, he thought. "Someone was trying to get our friend out." West was talking to himself, trying to organize his thought, to figure out who was behind the attack. "I know who did this," West said after a brief moment. It only made sense that the same people who rescued Senator Thomas had come for the professor. He looked at the other agent. "I'm going to anticipate their next move. They won't be able to get away from me this time."

Chapter 64

June 8
Fayetteville, North Carolina

Michael was tired of sitting in a hotel room with nothing to do. Agent Brown left him to go meet with the others. He refused to answer Michael's questions of whether they were fine or not. All he told him was that they were alive. He did not know what to make of the silence and wondered why everyone was kept separate.

He looked outside, pondering for a moment if he should attempt an escape. Then, he realized the reason why Brown was keeping him apart from the others. He would not attempt to escape, not without his friends.

While he was relieved to have been rescued, it felt strange to be with a Texas agent. It was starting to sink in his head that he was an enemy of the United States of America. The thought brought sadness to him. In spite of the differences he had with the current government, the last thing he wanted was to be an enemy of his country.

Michael heard the door open and was surprised to see Jackie.

"Mike!" She ran to him.

They embraced and kissed. Michael broke off the kiss, looked at her, felt so happy to see her. He touched her hair, softly kissed her lips one more time.

"I am so happy to see you," he said after they finished a long kiss. "Where were you?"

"Agent Brown is keeping us two doors down."

"Your grandpa is fine?"

"Yes, they had a lot of questions for him. He talked so much yesterday."

"Does he trust these guys?"

"You know Grandpa, he's skeptical of most people, but he realizes we have no choice but to trust them."

"Why did they separate us? I have been sitting here, not knowing a thing that's going on, bored to death."

"Brown said you would be disruptive," Jackie said it smiling, as if she agreed with that assessment. "They have been really nice to us. They want to take us to Texas. We'll be safe there. You should be happy."

"Spending the rest of my life in exile, never to return to my country . . . Not my idea of happiness."

"So you'd rather stay on the run forever?"

"No, I know, we have no better choice right now. I know."

"They want the letter, but Grandpa told them he lost it. I don't think they believed him. They searched him for it. They say it's part of their mission to retrieve it."

Michael walked away from her, pondering why they needed the letter badly enough to carry such an attack on Obama City. As he looked back at Jackie, he noticed her smile. Nothing was more important than that.

"They want Grandpa to testify before the UN," she said. "And you, about your dad's murder."

Agent Brown came in. "Sorry to interrupt the reunion," he said. "We'll be leaving soon. Before we do, I need that letter." He was looking directly at Michael.

"Why?"

"We intend to make a case before the UN regarding US suppression of political opposition. Senator Thomas is willing to testify . . ."

"Senator Thomas?" Michael asked, surprised. "Mr. Marshall says he was killed."

"No, he's alive. We rescued him. He's going to testify, and this letter is evidence of his testimony. A simple letter that they have gone through so much trouble to destroy because it doesn't fit their political ideology." Brown took out a cigarette. "Mind if I smoke," he said. "The subsequent persecution of Professor

Marshall and you over it validates his point." Brown looked like he was tired of giving explanations. Probably thought that since he saved them, they owed him total obedience.

"And you went through all this trouble just to get the letter?" Michael asked.

"The UN refuses to recognize our independence. It's very difficult for us to carry out commerce and treaties with other nations without recognition. By exposing your government's actions against a sitting senator nonetheless, we'll strengthen our case for independence. Besides, Professor Marshall is a good friend of the senator. He insisted on his rescue."

"What about me? Why did you bother with me?"

"When we learned of your father's murder over this mess, we figured it was worth the trouble. Now, you too are going to testify as to why your government killed your dad."

"No, I'm not."

"Yes, you are."

"I will not allow myself to be used for propaganda for your government. No matter what has happened these past few days, I am not about to become a traitor to my own country. Besides, I don't trust you," Michael said.

"Listen, I know you've grown up being taught how terrible we are. I'm not going to earn your trust in the next few minutes. I must point out there are people out there, out to kill you. You would likely be dead already if not for me. I don't think you have any choice but to help us, and I want that letter."

"Help me release it to the public. If the American people know its message and that our government has been trying to suppress . . ." He could see he was not going to convince Brown. He was wasting his time.

"Out of the question." Brown was shaking his head. "That does nothing for us. It's better we let Senator Thomas present it to the UN."

Michael thought of what he had gone through the past few days. His father was killed; he was captured trying to release the letter. He made a promise to the professor to protect it. He still intended to keep that promise. "The letter belongs to the American people," he said. "It was written for them, not for some

UN bureaucrat to place in a drawer while he considers whether you should or should not be free."

"Listen, kid"—Brown blew some smoke at him—"you don't understand."

Michael had never seen anyone smoke; it was illegal in the United States. The smoke was bothering Jackie who moved away from them.

"If this letter gets released"—Michael pushed forward with his point—"it might wake up people to what's going on. They'll be reminded of an America that used to stand for freedom. There are people throughout this country that still believe in it, that still wish it to be like that. They don't want to be associated with you Texans because they love America. They don't want to leave it. But they don't love what our government is making us be. They know something has gone wrong."

Brown blew more smoke at him.

Michael ignored him and continued, "Don't trust the UN, trust the people."

"You're young and naïve." Brown walked away from Michael "You say they love America. We love America too. We love the America that used to be. And that America is gone forever. Did you know Ronald Reagan's birthday is a national holiday in Texas?"

Michael was surprised at that revelation. He had grown up being told Texans hated everything about the United States.

"No, of course you wouldn't know that," Brown said, returning to where Michael was. "Know this, kid. We did not leave America. America left us."

The smoke and the smell coming out of his mouth were distracting. It was hard to continue a conversation like that.

"Are you going to give me the letter?" Brown asked.

Some lady interrupted them. Michael figured it was another one of their agents.

"We're going to have to leave right away," she said. "Get ready."

"Why the rush?" Jackie asked.

"We have reason to believe this location has been compromised," she said.

"What does that mean? Compromised how?" Michael asked.

"It means we have to go, period," Brown said.

Michael saw the fear in Jackie's eyes. He walked up to her and held her hand. The apprehension that soon they would be captured was returning.

Chapter 65

"It's good to see you again." Marshall hugged Michael. "I'm so glad you were not harmed."

They were aboard the Obama-Rail, on their way to a speed of 180 miles per hour. Marshall did not feel comfortable traveling in it, with surveillance cameras in all stations and in every passenger car. To top that, there could be community organizers doing their duty as civilian domestic security, going through the trains, making sure people were behaving.

They were traveling with Brown, and he would be staying with them the rest of their trip. He refused to elaborate where they were going, asked them to get comfortable, and left to go talk with the conductor.

"It's been a hectic past few days." Michael recapped his recent ordeal.

They were sitting next to each other, with Jackie on the other side of the train, her seat reclined as she tried to get some rest.

"Do you still have the letter?" Marshall asked.

"Yes." Michael reached into his pocket and handed him the letter.

"Thank God," he said. "How did you get out?"

"Well, thanks to Brown. He wants the letter."

"Yes, he told me. They're dreaming if they think this is going to help. But I can understand their desperation. Their people are tired of war, demanding some peace with America. But the UN has never solved any wars. They're wasting their efforts."

"What do we do about the letter?"

"The letter belongs to the American people," Marshall said. He seemed firmed and determined about that. "They can make a copy if they want to, but the original should remain with us, no matter what. Hopefully, we can still release it at some point."

"Do you think all of this sacrifice, the lives lost, all that we have been through, is worth it?" Jackie spoke with sadness in her voice. She was sitting in her reclined seat, her eyes still closed. "Mike almost got killed over that letter."

Marshall stood up, looked around the train car, and saw they were alone. "You don't think it's worth it." He shook his head. He had never been asked to make any sacrifices in the defense of freedom. Even when he was young and served in the army, he had never seen any kind of combat. In his classes, when he could have spoken up and awaken his students, he had chosen to be safe and stay quiet. Placing the comfort of his family and his career ahead of the liberty of his country. Most people, he imagined, were the same way. They loved freedom but also loved a safe, conflict-free life. One day he had been asked to protect a letter. A letter about freedom. Just a piece of paper with words in it. Was it worth it? Such a small request, so little was being asked of him. "For three hundred years, generations of Americans have given their lives to defend and preserve freedom. They did it for you, so you could be free." He was pointing at Jackie. "Free to read a simple letter about freedom. If those patriots were here, would you ask them if their sacrifice, their lives was worth it?" He had never been angry with his granddaughter. There was a first time for everything.

"Sorry, Grandpa."

"No, you don't need to apologize to me. I need to apologize to you. I failed you. My generation failed you. Never has a generation of Americans done so little to preserve their freedom as ours. Now, I leave you an America where you wonder if freedom is worth the trouble."

He sat down, feeling sad. The desire that made Americans, through the years, stand up for freedom, was gone, he thought. "No, it can't be gone," he murmured.

"What can't be gone?" Michael asked.

"The desire for freedom. It can't be gone. It's just suppressed. If people were reminded of what they've lost, they would wake up."

"Do you really believe that people still want to be free?" Michael asked.

"Absolutely. Every person has a desire to be free. Nobody volunteers to be a slave."

Marshall saw the attentiveness with which Michael was looking at him. He liked him. More than any other young person he ever met. Michael seemed to understand the American ideal. If he had been born in another time, another era, he would likely be in the military, answering his nation's call to defend freedom. He wished he could teach him more, tell him about the America that used to be, once upon a time, the last best hope on Earth. "Our Founding Fathers fought to live as free men," Marshall told Michael. "Those who died in the fight, died as free men. To them that was better than surrendering their liberty without a fight. They passed on that mentality to the generations that followed. For generations, Americans understood that living free was the highest value any human being could aspire to. We were the example to the world of the power of that idea, the power of that truth. The incredible power of freedom."

At that moment, Brown came into the train car. Marshall placed the Reagan letter in his pocket. He was more determined than ever to find a way to get the letter released to the public. If he died trying, at least he would prove that in America, there were still people willing to die in the name of freedom.

Chapter 66

Brown came in. There was something about him; Michael could not bring himself to trust that guy.

"We should be there in a few hours," Brown said.

"Where is there?" Michael asked.

"Our destination is Tampa. Hopefully, we don't get delayed. Once in Tampa, we will hide for a few days then take a boat and catch a ride across the Gulf to the Texas coast. Easy."

"Too easy," Michael said.

"Aren't you worried about us getting captured here? All these trains have extensive surveillance," Marshall said.

"Your government's most powerful tool in controlling you is technology. They do have surveillance cameras everywhere. However, technology is also their weak spot. Half of these cameras don't work. They break down and it takes forever to get them fixed. Most people don't know which ones work and which ones don't, so everyone behaves as if they were being watched."

"And you know which ones work?" Jackie asked.

"Yes, the conductor of this train is in our payroll. He's an informant for us and tells us which cars have a malfunctioning camera. The station in Tampa is a dump. Not even the toilets are working there, much less the cameras."

Michael was pleased to hear that. He felt completely exhausted. The tension and exhaustion of the past few days was catching up to him. Maybe it wasn't all that bad to be traveling with a Texas agent. At least, he would be able to move around the country without looking over his shoulder.

An oriental man with a broad smile came in. "Hi, everyone."

"This is our conductor," Brown said.

"Who's running the train?" Jackie asked.

"Don't worry, these things run themselves." He laughed. "We'll be in Tampa in just a few hours. There's a station coming up, and we'll be stopping there. Try to stay in your seats. There's always a risk of agents coming in. If so, I will turn the seat belt sign on. Notice that it is off right now."

"If he turns it on, we need to run, exit that way." Brown pointed to the back door. They were sitting in the last car.

The train slowed down. Michael looked out the window with concern.

"The train is slowing down because we're getting close to the next station. It will continue to slow down until it gets to the station and makes a full stop. I don't even need to be up there." He chuckled, as if amused that the train did not seem to need him at all. "It's all programmed, but it'll look suspicious if I'm not there when we reach the station." His smile seemed sincere. He looked happy to be helping. "You guys don't worry about anything. Everything will go okay. We do this all the time. We get people out like this without any problems."

"It must be such a risk to do this all the time," Jackie said.

"My grandfather was a political prisoner in China. I could never turn my back on freedom-loving people." His smile was gone for a brief moment. "Don't worry about getting caught. In all the years I've been doing this, no one has ever been caught. No one takes me too seriously. I'm always laughing and joking, so they would never suspect I'm pulling this off."

Michael heard a noise and his first instinct was to look out the window, thinking it came from outside. There was no doubt that it was a gunshot. However, it came from inside. He looked to the front; the smile and laughter of the conductor were gone. His gaze was fixed forward as he fell to the ground, dead.

Then Michael saw, standing by the door, Agent West. There were two other agents, one at each side of him. All three had a gun in their hands.

Michael, not moving, saw Jackie with a look of terror in her face. She was looking down at the dead body of the conductor. Brown was standing in front of the dead body.

"You don't think I know all your tricks, all your routes of escape?" West asked Brown, pointing the gun straight at his chest.

"If you were sure, this train would never have left the station. We would be surrounded by agents," Brown said.

"Don't worry. There are plenty of agents waiting for us at the next station. We'll be there in ten minutes."

The train was slowing down further. To have escaped Obama City, just to be captured again. With no place to run to aboard a fast moving train. The Obama Express to nowhere.

"Take this traitor garbage out of my sight."

The other agents grabbed Brown by both arms and pulled him forward.

West turned to Michael, pointed the gun at him. "I'm glad you ran into that Texas scum. You realize, now I can do anything to you that I want. You're a traitor, and no one will question me." He smiled, looked at Marshall, and pointed the gun at him. "Please sit in the seat behind. I don't like to see the two of you together."

Marshall complied with the order right away. Michael kept his gaze fixed on West.

"Now, Mr. Adams, the letter please, before we reach the station and my agents take you away. Give me the damn letter!" He pointed the gun at Michael's head.

"I don't have any letter."

"I think a man that risked his life to go in a library to try to log in, scan it, post it somewhere, or e-mail it to your friends, might be the one with the letter. I'm tired of chasing you for it. Give it to me."

Michael did not have a chance to say anything. Agent West took a step to his right, stood next to Jackie, and pressed the gun against her head. He pressed hard against her head.

"I'm getting tired. Give me the fucking letter before I scatter her brains all over the place."

Chapter 67

His heart came to a full stop. At least that was how Michael felt. West had a gun pressed against Jackie's head, and he was not bluffing—that much was evident.

"Give me the fucking letter!" he repeated.

"Wait a minute!" Marshall stood up.

"Brown has it," said Michael. "Agent Brown took it from me. I think he forwarded it to Texas."

West looked at Brown then back at Michael. "I don't think so. We have been monitoring the communications of Mr. Brown. He has been very quiet, no contact with Texas."

"Your surveillance of their communications was as incompetent as everything else you have done. I know he sent it, I saw it with my own eyes."

Michael succeeded in annoying West. He withdrew his gun from Jackie's head. "You know"—West nodded while aiming the gun at Michael—"I'm going to enjoy killing you. I probably have never enjoyed killing another human being as much as I'll enjoy killing you. I have to admit, I'm even excited about it."

A passenger came in and stood there with his mouth open. One of the agents kept his gun aimed at Brown while the other one was able to hide it the instant the passenger came in. West put his gun out of sight the moment he saw him. The passenger turned around and went back the way he came.

West turned to one of the agents. "Go back and make sure no one comes in here." Once the agent left, West took out his gun, looked at Brown, "I don't care who has the letter. I will shoot all of you until I get it. You are now traitors, cooperating with an enemy of the United States, and I can shoot you at my pleasure. I will likely get a medal for it."

Marshall was standing a couple of steps behind West who was staring at Brown. He never saw the kick the professor sent him. It knocked down his gun. Michael saw it, and before West was able to do anything, he jumped at him.

Michael pushed West toward the back of the train, making him fall. He heard a shot up front and looked to see Brown and the other agent struggling for a gun. It was hard to see if anyone was hit.

West stood up, and Michael received him with an uppercut to the abdomen. His previous two fights had gone his way. The first time, more luck and the advantage of surprise than anything else. Their second bout was one Michael was proud of, but so much had happened since then, and he hardly had any sleep or food since that day. His energy level was at the bottom.

West sent a right hook into Michael's face; the punch knocked him down to the ground. For a moment, he felt a strange desire to stay down. Everything would be better if he just did not get up.

West rushed to get him before he could get back on his feet, failed to see Jackie, who punched him right on the nose.

"You broke my nose, you fucking bitch," he said while holding his bloody nose.

"Jackie!" Michael came to his senses and was back on his feet in a second.

West received him with a right punch directly into his face. This time, Michael took it and looked straight at West. His eyes fixated on the agent's just as another punch came at him. He stopped it, grabbing West's fist with his left hand. West tried to hit him with his other hand, but Michael grabbed that other fist as well. They stared into each other's eyes.

"I've had enough of you," West said. "I am going to kill you!"

"Not today," said Michael while staring at him. Michael pushed him with all his strength. "Not any other day!"

West fell all the way to the back of the train. Before he could do anything else, Michael was already coming at him.

Brown could be heard cursing, struggling with the other agent. It caught West's attention for just a brief instant. It was enough of a distraction that before West realized it, Michael was right in front of him. He pushed him with his right shoulder, throwing him hard against a window. West hit his head, broke the window, and closed his eyes for a second, as if about to lose consciousness. When he opened them, Michael's right fist was landing on his face.

Kickboxing had been something that Michael had learned for fitness and relaxation. He never thought he would actually be using his skills to take down another human being. He avoided hitting fellow classmates with too much force. Typically, the hardest punches were saved for the heavy bag at the gym. With every inch of will power he had, he threw an uppercut to West's abdomen, destined to be stronger than any punch he ever landed on the bag. It hit West around the right upper part of the abdomen—his liver. He followed it with another punch to the stomach. All the air that West had in his stomach burst out, and he went down.

Michael saw Brown against a corner, beating up the other agent. He could take care of himself. "Let's go!" he cried out to Jackie.

The train was slowing down, probably not going at more than twenty miles per hour. He took Jackie by her hand and opened the back door. Marshall was right behind them.

Looking down to the tracks, it seemed as if the train was moving too fast. There was no hesitation from Michael; he jumped. Jackie jumped at the same time, and they both fell to the ground, rolling over a couple of times but were able to stand up right away.

Marshall hesitated to jump.

"Come on!" Michael screamed, the train moving away from him.

Marshall was about to jump when he was grabbed by an agent. Michael and Jackie ran back to the train. When they heard a shot, for a moment, they feared the worse. They stopped and saw the agent falling down on the tracks. He was dead, shot by Brown.

There was no hesitation from Brown, he jumped right away and ran toward Michael and Jackie. Marshall did not jump with him.

"Come on, jump!" Michael screamed.

Marshall jumped. He screamed in pain as he fell hard on the tracks. Michael was relieved when he saw him get up. He seemed all right, walking without problems.

Brown was quick to catch up with them. "Let's go," he said.

Michael was about to turn around when he heard a shot. He looked and saw Marshall falling to the floor. "No!" He ran to him.

West was a few feet away from Marshall with a gun in his hand. The shot had come from him. Marshall had been shot and was down on the ground.

Michael could not see if the professor was alive or not; he was too far. He had not run far when he felt Brown grabbing his arm.

"Let me go," Michael said, as Brown forced him to stop.

"He's been shot! You can't help him now! They likely have back up on the way—if we don't go right now, we're all dead. Including her."

Jackie ran past them.

Michael reached out for her and was able to grab her arm. "No, Jackie, Brown's right. He'll shoot you too."

"Grandpa!" Jackie cried out, tears coming down her cheeks.

Another agent, also armed, was approaching West. Michael saw him, knew there was nothing to do. Marshall was a dead man or a prisoner. If they went back, they would share the same fate. He pulled Jackie away, dragged her, and forced her to run with him.

There were woods to their left, and they headed that way. Brown took the initiative, running ahead of them, as if he knew where he was going.

Chapter 68

Marshall laid down on the floor in agony. It was the worse pain of his life. He felt it intense, in his back, as he tried to crawl. The effort was too much. There was no significant movement, just worsening of the pain.

He felt a foot on his upper back, pushing him down. He looked back and saw the smiling face of West.

"Hello, old man." He kneeled down. "Were you planning on going somewhere?"

Marshall looked ahead and could see Jackie and Michael running away. He was glad. If they had come back for him, they would have died.

"They've abandoned you," West said. "You're all alone now." West stood up. "I want this place surrounded. I want them captured." He was talking to another agent who had joined him. "Search him," he ordered.

The other agent turned Marshall over, searched him, found an envelope in one of his pockets. "He's unarmed. All he has is this." The agent handed the envelope to West.

Marshall tried to look back. It was hard to stay focused. The pain was getting worse; he was short of breath, light-headed, nauseous.

West walked toward a light post, stood under it, took out the letter from the envelope, read it. He walked back with a big smile on his face. Even in the darkness, Marshall could see the look of satisfaction.

"We have what I wanted. It is the Reagan letter. I still want the others, dead or alive. Make sure this place is surrounded. Those Texans are very good at finding places to hide." He kneeled down next to Marshall, showed him the letter, continued to display a smile. "All that running . . . All that hiding . . . And in the end . . . To what end? It was all for nothing."

Marshall closed his eyes. The pain in his back was secondary. Heaviness in his chest was overwhelming him; he wanted to cry, to scream. He failed. The letter he had sworn to protect, to make public one day, was in the hands of a man who wished to destroy it. Nothing could prevent it; it would be destroyed. He failed. He opened his eyes to look at West. For a moment, he considered begging to be shot. There was no longer a reason to live. His only desire was to die a quick death.

Part 3
It spoke of individual freedom

Chapter 69

"Where are we?" Michael asked.

"South Carolina," Brown said.

They had been running for twenty minutes. Michael was tired. He could only imagine how Jackie felt, dealing with the grief over her grandfather while running for her life.

Barking dogs could be heard in the distance. Michael could not tell whether they were running away from the barks or toward them. "Do you hear that?"

"I hear it," said Brown without slowing down.

"Do you have any idea where you're taking us?" Michael asked.

"This way." Brown changed direction. There were some lights in the distance.

Brown stopped and looked around. He was short of breath, with his shirt soaked in sweat. "If I'm right, there is a small farm about five miles south." He could hardly finish a sentence. After a few breaths, he continued. "The farm belongs to a political dissident. He will help us . . . If he's there."

"A friend of yours?" Jackie asked.

"No, but I've dealt with him. He has no love for the government. I can tell you that. He's a truck driver and has helped us transport . . . things in the past."

"What sort of things?" Michael asked.

"Weapons, of course." Brown's breathing was returning to normal. "Not long ago, he transported for us a cargo of weapons to the Arizona-Mexico border, where we were able to retrieve them. He is a fearless guy. I've been to his farm a couple of times."

Michael heard the barking getting closer. "We should go."

Brown took off ahead of them. Michael waited for Jackie, who seemed hesitant to keep going.

"We have to do this," he told her. "Your grandfather would have wanted for us to keep moving forward. We can't surrender."

She nodded in agreement, and off they went. Catching up to Brown was not that difficult; he was not going fast at all. They were never going to make it five miles running that slow.

"Let's go there." Michael pointed toward a house he could see, not too far from them.

"That's the wrong way," Brown said.

"We're going to get killed if we stay in these woods. They're getting closer."

Before Michael could say anything else, Brown grabbed his arm. "I have an idea," he said. "Follow me." He took the lead and headed toward the same house.

"Okay, what's the idea?" Michael asked.

"We're going to steal their car."

He reached a car parked in the driveway. The lights in the house were on. Brown took out from his pocket what to Michael looked like a phone. He pressed a code and pointed it at the car's digital panel. The doors unlocked.

"That's a convenient gadget," Michael said.

"Yes. It overrides the electronic system. No fingertip needed."

"I'm sure all good thieves must have one," Jackie said.

It was not a nice comment to make, and Michael could tell Jackie was sorry the moment she said it. In the news, there were constant reports of Texans crossing the border and stealing cars to take them back to Texas. It was the constant attempt by the U.S. government of portraying Texans as thieves, criminals, rebels.

"Yes, I guess so." He gave her an unfriendly look. "Get in."

He drove five miles and reached the farm, which looked deserted. Not a single light was on. As they came out of the car, a helicopter could be heard approaching.

"Get down on the floor, by those bushes." Brown pushed Michael down to the floor.

Michael looked up to see where Jackie was. He could not see her. The helicopter was going on the opposite direction, moving north, away from them.

"We're fine for now"—Brown stood up—"but they'll be back."

Jackie was kneeling down next to the car, full of dirt. She had dropped down on the floor, but she would have been spotted without difficulty if the helicopter had flown above them.

Brown rushed up to the door, knocked with desperation.

"Who the fuck is there?" A voice could be heard from inside.

The lights were turned on, and a man opened the door. He was the scariest person Michael had ever seen. A dirty, torn-apart, old shirt could be seen beyond a long and unkempt beard. The man looked like he had never shaven in his life. His face was filthy; he last showered the same day he last shaved, thought Michael. And, he had the smell to prove it.

He had a rifle, which he pressed against Brown's chest. "The fuck do you want?"

"Hey, it's me. Agent Rick Brown from Texas. Remember me?"

"What the hell are you doing here? You want to get me killed?"

"I'm sorry, but there are federal agents after us."

"Shit."

"They'll kill us—we need help. I'll make it worth your time. I'm good for it."

The man looked as if someone was trying to sell him a used car he had no interest in buying. Michael felt they were going to be turned away. They needed a plan B.

"Fuck. What the fuck did you do?" he asked Brown. "Is it because of you—all this police activity? I've been monitoring their communications. There's a lot of noise out there."

"It's a long story, but yes, it's because of us."

He looked at Michael and Jackie. "Who the fuck are they?"

"They're patriots. The government is trying to kill them."

The man stared at them for a second. His anger seemed to be dissipating. "Fine, come this way, quickly." He lowered the rifle and stepped out. He turned around as soon as he saw the car. "The fuck you want me to do with your car? They'll find it here."

"I had no choice. They're after us. I needed to get here as fast as possible."

"You're a dumb motherfucker." He stared at Brown and then walked away. "Good thing you came to me, or you'd be dead soon," he murmured.

They went to the barn. Inside there was a large semitruck. The man took them past the truck, all the way to the back. There he removed a dirty carpet from the floor. There was a false wood floor, which he took off to reveal a metal door. He took out a key and opened it. The door was heavy to lift, and Brown helped him. It opened to a staircase.

They all went down; he turned a switch on, bringing multiple lights to life. It was a well-lighted room, and Michael, right away, noticed they were surrounded by weapons.

"As you can see, I cannot afford the government to come in here looking for nothing."

"You're planning on declaring independence all on your own."

He ignored Michael's joke. "I could get life if you bastards have brought federal agents here," he said.

"We're going to die here." Jackie's despair was evident in her voice.

"You'll be safe here. There are food supplies back there, enough for a month. The generator is back there. You won't be out of power either or ventilation."

"What about the car?" Brown asked.

"Yea, you stupid motherfucker, very smart to bring that car in here." He paused, seemed to be contemplating what to do. "I have no choice. I'll take the car away in my truck." He paused for another couple of seconds. "I'm going to set the barn on fire."

Michael tried to clear his ear. Did he really say set the barn on fire?

"Don't worry," he told Michael "You lousy bastards will be safe here. I will park my tractor above this door. They won't find you. The firefighters are my buddies. They'll cover for me if federal agents come around. I care more about what's down here than the barn." He went up the stairs; before stepping out, he turned around and looked down. "I'll be back in two days. In two days, I have to go get a cargo in New York."

"Weapons?" Michael asked.

The man no longer seemed angry. He glanced at Michael with a peaceful look. "No, just food. I can take you guys along. You have until then to think where you want me to drop you off."

With that, he stepped out, and before closing the door, he gave them one last piece of advice. "Don't try to get out. You won't be able to with the tractor blocking the door. Wait for me, and if the feds do find you, feel free to use what I have down there. Don't let them take you like cowards."

The door closed. Michael felt trapped in a place from where escape was not possible. With a Texas agent who was proving himself to be incompetent.

"We'll be safe here," Brown said.

"Like we were in the train?"

Brown ignored Michael's remark, went over to a sofa in the back of the room, and sat down. "Do you have the letter with you?" he asked.

"Mr. Marshall had the letter."

"I searched the professor. He had nothing."

"I gave him the letter back in the train."

"What?" Brown brought his hands up to his face. There was frustration written all over him.

Michael thought about saying something, remind him of his own incompetence but decided the last thing everyone needed was an argument.

"You made copies, I hope," Brown said.

"Copies? How? Where? We haven't stopped running since this whole thing started."

Michael became aware of Jackie, sitting in the kitchen area, her head down on a table. She was crying.

Michael felt a tear coming down too as he remembered Marshall. The thought of the professor being dead was depressing. To make things worse, the letter the professor was so eager to make public was, without a doubt, in the hands of West. He would destroy it. Everything they went through the past few days was in vain. He felt like a complete and total failure.

Chapter 70

"And if you fail . . ." Marshall heard the words but did not know who was talking to him. He opened his eyes; it was all blurry as he looked around. Where was he? The first thought that came to mind was that he was in his room, back in Los Angeles. No, it was not his room. He tried to call his wife and wondered why she was not coming up. What was keeping her downstairs? Then, he remembered she died years ago.

His eyes felt heavy, and he could not keep them open for too long. He felt dizzy, disoriented. What day was it? He tried to remember but could not. Not the day, the month, or the year.

A noise made him open his eyes. He was in a hospital. At least, he thought it was a hospital. "Jackie." She was in danger; he remembered. What was she in danger of? He closed his eyes.

He opened them again; his wife was standing at his side. Why did she take so long to come and help him? It could not be her; she was dead. The woman standing by his bed was not his wife; she was a nurse. What was a nurse doing in his house?

"Now, Mr. Marshall, relax, you're very agitated. Those restraints around your wrists are so you won't hurt yourself." She took out a syringe. "That's just to relax you."

He looked down and saw his wrists tied to the bed. There was an IV with fluid running into his arm.

The nurse smiled at him. "Do you know where you are?"

What was she asking? It was hard to focus on her words. "I'm home." He said after a while.

"No, you're in a hospital. You were in a terrible accident. You fell off a moving train. It looks like you were disoriented, and you fell off. You injured your back and had emergency surgery, but you're better now."

He remembered a train. He did not remember what happened. His eyes closed again. There was a movie playing in his head, but it was blurry; he could not understand the images.

"You know the date? Do you remember what year this is?"

"It's . . . 1976." Why did that year come to mind? He did not know. It was a year of importance to him. If only he could remember why.

"No. It's 2076," she said.

A man opened the door behind her. It was hard to focus, to see who it was. Then, he recognized him. But it couldn't be. Ronald Reagan entered the room and approached the nurse.

"We don't know what kind of a world they'll be living in . . ." Reagan told the nurse.

Marshall closed his eyes. Why was he so confused? There had to be something wrong with him. Was it all a hallucination? It felt so real.

There was a man in the room; that much he was sure of, but who was it? He looked at him again, saw he was a doctor, standing next to the nurse, and asking her questions.

The doctor looked at Marshall and spoke to him. It was the voice of Ronald Reagan; he looked exactly like him. Marshall closed his eyes, convinced of his own insanity. The voice was so perfectly clear, as real as anything else he had ever heard.

"And if you fail . . . They'll never get to read the letter at all because it spoke of individual freedom, and they won't be allowed to talk of that or read of it."

"The letter!" Marshall tried to sit up. Light-headedness and the restraints made him fall back down. He also could not feel or move his legs.

"Easy, Mr. Marshall, I'm your doctor. You were in an accident. You're a little confused now, but try to relax."

The doctor no longer looked or sounded like Ronald Reagan. He realized he was in a hospital. There had been no accident. The memory of West shooting him in the back was clear. At least Michael and Jackie were able to get away, he thought. The letter, on the other hand, had fallen in the hands of West. His failure was one painful memory he wished he could erase.

The room he was in looked like a regular hospital room. The nurse was there with the young doctor. Suddenly, the door opened, and the last person he wanted to see came in. If only it was another hallucination, he hoped. However, he knew that it was not.

"Hello, Mr. Marshall. I'm so happy to see you're awake."

"Good morning, Dr. West," said the nurse.

Marshall wanted to scream, to tell everyone that was not a doctor, but a cold-blooded murderer. That would be pointless. They would just give him more drugs if he did that.

"This patient came in Monday night after a terrible accident," the doctor explained to West. "He has a past medical history of Alzheimer's and became disoriented while on a train to Tampa. He fell from the train, fractured his T12, sustaining spinal cord injury."

Marshall remembered the pain in his back. It was not from a fall but from a bullet.

"Tragic," West said, looking sad.

"He underwent surgery, but he's paralyzed from the waist down."

Marshall tried to move his legs but could not. From below his waist, there was no feeling at all.

"It is a truly sad case. His Alzheimer's dementia already carried such a poor prognosis. Now he had this accident. There is not much that can be done for him," West explained to the others.

The young doctor turned to Marshall. "Dr. West is a visiting physician, specialized in palliative care. I'm afraid that's all we can offer." The doctor walked away from the bed.

West approached the bed, gently tapped Marshall's hand, and looked at the nurse. "I spoke with his family earlier today. They have given consent to go ahead with euthanasia. You'll find the consent in the chart. It's the best for him at this point. If he was in full use of his faculties, he would not want to suffer like this."

It all made sense to Marshall. West was there to finish the job in a nice and clean setting. To send a message of fear to anyone who dared challenge the government. Who would want to end that way? Driven to the edge of insanity? Who would challenge a government with the power to eliminate someone in such a way? There would be no questions, no inquiries. He was an old man with dementia, confused, and hallucinating. The nurse, likely with no clue to what was going on, would document and confirm that he was disoriented, unaware of place or time. The diagnosis of Alzheimer's would not be questioned by anyone who reviewed his file. With his injury and subsequent paralysis, euthanasia would be considered appropriate. Everything was being done within reason.

West was right on one thing. Marshall did not want to continue to live like that. It was better to be put out of his misery. There was nothing left to live for.

Marshall closed his eyes and heard the voice of Reagan again. Not a hallucination but an echo playing repeatedly. He felt tears coming out.

"And if we fail . . ."

"No." Yes, his fear had come true. He wanted to hope against all hope, but he could not deny it. It was true. Freedom in America was dead.

Chapter 71

The events of the past few days kept replaying in his mind. He could not help it. Michael was sitting on the stairs as Jackie approached him.

"Are you okay?"

He had tears in his eyes. He wiped them as soon as he saw her. "Yes, I'm fine."

She sat on the step below him, placed her head against his chest. "I know," she said. "I feel the same way."

"I keep thinking I should have helped him jump. He was an old man."

The dangers they had managed to escape had been many. They escaped West, community organizers, rats, trains, some homeless punks, a malfunctioning ambulance, a terrible family dinner, a bad movie, more community organizers, the police, West again; they even managed to get out of Obama City. Then, one slip, and the professor was shot and captured. It did not seem fair after evading so much. To make things even worse, the letter Marshall was in trouble for, and which he wished to protect, was in the hands of the people he was protecting it from; the people who intended to destroy it.

"Everything happened too fast." Jackie tried to reassure him. "It wasn't your fault. We could easily all have been killed. We were lucky to get away."

Another tear came down his right cheek. "I promised him I would protect the letter. If I still had it, he would at least die with some hope. It meant so much to him."

Jackie cleared the tear from his face. "Don't blame yourself, you did all you could. Now let's just pray we can get to Texas. At this point, it seems like a fantasy."

Michael heard a noise and knew there was someone upstairs. He reached for a gun. There were so many to pick from, but he had one with him—all loaded and ready to go. "Rick! We have company!"

Brown woke up and leaped out of the sofa he was sleeping on. "Hide behind the corner," he ordered Michael.

The door opened. The sunlight blinded Michael for a moment; he could not see a thing.

"You dumb bastards down there?"

Michael smiled; it was as if Santa Claus had come to visit. A vulgar, dirty, smelly Santa Claus, but he would do. He lowered his gun, relieved that there was no need to use it.

"We're here," Brown said.

As he came down, Michael noticed the smell was gone. Wherever this guy went to the last couple of days, he found a shower, thought Michael.

"Good, you guys were ready, I like that." He observed they were armed. "The fire destroyed most of my barn but not all. You owe me big." He pointed a finger at Brown. "Most of the roof is still intact, which is a good thing. It will block our departure, in case someone is watching from the sky."

Michael knew he was talking about satellite surveillance. The whole area was likely monitored via satellite images.

"The firefighters called me right away, told me about the fire. They were able to save most of the stuff. They said some federal agents came, looked around a little while they were putting off the fire and then left."

"Now what?" Brown asked.

"They're crazy looking for you guys. I don't know what the fuck you've done, Brown, but you really pissed those people off. I haven't seen mobilization like this in a long time. There's a rumor about some attack in Obama City, but they won't say nothing." He went over to the bathroom.

Michael sighed and shook his head. It was hard to envision how they would escape to Texas with the federal government looking for them like that. Especially when West knew they were with Brown and therefore headed for Texas. Any way to get out of the country was, without a doubt, under surveillance. After all their escapes, he felt they were headed for a dead end.

After five minutes, their Santa savior came out of the bathroom, touching his long beard; he seemed lost in his thoughts. "It's going to be a risk to take you guys anywhere, but we have to. I don't trust you guys staying here. You'll do something dumb, and we'll have agents here. And they'll go looking for me all over."

"You said you were going to New York?" Michael asked.

"That's right. I can take you there. Where you go from there is your business. But that's as far as I'll take you."

"I want to go to Manhattan." Everyone in the room looked at Michael.

"You fucking stupid?" he said laughing. "I know you are fucking desperate, but I'm sure you can do a little better."

"We've talked about this," Jackie said.

"That's crazy. New York City is a radiation dump. Nobody goes there," Brown said.

"The radiation is not as bad as they've been saying. It's the perfect place to hide—they'll never look for us there. We can take some food supplies and hide there for a while."

"And then what? We can't stay there forever." Brown sounded skeptical.

"I have an idea," Michael said. He could see Brown was not going to go along with it.

Jackie rolled her eyes. "I don't like it." She looked at him with disbelief.

The last thing he wanted to do was upset her, with all the pain she was going through, after losing her grandfather. He walked up to her, held her hand. "Please trust me. If we try to make it to Texas, West will get us. He's anticipated all our moves. Going into Manhattan, he'll never expect."

"I can take you to Brooklyn. I can drop you off close to the Brooklyn Bridge. There's a gate, keeping anyone from getting in, but you can get past it. They don't expect anyone to be stupid enough to want to get in."

They all looked unconvinced. At the same time, no one had any better ideas.

"Brooklyn is actually not bad. We have an apartment there. We can hide, and I know people that can help." Brown turned to Michael. "If you want to go into radiationland, that's your problem."

Michael smiled. The more he thought about it, the better an idea it felt. Regardless of the objections, he had made up his mind. He was going to go into Manhattan, even if he had to go alone.

Chapter 72

"Just relax," West told his patient, who seemed to be agitated. The nurse and the other doctor had left. It was just him and the patient.

He took out a syringe from his lab coat. "This is thiopental. It's what we call a barbiturate. It will relax you a little, suppresses some of your brain's higher functions. It makes it difficult to lie." He smiled as he administered the drug.

West looked at the monitor. The blood pressure, heart rate, and respiratory rate were all within normal limits. "Do you have any idea where your friends might be?"

Marshall looked at him without saying a word. The drugs were not loosening his lips.

West did not mind. He had other drugs to try; the satisfaction would be greater, the more his patient struggled. "It's such a shame we have not been able to find your friends. Do you know how bad that makes me look?"

"I don't know where they are." Marshall finally spoke.

"Was their intention to make it to Texas?"

"Yes, but you knew that already."

"Oh, I know so much more than you think." West turned off the cardiac monitor; it was not necessary anymore. The next area of inquiry was about Senator Thomas. He first asked him questions he already knew the answer to, just to check if Marshall was telling him the truth. When he felt comfortable that he had inhibited the professor's ability to lie, he went deeper, searching for new information. Most of the questions were about the senator. Marshall told him mostly things he already knew; he gained little new information. Then, he turned to the letter. "Did you make a copy?"

"No."

"Good. Did the senator ever make a copy?"

"No."

"How can you be sure?"

"I've had the letter in my possession since he first retrieved it from Faulkner. He was too afraid of her to keep it."

West smiled. His biggest fear had been that they managed to make a copy and that all his efforts to destroy it were futile. Now, he knew the original letter was the only one in existence. Soon, it would be gone.

"Don't worry about your friends. They have to stick their heads out someday. When they do, we'll be waiting."

"The mind and will of one individual can tear down an empire," Marshall said.

West chuckled. "To the last moment, you hang on to this notion that the individual is more powerful than the State." He reached into his pocket and took out an envelope. "You recognize it? The letter Reagan wrote in 1976. The letter you've been protecting. He had your same stupid notion about the individual." He took out the letter from the envelope. "Maybe you think the letter will still find its way to the public. That someone will take it from me and someday, feel that it should be released."

There was a bassinette on a chair next to Marshall's bed. West picked it up. "I'm afraid the letter will never be read by anyone else. Its message will die with you." He took out a lighter from one of his pockets, turned it on, and set the letter on fire.

The expression in Marshall's face was priceless to West. He wished he could take a picture of it. When the letter was burned halfway, he dropped it inside the bassinette. When fully burned, he showed what remained to Marshall. He then walked to the garbage and dumped it.

"You can destroy the letter, but you'll never destroy its message," Marshall said in a defiant tone.

"That's the point, Mr. Marshall. That's the point. We already have."

West reached out for another syringe. "This is pancuronium bromide. It is a muscle relaxant. It will make it difficult for you to move or talk." That syringe was followed by another one. He held it in his hand, examined it as if he was considering whether to give it. "You think there is nothing medically wrong with you, but there is. This belief that you have in the freedom of the individual is a disease. Society needs to get rid of it—to cure itself from the menace that it represents."

Marshall attempted to talk. It was impossible.

"It is what people want. They don't want freedom. They want that security that everything is taken care of. We finally have a government that truly responds to those needs, to their every demand. That gives them that security they so much need. We now truly have a People's Republic. Someone like you comes along and confuses them. You remind them that they've lost their freedom and next thing you know, they'll be demanding it. And how can we refuse the people? So today, I am doing my social duty and getting rid of the worst disease a people's republic can ever have."

West injected the syringe into the intravenous line, paused before pushing all of the medication in. There was no need to rush it; he wanted to enjoy the moment. "The muscle relaxant is working, isn't it? It is becoming difficult to breathe, isn't it? Soon your diaphragm will be paralyzed, and you won't be able to breathe." His mission was accomplished. The letter destroyed, the professor about to die; the only thing missing was the capture of Michael Adams. He would be captured soon enough. "And this one is potassium chloride. It will make your heart stop."

Professor Calvin Marshall struggled to open his mouth. He wanted to say one last thing, but he was having a difficult time. "Freedom . . ." He did not finish his sentence.

West pushed the rest of the potassium chloride. "Good-bye . . . freedom man."

Chapter 73

June 30
Brooklyn, New York

The coffee was the best she had in a long time. Being on the run made it impossible to get the proper and therapeutic amount of caffeine her body needed.

It felt good being back to New York. The fear was still present, made it hard to fall asleep. There was no way of avoiding the feeling that, at anytime, federal agents would come in and capture her.

She approached the window, enjoyed the aroma of her coffee as she looked out into the distance. She sat at a desk and continued her writing while looking out into Manhattan.

"How's the coffee?"

Jackie turned around to see her new friend, the pizza lady—the woman who rescued her back in Obama City. The long hours of the day had been made more endurable by long chats with her. She had learned her real name was Elena, and she, too, had lost her beloved grandfather when she was younger. Her dad was a freedom-loving man who died in the war with America, and that had inspired her to join the secret service. She told Jackie her dad believed to the day he died that America one day would be free again, and Texas and America would be reunited as one country.

"It's wonderful, thanks," Jackie said.

"What are you writing?"

"I'm just writing down what has happened to us these past few weeks. So others will know."

Jackie was trying her best to stay busy, distracted, but it was hard to take her eyes off the window. She kept looking at Manhattan, wondering if Michael was safe. The feeling she had in Obama City, when he went to the library, was back. At that time, it had turned out to be a well-founded fear. This time, after a week of not hearing from him, the anxiety was growing stronger day by day.

"Don't worry, they'll be okay. Nobody is going to be looking for them there, and they have enough supplies for a month."

"I know. They're probably safer there than here." But she still couldn't avoid thinking that something was going to go wrong. Who could blame her after all that had gone wrong already?

"I am glad Rick agreed to go. He is a resourceful guy. He can improvise if something goes wrong."

"Is everything ready for the fourth?" Jackie asked.

"Oh yes, we have a rental truck that we'll take to Buffalo. There, on Monday, we'll get the documents we need to cross into Canada."

"And from there to Texas."

"Well, to Mexico first and then we cross the border into Texas."

The plan sounded simple. However, Jackie was realistic about their chances. Whether by air, car, or foot, crossing the U.S. border was difficult. A government that decades prior had proven itself unable or unwilling to keep unwanted visitors from coming in had become progressively more efficient about keeping people from getting out.

Jackie closed her eyes and prayed. She prayed that things would work out. Michael was out there, risking his life to try to honor her grandfather's memory.

Sitting there, writing, thinking about their ordeal, she realized why the government found the letter to be such a threat. Why a message of individual freedom posed an existential threat to those in power. The planners and schemers in Washington DC and in Obama City knew the one thing they could never control was the ingenuity of the individual. West was wrong. Power was not in the barrel of a gun. That was just a pathetic attempt to suppress it. True power existed in the mind of the individual. The greatness of America was that freedom unleashed that power. It was the power which allowed an actor to bring down an evil empire of intellectuals. That allowed a general with tired and outnumbered troops to defy one of the coldest nights of the year and cross the Delaware to free a Nation. A country lawyer turned president who, against all odds, refused to surrender the last best hope for freedom on earth.

The same power which sustained a tired old man who refused to believe he was the last freedom-loving person left, the last voice of sanity, in a world turned upside down. The power which made an idealistic young man go rogue and shock a nation.

It was what the control freaks in DC feared the most. The power of freedom. The power of an individual willing to do the unexpected.

Chapter 74

June 30
Austin, Republic of Texas

"Are you sure that's what you want to do, Senator?"

"Yes," Senator Thomas said.

The people around the table were looking at him as if he was some senile old man, who had just lost his mind. Perhaps they were right.

"It's crazy. They'll kill you." The lady who spoke was the assistant to the director of intelligence. The director sat next to her. Across from them sat the secretary of state, and the secretary of defense. At the head of the table was the president of the Republic of Texas.

"I must say, we've had a lot of people over the years ask us for political asylum. You're the first one to ask us to rescind it," the president said.

"You must still be upset about your friend's death," said the intelligence director, a man Thomas found obnoxious and irritating. "This is ill-advised, Senator."

The director was not completely off on this one; he was upset about Marshall's death. He wept the day the assistant director showed him the obituary and the lie he died due to complications from end-stage dementia. It did not help when she added that, according to their intelligence, they destroyed the Reagan letter. However, while the director believed these events were blinding his judgment, he felt the opposite. For the first time in a long time, he was seeing things clearly.

"What will you do when you get there?" asked the secretary of state.

"I still am a United States senator. I intend to walk into the Senate and address my fellow senators and my Nation."

"They'll never let you. They'll censure you," the director said.

"Given time, the White House would twist enough arms to force a censure vote." He wished he had a cigar with him. Having found a new purpose, he was determined to quit the bad habit once again. "I will not give them time. They'll never take a vote without closed-door meetings first, to know if they have enough votes. To make sure they do not have a humiliating loss."

"You're dreaming," The director said as he took out a cigarette.

Thomas wondered if he was doing it on purpose, knowing he had just quit smoking. "It won't be the first time," he told the director.

"Even if you give a speech, what will you accomplish?" The president asked.

"In my speech, I will expose everything that has happened, my persecution, my friend's death, the destruction of the Reagan letter, the murder of George Adams, and other things I haven't even shared with you."

The president looked skeptical. As much as Thomas disliked having to explain his decision, he was going to need their assistance to cross the border and make it to Washington.

"A speech won't change a thing. Even if it creates a scandal, they'll just blame it all on Faulkner. She is already retired anyways." The director said, taking another puff of his cigarette.

"It will be swept under the rug," the president said in agreement with his director.

"Not this time." Senator Thomas stood up. "We are the ones that have given these czars, these unelected bureaucrats this unlimited power they have. I will not allow my colleagues to pretend they are blameless in all of this."

The director was shaking his head, smiling. "The bureaucrats were appointed by the White House. Even if your fellow senators agree with you, what are they gonna do about it?"

Senator Thomas sat down. He looked around the table at the skeptical faces of his hosts. Patience needed to be exercised. He was thankful for their help. When Agent West came knocking on his door and took him, at gunpoint, to a hospital for questioning, it was the Texans who intervened, rescued him, and offered him political asylum. In return, they wanted him to testify on their behalf before the United Nations. It was part of their desperation to get international recognition for their independence. If he was going to walk away from his end of the bargain, he owed them a detailed explanation.

"I intend to offer the Senate a solution to our present crisis. A way to confront this White House with just minimal risk for them."

"What solution?" the assistant to the director asked.

"I intend to place my name before the Senate for nomination for president of the United States."

The director burst out in laughter. "Now we know you are senile."

"Maybe," said Thomas. "It was Ronald Reagan who once when confronted with the age issue said, 'If not for the elders to correct the mistakes of the young, there would be no State.' Well, there are a lot of mistakes to correct."

"The Senate will never approve your nomination," the director said.

"There is more opposition to this White House than it is known. Now with George's death, my persecution, those senators know any of them could be next. It will be close, but I know I can get the votes I need to challenge President Wilson in November."

There was an awkward silence. Everyone seemed to be digesting what they had been told. The director was going through his third cigarette. Thomas, once again, wished he had a cigar.

"There hasn't been a competitive presidential race in America for decades. The Senate has been, for years, handpicking who runs for president. It will be interesting if you pull this off," the secretary of state said.

"Please, don't encourage him. This is crazy," the director said. "Even if he gets nominated, he'll never win. The American people are not interested in change. They like their government the way it is, taking care of every aspect of their lives."

"That's bullshit!" Senator Thomas slammed his hand against the table. "Don't blame the American people for what's happened to my country. It's not their fault. It's mine. Mine and all of those in power. For many years, I saw what was happening. I saw the country deteriorating into this mockery of everything America used to be about." He stared at the director. "You said I was upset about my friend's death. You bet I'm upset. It was my fault. I have seen this intolerance coming for years. To voices of opposition. To dissent. And what did I do about it? Nothing! I didn't want to make too much noise, to rock any boats, to get the community organizers turned against me. I wanted to move up the political ladder. My country was going to hell, and I stayed quiet to further my political career!" He slammed his hand on the table, hard enough that the ashtray in front of the director tipped over, falling on his lap.

"Shit!" The director was not happy to see his expensive suit covered with ash.

"Please, Senator, calm down," the president said.

The senator stood up. He placed his hands in his pockets so that he would not slam anything else if he lost his temper. "I wanted to be the first African-American to win the presidency since Barack Obama," he said, walking away from the conference table. "The first Californian since Ronald Reagan. To advance, I stayed quiet, away from the big controversies, made the right friends, the important connections. What did I get out of it? A visit from one of Faulkner's assassins."

"They know you are here with us. They'll accuse you of collaborating with their enemy."

Thomas turned around; the secretary of defense was the one who spoke. It took him by surprise. He was known to be a quiet fellow; it was the first time he heard him talk.

Thomas walked back to the table. "I've lost my only son on this stupid conflict. No one has more reason to hate Texans than me. Most Americans are sick of this endless war as I am. I will promise not only to end it but to welcome Texas back into the Union peacefully."

The director laughed again. He was lighting up another cigarette. "What makes you think we would want to go back?"

The president gave the director a look as if pleading with him to be quiet. He then looked at Senator Thomas. "I understand your desire to change your country, but I must say that I agree with Smokey here." The president pointed at the director. He was notorious for giving everyone around him a nickname. "The American people have not shown any desire to change the way things are. For years they have seen their government grow, their liberties erode, and to us, they just do not seem to be willing to change their leadership."

Senator Thomas sat down. He was feeling more relaxed, at peace with his decision. "The American people, for years, have been made to choose between bad and not as bad, and year after year, things get worse. They needed leadership that would tell them not to look at the government for the solution to their problems. That all government can do is get in their way, restrict freedom, and create more problems. They have not heard that in decades. Instead, the American people have received nothing but mediocre leadership. It is due time for someone to stand up and remind them what it means to be an American."

Chapter 75

July 4, 2076
New York City, New York

The Fox News studio, located in midtown Manhattan, had returned to life. Abandoned in 2055 when the entire city was evacuated, it would never resume broadcasting. Other media outlets transferred their operations to what was to become Obama City. Fox News, which for years had been critical of the government's agenda, was not given a license to resume transmission. The other networks were government-controlled and did not have difficulty securing their licenses.

"How are you doing?" Brown approached Michael from behind.

Michael was looking at several screens in front of him. "It's great," he said, turning to see Brown. "I'm ready."

He was sitting at a production console, with several monitors and screens turned on in front of him. One of them was playing Ronald Reagan's speech from the 1976 convention. Thanks to his father's account and password which were still active, Michael gained access to the Department of Communication's main database. From there, he was able to download a multitude of speeches, videos, and documents from previous presidents—all leaders who had spoken up about freedom in America.

"And that's the letter? Word by word?"

"Yes. That's the Reagan letter. The one he spoke of in his 1976 speech." Michael looked down at the letter he had typed, which was displayed in a monitor to his right.

Brown picked up a paper copy of the letter and looked at it. "You haven't missed a word?"

Michael took the letter from him; he wanted to make sure it was right in front of him as he went on the air. "That's the Reagan letter. Every word, every comma, every period as he wrote it. Except it's not in his handwriting. I wish I had the original, of course, but at least, the message is preserved." He looked at Brown. "I have a photographic memory. I don't even need to read it when we go on the air. I know it, as I said, word by word."

"You better read it. You don't want to miss something, forget something, and sound foolish."

"I am incapable of forgetting." The smile was immediate as he remembered Jackie. She made fun of him the first time he made that statement in front of her. Told him he was conceited and immature.

They both went back to their respective consoles. There was a lot of work to do before broadcast time.

"You know," Brown said as he continued to work, "there are agents in Texas who would give an arm and a leg to have this access code to the Communications Department."

"See? And I gave it to you for free."

"I still can't believe you had this kind of access."

Michael chuckled. He had access since he was a child. That was when he first memorized his father's account number and password. When his dad was sleeping, he would spend hours reading news reports as they came in for the department's approval. "How do you think I learned that New York was not a radioactive wasteland? A report came to my dad for approval, detailing how there was no significant radiation in New York City. Faulkner did not want the truth to come out. The whole campaign against nuclear power was based on having people fear that their city would be the next Manhattan."

"So he rejected it?"

"Yes. That made me suspect it was accurate. I had read the whole report. It was very detailed, with a lot of opinion in it but a lot of facts." Michael saw that Brown was looking at him with amusement; he was learning something that his agency could take years and great effort and would not be able to find out. "I still remember it. I could probably rewrite it if you are that interested."

"Interested? You bet I'm interested. You've given me so much information. They better give me a promotion after I take this back to them."

"I'm glad I could help."

"I'm glad you were able to figure out the password. I thought they would have blocked your dad's access after his passing."

Michael was distracted, downloading a final list of emails. When he completed it, he turned back to Brown. "I was confident about the password. The new acting communications czar or someone like the chief of staff at the White House would be the only ones with enough access to go in and block my dad's account. They would have no reason to make this a priority." Michael was getting nervous as the time was getting closer. There was only a few minutes left. "My dad's password was not hard to figure out. He had three sets of passwords that he recycled, just changed a character here and there. I knew it would take me just a few minutes to figure it out."

"It took you an hour."

Michael returned his attention to the console. One last time he checked the signal to make sure it would be going out to every channel, every broadcast station, and multiple internet sites.

"We're ready to go national," he said.

"They've been showing that Obama message all morning long, every hour on the hour."

"And President Wilson is set to speak from the Rose Garden at noon," Michael added. "That's when we'll go on the air."

"They won't be able to abort our signal?" Brown asked for the tenth time.

"No. I have revoked access to Faulkner, to the new acting Communications Czar, to the White House. Actually, thanks to Faulkner, very few people have the level of access needed to stop me." Michael loved the irony that he was going to use Faulkner's tools—the same ones she used for years to silence dissent, to spread a message of freedom. "They will jam our signal locally, station by station, but that takes time," he said.

Michael took the mouse, and with one click, he reintroduced America to the Great Communicator. "I have now sent an email to every account in the department's database. The letter is attached to it and pasted on the email itself. Every person in America has now received a copy of the Reagan letter." He smiled. The first step was a success.

Michael went to put on his suit. He had borrowed it from one of Manhattan's abandoned stores. He returned to the studio and sat behind a news desk. Brown would be behind the camera.

"All right, it's noon. Ready or not, here we go," Brown said.

At twelve noon, in midtown Manhattan, the broadcast signal of the Fox News channel went live from coast to coast. To all fifty-six states and Texas.

"Good afternoon and happy Fourth of July." Michael took a deep breath. His hands were shaking a little, and he prayed he was not looking nervous. It was what he wanted to do since he was a kid. To sit in front of a camera and report on an important event to a national audience. "I am sure most of you were eager to hear how President Wilson is going to now be able to control your lives from the comfort of the Oval Office. We can return to microchips and tyranny tomorrow. Today, being the Fourth of July and all, I figure, let's talk about freedom." The teleprompter in front of him was displaying the speech he had written earlier. As nervous as he was, it was reassuring to have it there.

"Three hundred years ago, our Founding Fathers conceived a nation where all men are created equal, where we believe we have certain inalienable rights. That those include life, liberty, and the pursuit of happiness. For the last three hundred years, great patriots have done the necessary work to keep this nation free, to keep those founding ideals alive. To keep this a land of freedom." He felt calmer as he continued to read the words he carefully wrote.

"One hundred years ago, a former president of the United States wrote us a letter. Ronald Reagan wrote a letter for us. He was a great leader, a freedom man. His message was meant to be kept in a time capsule and to be opened today, so you could hear it and read it." Michael picked up the copy he had printed so the audience could see him holding a letter. It was not the original, but he was nonetheless excited to be delivering its message.

"Our government has done everything it can to destroy this letter, to keep you from hearing Ronald Reagan's message to our generation. His message is a message of individual freedom. In this age of social justice, our government has no tolerance for such talk." He tried to remain calm, even as he remembered Marshall being shot over the letter.

"I am defying our government by interrupting this broadcast, to bring you his message. But our history is one of Americans defying those who try to oppress our freedoms." Michael hoped West was watching.

"So please join me as I read to you the letter that Reagan wrote for us. He was concerned whether we would ever get to read this letter. He was concerned that if our government continued to grow and become progressively more intrusive, that we would never get to read the letter, because it spoke of individual freedom. He believed that an all-powerful government would not allow us to talk about that or read of it. I intend to talk about it as I am doing now. I intend to read about it as I am about to do.

"Join me in this moment of defiance," continued Michael. "Join me to tell those who try to oppress us that we are free to read a letter that was intended for us. In this anniversary of our independence, I cannot think of a more American thing to do. And by doing this we can send a message back to Ronald Reagan, as he watches from heaven, Mr. President . . . We still are a free people! In spite of our government's best efforts, America still is the land of the free."

With that, Brown pressed a key, and the image of Ronald Reagan came on.

"My fellow Americans . . ." Michael started to read the letter, trying to keep his composure, reading it slow, so he would not sound in a rush.

The picture of President Reagan being broadcast was one with an American flag behind him. He was displaying the optimistic smile he was well-known for. Below the picture, Brown typed, "Ronald Reagan: Fortieth President of The United States." Below that, "Addresses us today on our Tricentennial."

And so, seventy-two years after his death, the Great Communicator was addressing a new generation of Americans. A generation unfamiliar with his message of individual freedom. During his political career, his words inspired millions of Americans and freedom-loving people throughout the world. Now, a new generation was ready to hear the words that would spark their own love for freedom.

A young college student was getting ready for a day out with her friends. Just as she was about to leave, she paused to look at the broadcast. The message she heard was unlike any she heard before, certainly never heard it from any of her college professors.

A construction worker tried to enjoy his day off, watched TV during lunchtime. He was hoping to have a quiet meal. When Michael came on the screen, he became curious, wanted to see what it was about, and when he heard the request to join him in a moment of defiance, he was shocked. Never, in the public airways, had he heard such words. Then, a political leader he had never heard of made him forget his food. He called his buddy right away to ask if he was watching.

An eighty-year-old man paused as he was about to start a barbecue in his backyard. There was no one to cook for, but a barbecue had been a tradition in his family throughout the years. It seemed that to celebrate the Fourth of July was old-fashioned. That was not going to stop him from carrying out his own private celebration. He displayed an American flag in his porch with pride. A radio station was playing patriotic country music, which was a rarity, when the broadcast was interrupted. At first, he felt it was some jerk, and he was about to turn it off when his curiosity kept him listening. Once he heard President Reagan's words, his feelings of patriotism and love of country intensified. It was the same way he felt when he was a kid, celebrating the holiday with his dad, who would talk to him about the history of America, telling him stories about his personal hero, Ronald Reagan. He found himself pulling back tears.

A young mother approached the American Electric store in Queens Boulevard. She saw a crowd of people gather, looking at something, and she approached them to see what the fuss was all about. They were listening to Reagan, and she, too, paid close attention to every word. For many years, she had felt there was something wrong with the world around her. She did not have control over personal decisions for herself and her family. She had to obey rules she felt lacked any common sense. Now, someone was talking about freedom. "Freedom? Is there still such a thing?" she murmured.

A young community organizer stood at a community center. One of his friends tried to turn off the TV; he asked him not to. He was curious to see what was going on. He never understood why he volunteered to be a community organizer. Most of the time, he was pushing people to do things they did not want to, and he did not like it. But there was no choice. Having a choice was never something he had considered. Being an individual, free to make his own decisions, was not something he understood. The word free did not make sense to him. The words in the national anthem, "the land of the free," were meaningless to him. It did not make any sense. As Michael finished the broadcast, it all made a little more sense. Perhaps, there was such a thing as freedom. It just had been lost somewhere.

"Senator, you better come see this they're showing on TV."

Senator Thomas was in his room, packing his suitcase. "I'm not interested in hearing President Wilson's nonsense."

"It's not Wilson. It's a message from a former president."

"I'm not interested in hearing Obama's nonsense," Thomas said.

"It's not Obama. It's Reagan."

Thomas rushed after the agent. He was on time to hear Reagan's last words. "I hope you're recording this," he told the agent.

People in every state, every city, every town in America saw the broadcast, heard Reagan's message.

Michael's image came back after the letter was read. "People have died to bring you this message, to make sure you heard Reagan's words. Even more important, throughout the years, many Americans have given their lives to make sure you are free to hear it."

Michael placed down the letter. His prepared remarks called for him to thank his audience for listening. He had said what he had to say. However, something more remained to be said. Something he wanted to share with his national audience. It went back to his article, the one that got him into trouble. "Some of you may wonder why I have risked my life, undergone persecution, risked the lives of family and friends? Why have I bothered? I've upset my government over this letter, turned it against me. All to preserve this letter and be able to come and talk to you about its message about freedom. I have further defied them by bringing you this broadcast. They are likely trying to figure out where I'm transmitting from, so they can find me, arrest me, or kill me. Why bother going through all this trouble just to talk about some letter with some outdated concept of freedom." He paused for a moment. "I did it. Because . . . I am an American!"

Chapter 76

October 29, 2076
Santa Barbara, South California

"This generation has a rendezvous with destiny."

Mike and I were impressed with the size of the crowd. Senator Thomas was attracting large crowds wherever he went. Days after Mike's national broadcast, Thomas had shocked the nation by returning to the Senate, giving a speech in which he reread the Reagan letter, and exposed the abuses of an out-of-control government. He placed his name before the Senate for nomination for president of the United States and promised to restore the vision of limited government, personal freedom, and reward for hard work. In a move that sent shockwaves across the nation and the world, the Senate, by one vote, approved it. President Wilson was going to have real opposition against him in the November presidential election.

"The challenges are clear. We will confront the erosion of freedom that has taken place in this country for the past seventy years. We will demand that our government get back on our side and that it stops controlling and restricting every aspect of our lives."

The enthusiasm of the crowd was contagious. Neither Mike nor I had ever attended a political rally before, and we were enjoying it. The government could no longer do anything to silence all the dissent; it was too widespread. The entire country was caught in a wave of change. Even the new Communications Czar had stopped restricting media outlets. He did not want to be in the losing side.

Ever since Mike's national broadcast, there was fervor among the people to hear and read anything to do with Ronald Reagan. They wanted to know more about this long dead leader, who seemed more concerned about their freedom than their current leaders. Senator Thomas was taking full advantage of the situation, quoting Reagan at every event he attended.

"Government is not the solution to our problems, government is our problem," Senator Thomas said as the crowd erupted in applause.

When did you ever hear any modern politician say anything like that? When asked in an interview if he was exploiting the memory of Reagan, Thomas said he was humbled and proud to be leading a new Reagan Revolution. That his only regret was that he had not had the political courage to do it earlier.

"We are five days away from fundamentally restoring these United States of America to greatness." It was the biggest applause line of his speech.

It was felt that Thomas was headed for a landslide victory. The enthusiasm was growing day by day. The crowd knew that in a few days he would be president-elect Thomas. Of course, I admit I had my own personal reasons to hope for the senator's victory. A few months ago, I met the senator; it was at my grandfather's funeral. Federal charges were never brought against me, unlike Mike, so I was able to attend. Thomas met me afterwards. He expressed to me how sorry he was for what was done to my grandpa. Provided me with a secret report, part of an ongoing investigation on West's conduct and the division on antisocial behavior. In the report, a nurse who was caring for Grandpa gave a detailed account of what was done to him. Needless to say, I cried, but I was glad he let me see it. Afterwards we talked about Mike, I even got him on the phone, and they had a long chat. The senator first told Mike that he had broken into sensitive databases in the Communications Department, accessed private email accounts, and shared the information with a foreign government, not to mention previous charges of attacking a federal officer, and resisting arrest. It could all land him in jail for a long time. Then, he thanked Mike for his love of country and for igniting a new patriotic fervor throughout the nation. He hinted to Mike that he would consider granting a full pardon as soon as he became president.

"We will meet our destiny," the senator continued his speech. "In another hundred years, that next generation will look back and thank us because we did head off our loss of freedom. We did do our part to keep this nation free."

Mike looked at me, no need for him to say anything else. With Senator Thomas wrapping up his speech, it was time for us to go. It was still not safe for Mike to be out in public like that. Nonetheless, I was glad to see him. It was our first chance to be together in over one month.

"Those in power will oppose us with every weapon at their disposal. But in America's never ending struggle for freedom, surrender will never be an option. Yes, we are a free people! Thank you. God bless."

The applause from the students was warm and prolonged. Thomas was making many promises, getting people all excited. I was not immune to it; I stood there, clapping, hoping he would be able to deliver. He promised to immediately reverse the passage of the outrageous consumption chip that Wilson signed into law on the Fourth of July. He also promised to reform the health care system, to tear down the bureaucracy, so we can start saving precious life rather than disposing of the unwanted. To return market principles and once again have innovation in the system.

During our meeting, he asked me if I intended to return to the practice of medicine. I told him when I can start taking care of people rather than budget items, I would love too. In return, I asked him, considering it will likely be his most challenging task, if he was serious about reforming health care. All he said to me was, "You bet." Emphasized to me that, like my grandfather, he believed the government takeover of our health care system had been that first step into our current state of affairs. We shall see if he delivers.

As Mike and I walked away from the rally at the Santa Barbara City College, we noticed how beautiful it all was. In front of us, we could see the sunset over the pacific, and behind us, the Santa Inez Mountains were equally impressive. I wished we could have stayed and enjoyed the beauty of it all. It was not possible. Mike had to go on the run again.

"You sure you don't want to stay?" I asked him.

"No, it's too risky."

"I wish we were volunteering with the campaign, it's exciting." I was looking back toward the rally, seeing the volunteers passing pamphlets around.

"You know how I feel about volunteer work. Besides, we've done our part."

"It's so beautiful, isn't it?" I said as I looked at the sunset, which had caught Mike's attention.

"Yes." He smiled.

He placed his arm around my waist and brought me close to him. His smile grew broader; his eyes were sparkling with enthusiasm. "I'm just happy that the most beautiful woman I have ever seen is here with me."

We kissed. A soft touch of the lips which turned into a long and passionate kiss. (Again, I hadn't seen him in a month). The sunset, the mountains, the students, the rally—everything became a secondary thing.

It took Mike a few seconds to realize his phone was ringing. There were only two people with knowledge of his new phone number, and he was kissing one of them. The other one was the man who gave him the phone, his new friend from Texas, Rick Brown. Mike picked up the phone; he turned the speaker on so I too could listen.

"Mr. Adams."

We knew that voice right away. There was no confusion on who was talking.

"I must admit that you ended up being a more resourceful idiot than I ever thought. That little stunt of yours on the fourth was unexpected."

"I'm glad you were watching. I heard Faulkner threw you under the bus. And she looked like such a sweet old lady."

The Wilson Administration was under a lot of heat as the events surrounding the attempt on Senator Thomas, the murder of George Adams, and my grandfather's death were all becoming public knowledge. The president had avoided most of the blame by throwing Faulkner under the bus. She, in kind, had blamed everything on West, who was now suspended, as an internal affairs investigation was conducted.

"Don't worry about me," said West. "I've started a new hobby."

I was worried; Mike could see it in my eyes. I asked him to hang up, but he continued.

"What's your new hobby? Dressing up for kids' birthday parties?" Mike took my hand and we continued to walk away from the rally while listening to West.

"It's hunting. And I am eager for you to join me."

"I think I'll pass on that one."

"This letter created a little excitement, like when a car crashes in the highway, everyone stops to look. It doesn't mean everyone wants to be in the crash. It will all be forgotten in a few weeks. And you'll still be a fugitive."

"What happens to me is irrelevant. That letter was like letting a genie out of its bottle. It took you decades to get the genie in there, and now it's not going to be easy to get it back in."

"It took decades to make the progress we have, and you're dreaming if you think it's going to be reversed. Social justice . . ."

"Social justice is bullshit! And you're full of it!" Mike stopped. I signaled, once again, for him to end the conversation.

"Do you honestly think you have any chance against us?"

"Freedom will not be denied!" Mike turned off his phone. He had nothing further to say.

Mike kissed me on the lips once again; a soft, short kiss. "Don't worry about West. He won't find me."

We heard someone shouting at us.

"Hey!"

It took a second for us to see a student staring at Mike. He looked like he had a Che Guevara T-shirt, and we were about to turn away, worried he was a community organizer, who would call the authorities on Mike. Then, I took a second look, realized it was not the image of Che Guevara on the shirt. I pointed it to Mike. The image on the T-shirt was that of Ronald Reagan.

"That's that guy from the Fourth of July," the student told his friends, who were next to him. He then waved and yelled, "Hello, freedom man!"

A small moment with a big meaning. That's what it felt like to be an American once again. Freedom had returned to people's hearts. I know it's probably been there all along, but now, in a way, we were rediscovering it.

Mike smiled and waved back. He was interrupted by another student who came up to him.

"Your words were very touching," the student said.

"Thanks."

"Do you think we can still make it, you know, that shining city upon a hill?"

Mike smiled. In just a few weeks, we had gone from not being allowed to talk about the Reagan letter to now everybody quoting him. It gave us so much hope for the future.

"Yes, you can." He emphasized the "you." "And why not? You are an American."

That brings our story to its end. I hope you have enjoyed reading our version of the events. This book was my most sincere and honest attempt at letting people know exactly what happened. It seemed fitting that since Reagan sent us a warning through time about our freedom that I should write an account of how close we came to losing it.

Before I conclude, I need to address a few points. First, let me say, I have no idea whether Baron West and Olga Parker ever had an affair or any kind of romantic involvement. We do know she cooperated with him; he knew of Mike's editorial, and only she could have shown him that, since it was never published. In addition, Mike felt they were made for each other. For that reason, I took some artistic liberties in describing their relationship. If Olga Parker gets to read this book and is upset about this, all I can say is—it was Mike's idea.

Next, you might ask why Mike didn't write this book. He is the journalist, the one who wanted to expose this story. That's true, but as you can imagine, being on the run does not provide for the best writing environment. For that reason, the task has fallen upon me. The Lord sometimes gives us tasks we never knew we were up to and never asked but need to, nevertheless, give it our best effort.

Some out there will ask, "That was your best effort?"—being critical not of the substance of this book but rather the manner in which I have written it. All I can say to those critics is: I'm a doctor, not a poet.

Finally, I want to address the events of Obama City. Neither Mike nor I condone the violence that took place there. Even though it allowed us to escape Baron West, we do understand property was damaged, innocent bystanders were injured, and some people died. I can only say how sorry I am that any of this ever happened. My prayers will always be with those who lost their life that day.

The incoming Thomas Administration will not be happy of my revelation here that the senator not only knew but encouraged the attack. I can only hope people understand the circumstances of the moment.

It was never my intention to write a book that would throw a black eye on a new administration so early on. However, as Mike told me when I was writing it, the age of censorship is over; we must tell the truth boldly. If we do not have the truth, we can never be free.

Ultimately, I did not write this book to promote a politician, even one I like as much as Frank Thomas. I did not write it to earn the praises of literary critics or the approval of Olga Parker. I wrote and dedicate this book to all those people out there who must have freedom. To all the brave patriots who for the last three hundred years have sacrificed so much, sometimes their very lives, to keep this great land of ours free and to give the rest of us a chance to dream of that shining city upon a hill. Thank you. The dream lives on.

My grandfather was one of those patriots. I, Jackie Adams, will never forget his sacrifice and the cause he died defending. I should not call it sacrifice because for him, freedom had more value than life itself. Had he surrendered his freedom to stay alive, that would have been a sacrifice. It was a sacrifice he was not willing to make. A sacrifice Americans have never been willing to make.

This book is dedicated to him more than anyone else, and his approval is all I'll ever need. As he watches me from heaven, I close my eyes and can see that warm, gentle smile of his, and hear his humble, optimistic words. They are words of approval. Not only of this story or the events narrated in it, but also of something larger and far more important. Approval of a story whose last chapter has not yet been written. The American story. A simple story about simple people who fell in love with freedom. Not a perfect love for each generation has brought its own set of flaws. However, it has endured the test of time. And, after three centuries, many trials and tribulations, war and peace, wealth and debt, the love affair continues.

All in all. Not bad. Not bad at all.

The End

Ronald Reagan's remarks at the 1976 Republican National Convention

August 19, 1976

Ronald Reagan ran against Gerald Ford for the 1976 Republican Presidential nomination, and lost a close race. At the close of the convention, President Ford asked Governor Reagan to make some impromptu remarks.

Thank you very much. Mr. President, Mrs. Ford, Mr. Vice President, Mr. Vice President to be—the distinguished guests here, and you ladies and gentlemen: I am going to say fellow Republicans here, but also those who are watching from a distance, all of those millions of Democrats and Independents who I know are looking for a cause around which to rally and which I believe we can give them.

Mr. President, before you arrived tonight, these wonderful people here when we came in gave Nancy and myself a welcome. That, plus this, and plus your kindness and generosity in honoring us by bringing us down here will give us a memory that will live in our hearts forever.

Watching on television these last few nights, and I have seen you also with the warmth that you greeted Nancy, and you also filled my heart with joy when you did that.

May I just say some words. There are cynics who say that a party platform is something that no one bothers to read and it doesn't very often amount to much.

Whether it is different this time than it has ever been before, I believe the Republican Party has a platform that is a banner of bold, unmistakable colors, with no pastel shades.

We have just heard a call to arms based on that platform, and a call to us to really be successful in communicating and reveal to the American people the difference between this platform and the platform of the opposing party, which is nothing but a revamp and a reissue and a running of a late, late show of the thing that we have been hearing from them for the last 40 years.

If I could just take a moment; I had an assignment the other day. Someone asked me to write a letter for a time capsule that is going to be opened in Los Angeles a hundred years from now, on our Tricentennial.

It sounded like an easy assignment. They suggested I write something about the problems and the issues today. I set out to do so, riding down the coast in an automobile, looking at the blue Pacific out on one side and the Santa Ynez Mountains on the other, and I couldn't help but wonder if it was going to be that beautiful a hundred years from now as it was on that summer day.

Then as I tried to write—let your own minds turn to that task. You are going to write for people a hundred years from now, who know all about us. We know nothing about them. We don't know what kind of a world they will be living in.

And suddenly I thought to myself if I write of the problems, they will be the domestic problems the President spoke of here tonight; the challenges confronting us, the erosion of freedom that has taken place under Democratic rule in this country, the invasion of private rights, the controls and restrictions on the vitality of the great free economy that we enjoy. These are our challenges that we must meet.

And then again there is that challenge of which he spoke that we live in a world in which the great powers have poised and aimed at each other horrible missiles of destruction, nuclear weapons that can in a matter of minutes arrive at each other's country and destroy, virtually, the civilized world we live in.

And suddenly it dawned on me, those who would read this letter a hundred years from now will know whether those missiles were fired. They will know whether we met our challenge. Whether they have the freedoms that we have known up until now will depend on what we do here.

Will they look back with appreciation and say, "Thank God for those people in 1976 who headed off that loss of freedom, who kept us now 100 years later free, who kept our world from nuclear destruction"?

And if we failed, they probably won't get to read the letter at all because it spoke of individual freedom, and they won't be allowed to talk of that or read of it.

This is our challenge; and this is why here in this hall tonight, better than we have ever done before, we have got to quit talking to each other and about each other and go out and communicate to the world that we may be fewer in numbers than we have ever been, but we carry the message they are waiting for.

We must go forth from here united, determined that what a great general said a few years ago is true: There is no substitute for victory, Mr. President.